VIKING WARRIOR

Gina Dale

Gina Dale Publishing
United Kingdom

Disclaimer
This novel is entirely a work of fiction. The names, characters and incidents
portrayed in it, while at times are based on historical figures, are the work
of the author's imagination.

Printed by Ingrams UK
A CIP catalogue record for this book is available
from the British Library
978-1-9996610-38-8

Also available as an eBook
ISBN 978-1-999610-39-5

ACKNOWLEDGEMENTS

I would like to thank the following for their help, expertise and encouragement in producing my second indie novel in the Viking Series 'Viking Warrior'.

Editor Rachel Gregory, pedanticpolly@gmail.com
Cover designer Jenny Quinlan, USA www. historicaleditorial.com.
Typesetter Catherine Cousins, 2QT Limited.
Marketing & Media, Clancy Walker, Leeds
Photoshoot for cover, Katie Amos, www.equineshoot. com

PHOTOSHOOT ACKNOWLEDGEMENTS

Photography: Katie Amos Photography
www.equineshoot.com, Todmorden.
Hairstyling:Kaye Volante (07791 546617) from
Zeitgeist Hair, Hebden Bridge,
Tel: 01422 844974
www.zeitgeisthair.com
Model:Ben Glynn, Todmorden.
benalanglynn@hotmail.co.uk
Costume Hire: History in the Making Ltd.,
 Portsmouth. Tel: 023 9225 3175
 www.history-making.com
Horse:Sorrento, owned by Helen Kettle-
borough, groomed by Alanna Pilling,
Hebden Bridge
www.blackshawroyd.co.uk
Bridle:Designed and produced by Ryburn
Leather, Sowerby Bridge. Mob: 07512
996339 - Tim@ryburnleather.co.uk
Venue:Shaw Farm Equestrian, Todmorden,
Tel: 01706 819467

Other Titles

Viking Series

Viking Wolf (Book 1)

Brushstrokes Trilogy

Brushstrokes (Book 1)
Darkness Falls (Book 2)
Drama Unfolds (Book 3)

The author has her own website
www.ginadalepublishing.com
where pictures relating to all these books
can be seen.

Social Media posts for Gina Dale Author are
available on FB, Twitter and Instagram.

ONE

Ubba lay on his side with his arms cocooned around Torri's body, as he recovered from their passionate lovemaking. He could not believe his passion and lust for his wife could rage as strongly now as it had when they had first met and when she had finally become his wife.

He kissed and nibbled her right shoulder and whispered, 'My darling wife, I love you more each day and just want to stay here by your side forever.' Just then, he heard hesitant footsteps pausing at the door; a timid knock sounded.

'Father, a lone Dane visitor has arrived and is asking to see Ivar. He claims he was invited to stay when they met in Ireland.'

Ubba jumped up and strode to the door, still naked, unlocked it and ushered Arne into the room. 'Christ Arne, there's no such thing as a "lone Dane" – especially an Irish one.' He started pulling his clothes on quickly. 'Where's Frank? We need to send a scouting party out; we could be facing an attack.'

Torri leapt, still naked, out of bed.

Arne gasped, 'Mother?'

Ubba laughed, 'Oh, I see what you were thinking, Arne. Yes, of course it's your mother; who did you think it would be? Teenage sons cannot reconcile that their parents actually have sex, especially when they are over forty. Here you have the proof of what a real loving marriage is, and I hope you will one day find a woman whom you love, respect and worship as much as I do your mother.'

Arne was bright red and stammered, 'I am sorry for my intrusion, but I considered it important. The Dane *is* alone – Einar and I were out hunting in the woods. We spotted him on the Pennine drover's track and followed him from a safe distance down into Jorvik. He is riding a Shire horse and is very tall with shoulder-length dark blond hair. He has a disfigured eye and looks like he is in his late teens. Frank is with him in the hallway of the palace and sent me to find you.'

'Did he give his name?'

'No, he said Ivar would know him. I didn't reveal that Ivar was away.'

'Good lad; you used your head.'

Ubba finished pulling on his boots and said to Torri, 'Make sure all the children are supervised in the palace. None of them should leave.' He swept out of the room at speed, with Arne in tow. He paused briefly to assess the horse being held by a groom at the entrance; it was a huge beast. Ubba ran up the steps and into the palace hallway. Frank was with the young man, who turned to face him as he approached.

He smiled and said, 'You can only be Ubba Ragnarsson, the great warrior and brother of Ivar.'

Ubba stopped and realised that the visitor was taller

than him and clearly blind in one eye, but emanated authority and power through his deep voice and stature.

'Perhaps, but who are you?'

'Sigtryggr of Ireland, my lord. I was invited by Ivar to visit him here and observe his territory.'

'But that was over 18 months ago. What kept you?'

'The many twists and turns of Irish politics and war intervened and I have only just found the time to come over. Did Ivar not mention me when he returned?'

'Oh, yes, he did, and you certainly made a lasting impression on him... but he never mentioned you being blind in one eye.'

'Well I wasn't back then; I received a glancing blow from a sword when I jumped off some ramparts in a recent skirmish in Ireland, losing the sight in my left eye as a result.'

'Where precisely are the rest of your men?'

'Lord Ubba, I can understand your caution, but I am alone. I came on a trading ship between Dublin and Ceaster and purchased the Shire for my journey over the Pennines as there were no decent riding horses suitable for a man of my height. I am not a leader of an army; I am only eighteen years old. I know I was seen by two young men, one of whom appears to be your son, but I swear I am not here to cause trouble. I merely wish to accept Ivar's invitation. I assume he is not available to greet me. Perhaps Ralf Lindholm and his son Ranulf can assure you of my identity, if they are here?'

Suddenly, Freya arrived in the hallway and came

running over when she spotted the stranger standing with her father. 'Daddy, have you bought that big horse outside?'

'No sweetheart, he belongs to our visitor. How many times has your mother told you never to interrupt adult conversations? Have your manners deserted you?'

Freya grimaced, 'I know "little girls should be seen and not heard" Daddy, but I want to see this man's face. He is too tall – please lift me up.'

'Only if you keep quiet!'

He picked her up and she looked closely at the vivid red scar on Sigtryggr's face. 'I know who he is; you told me all about him last night before bed. His hair isn't red though.'

Ubba looked aghast. 'Who do you think he is?'

Freya replied, 'Thor, God of War, of course.' She turned to the visitor. 'Can I see your hammer?'

Arne and Frank burst out laughing and Sigtryggr struggled not to laugh as well. He smiled at Freya, took her hand and kissed it. 'No, little princess, I regret I am not Thor – just Sigtryggr of Dublin – but I am honoured you should think me worthy of being Thor.'

'No, I am not a princess because Daddy is not a king...'

Ubba shouted loudly, 'One more word, young lady, and you will receive your first ever thrashing from me.' He turned to Arne, 'Take her to her mother and insist she keeps her out of my way before I have a breakdown.' He put her down on the floor and she was about to protest until she saw his angry face.

'My sincere apologies Sigtryggr, for my daughter's loose tongue and vivid imagination. Ivar is away on business until Monday, but Ralf and his son are coming here to dine tonight and hopefully can confirm your identity. Now, let me oversee some food for you before *my* manners escape me.'

Frank spoke, 'Lord, young Ranulf is schooling one of the troop horses in the arena now.'

Ubba responded, 'Well, ask him to come and see me before he goes. Please ensure you find a stable for Sigtryggr's horse... provided it can get through the door.'

'Yes, my lord.'

He turned to their guest. 'Come, I will take you to the kitchen and charm someone into making you a hearty breakfast.'

'Thank you. I would love some hot food.'

Ubba led him to the kitchen. They received astonished looks when they arrived. Edith the middle-aged Saxon chief cook rushed over, very flustered. 'Lord Ubba, what can I do for you? This is not your normal territory.'

Ubba smiled at her and she blushed. 'Now Edith, this young man has sailed across the Irish Sea and needs to fill his boots with some hearty Yorkshire food. As a talented cook, what can you rustle up for him as quickly as possible to keep him content until dinner?'

'Well lord, I have some bacon, ham, eggs, liver and sausages that can be ready quickly – and a loaf of fresh bread and butter.'

Sigtryggr replied, 'Oh, what perfect heaven that

would be.'

Ubba turned to Edith, 'We will eat in here as we are going to the stables next.'

'And what would *you* like to eat, my lord?'

'I fancy some of that cold roast ham and pickle inside some thick bread and butter. I have had breakfast and have to curb my food intake.'

'Rubbish, lord! You are as fit and lean as a butcher's dog!' She scurried off to the fire pit where one of the kitchen maids already had Sigtryggr's breakfast sizzling in a pan.

They moved to a quiet spot with a small table and a young girl brought them ale.

'So, what role do you have at Ivar's court?'

'I am commander of his troops, responsible for protecting Ivar's territory in North Yorkshire, which covers a considerable area. There are the North York Moors and the Wolds, which are high and wild, and then the Vale of Jorvik, which has rich agricultural land.'

'Ivar said you were like your father and would have been content to be a farmer.'

'I would have been a horse breeder and farmer. The land round here is perfect. I like the rugged moors, wonderful coastline and the rich fertile land. The weather suits me perfectly. I was impressed with Halfdan's fertile land in Lincoln, but it is very flat and boring when compared to here.'

'Ivar said he feared that the Saxons would try to procure Alfred's dream of a united England.'

'We have been expecting it since his son Edward

became king, but Wessex, Devon and Mercia have been experiencing attacks from raiders on the coast and over the border from the Welsh. They have been unable to leave their own lands for fear of invasion and although Athelstan (formerly the Dane convert Guthrun) holds East Anglia, it has been subject to attack. If it does happen we would need the Danes to unite, and you know how difficult that would be to achieve. Look at us – five brothers and we can't agree. We did achieve revenge for our father's death, but it did not come easily, of that I can assure you. Bjorn and Ivar clashed swords, Sigurd would not come over because of Ivar, and we all ended up leading our own troops into battle supported by various groups of Norsemen intent on keeping their Danelaw land.'

The food arrived and Sigtryggr tucked in as if he had starved for a week. Edith chuckled, 'Jesus lad, are all the Irish Danes as tall as you?'

'No, lady. If you spend your life up to your knees in Irish peat bogs it stimulates growth to protect you from drowning. The born and bred Irishmen are small, fit and lean and are better suited to the rain.'

After Sigtryggr had eaten his breakfast with relish, Ubba took him down to the stables. Ranulf had just returned the horse he had been schooling to the stables and came over to greet them.

'Sigtryggr, how are you?' As he came closer he saw the scar. 'What happened to your eye?'

'I was making a hasty exit and caught a glancing sword swipe from an angry Irishman. It could have been a lot worse; it hasn't stopped me fighting my corner. If you lose a vital sense you learn to compensate and draw on other senses to aid you. I have retrained in sword fighting to adjust for the lack of vision on my left side. I can differentiate between light and dark, at least, and can see shadows across my lens.'

Ubba asked, 'So can you assure me Ranulf, that this is Sigtryggr, before I send out a scouting troop looking for an army?'

'Oh, yes, this is indeed Sigtryggr. He appears just as cocky and arrogant even though he has lost an eye! He is very different from other Danes. You and he have a lot in common; he adores women and horses.'

'Sensible lad. Like you Ranulf, he has the right priorities, but obviously is slightly too impetuous when it comes to fighting.'

'I am sure under your guidance Ubba, he would soon learn discretion.'

Sigtryggr replied, 'I would prefer to avoid a fight if possible by sensible negotiation rather than losing good men, but with the Irish you are dealing with seasoned warriors who are always outnumbered. They trust nobody and rely on their God to sustain them. Sometimes their bravery outweighs their ability and downright cunning, but often it triumphs.'

Ubba replied, 'Ivar said you were a deep thinker and a bold strategist for someone so young.'

He smiled, 'Ivar and I spent many nights arguing over battle tactics, ending in drunken arguments. I did not approve of Ivar's impulse to engage the enemy in battle rather than achieving victory without slaughtering good men on both sides.'

Ubba laughed, 'Well, to Ivar, battle reputation is most important. As he never wishes to conciliate – he considers it a weakness – I can understand why you argued.'

'Ivar said I was more like you than him and I take it as a great compliment my lord, as I have huge respect for you.'

Ubba laughed, 'That surprises me! I would expect you to consider me lacking in ambition as I never wanted to become a king.'

'Not at all, my lord. I admire your tenacity to pursue the path in life that makes you happy.'

'I learned from my father that being a king creates more sacrifice than joy.'

He gave Sigtryggr a tour of the stables and was delighted to find he was indeed devoted to horses. He promised him a ride on Sleipnir another day. He then took him to his house to meet his family.

TWO

orri was dressed for courtly duties. She had plaited and weaved her hair, which she would not normally have done until just before the dinner party. Ubba observed her closely as he introduced her to Sigtryggr, who bowed low and kissed her hand.

'My lady, the rumours of your beauty do you no justice whatsoever.'

Torri blushed and replied, 'Maybe 20 years ago, but not now... and neither did Ivar describe you as the fit, tall young man I see before me.'

Ubba flinched and could not stop a flash of anger sweeping across his face. *For heaven's sake, he was a mere pup young enough to be her son!* She was generally referred to as the "ice maiden" as she rebuffed sexual advances from any man who dared to flirt with her.

The peace was shattered by Freya and Astrid chasing each other into the room. Astrid was screaming for her doll back from Freya.

Torri shouted, 'Girls, where are your manners? We have a visitor – behave!'

Both girls stopped dead and Freya threw the doll to Astrid. 'I know, Mama. He is a warrior from Ireland but because he is so tall I thought he was Thor, even though he is blind in one eye.'

Serena, Ubba's lover, appeared holding Theo's hand – their toddler of two years old – in pursuit of her charges. 'Apologies Torri, they escaped the playroom. Perhaps I should take them outside to let off some steam.'

Ubba said, 'Sigtryggr, may I introduce you to Serena and my daughter Astrid and son Theo.'

Sigtryggr was visibly shocked by the sudden intrusion but recovered sufficiently to kiss Serena's hand and bend down to Astrid and Theo to say hello.

Jealous of her siblings being the centre of attention, Freya shouted, 'Look Theo, he was blinded by a sword in his eye.' The children's eyes were riveted on Sigtryggr's face and Theo put out a hand to touch the scar, intercepted by Serena.

Ubba snapped at Freya, 'What did I say to you earlier, young lady? One more word and you will be sent to bed.'

Freya realised she was in trouble again and said, 'Sorry Daddy, I won't mention it again.' She gave Ubba a dejected look with a trembling bottom lip, to gain as much sympathy from her audience as possible.

Serena picked Theo up. 'Come along, children – outside for a walk we go.'

The others retired to the salon and discussed Ivar's stay in Ireland and his sudden decision to come to England.

There was a loud knock on the front door and they heard Arne answer it. Ubba recognised Frank's voice; shortly, he came into the room accompanied by Arne.

'Lord, may I speak with you privately for a moment?' He was looking across at Sigtryggr.

Ubba jumped up. 'Certainly, Frank.' He turned to his guest. 'Please excuse me.' Frank and Arne left the room with him.

Torri chatted politely to Sigtryggr until Ubba returned to the room. Straight away, she noticed he had donned his sword belt.

'I have some business to attend to, but I am sure Torri will keep you entertained in my absence. I hope I won't be too long.'

Frank and Arne were hovering in the doorway and then they left the house at speed and headed towards the palace.

Sigtryggr exclaimed, 'Nothing serious, I hope?'

Torri sighed, 'Who knows? It could be anything from a lame horse to a petty squabble between the men.'

'May I ask you something rather personal, my lady?'

Torri directed an imperious look at him. 'You may ask, but I don't promise to answer.'

'Is Serena Ubba's mistress?'

Torri paused before she answered, 'Yes she is, and with my full knowledge and consent. When I came over two years ago Ubba had taken her as his mistress and she was carrying Astrid. I already had Arne, Viggo and Freya to Ubba, as well as three other sons: Erik and Refil to Bjorn and Guthrun to Jarl Lund. I decided my breeding days were over after a difficult pregnancy with Freya. Ubba is ten years my junior and I had no wish to deny him more children. We agreed that

Serena and her children would be included within the family as long as I remained his wife.'

Sigtryggr watched her face carefully. 'Not what I would expect from a former queen and shield maiden. Does this arrangement apply to both of you?'

The ice maiden turned to him and gave him a look that would have turned most men into solid ice. 'No, it does not. I have no need of any man in my life but Ubba. As Queen, I know that in order to fulfil your heart's desire sometimes sacrifices have to be made... and this was one I was prepared to make. I represent Ivar as Queen Consort of Jorvik and am therefore bound to three Ragnarssons as well as being mother to five Ragnarsson children. In fact, two years ago in a ceremony Ivar, Halfdan and Erik (representing his father Bjorn) swore fealty to me and of course, Ragnar spared my life after he retook Jormund from my husband. It would appear that the threads are inexplicably bound between us.'

'Deservedly so, my lady. You have fought alongside them to extend their empires, and founded a dynasty. My admiration for you is genuine; dealing with such volatile characters cannot have been an easy existence. Ivar told me that Ubba was the one who kept his anger and impetuousness under control before you came back.'

'Ivar and I have forged a good relationship governing Jorvik. I don't hold back on my views and even though we may disagree, he does listen to my opinions and often takes my advice. He has mellowed now he has me and the children beside him. He has formed a strong bond with Viggo and he has moved mountains to find the most learned tutors for all of them. He proved to be a firm guiding light with Erik and Refil, preparing them to aid their father's quest to become King of Norway, even though he and Bjorn don't always follow the same path.'

'Are Bjorn's sons still here?'

Yes they are, but they are living over on the East coast for a month learning about fishing in the North Sea. Bjorn was insistent that they both mastered every aspect of sailing whilst they were over here on as many different boats as possible. Refil has a real fascination for the sea and is a born sailor and lover of marine life. Erik is polishing his navigation skills at the same time. They have inherited Bjorn's curiosity and love of the sea. Unlike Ubba who is a 'landlubber' and prefers his feet firmly on solid ground.

'So why exactly are you here? Isn't Ireland big enough for your ambitions?'

'Ivar suggested I come here and observe the Saxons at close quarters. What opinion do you have of them, my lady?'

'I find these northerners very different from the southerners. They are very resilient, and their life is bound by the weather very similarly to our life back home. Initially, they can seem rather brusque and untrustworthy of strangers and they bitterly resented our brutal ways and raids of their land, as they are very family orientated. Don't ever believe the myth that they lack courage, though; I can assure you they do not. What they lacked until we arrived was fighting skills, but they paid us to teach them and their strong family bond, religious beliefs and desire to protect their land has forged them into formidable warriors.'

'So, if King Edward attacks Jorvik, will they turn against you?'

'Well, that remains to be seen. They don't necessarily trust Edward any more than us. They are heartily sick of seeing their homes destroyed and families torn apart. They just want to get on with their lives in peace. You have met Ralf and Ranulf and tonight you will meet Gytha his wife, Skye his teenage daughter and Thorin their seven-year-old son.'

'Does Ralf serve with Ubba's warriors?'

'No, he pursues his own horse breeding, training and farming interests but has sworn fealty to Ubba and will join him on request. Ubba wants Ralf to breed and train horses for him. Both he and Ranulf teach riding skills to his men.'

'I have seen the quality of his horses and am delighted to know he is using Irish mares crossed with Barb stallions as they have such wonderful temperaments and a strong work ethic. I am very jealous of you owning Sleipnir – he is an outstanding horse. Ubba has promised I can sit on him.'

'Sleipnir is Ubba's pride and joy and if anything befell him he would be mortified. He uses Raven for scouting forays and although he and Sleipnir have a great rapport he will be reluctant to risk him in battle although he is fully trained as a warhorse. They work as a team. Sleipnir knows that he has to protect his master and he will take out another horse if necessary.

Ubba loathes harming horses in battle and detests the practice of digging ditches and using stakes to repel an attack; he considers a horse a noble beast that should not be harmed.'

'I totally agree... but sometimes, needs must. Sleipnir protects your husband, but who protects you?'

She gave him a withering look. 'I think I have proved capable of protecting myself. I may not fight on the frontline anymore young man, but I am still capable of defending myself against an attack. Sheer size and strength do not always triumph. Brains, speed and agility often conquer.'

'My lady, I don't underestimate your capabilities in any way. In fact, I wish I could have fought alongside you myself. In Ireland our women do not fight; they protect our children and homes. Most of our battles are in open terrain or attacking burghs and battlements.'

'Sigtryggr, you appear to be under the impression that I planned my life down to the last detail, but let me assure you that in reality, that doesn't happen. I made choices based on the position I was in at the time. I did not intend to found a dynasty of Ragnarssons; it just happened because I married two of them. Bjorn and I were incompatible as he was always susceptible to chasing other women and I would not tolerate that. Lagertha begged me not to marry him. She knew that Ubba was the right man for me but like most foolish women in love, I did not heed her.'

'Yet, you permit your husband to have a mistress and a second family.'

'Well, we had been apart for 18 months after we

killed King Aelle in revenge for Ragnar's death. I lost Guthrun in that battle at only seventeen years old and returned to Jormund with both Bjorn and Ubba's children for safety. Ubba was free to take other women as I was to take other men, but he never fell in love with one until Serena crossed his path. Shared grief and loneliness brought them together and Ubba is far too honourable a man to abandon her and his child. The arrangement works well; Ubba always puts me first. It was my choice not to have more children and certainly, he is the perfect father. He took a serious role in guiding his stepsons and sons in their careers. Amazingly, so did Ivar, and it changed him. He enjoyed an active role in creating the future of the Ragnarsson Dynasty, because he can't reproduce himself.'

'So, Ivar has mellowed since I last saw him.'

'Only because there has been relative peace over the last two years. But war is coming – make no mistake – and it will have serious repercussions for us all.'

'It must be a concern for you my lady. One thing I have already learned is that to be single allows more freedom. I am not concerned about protecting a family and that makes me less of a target.'

'It may suit you at eighteen young man, but when love strikes be prepared to change your mind. We have no control over destiny; our path is woven by the gods.'

When Ubba returned he took Sigtryggr over to the palace and showed him to his room. By chance, Ralf and his family arrived in the courtyard before they reached the front steps.

They were all on horseback and Sigtryggr was impressed with the quality of their mounts. His eyes fell on Skye and he was captivated by her beauty. He strode over to her and took the reins of her horse. 'May I assist you in dismounting, young lady?'

'Skye gave him a bold look. 'I think I can manage, thank you. You must be Sigtryggr from Ireland? My brother failed to report on your exceptional height and good looks, even though marred by a sword swipe across your eye, which only helps to accentuate your demeanour.'

'Alas, the injury was fairly recent, but I have retrained to compensate.'

Grooms appeared, to take the horses. Sigtryggr turned to young Thorin. Ubba had said he was only seven years old, but he was as tall as a teenager with a body made of pure muscle. As their eyes met he saw a flash of the warrior he would become. Thorin nodded at him as if he recognised him.

Ralf said, 'This is my son Thorin, who has been excited to meet you since Ranulf confirmed you had arrived.'

Sigtryggr nodded to Ralf and then looked across at his wife, who was chatting to Ubba intently. She was as blonde as Torri, with deep blue eyes, and had a smile that lit up her face. Ubba brought her over to him. 'Gytha, may I present Sigtryggr of Dublin.'

He took her hand, kissed it gently and bowed. 'My lady, I am delighted to meet you.'

'Heavens above! Are all Irish Danes as tall as you?'

'Yes, my lady. We spend so much time in peat bogs and driving rain, it increases our growth rate.'

Gytha laughed, 'I love a young man with a sense of humour; it is so endearing.'

Ubba led them into the palace and the servants hovered, ready to escort them to their rooms.

'Dinner will be served at my house at 7:30 p.m. so you have time to relax, bathe and change first. Thorin, would you like to come down early to mix with my offspring? There is a young lady dying to see you.'

Ubba turned to Ralf and winked and Sigtryggr assumed this was so that Gytha and Ralf could have some time alone. The servants ushered them upstairs and Ubba returned home to have his shower and relax before dinner.

Torri was supervising the boys who were changing into their tunics and he went straight into the shower after unbinding his plait. He came out, grabbed a towel and wrapped it round his waist, then flung himself onto his bed for a rest. He lay with his eyes closed, thinking about the two suspects that a patrol had brought in, who had been acting suspiciously. He had not been satisfied with their answers to his questions so decided to detain them and let Ivar carry out the interview when he returned on Monday. It was amazing how people suddenly found their tongue in the presence of Ivar the Boneless.

The door opened and he heard little feet padding across the room and approaching his bed. He knew exactly who it was but kept his eyes shut to tease her. She climbed up next to him and kissed his cheek. He grabbed hold of her and lifted her up in the air. 'Is this the little minx who needs a good smacking for talking too much?' After her initial shock he threw her up in the air and then caught her, and she giggled as he placed her across his waist.

'Can I comb your hair out now you have washed it?'

'If it pleases you my dear, as it is obvious I am not going to get a snooze before dinner.'

'You will have to move to the chair.' As he got up and she scrambled down, his towel unravelled and fell to the floor. He grabbed it, flustered. Freya roared with laughter. 'I have four brothers who walk between the washroom and their bedrooms stark naked. I know exactly what men have between their legs, Daddy.'

'Freya, are you trying to shock me? I will speak to Arne and Viggo about parading naked in front of you. I trust you are not in the habit of emulating them.'

'Why not? I have swum naked with them since I was a child – even Erik, Refil and Thorin. What's the big deal?'

'Well, you are eight years old now and this has to stop. I will speak to your mother about this.'

'But why, Daddy?'

He sighed in exasperation, 'You are approaching puberty now and you should cover your body from men or they may take advantage of you.'

'Does that mean they may want to have sex with me? I am not that innocent Daddy; the boys talk about sex all the time and the antics Erik used to get up to with the milkmaid would make even you blush. Besides, Arne says he will chop the balls off anyone who thinks he can have sex with me. Thorin has made me a silver hammer, which has a very high-pitched whistle inside. He says if ever I am in trouble I should blow it and he will come to rescue me.' She pulled a leather thong out over her dress and showed him a three-inch-long silver scrolled hammer. 'Thorin says only birds, dogs, wolves, horses and he can hear it.'

Ubba groaned and ran his fingers through his silken blond hair, then Torri appeared. 'Come on Ubba, get dressed. Our guests will be down in ten minutes and you are just lounging about letting Freya comb your hair. Off you go, Freya. Thorin has been looking for you.'

He couldn't speak after hearing these revelations from his beautiful "innocent" daughter. Torri looked at him. 'What on earth's the matter with you, Ubba? Have you been struck dumb?'

In a very shaky voice he replied, 'We need to talk about Freya and her knowledge of sex. She has shocked me to the core. I had no idea my beautiful eight-year-old daughter understands all about sex. You have failed in your duty to protect her innocence and I am appalled.'

'Ubba, stop being ridiculous. Do you seriously think your daughter is unaware of what goes on in our bedroom between you and I, or doesn't join in the conversations with her brothers and servants about their sex lives? She has been surrounded by nature from the day she was born; she has seen dogs and horses mate and watched their offspring being born. Of course I have discussed the repercussions of experimenting with boys and sex and bringing shame to our door. You were reared in an all-male household. Girls are a lot quicker to learn about sex; they have to be.'

'But she admits to swimming naked with her brothers and Thorin... and what's even more horrifying is that she said, "Daddy, the boys talk about sex all the time and the antics Erik used to get up to with the milkmaid would make even you blush."'

Torri roared with laughter. 'For God's sake Ubba, children are best exposed to sex at a young age in a family environment, so they learn the dangers that may befall them as they mature. You don't need to hide her body away at eight; she knows all about puberty and that she can't conceive until her bleeding starts. Get a grip on yourself and leave this for another day.'

Ubba sighed then jumped up and quickly dressed in a navy tunic embroidered in silver thread across the chest with a stag's head. He tried to banish his thoughts about Freya and went to greet his guests.

Dinners were always less formal at home and the younger children were allowed to sit at the table. Serena had Astrid and Theo with her and he swept Astrid into his arms, kissed her and complimented her on her pretty dress. Freya was talking to Thorin and judging by their glances in Sigtryggr's direction, he was the topic of conversation. Ranulf, Arne, Skye and Sigtryggr were chatting together and Ralf and Gytha were chatting intimately, looking out of the window.

Torri showed their guests to their seats then took his place at the head of the table. Torri was on his right, with honoured guest Sigtryggr on the left. Skye was next to him and Gytha was opposite. Gytha was grilling Sigtryggr about his home and family in Ireland and flirting with him at the same time. Torri was also enjoying the conversation and in his opinion, trying to "out flirt" Gytha. Skye was listening intently and doing her best not to show any undue interest in him, whilst chatting to her father on her other side.

Ubba could not understand why the females were so keen to impress Sigtryggr when to him, it was obvious that he only had eyes for Skye. However, it amused him that Torri and Gytha were sparring for his attention and preventing him engaging Skye in conversation. He even noticed Serena giving Sigtryggr several searching looks, but he could not see any reason why this young arrogant pup should be so popular with women, most of them old enough to be his mother. He applied himself to the excellent French wine he had purloined from Ivar's extensive wine cellar.

THREE

After the meal Ubba had a few moments alone with Serena, who was returning to the palace with her children. She asked him whether he would be joining her later and he declined, saying he expected the night to turn into a long drinking session between the men. He felt slightly guilty for using this as an excuse as his intention was to remonstrate with Torri for flirting. The fact he was jealous never entered his head, as he had never encountered the feeling before. Torri had never given him cause to feel jealous in all their years together; her rebuttal of amorous men had led to her "ice maiden" nickname. He had always enjoyed seeing men clamouring for her attention, safe in the knowledge that his beautiful wife belonged exclusively to him.

Freya was not best pleased to be dismissed by her mother. She was on the verge of a tantrum, complaining that Thorin was over a year younger than her.

He approached her and whispered, 'Bed, young lady, or I will give you a good thrashing.' He watched her eyes flicker as she assessed whether her precious father would dare to carry out his threat. In return he gave her one of Ivar's fierce looks. Knowing that her brothers had never been spared punishment for their misdeeds, she capitulated, but scowled at him in return.

They moved into the salon. Sigtryggr tried to engage Skye in a private conversation, which was interrupted by Arne. Ubba chuckled to himself, reflecting on what the outcome would be if Skye succumbed to Sigtryggr's charms. Ralf had told him that Skye had flatly refused to consider an arranged marriage and would only marry for love. He did not think Ralf or Gytha would be too pleased if their precious daughter moved to Ireland. He remembered the night Ivar had told him he was going to marry Skye. He himself had held an axe to his throat, coming close to killing his brother to protect her freedom. Ivar realised he couldn't keep his throne without his brother, but his vanity had made him ask her still. She had declined, much to Ivar's surprise, claiming she had no desire to become a queen.

Ubba ensured the evening did not end in a male drinking session, citing Sigtryggr's long journey as an excuse. He suggested that he and Sigtryggr would ride home with Ralf's family the following day and then he would take him on a brief tour of the area.

When they reached their bedroom, Torri started removing her hair ornaments while sitting at her dressing table. Quietly, he moved behind her and unclipped the sapphire necklace he had given her, and she watched him with mounting curiosity in the mirror. She hadn't picked up on any sexual signals from Ubba during the evening, but wondered whether the wine had made a difference. He undid the back of her dress and slid it down to her waist. She lifted her bottom so he could slide the dress down over it.

'You're keen tonight! What brought this on?'

He pulled her to her feet and wrapped his arms around her waist, removing her undergarments with one hand. 'You gave me the impression you were craving a good humping, lady, so I shall grant your wish.'

Torri gasped in shock as he picked her up and took her over to the bed, depositing her on her knees at the same time as removing his tunic. 'I think you need reminding that you are not a simpering teenager lusting after an arrogant Irish pup, but my wife.'

'Ubba, how dare you speak to me like that?' She struggled to twist away but he had her pinned to the bed with one hand on her shoulder, the other on her hip and his legs between hers. She knew she did not have the physical strength to break free.

'Do you deny you were flirting with Sigtryggr? Considering you were openly doing it in front of me, I don't see how you can.'

'But flirting is not indicating I want sex with him. Gytha was just as bad. He's an attractive young man.'

'And you are my wife and will refrain from such unseemly behaviour. If you were trying to do it to annoy me then well done, you succeeded... and this is your punishment.' He forced her legs apart and entered her with no foreplay.

'How bloody hypocritical from my husband – who has a mistress, too.' She lay still, devastated that her "perfect" husband could display such anger.

When he had finished he lifted her onto her back and lay beside her. 'Now I will attend to your pleasure, my dear.'

She slapped his face and shouted at him, 'Don't dare touch me again. I cannot believe that you were capable of raping me Ubba, for something I did not do. That was pure male dominance and I can't believe you did it. It was a sheer act of violence and one that neither your esteemed father, Bjorn nor Ivar would have done. You were jealous and allowed your anger to escalate. When Sigtryggr asked why I tolerated you having a mistress I replied that I loved you. Then he asked whether our arrangement worked both ways and I replied, "No, it does not as I have no need of any other man in my life but Ubba." Ask him yourself if you don't believe me. You have shattered my faith in you. Now go and sleep in Viggo's bed; I can't bear to look at you or have you near me. Feel free to go to your mistress, because you won't get the chance to touch me again.'

Now the jealousy, lust and anger had dissipated he suddenly realised what he had done, and he was horrified. He had not considered it rape when he did it but now Torri had condemned him he could see that it was, and he was ashamed.

'Torri, I didn't mean...'

'Get out before I scream the house down and I have to explain to your son and daughter what their dishonourable father did to their mother.'

He reached for his clothes and dressed. Torri pulled the bed covers over her and turned her back to him.

He desperately wanted to take her in his arms and beg for her forgiveness, but he knew she would not accept it. He opened the door with no idea of what he was going to do next. He paused and listened and could hear Torri sobbing into her pillow. The door defined the barrier that had come between them and he made his way to Viggo's room, threw himself on the bed and let his emotions flow. He tossed and turned until finally dawn came. Eventually, he gave up on trying to sleep and went to the bathroom to wash, where he saw the red outline of Torri's fingers across his left cheek. His misdeed was imprinted on his face for everybody to see.

He headed out of the palace grounds and into the empty Jorvik streets. He went to the church and opened the door, praying it would be empty. He forced himself up the nave to the altar steps and then knelt below a statue of the Virgin Mary. He had been baptised as a Christian when he first arrived in Mercia with his father, and he had some knowledge of the Christian faith. He knew that the Christian God forgave sins and he thought that He might help him resolve his problem.

Ironically, he knew some of the Latin texts used by the Church but wondered whether the Christian God could understand him in Danish when he entreated him for help. *Why did he even think Christ would want to help a heathen like him in the first place?* He told him of his despicable act, asking for forgiveness and a solution to heal the rift with his wife.

A priest appeared at the altar, preparing for mass.

As Ubba turned around, aware there was someone behind him, he recognised Father Abraham.

'My lord Ubba how delighted I am to see you praying in our church. Can I be of service to you?'

Ubba was relieved and replied, 'Yes Father, I would like to confess to you and ask your help in righting my wrong.'

'Come through to the vestry, my son. Nobody will disturb us.'

Ubba walked up to the altar, remembering to bow and cross himself in front of it. He went through the vestry and then into an office down the corridor. Father Abraham took his seat behind the desk and he sat facing him.

'Well, lord, tell me how you have sinned; I can see it is bothering you. But tell me why you came here, first, rather than praying to your own gods?'

Ubba hesitated and Father Abraham continued, 'Now, I want the truth or there is no point in hearing your confession.'

'I wasn't sure my gods would consider what I did a sin.'

Father Abraham laughed, 'So you thought you would ask the Virgin Mary to forgive your sin and help you resolve your problem because Odin may not.'

'Something like that, Father. The Christian faith always preaches about forgiveness of sins.'

'Go on, I don't shock easily but you must be contrite and prepared to absolve your sin and make amends. The Church doesn't let you off the hook just because you admit your guilt.'

'I am ashamed to admit that in a jealous rage, I accused my wife of flirting with another man, knowing full well she would never commit adultery… and I raped her.'

'Ubba, rape in marriage is not a sin, nor is it against the law.'

Well, Father, it should be. I have beheaded two of my own men who committed rape during a raid, even though they knew I forbade it. Where does that leave me as a commander when I have raped my own wife knowing she was innocent of infidelity? I have shattered her trust and faith in me and worse still, I have a mistress with my wife's approval, so I am nothing but a hypocrite.'

'Ubba, had you been drinking before this act? Drink is often the root cause of many evil deeds.'

'No Father, I was not drunk. I will not use that as an excuse for my wicked behaviour.'

'I don't know your wife well – only through her reputation and the many good deeds she has done during her governance as your brother's consort. She has done a lot to improve the poverty of families and has championed women's rights. She is an able judge and presides over the petty court sessions better than any man could ever do. She gives fair and just punishment and I can totally understand her devastation over what you did, and her loss of trust in you.

'You have also done many things to improve the city and steadied your brother's hand in office. Your skill as a trainer of men is a legend in itself and your kindness and understanding are appreciated by everyone. Jealousy can be a cruel emotion and can twist the mind into thinking one partner has deceived the other. Your contrition is obviously genuine. There is no doubt about your love for your wife, or hers for you. I am sure you can persuade her to forgive you in time.'

'Father, I didn't think about what I was doing and how Torri would view it. She has told me she can't bear to look at me. She said my father Ragnar, brother Bjorn and even Ivar would not do what I did, and she is absolutely right. I have shamed not only myself but my entire family.'

'My son, you are being overly harsh on yourself. This incident is between you and Torri. She has been an admirable mother to six children and she will not tell them; what you did was so out of character, she will not want them knowing that Ubba the warrior is only human and can make mistakes. Torri will know in her heart that you made a mistake. She is a wise woman and has been wife to some very volatile characters whose inadequacies she knew only too well. It will have come as a shock to her that her idol is only human after all. She will forgive you... although I would keep a watch for flying arrows and axes as she has the skills to take her revenge.'

'I hadn't thought about that, Father. She can be very cunning and will bide her time. The last man who tried to rape her had his balls chopped off and then his body ripped from throat to crotch.'

'I heard the story and under the circumstances I am more than happy to leave your punishment in the hands of your wife. You are a very brave or foolish man to take on such a proficient executioner. You may find you no longer have the upper hand in your marriage.'

'Believe me Father, I never did... but she is such an incredible woman, whom I have loved since I was sixteen years old.'

'Go with my blessing, son. You may have to crawl on your knees for forgiveness, but she will let you back into her arms because she cannot deny her love for you. She has a similar profession to me in dealing with errant members of our flock and I trust her punishment will be fair and accepted by you.'

FOUR

Ubba went back to the palace, to sit in Serena's rooms. She was dressing Theo and Astrid was running around in a nightie. She ran up to him and stroked his hair. As she pulled it back, it revealed the red mark across his face.

'What have you done to your face, Daddy? It is all red.'

'I got caught by a branch while riding through the woods yesterday.'

Serena strode up to look at his face, then gave him an enquiring look before shouting for one of the servants and asking her to supervise the children at breakfast.

When they were alone she said, 'Now, that is a female handprint. I want to know who administered it, and why?'

He snapped, 'It is none of your business, Serena – remember your place.'

'Have you been chasing another woman, Ubba?'

'Certainly not. Torri and I had an argument last night. She lost her temper, lashed out and caught my face by mistake.'

'Torri does not lose her temper without good cause, and never with you. You must have provoked her.

What did you say?'

'We had a row because Freya told me that she had seen her brothers naked around the house and swum with them last summer and I did not think it appropriate.'

'She's only eight years old and nowhere near puberty yet. She knows about sex as she sees it going on around her with both animals and people. She is renowned for spying on courting couples; she has caught Arne testing the water on more than one occasion.'

'Perhaps I was just being an over-anxious father, as my darling wife pointed out. Have you got some cream that will cover up the fingermarks?'

Serena ushered him into her bedroom and found some unguent to put on his face. As she finished, she kissed him and whispered, 'There's time for a quick one before breakfast if you like?'

He pulled away and snapped, 'No, I am not in the mood and there are guests for breakfast who must be entertained.' He strode out and she followed him, frowning at his reaction. It was completely out of character and she could only conclude the row had been more serious than he was prepared to admit.

She observed him over breakfast. He put on a brave face, but his smile never reached his eyes and his cheerful banter was missing. Gytha commented to her that he must have overindulged in wine at dinner. She knew he was perfectly sober when she left his house the night before, although he expected to have a late drinking session. She questioned Arne about what time they had dispersed last night and was surprised to hear that Ubba had suggested they have an early night as Sigtryggr would be exhausted from his travels.

Ubba and Sigtryggr accompanied Ralf's family home and he was relieved when Ralf and Ranulf offered to show his guest the horses. Ubba joined Gytha in the kitchen. She had observed his unusually quiet demeanour.

'Come on then, what have you done? That is a woman's hand mark across your cheek. Which lady have you offended since 11 p.m. on Saturday night? Don't tell me you have dallied with another woman and been found out? If you have, you are a bloody fool.'

He rubbed his hands through his hair, which she knew was a sign of his despair and embarrassment. 'Torri and I argued last night. I accused her of flirting with Sigtryggr and I told her that her behaviour was unacceptable... and then I... I saw red thinking she might have been unfaithful to me, and I forced her to have sex.'

'No, you couldn't possible have done that; you love every bone in her body and could never violate her. I flirted with him too – he is a very handsome young man – but Torri would never sleep with him.'

'I know that now. She just lay there and let me do it. It wasn't done in love but in anger. She didn't cry out, just called me a hypocrite and said I was punishing her for something she would never even contemplate.' Tears ran down his cheeks as he continued, 'And afterwards she said that never would my father, Bjorn or Ivar have done such a wicked deed and used male dominance to make a point. And she is absolutely right. She told me she couldn't bear to look at me.'

Gytha gathered him in her arms. 'Oh Ubba, where did this wicked act come from?'

'My warped wicked mind. I have never experienced jealousy over Torri before because I am always so sure of her fidelity. She didn't take a lover when she returned to Jormund. She was so distraught over Guthrun's death and I should have helped her through her grief; I wasn't there when she needed me most. Please don't tell a soul, even if Torri confides in you.'

'Torri is an experienced woman and would know that you were just lashing out through jealousy. You will both find a way through it when you have come to terms with what you did. Your grief is obviously genuine.'

On the return journey Sigtryggr asked, 'Ubba, have I offended you in any way? If I have, I apologise profusely.'

'No, not at all. I have a throbbing head, probably from the wine last night. I don't normally drink much and it's a while since I've had wine. Come, let's canter up this hill from which you can see Jorvik and the valley below.'

When they returned to the palace Arne met them in the courtyard on his horse and suggested he take Sigtryggr to see their troop's longboats on the river. This was the perfect excuse to leave Arne to entertain their guest until dinner. Ubba's lack of sleep was catching up with him and his despair was deepening. He returned to the palace and decided to send a note to Torri saying he would stay there to entertain Sigtryggr tonight. He desperately wanted to run home, throw himself at his wife's feet and beg for her forgiveness. The look she had given him when she ordered him to leave would be with him forever. He appreciated that Torri would need more time before he did so.

He had an hour's snooze before dinner, followed by a shower and then an uneventful dinner with Serena, Astrid, Sigtryggr and Arne. He picked at his food as his appetite had completely gone.

Serena looked on with concern as Ubba sank deeper into a black hole that even she could not see any easy way out of. By now, she knew what had happened. She knew, too, that Torri would not end their marriage, as their love for one another ran so very deep. How on earth this situation had occurred was beyond her wildest imaginings. Ubba had the sunniest personality of any man and was loved by everyone. He rarely lost his temper and wouldn't harm animal or human. She observed that Shadow, who normally curled up under the table at Arne's feet, had deliberately moved to Ubba's side without any signal from him. Even the wolf knew that he was upset and when Ubba ignored him he put his paw on his knee until he responded by giving him a pat.

After dinner Arne and Sigtryggr left. Shadow reluctantly left Ubba's side to follow his master. While Astrid was distracted playing with one of her dolls, Serena pulled Ubba to one side. 'Ivar will be back tomorrow, and he will sense there is something wrong between you and Torri. She spent the day at home confined to her room, feigning a stomach ache, but was heard crying by one of the servants. Ivar adores her and he will be angry with you. This was so out of character. Rumours are circulating already about a rift between you, and Arne has already asked me what is wrong.'

'I will tell Ivar. I know he will be angry with me. His love for Torri runs very deep and he will be so ashamed of me – probably even more than I am of myself. His reaction will be volcanic, and rightly so.'

'Are you joining me later?'

'I need to be alone and do nothing to make matters worse. She told me to go to you because I wouldn't be touching her body again. You know under Danish law she could divorce me for this, just like she divorced Bjorn for infidelity.'

Ubba, although it is hard to understand that you could have done this ugly deed, I think it highly unlikely she will divorce you. She is devoted to you and she would not deny her children their father.'

Astrid ran over and he picked her up and cuddled her. 'Goodnight my little angel, sleep tight.' He put her down and Serena could see tears in his eyes. He kissed her and left the room at speed.

The next morning, after another night of tossing and turning and minimal sleep, he realised he could not train. He knew it would cause more rumours, but he sent a message to Frank saying he was ill and to take over the sessions. He ordered breakfast in his room and forced himself to eat something.

He went to his office and awaited his fate, going over in his mind how Ivar might react. There was the prospect he might kill him. The way he felt at that moment, it would have been a blessed release.

At midday he heard Ivar arrive and he stood back from the window to observe.

Viggo and two guards on horseback accompanied Ivar. On the cart he had some crates containing more raptors for his aviary. Viggo helped him down, took the wagon round to the aviary and supervised the birds.

The head of his household Egil greeted him at the bottom of the steps. 'Good afternoon lord, I trust you had a good trip. Would you like some lunch?'

As they climbed the steps Ivar replied, 'Yes, we had a pleasant weekend and restocked. We have eaten already. Anything unusual to report?'

'Sigtryggr of Ireland has arrived.'

'Oh, good! Finally he has made it. Did Ubba entertain him?'

'Yes, lord; he included him at a private dinner with Ralf and his family on Saturday evening and Master Arne is with him now.'

'Is Ubba out on patrol?'

'Lord Ubba is ill and in his office. He ordered Frank to supervise training this morning.'

'Ubba has never had a day's illness in his life! What ails him?'

'I don't know, my lord... possibly overindulgence from Saturday night.'

'Egil, why are you avoiding looking at me? Something is wrong; I can smell a rat. I will get to the bottom of this immediately.'

He made his way to Ubba's office, convinced that something serious was afoot. He flung open the door and saw Ubba leaning against the far wall. Apart from being pale, he could see nothing outwardly wrong with him.

'What ails you, brother?'

'Nothing but fear, deep remorse and shame.'

'What have you done?' Ivar approached him and he saw Ubba flinch and turn his eyes away.

'On Saturday night at dinner, Torri flirted with Sigtryggr and I was, for the first time ever, jealous. It's an emotion I have never encountered before. He did nothing out of order and Gytha was also flirting with him. It was just gentle banter, with the women trying to outdo one another. It angered me though, and as I had left the two of them alone together earlier in the afternoon my mind raced – and the possibility that Torri may have gone further reared its ugly head. I thought her behaviour was inappropriate and when we went to bed I remonstrated with her.'

Ivar interrupted, giving him the fiercest look he had ever seen. 'If you laid a finger on Torri you know I will have to kill you.'

'I didn't beat her, but I did force myself on her.'

Ivar screamed, 'No, you cannot have raped her! You love her so. She is the mother of your three children and Bjorn's two boys. You are my hero too, the honourable warrior whom everyone loves. I am the evil, wicked monster Ragnarsson and you are the saint.' He came closer and Ubba froze. Ivar punched him across his cheekbone and continued to rain blows on his face and chest with increasing force. 'Defend yourself you bastard, before I go any further.'

Ubba gasped, 'I won't. I deserve every one of your blows.' Blood was pouring down his face from his nose, lips and cheeks.

'Had you been drinking, taking drugs or been poisoned? I can't believe you would do this to Torri in cold blood.'

'No. I did it and she lay there and let me; she didn't cry out or struggle to free herself. She said afterwards that I had done it in a jealous fit of rage knowing that she would never have been unfaithful to me, to exert my dominance and make a point. She said even you would never have done that, and my father would have been mortified by my actions. She told me to get out and sleep in Viggo's room as she couldn't bear to look at me.'

Ivar punched Ubba in the chest one last time and then staggered to the door. He flung it open and screamed to the guard outside, 'Fetch Torri.'

'The guard stuttered, 'I will send for her, my lord.'

He shut the door. Ubba was still propped against the wall, struggling for breath.

'I can't believe that you did this. You would never rape a woman, never mind your wife. What came over you, and what are you going to tell your children?' He wrapped his arms around Ubba and sobbed on his chest. He guided him over to the sofa and they both collapsed. Ivar pulled him closer, still weeping, and then Torri arrived. She stopped dead, surveying the scene.

'God forbid Ivar, what have you done to him?' She ran back to the door and told the guard to fetch hot water, soap and towels, and returned to the sofa.

'I haven't done anything that will kill him but if you want me to, I will. Why have you not had him confined to a cell and strung up by his balls?'

'Ivar, when will you learn that violence only ever breeds more violence? He made a mistake in a jealous rage without any thought to the consequences, and he is devastated. How many times have you done things that you shouldn't and regretted it later? You experience the red mist in battle to extend your power and assert your dominance. He did the same with me and if that's the only mistake he makes in life then I can forgive him, because I love him.'

'How can you forgive him for this Torri? I swore fealty to you, as did Halfdan and Bjorn. I am duty bound to protect you. What if he does it again?'

'Ivar, I can assure you that he will never harm me again – and if he does, I will allow you to kill him if I don't do it first. Now listen to me! I will not let this ruin my marriage, or my relationship with you, Ivar. We cannot afford to be distracted by this when war is imminent.'

A servant came in with water and cloths and put it on the table closest to the sofa. He glanced at Ubba and left in a hurry.

Torri knelt and bathed Ubba's face. The blood had

stopped oozing. Bruises were already starting to form around his eyes and cheeks. When he winced, she knew there may be a break in the bone. There was a possibility he had a broken nose. She pulled his tunic and shirt off and was shocked that his axe and seax were tucked into his belt.

'Why didn't he defend himself?'

'He wouldn't – he said he deserved every blow.'

She checked his ribs and although they looked sore, she didn't think any were broken. His breathing had steadied and although his face was a mess, she knew that time would heal the skin. She kissed his cheek. 'I think you may live to fight another day.' She put the tunic back on over his head.

Ubba whispered, 'I am so sorry; please forgive me. I don't know what came over me.' Tears rolled down his cheeks.

Ivar hugged Torri. 'I'm sorry. I shouldn't have punched him, but I could not believe my compassionate gentle brother could ever do that to you.' He also started crying.

'Look at you both! Victims of that terrible Ragnarsson temper. I didn't know you had it in you Ubba, but I suppose you displayed it whenever you got hurt in battle, so deep down it has been lurking.' She put cushions behind him to prop him up, and kissed his torn lips.

Ivar started pacing up and down. 'How are we going to deal with this? What I have done will be common knowledge around the palace by now. Your children will have to be given an explanation.'

Torri replied, 'We shall say you two had a violent disagreement that turned into a fight.'

Ivar interrupted, 'Torri, look at him – and there's not a mark on me! All my brothers know to keep their distance when I am angry.'

'Well, you could have had him tied up by a guard?'

'That still won't make any sense; he has the strength and agility to knock two of us out and nobody will believe he would not defend himself.'

'Let's get him into a bedroom and I will go and tell the children that you have been fighting and he will have to stay out of sight until the bruising goes down.' She bent down to Ubba. 'Sweetheart, can you stand if I support you?'

Ubba moaned but nodded his head and put one hand on the arm of the chair and the other around Torri's waist. He yelped as his ribs hurt but he managed to stand and keep his balance. Ivar opened the door to discover three men outside; he asked Frank to help Torri. Frank was horrified when he saw Ubba's face. After a few steps, Ubba asked to stop as he was feeling dizzy; they halted until he regained his balance.

Ivar opened the door to check that nobody was in the corridor. Torri and Frank led him to the bed and lowered him gently onto it, then Torri propped him up with the pillows.

Ivar said, 'I need to go and welcome Sigtryggr. If you want I will sleep here with him overnight.'

'No, I will tend to him once I have spoken to the children.'

Ivar left the room sensing Frank's anger, and realised

he was going to have a difficult time overcoming everybody's shocked condemnation.

Frank started undoing Ivar's boots and said quietly, 'Why did you not defend yourself, Ubba? I know Ivar has incredible strength, but you could have knocked him off balance in a second.' As Torri removed his tunic Frank saw the bruising breaking out on his chest and the axe and seax still fastened to his belt.

Ubba said nothing. Torri said, 'Ivar did not intend to kill him; he just saw red and wanted to hurt him. You know how volatile Ivar can be. Would you stay with him until I come back? I need to go home.'

Frank undressed Ubba and helped him into bed.

'Can you talk about it?'

'No, I can't... but you must stop the men blaming Ivar. It is not his fault; I deserved every one of his blows. I shattered his faith in me and he took it very badly.'

'But Arne and Viggo will never forgive Ivar for harming you. Arne has more of a temper than you and he won't reconcile until he knows the truth.'

'Well you must advise him to let it go and convince him that Ivar was not to blame; the fault was all mine.'

FIVE

Torri returned carrying a tray of food for both of them. Ubba had drifted off to sleep and Frank had been left to wonder at what this huge argument had been about between the two brothers. He saw by her face the traumatic ordeal she had faced telling her children, but said nothing and left her to care for her wounded husband.

She poured the soup into a bowl and gently woke Ubba. 'Sweetheart, I need you to eat some soup to preserve your strength overnight.' She pulled him forward, shook out the pillows and propped him up. He groaned from the pain in his ribs. He agreed to eat but wanted to know what she had said to the children and how they had reacted.

Torri explained that she had told them that the two brothers had argued but did not disclose why, despite repeated pressure from the boys. She told them it was a private matter and had now been resolved. She admitted to them that he had been badly hurt because he had not defended himself. Freya had been very quiet but asked if she could come to see him. When Torri had told her to wait until he was feeling better, she cried.

'Oh, Torri! I am so sorry. I should have realised that

Ivar would lash out; he worships you like a goddess and I didn't realise how much he looked up to me. I have shattered both your opinions of me in a single moment of jealousy. I don't deserve you and yet you have forgiven me.'

'Ubba, you are only human and you made a mistake in a moment of madness. Of course I was shocked and disappointed in you, but I wasn't entirely blameless. I flirted with Sigtryggr and I should have known better. Many men rape their wives to instill authority and obedience, but you are such a gentle man and such a compassionate lover that I never expected you to react so badly. I know I have never given you cause to be jealous before but as I have forgiven your infidelity with Serena, it *was* very hypocritical of you.'

Ubba reached out, touched her face, pulled her forward and kissed her nose. 'My wonderful wise queen. How do you cope with all the things that life throws at you, with such skill and determination? We Ragnarrsons have made your life a constant battle for survival and you have been steadfast while guiding us through all the traumas we encountered, fighting by our side and raising our children. Without you and Lagertha none of us would have survived.'

'And if your father had exerted his dominance and authority by killing me, the pregnant wife of the man who usurped his throne, then I would not have been here. Was it an act of mercy and compassion, or did the gods intervene? It may have been that Ragnar was highly susceptible to pretty blonde blue-eyed women. He never made a move until after Guthrun was two months old. I was effectively his slave, so wasn't in a position to object – and why would I? We knew it could not continue as when Aslaug found out she would kill me.'

'I will never forget that day. Bjorn, Halfdan and I were considered old enough to witness our father blood eagle your husband. He died in true Viking fashion without uttering a sound. You witnessed the cruel torture of your husband, knowing that you and your child's life were forfeit too. You never begged for mercy whereas I threw up several times and would have run away without Bjorn's steady hand holding me up. What we didn't know is that eight-year-old Ivar was watching it too, from a rooftop. We all saw your outstanding courage and bravery and it had a profound effect on us. We were terrified that our father would kill you and yet he stepped down from the platform covered in blood, walked over to you, took your hand and kissed it, proclaiming, 'I do not wage war on innocent women and children.'

'I was so shocked, I didn't believe him. I thought he would bide his time and then slit my throat one night and blame it on someone else. Your father was a good man, Ubba, firm when he had to be but not a cruel or vindictive man. You are just like him and he knew you struggled with your conscience to become the outstanding warrior you became; he admired your courage and resilience.'

She fed him portions of orange, strawberries and grapes she had raided from the kitchen stores where expensive rare food that had been purchased from merchants coming from Mediterranean countries were stored under lock and key. Finally, she prepared for bed, realising she had no nightgown and would have to lie naked next to her injured husband. She saw him register this as she approached the bed.

'I am here to nurse you and nothing else, Ubba; refrain from any sexual advances towards me. You have shattered the trust I had in you and it will take me a while to want you again. Attempt to force me and you will end up in the same state as the last man who raped me.'

Ubba groaned, 'I am in no condition my love to attempt such a deed. I know I have to regain your trust before I can expect to resume our sex life. I am just grateful you are willing to forgive me.'

It was a difficult night for both of them. Ubba was in severe pain from his ribs and when he turned over he yelped. His head felt like he had been kicked by a horse and his cheeks were swelling across his eyes. Once, he had staggered to the bathroom and struggled with dizziness and disorientation. Torri had supported him back to the bed as he could not cope with the pain, or see properly.

The next morning, Ubba woke early and crawled on his knees to the dressing table to look in the mirror. He didn't recognise the swollen face looking back at him. He had bruising over both eyes and his cheeks. His nose had swollen and his lips were torn. His chest was covered in bruises and he could not take a deep breath as his ribs were sore. Ivar could certainly punch hard; all his strength was in his upper body. He remembered

Frank taking a crashing fall from his horse in battle and being trapped underneath it while it thrashed to get up, kicking his upper body, face and chest. He had ended up looking like this.

Torri put her arms around him from behind. 'You idiot, Ubba – you had no need to take such a beating. And if Ivar had used his seax or axe you would certainly be dead.'

'I didn't realise just how much Ivar worshipped you and me. He could not believe that I could do such a wicked thing. He said he was the cruel wicked one and I was the saint and could not possibly have harmed the woman I had loved since I was sixteen. But I did. I let you all down.'

After a light breakfast, when Ubba discovered his jaw was preventing him from opening his mouth, they were discussing his next move when Ivar swept in accompanied by an older man dressed in flamboyant blue and yellow silk who could only have been of Arab origin.

'This is Sulamain, one of the tutors I have engaged to teach Viggo. One of his many skills is as a healer and I have brought him to check you over after your drunken brawl yesterday. I will leave him to examine you as I have matters to attend to. Torri, he will prescribe potions to assist in healing and give his advice to aid recovery, which must be followed to the letter. Do not let my brother do anything stupid or ignore his advice.' He then left the room, trying to avoid looking at Ubba's battered face.

Sulamain smiled as the door closed. 'Your brother asked me to take a look at you, but wasn't quick enough to put his gloves on to prevent me seeing his swollen hands. I have served three different *emirs* in my lifetime and I know just how volatile brotherly relationships can be. I can tell just by looking at you that you are not a man who overindulges in alcohol. Now, let me take a look at you and assess the damage.'

He pulled the covers off Ubba who was sitting propped up by pillows. He produced a small metal instrument from his bag, which had a bright light that illuminated Ubba's face. He carefully examined his eyes. 'Such beautiful blue eyes, which I am delighted to report do not appear damaged behind the eyeball. The swelling is causing the discomfort and blocking your vision.' He ran his thumb and forefinger down his nose. 'There is an old break here, probably caused by a sword, and the tip has been hit hard but not broken.' He carried on his gentle examination of his patient's cheeks and mouth. 'The right cheekbone is cracked and your lips are torn but they will heal. Did you lose consciousness at all?' Ubba shook his head in response. 'Now let's examine this muscular chest. I must declare that you are so physically fit you have provided your own armour to protect your vital organs. Unlike some of your race, you do not carry any fat and I suspect you are extremely agile and can run as fast as a horse if necessary.' He checked his heartbeat and pulse with his fingers. 'Very impressive readings – better than most Saracens – and they are fit fighting men.'

Ubba replied, 'I have been to Jerusalem and Alexandria and ridden across the desert on a camel and on horseback. I have to admit I struggled with the oppressive heat, but not as badly as some of my colleagues. I much prefer a colder climate to your country's excessive heat.'

'Your body would have learned to adapt to the conditions if you had persevered, as your level of fitness is excellent.' He was examining his back now.

'I was leaning against a wall, so Ivar did not hit me there.'

'You will have been banged against the wall and I need to check your lungs and kidneys to be certain. You have no broken ribs so there is no danger of a punctured lung, but you will be sore. I will show your wife how to strap your ribs up to give you support. I have some arnica ointment that your wife can put on your face to relieve the swelling. It will reduce the healing time considerably. Tell me, what is hurting you most right now?'

'I seem to have balance issues. My head wants me to lie down even when I am standing upright. I feel dizzy, sick and disorientated like I do when I am seasick.'

'Ah, well what you describe is caused by an imbalance within the inner ear. The punches you received will have disturbed it and it will settle down in time.'

Torri asked, 'Should he remain in bed and avoid exercise?'

'Certainly not! He needs to keep moving to drain the swelling from his body. He must not partake in sword fights but gentle exercise such as riding and swimming will speed recovery.' He turned to Ubba. 'I saw you riding that grey stallion of yours from the window and although I am not an accomplished horseman I can tell that you are. The lightness of your hands and the balance in your seat was a joy to behold; it was as if you and the horse were welded together.'

Ubba replied, 'Thank you. I am honoured by your compliment, Sulamain. Sleipnir is a very special horse; he has a prophet's thumb-mark on his wither.'

'Ah, if Allah has blessed him then he is indeed very special – and named after Odin's horse, too. Perhaps both our gods have sent him to protect you.'

Torri said, 'Well, somebody needs to protect him… but not usually from his own brother.'

Sulamain turned to Torri. 'Did you accompany your husband to Jerusalem?'

'No, I was married to his older brother at the time, back home in Jormund, rearing my sons.'

'You have married two brothers my lady and are Queen Consort with Ivar. That shows a great deal of devotion to the family and cannot have been an easy commitment.'

'I owe my life to their father and have been inextricably bound to them ever since.'

'It's probably as well you didn't come over my dear, Western women with your looks and features are greatly admired in my culture. Several *emirs* have married them, but the life would not suit a woman of your intelligence and courage. I see now where Viggo's intelligence and appetite for knowledge stems from.'

Ubba asked, 'What exactly are you teaching Viggo?'

'Whatever he wants – he has a fine brain. He reads and writes Latin and Greek. He studies Astronomy, Geography and History with verve. He is very good at Mathematics and Science. He has also learnt to play the lyre and has a fine voice. He is a true scholar and a very quick learner. Viggo is so talented that when he finally decides what area he wants to pursue he will be exceptional. Your eldest son Arne appears to favour you. He is a true nature and animal lover and will no doubt be an accomplished warrior just like you. I have finally become accustomed to teaching with a wolf in the room. In my country *sheiks* often have cheetahs roaming free, so I suppose it is not so very different.'

'Sulamain, has Ivar asked you about his illness? Is it just a birth defect or in fact a physical condition that means his legs are like that?'

'I think it is possibly an hereditary condition as his legs are formed with muscle and cartilage, but not bone. He also has uncontrolled attacks when his bones literally break without much warning, although his eyes shine bright blue before an attack.'

'My mother noticed that and tried to keep him off his legs when he was like that, but that made him angrier; he would go mad if shut inside. She basically had to confine him to a padded cell as he would destroy any object in his path.'

'I do know that every day of his life he lives with pain and some days it would drive a normal human being to kill himself. Your brother's brain is equal to Viggo's and the sheer frustration at being crippled has driven him to find the best way he can of coping with his physical disabilities. His drive, ambition and determination to succeed have made him the man he is, but at great cost. He asked me to define jealousy. He told me then that he has lived with jealousy every day of his life – especially within his family. The mere fact that his brothers could walk and he could not, has ruled his life. His father, I believe, took him out into the forest to dispose of him shortly after his birth but could not bring himself to kill him, so left him to die. His mother rescued him and took on the task of caring for a severely disabled child with three other children to rear as well, and that would adversely impact on all of you.

'He says you were the only one who reached out to him and gave him love and compassion. Whatever happened yesterday between you was triggered by a shattering of belief or loss of respect for his hero. The only way Ivar can accept that is to punish you for it. The fact he did not use weapons indicates he did not intend to kill you.'

'I know that Sulamain, and I deserved every blow he meted out. I was too ashamed of myself to try to stop him.'

'He did it out of love Ubba, not malice. You need to forgive him as he is horrified at what he has done, and your love is very important to him.'

'I know that now and I will make my peace with him.'

SIX

Ivar and Sigtryggr were in Ivar's office, tiptoeing around the major event of the previous day. Sigtryggr was unaware of the details but knew that he had been the cause of the rift between Torri and Ubba. A knock came at the door and Egil entered. 'My lord, Freya would like to speak to you about a matter of great importance. Shall I ask her to come back later? She seems rather angry and agitated.'

'Show her in; she will only become more agitated. I would never harm my beloved niece Egil if that is your concern.'

Sigtryggr interrupted, 'Ivar, I will come back later.' He jumped up and headed for the door with Egil, giving Ivar no chance to deny him.

Freya entered and scowled at him.

'Come and sit down my dear, you obviously have something on your mind.'

'Why did you fight and injure my daddy?'

'It was just a disagreement that spilled over into a fight. Nothing more than you will have seen your brothers do many times.'

'But the argument was between my mother and father, not you.'

'Well, it was because I took her side because I

considered your father was in the wrong.'

'Why? What did he say or do?'

'I cannot say, sweetheart; it was really none of my business and I should not have intervened. I promised both of your parents I would not speak to you or the boys about it.'

Freya's bottom lip wobbled. 'I know what happened as I was outside their bedroom door on Saturday night. I heard what was said and I know my father forced my mother to have sex and he was angry with her.'

Ivar threw his arms in the air. 'Freya, come round here and let me cuddle you, but I cannot discuss it with you.' He lifted her onto the desk, hugged her and sighed. 'You are only eight – admittedly, more like thirty-eight in your head – but eavesdropping on your parents is not advisable.'

'Well, you do it all the time and have done it since you were way younger than me. Don't deny it.'

Ivar smiled and came up with a quick response, 'Ah, but I am King now and I have to guard my throne as there is always someone ready to take it from me. Eavesdroppers never hear any good things about themselves, you know. I think you need to talk to your mother about this; you are not old enough to understand the concept of love and the relationship between man and wife yet.'

Freya snapped back, 'My parents love each other to bits and their lovemaking brings great joy to both of them. My father has never raised a hand to my mother but this time I heard the anger in his voice.'

'Freya, I cannot speak to you about this subject. I

have done enough damage already.'

'Why did you fight him over it?'

'Because I was angry that my brother had hurt your mother, who I have great love and affection for. Controlling my temper has always been a difficult thing for me to do.' He went to the door and asked the guard to fetch Torri.

'My mother won't be too pleased with me, will she?'

'Sweetheart, she needs to know you are aware of what happened. We don't want it to spoil your relationship with your father because he loves you very much and he is mortified about what he did.'

Torri arrived and was astonished to see Freya in Ivar's office.

Ivar spoke, 'Freya came to see me, very angry that I had hurt her father. I promised you both I would not speak to the children about it. However, it appears Freya was outside your bedroom door and knows exactly what transpired.'

Torri hugged Freya. 'Oh, Freya, why?' You are not old enough to understand yet about the relationship between a husband and wife.'

'Mama, all I want to know is why did he rape you?'

'Freya, you must understand that what your father did was not in the same league as what that evil man did to me when he kidnapped me. Your father loves me so much that he mistook my harmless flirting with Sigtryggr as a serious threat. He has never had cause to be jealous before and he overreacted and did it to remind me of my place. He did not hurt me; he just wasn't his usual caring self and it was very out of character. In marriage a wife should obey her husband but because I have been married three times, am older than your father and have been a queen, I have had more freedom than most wives. Although I was very hurt by your father's reaction I wasn't going to let it ruin our relationship, so I have forgiven him. We all make many mistakes in life and this is the first one your father has made with me. You know the Ragnarsson temper affects them all and this is the first time your father has ever lost it with me.'

'But Ivar hurt him.'

Ivar said, 'You know what a very short temper I have. I overreacted. I did not intend to kill him. I love your mother as a friend and a sister and I was mortified that my brother could do that to his devoted wife.'

'Can I see Daddy now please?'

Torri replied, 'If it will make you feel better. Now you must not discuss this with your brothers as I do not want it casting a cloud over their relationship with Ivar or your father.'

They returned to Ubba's room and Torri held her hand to prevent her running up to her father and causing him pain by throwing herself at him.

'Hello, my little angel. Have you come to see your bashed-up father?'

Freya gasped when she saw his battered face and bruised arms. 'Oh, poor Daddy! I went to tell Ivar off for fighting with you, but I did not realise he had done so much damage. Why didn't you stop him?' She knelt down by the side of the bed and held his hand.

Torri interrupted, 'Ivar fetched me because Freya

was listening behind the bedroom door on Saturday and heard what we were arguing about.'

'Oh, sweetheart, I did not mean to hurt your precious mother. I was jealous and angry thinking she may have been unfaithful, when she was not.'

'Mama would never be unfaithful to you but you have Serena as your mistress, so you are the unfaithful one.'

Torri said, 'I agreed for your father to continue with Serena as his mistress because I did not want to have any more babies, but I still wanted to remain his wife.'

'But I think it unfair on you, Mama. Shouldn't you be free to choose someone else yourself?'

'No pet, coping with the three husbands I had was quite sufficient and I love your father so much even though he shocked me with this one flash of anger. It is difficult to accept but shows he is only human and makes mistakes like everybody else.'

'But why did Ivar get so angry? Does he love you too?'

'Ivar loves me as his sister-in-law, consort and good friend. Because of something that happened a long time ago when Ivar was only eight, like you are now, our lives became entwined. You remember when Ivar, Halfdan and Erik all swore fealty to me? That means they swore to protect me for life; that was why Ivar was so angry with your father for doing what he did.'

Ubba said, 'Your mother has borne five Ragnarsson grandchildren; she has founded a dynasty. Ivar cannot have children and Halfdan does not want any children, so she alone is responsible for keeping Ragnar's line going. I think she deserves a medal for that; there can't be many families as volatile as we are. She also fought beside us many times as a warrior and we honoured her for that too.'

Torri responded, 'When you are older you will understand how empowering love is. I am proud to have been an integral part of this family. If your future husband can make you half as happy as your father has made me then you will be a very lucky girl. Being a woman in a man's world is hard but I have every confidence you will make your mark in life, just like your brothers.'

Later that afternoon, Ubba was becoming restless and refused to stay inside any longer. Torri bound his ribs as she had been shown how to do, and agreed to let him go down to the stables as long as he did not attempt to ride. She insisted on accompanying him to ensure he obeyed.

'You will have to wear a cloak with a hood to cover your face. If your troops see the real state of you they could start to turn on Ivar's men. You see, you and Ivar, with your male pride, never consider the consequences of your actions. I will not let this destroy the work you have done to turn these men into the best warriors we have ever had. We are going to need every one of them in the battle to come.'

'Spoken like the wise queen you have always been, my dear.'

They were disturbed by a knock. Torri went to answer it to find Gytha outside. She ushered her inside and she went over to Ubba, who was still shirtless from

Torri strapping up his ribs.

She stared at his ravaged face and bruised chest and arms. 'Did Ivar do that with just his fists?'

'I'm afraid so. I didn't try to stop him. The good news is there is no damage to my major organs and I will live to fight another day.'

Gytha sank into the chair at his bedside. 'Vidar came last night to tell us what had transpired. Ralf is very angry with Ivar. I have come to offer both of you sanctuary on the farm while Ubba recovers. You have not had a break together for ages and we are just starting the breeding season with the mares. I'm sure Ubba, you would be more than content to help us; you so love seeing them being born and developing.'

Ubba's face lit up with delight. 'Oh, that would be wonderful. A chance to be out in the summer sun and be with horses all day. I could swim, ride and fish to regain my strength. Please say you will come, Torri? We need time alone together.'

'I suppose we could ask Serena to move in to care for the boys, but I think we should take Freya with us. She has been badly affected by this and you need time to get to know and understand her, Ubba.'

Gytha replied, 'Of course, bring Freya. I will keep an eye on her when you want time alone together, and Thorin will be delighted.'

Torri said, 'I will inform Ivar. He can't object; he injured you in the first place. You need to speak to Serena. She will be very concerned about you. If we walk home now I can pack a bag, which somebody can drop off at the farm later, and we can accompany

Gytha back to the farm if you are up to riding. Remember what Sulamain said about your balance issues. You must not ride if you feel dizzy.'

Ubba said, 'What about Arne and Viggo? I can't leave without seeing them.'

Torri replied, 'Viggo will be at his lessons but Arne is probably with your troops. We can call on Viggo and if Arne is away from home he can always come over to the farm to see you later. Go with Gytha to see Viggo and Serena. I will find Ivar. We can meet in the entrance hall but if you two get there first, keep out of sight. Gytha, you must be with him because he can become dizzy.'

Torri made her way to Ivar's office and was thankful he was alone. He looked up as she entered, and she noticed a flicker of something like fear in his eyes. 'Torri, how is my brother today?'

'Battered and bruised, but desperate to go out. Sulamain says he must exercise to reduce the swelling. Gytha has extended an invitation for the two of us to stay at the farm until the bruising subsides. I think it would do him the world of good to commune with nature, given his love of horses. The breeding season is starting and he loves to help the mares, and see their foals develop. It will give us time to talk. I intend to take Freya as she needs time with her father too. It will take the heat off you as well Ivar, because we can't afford to have a rift between troops that Ubba has turned into the best warriors we have ever had.'

Ivar looked relieved. 'Yes, my dear, it is an ideal solution. Both of you take as much time as you need.

Frank and Arne can oversee the training of troops in Ubba's absence. I bitterly regret harming him, Torri. Do you forgive me?'

She kissed his cheek. 'Yes. I know you found it as hard to accept as I did but he deserves forgiveness as much as you do. Forgiveness is not a sign of weakness, Ivar, but empathy. We all make mistakes – you more than most.'

'Torri, tell him I love him and am so very sorry.'

'He knows that Ivar, but at the moment he can't forgive himself. But he will in time; I will see to that.'

Gytha and Ubba made slow progress to the library where Viggo was studying. He was alone and when they arrived he ran over to them. 'Father, you look dreadful. I can't believe what happened. Please tell me why?'

'Viggo, I can't. All I can say is that I do not blame Ivar. I would have done the same to him if he had done what I did. Please do not take revenge on Ivar, and you must prevent Arne from doing the same. Gytha has kindly invited your mother and me to stay with them until my wounds heal, and we are taking Freya with us. I want you to be the peacemaker like your mother, and calm Arne. You may both come and see me if you wish, but Serena will see to your daily household needs.

Viggo nodded. 'I will do my best Father, but you know Arne is wilful and hot headed; he will be like a dog with a bone until he finds out the truth.'

'Promise me you will send him to see me before he

does something stupid.'

'I will try, Father.'

Ubba hugged Viggo, turned away with tears in his eyes and took Gytha's arm for support as they slowly left the library. She whispered to him, 'He is such a lovely boy. You must be very proud of him.'

'You know, I learned today just how intelligent he is from one of his tutors. I was astounded at the knowledge he has acquired over the last two years, and it's all down to Ivar.'

They arrived at Serena's apartments and when she opened the door her face registered shock as she pushed his hood back. 'Oh God, Ivar did that to you with just his fists? Come sit down; you are unsteady on your feet, Ubba.'

Tears ran down her cheeks. Ubba hugged her and said, 'Sweetheart, I am fine – no broken bones, just a smashed-up face. Now I want you to do me a big favour.'

'Anything you ask my love, I will do for you.'

'Gytha has invited me and Torri to stay at the farm until my wounds have healed, and we are taking Freya. Will you move into my house with our children and keep a watchful eye on my sons? I fear Arne in particular will try and wreak revenge on Ivar. If you hear he is up to something you must tell Frank and get him to bring him to me or throw him in a cell before he does anything stupid.'

'I will, but are you sure you are all right? Has Torri forgiven you?'

'Yes, sweetheart, she has... not that I deserve it. But

I need to regain her trust, and this could work well for both of us, so I must go with her.'

'Of course you must, Ubba.' She hugged him gently and turned to Gytha. 'Look after him, Gytha.'

'I will, and you must bring the children and visit him. Torri will not deny you access.'

He kissed her cheek and left before he broke down. They made it down the sweeping staircase and thankfully, did not pass anyone. At the bottom, Egil met them. 'My lord, is there anything I can do for you?'

'Could you send a message to the stables to have Sleipnir, Blondie and Freya's pony saddled and brought to my house along with Gytha's mare?'

'Certainly sir, may I wish you a speedy recovery.'

Both Gytha and Torri supported him down the steps as he was unsteady on his feet, and they made the short walk home without being observed. On arrival Torri told an excited Freya that they were going to Gytha's for a short break. They went upstairs to pack a trunk that would be transported to the farm later.

Gytha offered Ubba a drink and insisted he sit down and rest before his ride to the farm. His head was throbbing and his ribs were aching. He said, 'Why have I been blessed with the lowest pain threshold of all my brothers? Considering what Ivar copes with on a daily basis, this wouldn't even register as painful to him.'

Gytha replied, 'Well, you chose not to defend yourself remember, and you could have got away from him if you had tried, so you have only yourself to blame. You do look as though you have been set upon by thieves that have beaten you with clubs.'

'Ivar told Sulamain I was involved in a drunken brawl, but he sussed out that it was a lie.'

'Has Torri been sympathetic?'

'Of course she has. She had already decided to forgive me before Ivar beat the hell out of me. She has, however, banned sex until she is ready to resume.'

'Well don't whinge about that Ubba, I would certainly have done the same. You shocked her and she needs time. I am sure once you have time to devote to pleasing her, your charm will overcome her reticence.'

'I wouldn't be so sure; they don't call her the "ice maiden" for nothing. Besides, it will be a while before I feel capable of initiating sex, with my ribs as sore as they are.'

'Serves you right! At least Ivar did not damage your balls.'

'That doesn't mean Torri won't! She can be just as vindictive as Ivar.'

Torri came down the stairs along with a very excited Freya. 'Is there anything else you need, Ubba?'

'Yes, help me put on my sword belt and leather boots please.'

The horses arrived outside. Ubba pulled his hood over his head and was pleased to see old Sam the stud groom and his own groom Josh leading the four horses. Sam held Sleipnir and Freya's Dales pony. Freya ran out, took the reins and vaulted onto his back.

Josh raised an eyebrow when Ubba got closer. 'Will ye be all right with Sleipnir? He is a bit fresh, my lord.'

'He will be fine next to Blondie. He adores her company; that will slow him down. My problem will be getting on him. My ribs are giving me considerable pain even though they have been strapped up.'

Josh said, 'Can you manage to stand on the water trough and then put your foot in the stirrup?'

The ladies joined them and were each given a leg-up onto their mares by Sam.

Ubba walked over to the trough. With the help of the wall, he pulled himself up. Josh led Sleipnir as close as he could so that Ubba only had to put his left foot in the stirrup and swing his leg over. As soon as he was in the saddle Sleipnir was impatient to show off to the two mares. Ubba took up the reins and growled at him, 'Now behave yourself and stop flirting!'

Sleipnir was shocked and turned his head right round to look again at this imposter who could not possibly be his beloved master, growling at him like that. Ubba turned to the others and said, 'We will walk out of the city gates and there will be no trotting. When we leave the road, we can have a quiet controlled canter. Torri, you will ride next to me, with Gytha and Freya behind.'

He turned to Josh, 'There is a trunk packed in the house. Could you ensure somebody delivers it to the farm?'

'Certainly, my lord.'

SEVEN

They spent an idyllic three weeks at the farm. Ubba revelled in activities he usually had little time to pursue. He was delighted by Freya's riding ability and he taught her to jump properly without galloping full tilt at every fence. She was untutored, but her balance and soft hands were a gift from him. She cantered around standing up on her pony's back and could fire a bow and arrow at full gallop and hit a small target. He let her ride Blondie and decided she was ready to move on from ponies, so instructed Ralf to find her first horse. He even put her on Sleipnir and instructed her in dressage. His horse responded beautifully and never took advantage of her small size.

He went swimming, fishing and riding, sometimes with Torri and often with Freya. Viggo brought over some of the raptors and they all went hunting one Sunday. Ubba observed the birth of five foals and assisted with one that was stuck. He allowed Freya to be there too and she was delighted. He was ashamed he had overlooked his daughter's education and was determined to ensure she received reading, writing and language lessons when they returned to York. It appeared that Thorin had been her riding and weapons instructor. He observed how close they were.

He watched Thorin closely and asked him some interesting questions. The answers convinced him that he could not be Thorsten's son. He admitted to having had visions, and confirmed that he had seen Sigtryggr in one of them. Having been sent by the gods seemed to be the only explanation for the phenomenal strength he possessed. He was only seven but looked twice that age in both build and stature. He watched him in the forge and observed that his skill at making swords was comparable to Ralf's already.

They had long discussions about the prospect of war. Torri accepted she could not fight beside him and would have to withdraw to safety with the children when the time came. Ubba was convinced Ivar would leave for Ireland if he was in danger of losing Jorvik. He did not want to go to Ireland and neither did he want his family over there. He knew the prospects for his survival were low. Unexpectedly, it was Ralf who came up with a solution. He suggested Torri, Serena and the children moved to his farm at Terrington where they could remain hidden from sight whilst a plan of survival was created. He could not allow Arne, at fourteen, to fight in his first battle, even though he had only been twelve himself at his first battle. Convincing Arne of this would not be easy. Arne took his Ragnarsson bloodline very seriously. Their only hope would be that they could convince him to be his family's protector in case he himself did not survive. However, they both knew that Arne and Viggo would be slaughtered by the Saxons if they were captured. He could not bring himself to consider the fate of Freya,

Astrid and Theo – not to mention that of Torri and Serena.

Ubba was looking forward to being left in peace on the farm for the full day with the responsibility of overseeing the birth of a foal to a seasoned broodmare who was grazing contentedly in the foaling paddock. She was imminent but as mares generally foaled at night, he hoped he would not be needed. Ralf, Ranulf and Thorin had taken some young horses to Ralf's Terrington farm to graze for the summer and would not be back until later that night. Torri, Freya and Gytha had returned to Jorvik to inspect a visiting merchant's cargo of fabrics newly arrived from the Mediterranean and beyond, which had caused great excitement. Torri insisted on leaving to purchase dress fabric immediately. He was left to oversee the farmhands and Vidar, along with Skye, who had flatly refused to go.

He checked the three stallions. They were calmly munching their hay and seemed content to be inside, away from the flies. He was just contemplating schooling Sleipnir in the paddock when Skye came looking for him. He had noticed her and Sigtryggr together and was in no doubt that she intended to seek his advice on this matter. He suggested they sit in the garden where he could observe the broodmare at the same time.

'Ubba, I am so glad there are just the two of us. I need your wise counselling on a delicate matter.'

He laughed, 'I think I know what you wish to talk

about, but I suspect you should be seeking advice from your mother or Torri rather than me, if this is to do with your relationship with Sigtryggr.'

She blushed. 'Oh, is it that obvious to everybody?'

'You only have to look at the stars shining in your eyes whenever you see him to know, Skye. Thankfully, as good as he is at trying to mask his feelings, his eyes give him away, too.'

'You once told me that I would know when I was truly in love with the right man, but I am concerned about some aspects and would appreciate your help. I know I should be consulting my parents, but I would find it difficult and I don't want to hurt them.'

'Perhaps you should start by telling me how far this relationship has progressed.'

She recoiled in horror. 'Oh, believe me, it has not progressed sexually.'

Ubba laughed, 'Then I must commend you both for your restraint. Tell me how he makes you feel when you are around him?'

She blushed. 'Hot and bothered, breathless and I have to stop myself kissing him. The fact I would not be able to reach his luscious lips without standing on something is the only thing that stops me. I can hardly sleep for dreaming about him.'

Ubba laughed at the image she portrayed. 'And how has he expressed his feelings towards you?'

'He has told me he loves me, but apart from holding hands and a chaste kiss on my cheek... and once, when helping me down from my horse, he held me a little too close... he has been a bastion of self-discipline.'

'What exactly has he said about your future together? He is a very ambitious man who craves power and influence and has huge determination to succeed. He is a born leader, and clever with it. Are you sure you want to tie yourself to a man who could be killed long before he achieves his potential? He has had one near miss with the loss of an eye. He will never be a man who puts his family before his ambition and if you want a quiet family life, he is not the man for you.'

'I know that already. We have discussed me returning to Ireland with him to experience life there because as much as I want to be with him, I would have no family support. I know I am no shield maiden either; I could not fight alongside him. I was hoping that perhaps we could remain friends rather than be lovers or marry, until I am sure of my feelings.'

Ubba threw his hands in the air. 'Are you mad, woman? Neither of you would be able to do that. Once you have become intimate you will be unable to stop. The question is, is it real love or just sexual attraction? Skye, there is a hell of a difference between a sexual relationship and marriage.'

She raised her voice in anger, 'Well, you should bloody know, having both a wife and a lover to keep your bed warm!'

He glared at her, trying to control his anger. 'Sigtryggr is not like me; he has all the worst qualities of Ivar, Halfdan and Bjorn in one, but none of the good ones. When he achieves his goal he will be content for a while, but you will always play second string to his ambition… and if you become a nuisance, he will discard you instantly, regardless of whether you are the mother of his children.'

She burst into tears and shouted, 'You don't like him because you thought he had seduced your wife. But she was entirely to blame, not him.'

He pulled Skye to her feet and hugged her. 'Sweetheart, I know, but you have to ask yourself why I think him capable of doing such a thing when I have only just met him. I admit I have a grudge against him but if you don't believe me then ask Ivar for his opinion of him, or better still, consult Torri because she has known many men like him over the years and knows how hard they are to live with. I am telling you the truth, Skye. I didn't attempt to kill Ivar when he threatened to take you for his wife, only to stand back and watch you make the same mistake. I want you to be happy and content and I fear he will not put your needs before his own.'

'But Ubba he is brave, strong and courageous and life would never be dull – married to him, it will always be exciting. I know he has ambition and I am certain Ireland is not big enough to contain his talents. Who knows what the future holds? But I want to be a part of his life.'

Ubba grabbed her hand. 'But what if he dies in the process? Your life will then be forfeit too, as will any children you have. Ireland can be a dangerous place – ask your father. Do you think your parents will be happy to let you go, especially as a single girl?'

'They agreed I could choose my own husband when

I was ready. I don't want to marry him until I have been there and seen Ireland. I will return home if I don't think a marriage could work. Now, can I rely on your discretion to keep this to yourself? I will tell my parents when I have made my decision.'

'I will keep quiet, but only if you promise to discuss this with Torri before you make a final decision. She has years of experience of dealing with men like him, and she knows how hard life can be with a dominant ambitious husband who won't accept advice from his wife. I am only trying to warn you so you consider your options very carefully. Love can be a wonderful emotion, but it can also blind us.'

'I know you are only looking out for my welfare, Ubba. I will speak to Torri. You are right – to have survived three husbands and reared six children she must have encountered many difficulties throughout her life.'

After dinner that evening when they had all returned, Ubba asked Torri to join him for a walk. The sun was shining but there was a welcome breeze. Torri had been observing her husband at dinner and she knew that something was wrong.

'All right Ubba, what's wrong? Something has upset you today and I suspect you want to speak to me in private, not whisk me away for outdoor sex.'

Ubba's face was a picture. 'Torri, be serious. We have been romping like teenagers since we arrived; how we haven't been caught "in flagrante" by Freya is a miracle. Perhaps if you can put my mind at rest I might be able to concentrate on sex later.'

Torri roared with laughter. 'I was only joking, Ubba. Now, what can possibly have made you so anxious? Let's sit down on this fallen tree stump and you can tell me?'

'Skye approached me today about Sigtryggr. She has fallen in love with him. Nothing improper has transpired but she is seriously considering going back to Ireland with him and provided she likes it there, she may consider marrying him. However, they will inevitably become lovers in the meantime so if she decides to return home instead, her reputation will be ruined.'

Torri took a minute to answer, 'From Skye's point of view I think she is being careful, although *how* she would come back from Ireland alone, I don't think she has considered. Has Sigtryggr actually proposed to her?'

'No, she never confirmed that, which is precisely why she should be running in the opposite direction. He is not the right man for her; he has all the worst qualities of Ivar, Halfdan and Bjorn, and none of their good qualities. He is ambitious, craves power and influence and will trample over anybody to achieve it. He will not tolerate any interference from anybody, least of all a wife! Skye is not shy of giving her opinion and if it doesn't agree with his, he will dispose of her.'

'But you don't know him Ubba, and you bear a grudge about me flirting with him, which he did not initiate at all. He is young, possibly hotheaded and he does crave power, but he has a fine brain, he uses it confidently and men follow him. I know he has criticised the tactics of some of our generation of Norsemen for losing too many lives, but he has proved he can win by negotiation rather than outright war. He has said he wants to be King of Ireland, not just King of Dublin, and I don't think for a moment he will be satisfied with that, even.'

'He doesn't even rule Dublin yet, never mind Ireland!'

'But if Ivar is overthrown in Jorvik and heads over there then between them, they will conquer both crowns. You have said yourself that Ireland is the hardest land to hold because of all the different tribes fighting for control – but with Ivar's reputation the battle is half won already.'

'Perhaps, but Skye may be dead long before that becomes reality. He has no incentive for marrying her; she doesn't have land or power to offer him.'

'But isn't love enough? How do you know he doesn't love her for the beautiful and outspoken woman she is and the team they would make?'

'Only for as long as it suits him. If he gets a better offer then she will be disposed of.'

'Ubba, much as I trust your judgement in assessing character, are you not falling into Ivar's trap of spinning lies to frighten your enemies? I admit to misjudging your father as a man because of his reputation as a warrior. I was convinced that he would kill me in revenge for my husband's capture of Jormund as he was renowned for destroying anyone who crossed him. When he took me as his lover I was certain he would kill me, but he had no intention of doing so. He told the truth – he does not wage war on women and children, especially not blonde blue-eyed Danes – but we both knew our relationship could never last. It was great fun while it lasted, particularly when Bjorn declared his interest in me. Ragnar wasn't best pleased about losing me to his son, but he accepted it gracefully. He was even more amused when I divorced Bjorn and then married his second son!'

'Torri, don't tell me you only married me because you wanted a replacement for my father.'

'Oh, Ubba! You are impossible! I married you because you were the perfect man for me. You had quietly worshipped me with devotion for a long time. You were honest, trustworthy, compassionate and so very handsome. I knew that together we would produce some incredible children. Your father was a clever man; he ensured the Ragnarsson dynasty would survive with me as the matriarch.'

'Well, put yourself in Skye's position. Is she too besotted with Sigtryggr to acknowledge he would not be right for her? She would have to be very brave to walk away.'

'Skye does not lack courage, despite never having fought in a battle. I think she will have the chance to see how he operates under pressure and she may just be canny enough to manoeuvre him towards the right decisions without him realising. I did it with Bjorn and Ivar and she's clever enough too.'

'I notice you didn't mention me!'

'Well, of course not. You may have been a reluctant

king, but you have always made the right decisions.'

'I take that as a massive compliment, my dear. I promised I would not reveal Skye's intentions to anybody provided she speaks to you before she makes her final decision. How the hell Ralf and Gytha will take this, I dread to think. Now I have designs on your body, my dear, and intend to banish all thoughts of my father from your mind forever.'

'You know he would be so proud of you. It's a tragedy he is not here to see the great man you have become.'

'Perhaps it's for the best! I wouldn't want him to see us lose control of Lincoln and Jorvik.'

EIGHT

Skye approached Torri while she was reading in the rose garden. Ubba was with Ralf tending to the stallions, Gytha was baking and Thorin and Freya were playing somewhere on the farm.

Hesitantly, Skye said, 'Torri, may I ask your advice about Sigtryggr? Ubba insisted I speak with you as you understand ambitious men. I don't quite comprehend Ubba's objections to him but I am concerned because I know he seeks my happiness.'

Torri pointed to the swing. 'Come and join me, Skye. Ubba has told me of his doubts. Ordinarily, there is no man better at judging another person's character than him, but I fear he bears a grudge against him through no fault of Sigtryggr. I have not spent much time alone in his company for obvious reasons, but other people seem to admire and like him. I think his confident manner hides quite an inferiority complex and he is frightened of making the wrong decisions, so he can come across as a little arrogant at times.'

'He is not like that with me. He will talk to me about his ambitions and plans for the future, but Ubba seems to think he would not take advice from a woman... and Ubba is right – I am not a woman to be ignored.'

Torri laughed, 'Well good for you, Skye – but you have to learn how to get your own way with strong opinionated men without them realising. You have to sow the seed and then back off until they suddenly come round to pursuing your idea as if it was theirs in the first place. Bjorn could be the most stubborn man for accepting advice, but behind that was his fear of failure. You had to leave a thought to germinate in his head for a while, but it usually worked.'

'We have not indulged our passion yet, but I have no sexual experience and feel so inadequate. I was hoping we could avoid it until I had decided whether I wished to become his wife or not after we go to Ireland, but Ubba said that would never happen.'

'Skye, you are both only eighteen. Sigtryggr may have a little experience but there's a huge difference between casual sex and marriage. Danes can be a little too hasty in seeking their pleasure, but he should put your needs before his own and take his time. Do not let him dictate the pace or frequency of sex and you will soon learn what turns him on. After passionate lovemaking that is when you plant the seed of the path you want him to follow. Believe me, arguing and shouting to get your own way will have little effect on men as stubborn as him. And tears and tantrums will never work with them. They can't cope with highly emotional scenes; they are too self-centred. They may be vicious warriors in battle, but they are still little boys at heart. They need guidance, food, sex and occasionally a severe hiding or tongue-lashing to keep them in line.'

'But how did you make the right choices in life?'

'Skye, don't assume I have always made the right decisions; that's just not true. My first husband was forty. I was sixteen and had been wrenched from my own family to marry him. I didn't even know him before we married but he was as gentle as a lamb with me and although it was never a love match, I respected him. When I realised he intended to raid Jormund whilst Ragnar was overseas I knew my days were numbered because I knew Ragnar would win it back and usually, all the family would have paid with their lives.'

'How come Ragnar spared you when he blood eagled your husband?'

'Who knows for sure? He announced to his subjects that he did not wage war on innocent women and children, but I was convinced he would kill me anyway. However, he bided his time and eight weeks after Guthrun was born he wanted his reward. I gave myself to him willingly, fully aware that I would be in more danger from his second wife Aslaug than from him. You have to remember I was his slave, so I really had no choice. It could never have lasted and when Bjorn showed interest in me, Ragnar backed off.'

Skye laughed, 'And was Ragnar the sex god that his reputation implied?'

Torri smiled. 'Oh yes, he knew how to please a woman. He was innovative, exciting, passionate and caring. When you were in his arms the world stopped and he made you feel so safe and very special. However, never discuss past sexual relationships with a new partner or husband. That was one decision I made that proved to be correct. Bjorn knew we were lovers thanks to Ivar's insatiable appetite for spying as a child. He could not resist asking but I would never reveal any details of my relationship with Ragnar to either Bjorn or Ubba. Male pride is very delicate and competitive. If you don't give them any ammunition, they can't fret about it. Bjorn didn't like it of course, and tried many times to draw me into making comparisons, but I would not tell. Ubba was far too much of a gentleman to even ask about my previous sexual relationships, but he has all the qualities of his sainted father and has always been loyal and trustworthy. Those qualities are not often found in a Ragnarsson.

'Marrying Bjorn was not one of my best decisions as he had an insatiable appetite for life. He always wanted to explore new adventures, as well as new women. His own mother warned me that he wasn't the right Ragnarsson for me but you have to remember, Ubba was only sixteen when our paths first crossed. I was ten years older than that when I finally decided to divorce Bjorn for my own sanity.'

'And has Ubba lived up to your high expectations?'

'In every single way possible. He has made me the happiest woman alive. He is the perfect husband and father. You have to decide whether Sigtryggr is right for you; I think you are very wise not to rush into marriage or having children until you are sure. High achieving ambitious men are always selfish and hard to live with, and only you can make that decision. Remember, when things go wrong they can twist reality and blame everyone but themselves, including you. When everything goes well they can be pussycats but when it doesn't, they can be lions and destroy everyone around them.

Placating your mother and father will be difficult, but I will try and ease their pain. Letting their daughter leave the country with a man they hardly know, and an unmarried one too, will be extremely difficult for them.'

Skye threw her arms around Torri and hugged her. 'Oh, thank you for believing in me. If I can be a fraction of the woman you are then I will be satisfied. I know it is not going to be easy adapting to a whole new life in a dangerous country, but I will do my best. If it doesn't work I shall come home, depending on the situation here.'

Ubba had seen Torri deep in conversation with Skye so he went to help with the horses. Torri headed to the stables afterwards and he joined her outside. They walked away from the buildings so they could not be overheard.

'Well, could you dissuade her from running away to Ireland with him?'

'Not exactly, my dear. I agree with the logic behind what she is doing and think she is being very brave and sensible about it.'

Ubba stared at her in disbelief. 'What – are you mad? Ralf and Gytha will be devastated. Remember he hasn't even proposed marriage and she won't marry him until she is in Ireland... and by then she could already be pregnant!'

'Calm down, Ubba. If you are like this over Skye, what will you be like when Freya takes a lover?'

'No man will ever be good enough for our daughter! I will confine her to a nunnery; no man is taking my daughter's virginity and taking her away from me.'

She turned to him, 'You cannot keep her locked up for life; her virginity is hers to bestow on the man she loves. All we can do is guide her in selecting the right man and lead by example. Freya knows how very important love is in a marriage. And remember, we may not be alive when she takes this important step in life.'

Ubba grabbed her. 'Promise me you will leave with the children before we are attacked, like we agreed.'

'Of course I will, Ubba. I have no desire to be there when you die. It is my responsibility to ensure our children survive, and I intend to do so. That includes Serena – and your children Astrid and Theo. They are also grandchildren of Ragnar.'

He looked deep into her eyes. 'You are the most incredible woman, mother and lover Torri, and I worship every bone in your body.'

The following day, after their evening meal, Skye took her parents out to the garden and told them her plan. Gytha screamed in despair, which brought everybody running to see what was wrong. Ubba and Torri knew immediately; Torri hugged Gytha to her and Ubba ushered Ranulf, Thorin and Freya back into the house. Ralf was holding onto the fence for support and Skye looked terrified.

He turned to Ubba, 'You know what she plans to do with her life?'

'Yes, and as a father I know exactly how difficult this is for you, but listen to what Torri has to say.'

Torri made Gytha sit in the swing and then took Skye's hand. Before she could speak Ralf shouted angrily at Skye, 'Are you still a virgin?'

'Yes Father, of course I am.'

He grabbed her arm. 'Then I am locking you up until that bastard has sailed for Ireland.'

Torri pushed between them. 'Ralf, that is not the answer. Please listen to me first. I know this must be a terrible shock to you, but please try to look at the situation from Skye's point of view. She is an adult now and knows her own mind. She has assessed the situation and realised what she would be giving up by leaving her family and going to Ireland with Sigtryggr. She is not just a lovestruck teenager or she would not have considered her options so carefully. Neither is she being forced into this. She wants to be sure that their relationship will work before she takes the next steps towards marriage and children. You have to give her credit for that.'

Gytha cried, 'But if she returns she will be outcast by the Church for becoming his mistress – no Saxon would take her as his wife.'

Torri responded, 'Gytha, I know that, but which would you rather have her do – give her virginity to Sigtryggr and avoid pregnancy, or marry him, become pregnant and discover it won't last? She has thought it through very carefully.'

Gytha replied, 'But he could be killed in battle in Ireland.'

Ralf groaned, 'And she would be taken as a prize and raped and enslaved by his enemies. What sort of life would she lead then?'

Ubba intervened, 'Ralf, all our wives have this prospect to consider. At least this way, she can walk away if it's not for her – but married to him, she cannot.'

Ralf shouted angrily, 'So where is your hero now? Not here to face the anger of your family... that hardly shows love, devotion and courage.'

'Father, it was I who insisted he stay away. I knew you would not welcome the news. I did it to avoid any bloodshed.'

Ralf turned to Ubba, 'And you were prepared to kill your own brother when he threatened to take Skye as his wife. Surely you cannot consider Sigtryggr a better proposition?'

Torri gave him a searching look, then Ubba replied, 'Ralf, I have known my brother a long time and I did not consider him to be a suitable husband for Skye. I do not know Sigtryggr at all, but I do think he has the potential to be a great leader despite his impetuosity and youth. He has a good brain and, I hope, a kind heart. I admit he craves ambition and power but I'm certain that Skye is very special; perhaps they will make a great team. I have been blessed with Torri as my wife. She has been a guiding light to four sons of Ragnar, and bred four grandsons and one granddaughter. To succeed as a king you must have a strong woman beside you. As a father I know it is hard to let a daughter fly the nest, but it's her life and she has to live it her way. Trust her judgement and give her the chance; she has never been found wanting.'

Torri said, 'Look, sleep on it; you need time to take everything in. I think you need a meeting with Sigtryggr to understand his motives. Ubba and I would be happy to be there if you want our support.'

Torri and Ubba left and as they passed Skye she whispered, 'Thank you so much – and Ubba, I know that was especially hard for you.'

Two days later, Sigtryggr visited in the late afternoon for a meeting with the family. Gytha had insisted Torri and Ubba be present because she feared Ralf might lose his temper. Ubba had spent time trying to calm Ralf down, but he was no closer to accepting losing his daughter.

Sigtryggr and Skye came into the room holding hands. Both of them looked anxious. Gytha told them to sit down and suggested Sigtryggr explain the situation. He looked briefly at Ralf's hostile expression and at Ubba, then took a long deep breath. 'I know this is hard for you to understand and accept as parents, but I assure you that I will do everything in my power to love and protect your daughter and respect her wishes.'

Ralf growled, 'Why have you not asked her to be your wife? Surely even in Ireland men court their women and marry them before taking their virginity?'

'Sir, marriage is not what Skye wants until she is

sure that both Ireland – and I – suit her. I would marry her now in front of you as I love her so much, but it is me who is on trial until she decides whether she wants me and is prepared to live in Ireland. I know it is a dangerous place for a single woman, but I totally agree that the decision has to be hers and she wants the opportunity to experience it for herself before she makes her decision.'

Ralf said, 'So there will be no sex before marriage?'

Skye interrupted, 'Father, I want to experience all aspects of our relationship before I make my decision. However, I will try not to become pregnant until I am sure of my feelings. I know that I would be outcast and considered wanton if it did not work out and I were to return to Jorvik.'

Sigtryggr said, 'I know that currently I have little to offer Skye, such as a permanent home or land, but I intend to become King of Dublin.'

Gytha interrupted, 'But what happens to Skye if you fail and are killed? She will still be classed as your "woman" – and what punishment will your enemies meter out to her then?'

'I do not intend to have Skye with me when raiding. She is not a shield maiden and I will ensure she is safe and protected by people who will ensure she returns safely to Jorvik should I die in battle.'

Ubba said, 'And will you take advice from Skye? She has a fine analytical mind and women see disadvantages and pitfalls far quicker than men do.'

'I am well aware of Skye's many talents and if she is to share my life then her opinions are important to me. I am aware of the part played by your wife when dealing with volatile husbands throughout her life, and I appreciate a female perspective. Indeed, Ivar warned me that without a strong woman as my wife I would not succeed... His respect and admiration for Torri is beyond doubt.'

Gytha sighed and took hold of Skye's hand. 'As a mother you know how difficult this is for me because I can see the dangers you may be walking into, but I have to admit that you have thought deeply about your decision and not let love blind you. You have my blessing to go with Sigtryggr.' She pulled Skye to her, kissed her and turned to Sigtryggr. 'Don't let me down; you must cherish and protect her.'

Ralf groaned, 'What say you, Ubba? I respect your opinion more than anyone else's. You know how to assess a man's strengths and weaknesses better than any man.'

Ubba sighed, 'Yes, but remember I have only known Sigtryggr for three weeks – and as you well know Ralf, it is only under battle conditions that you see the real character of a man. There is no doubt that he has proved his worth in battle, but he has already lost an eye. However, he has also prevented a sustained battle by negotiation and this has to be admired. You may recall Haesten saying when we were at Repton that, "You always need to have an exit strategy and not be ashamed to admit defeat." In my opinion Skye has looked at the situation and planned her exit strategy well. As difficult as it is to let her go unmarried into a relationship, you have to let her fly the nest on her terms. Sigtryggr knows he will have me to answer to if Skye is harmed in any way whilst in his care, so that should put her safety at the top of his list.'

Sigtryggr smiled. 'Don't worry – Ivar has already threatened me with a similar demise. I would be very foolish to take on two Ragnarssons and my future father-in-law by failing in my duty of care.'

Ralf shook his hand. 'You have my permission, but don't let me down. Skye is very precious to me.'

NINE

Sigtryggr and Skye set off for a ride together. Skye was mortified about upsetting her parents. The reality of what she had done was beginning to dawn.

Sigtryggr saw her remorseful look. 'Sweetheart, are you having second thoughts? It is only natural you will feel bereft at leaving your family and country, but I promise I will take care of you.'

'Did you really mean that you would marry me now? It's just that you've never actually said it before.'

'Only because I did not want to put any pressure on you. I understand why you want to be absolutely certain of our relationship before you take that step. To be honest, I didn't dare kiss you or touch you for fear of going too far. Taking your virginity would only have led your family to think even less of me than they do now. It is entirely your decision when and whether you want to have a sexual relationship.'

Skye halted her horse and said, 'Then show me how much you love me, right now!'

He spun his horse around. 'What!? Are you mad, woman?'

'Mad for your body, yes! I just need to know how you feel about me, and I want to know you intimately. There's the perfect spot about a mile away that would offer us privacy and space – follow me, sir, right now!' She kicked her horse into a canter and took off up the track.

Sigtryggr paused in shock as he thought about her proposition, then galloped after her, roaring with laughter. She was never going to be predictable, which was one of the many things that attracted her to him... and besides, one should never disappoint a lady in distress.

When they arrived in the copse he tied the horses to a tree and relaxed their girths. Skye had run over to an overturned tree stump where they could sit together. She watched him approach her with caution, never taking his eyes from hers.

'Skye, are you absolutely sure that this is what you want? I have dreamt of this moment, fearing it would not happen for a long time. You are an innocent girl and I want you to be certain that this is what you want before I lay a finger on your beautiful body.'

'Kneel before me, my love.' She held out her hand and he did as she asked. 'I may not have experienced sex before, but I am not entirely unaware of what happens. I am a Dane both spiritually and sexually – not a Saxon. I want your body now and hope to possess your heart and soul in time, as well.' She kissed his hand and guided it to her heart.

He moaned and put his arm around her, pulling her close. 'I love you Skye, as I live and breathe, and will protect you forever.'

Two hours later, they set off back to the farm, overwhelmed by their emotions and their shared intimate experience. Skye felt like she was in a fantasy world. However, the ride home helped remind her that it had been a reality as she felt quite uncomfortable in the saddle.

They unsaddled their horses and put them in the stables. Sigtryggr grabbed her hand in the tack room and told her to say nothing about what they had done, but to act perfectly normally over the meal. He would then return to the palace and start making final arrangements for their departure.

Thankfully, Freya was telling everybody about her jumping lesson on Blondie, and was full of enthusiasm. Ubba had promised she could have her first horse and she was asking everybody's opinion on the type of horse she should have. This hid Skye and Sigtryggr's quietness. Skye noticed her father looking intently at her and she looked away quickly, afraid her guilt would show on her face.

Torri knew straight away, by Skye's avoidance of looking at Sigtryggr, who was sitting directly opposite her. She sensed the change in their relationship. She considered they had both shown considerable restraint to wait as long as they had. Both parents had accepted Skye's wish to go with him and in her opinion, nobody could blame Sigtryggr for forcing her hand.

As the meal ended and Skye collected the dishes from the table, Sigtryggr was startled by Ralf as he leant down and whispered in his ear, 'Outside, young man. I want a word with you.' He knew instantly what this "word" was likely to be about, but obediently followed him outside.

Ralf was pacing around the raised porch area. He tried to suppress his anger but said, 'Have you seduced my daughter?'

Sigtryggr paused, trying to think of the best way of appeasing Ralf. 'Yes, sir. I have, and I know how difficult this must be for you as her devoted father...'

Ralf bore down on him and he stepped back towards the steps, hoping for a quick escape. Ralf charged and shouted, 'Bastard!' He punched with all the force of his many years of forging metal, catching Sigtryggr on his left cheek. He overbalanced and fell backwards down the six wooden steps to the yard.

Skye had noticed they were both missing and arrived just as her father hit him, quickly followed by Thorin and Ubba, who had heard Ralf shouting.

She screamed, 'Father, stop this at once! Sigtryggr did not seduce me – I seduced him.'

Ralf was already at the bottom of the steps as a very dazed Sigtryggr tried to stand up. As Ralf raised his fist to strike again, Thorin grabbed his arm and shouted, 'No, Father! The Norns have spun their threads; you have to leave them to fulfil their destiny.'

Ubba grabbed Ralf's other arm and pulled him away from Sigtryggr while Skye helped him to stand.

Ubba shouted, 'Ralf, calm down! This is not the best way to deal with this. They are both adults and have explained their reasons for their actions, and you have to accept it. Thorin, if you know anything about their future then you should tell us all, right now.'

Thorin replied, 'I do not know what their future holds but I have seen a vision of them together. We all have choices to make. Sometimes we make the right one and sometimes we don't. All I can say is that the gods brought them together for a reason and I know that I will be with them at some point in the future – but how, why, where or when, I don't know.'

Ubba said, 'Sigtryggr, I suggest you go back to Jorvik now and Skye, you go to your mother and explain what has happened.'

He turned to Ralf, 'Now, are you going to be reasonable and leave him alone? He made no attempt to defend himself against your attack and your daughter has admitted she was the instigator.'

Sigtryggr and Skye went to the stables to fetch his horse. Thorin had disappeared. They were alone for the moment.

Ralf turned to Ubba and said, 'Explain to me how she could seduce him without any experience? Skye must have been with another man.'

'Ralf, there is a huge difference between being told how to do something and experiencing it firsthand. Women are just as entitled to have sexual feelings as men are. If she offered herself to him then you have to be satisfied that he did not force her. It does not mean she was not a virgin; she has never given you cause to think she has had a sexual relationship with any man. She has been a model of propriety and has chosen her own partner. Trust her and let her make up her own mind about Sigtryggr.'

Suddenly, a little voice above them on the porch said, 'Daddy, how can a woman seduce a man? Surely only a man can seduce a woman?'

Ubba groaned, 'Freya, your capacity for spying is beginning to exceed even Ivar's skill and proficiency. Your mother sent you to bed, so what are you doing in your nightgown out here?'

Freya stood at the top of the steps with her hands on her hips as she launched into a tirade, 'You said that I was not to ask my brothers, the grooms, the milkmaids, the servants or anybody else about sex because they may not tell me the truth, and that I had to ask you or Mama if I had any questions.'

Ubba shouted, 'Freya, this is not the time or place. Go to bed and I assure you your mother will discuss this matter with you another day.'

She stomped off angrily and both of them burst out laughing. Ralf said, 'Torri is going to be so mad with you. You had better warn her, because I don't know how she is going to get out of giving her an honest answer.'

Ubba giggled, 'Neither do I, but it is not a father's place to teach girls the facts of life; surely it is their mother's responsibility? I have had enough grief keeping my sons – and Bjorn's – under control.'

They went back into the house. Skye followed a few moments later. Ubba made his way to his bedroom, where Torri was still up. 'Where have you been?'

'Preventing Ralf from beating the hell out of Sigtryggr for taking his daughter's virginity.'

'Oh, he noticed too.'

'Well you could have warned me. Thankfully, he chose to thump him rather than behead him with an axe. To Sigtryggr's credit, he did not fight back.

He took the first punch but unfortunately, Ralf is so strong that he ejected him down the steps and into the yard. His bad eye is now a black eye and he's cracked a cheekbone, too. Skye came flying out and heard Ralf say that it was for seducing his daughter, and she revealed it was her that had seduced him! God forbid! That made it worse. Now he thinks she has been with someone else already.'

Torri laughed, 'I am very proud of her. I told her to be wild and unpredictable and make sure he was not going to dominate her.'

'I might have known you had coached her. Then a little spy in her nightdress demanded to know how a woman could seduce a man, so I told her you would discuss it another day. Sort that one out, my queen; I have enough to do trying to guide my sons.'

'Oh great, Ubba. Where do I even start with that one?'

He leaned over her and played with a strand of her hair. 'You know you said that when you returned to Jormund you'd had no sexual partners? Are you sure no stranger sent by Odin sneaked into your bed one night and sired Freya? If Odin can recreate Thor in Thorin, did the goddess Freya recreate our daughter in her image? Because they have both been here before; she is eight going on thirty-eight and he is seven going on twenty-seven!'

Torri laughed,.'Oh Ubba, I love you! The proof of her ancestry shines out from her little face. You stamp your progeny as truly as Sleipnir. She has all our best features with a brain as sharp as Viggo and

Ivar's. Her curiosity knows no bounds and she will employ all Ivar's skills to achieve her goals. If she was a reincarnation of Freya she would not need to ask us about sex; she would know it all already.'

'I don't envy your task of guiding her through puberty my love, but she does have sound judgement of character already, so heed her reasons for picking her mate.'

'And why won't you be there to guide her too?'

He paused then sighed, 'I'll probably be dead!'

She wrapped her arms around him tightly. 'Don't you dare even think of death Ubba; you must always believe you will triumph. Have you had visions of your death?'

'No, sweetheart, I haven't... but ignoring death will not prevent it. You will promise to escape with the children when the time comes.'

'Of course I will, as their survival is more important than ours. We have both had a longer life than expected and I will fight to the death to keep them safe. Now promise me no more talk of death, Ubba. You have to believe you are invincible – and never have you been more prepared or fitter to fight than now.'

o0o

Ralf was teaching the boys the basic skills of being a farrier, in the stable yard. He was demonstrating how to recognise a broken nail and spot signs that a shoe was coming loose. Ubba had insisted they must be taught how to care for their own horses and must appreciate that their survival depended on their horse.

They must be able to care for their every need.

Ralf had one of the troop horses tied up and was demonstrating how to remove a shoe that may have started to come undone and spread across the foot. The quickest approach was to remove the shoe completely – if a protruding shoe caught the horse on an opposing leg it could lame the horse immediately.

Erik was the first to try to remove a shoe and he tackled the job easily. He was slightly more hesitant when asked to replace the shoe, as he knew that if he inserted the nail into the foot incorrectly, he could lame the horse.

A wagon and two horses appeared in the yard and it was assumed it was bringing supplies to the stables. Viggo wandered over, surprised to see a Dane merchant in the driving seat whom he recognised. Sam the groom came out to greet him with two stable lads, carrying pigeon crates containing six in each. There were already another two on the wagon as well as feedstuffs.

The lads loaded the crates and Viggo could not resist asking a question. 'Sam, where are those pigeons going? Have you sold some of your own?'

'Nay, Master Viggo. Those pigeons belong to a friend of mine who lives outside Loidis, and these are mine. We have a little wager once a month to see whose pigeons are the fastest to get home. The merchant is going north, and he will release them when he reaches Durham at a specified time, then we will wait for the pigeons to fly home and record their time and declare a winner. Our mates bet on the outcome and the winner receives a cash reward. The pigeons always make their way back to their own lofts, so we have turned it into a bit of sport.'

'But how do you know whose pigeon is whose?'

'We ring them, put our names and the bird's identity number on them and wrap it round their foot.'

Viggo was getting really excited. 'How long do they take to fly the distance?'

'Depending on the weather, around two hours. My pal knocks ten minutes off his flocks' time to compensate for the extra distance from Jorvik to Loidis.'

'Oh, Sam! Why didn't you tell me about this before?'

'Well, you only regard pigeons as food for your raptors; you've never shown any interest in them as birds before. Sulamain mentioned that pigeons have a homing instinct and they use them in his home country, which is what gave us the idea.'

Viggo was dancing around. 'But Sam, this is unbelievable! If you can take a pigeon from its home and release it many miles away and you know it will come home, you can attach a message to its other foot.'

'Aye, I can see that may be possible, but not every pigeon will make it home – that's why we release 12. They could be killed by raptors like yours, or hit bad weather, or some of them just get lost.'

'Yes, but you could work on that by training them with rewards for fast flying. Just imagine! If the Saxons attacked my Uncle Halfdan in Lincoln and he had some of our pigeons he could release one or two with a message, which we would have within an hour to warn us to prepare for an attack. I must go and tell my father and Ivar and we must build up our own pigeon stock.' He ran off, forgetting he was supposed to be learning about shoeing horses, straight back to the palace. He ran through the entrance hall and Egil was there. 'Now Master Viggo, slow down. You will collide with somebody at that speed.'

'Egil, where are my father and Ivar?'

Egil glared at him. 'The King and Lord Ubba are in a meeting with Sulamain and your mother.'

'Where? I need to see them.'

Egil raised his voice, 'Master Viggo, you will have to wait until later. You cannot interrupt the King whilst he is in a meeting.'

Viggo set off running towards the state rooms and shouted, 'Sorry Egil, this is a matter of urgency.'

Egil shouted after him, 'Don't you dare interrupt, you young scallywag.' But Viggo had found the right room already.

The occupants all looked startled. Ubba leapt to his feet and barked, 'What is it, son? Are we under attack?'

'No, Father. I am sorry; I just need to speak to you all urgently. You said when we first arrived that communication is vital, and I have found a way of doing it.'

His mother retorted, 'And it was so important you felt you had to interrupt our meeting? Apologise to Ivar for your churlish manners and leave.'

Ivar raised his hand. 'No. Viggo, I know you well

enough to know that you would not do this lightly. What have you discovered?'

They all sat down and Sulamain looked at Ubba and smiled as Viggo explained. 'Sam the groom keeps pigeons in the backyard at his home and has a friend in Loidis who also has them. A merchant has just picked up 12 of Sam's pigeons and already has his friends' stock onboard. They will then be loaded onto his boat for the journey north. He will release them at an agreed time from Durham and they will fly home. The first one back to their own pigeon loft is declared the winner, with the Loidis pigeons allowed an extra ten minutes to account for the extra distance. Their pals bet on who will be the winner and it provides an extra sport for them. They can fly this distance in less than two hours, which is very quick, and they have a metal ring on one foot stamped with their name and owner. They could carry a coded message on their other foot to warn well in advance of danger.'

Ivar interrupted, 'I never knew they raced pigeons, but now I know why Sam gets anxious when we hunt with the raptors.'

Viggo turned to Sulamain, 'You explained to me that migrating birds, mammals and fish navigate by using the Earth's magnetic field to reach their destination and return to their breeding grounds. We know that many species of birds fly here from Europe and Africa in the spring and breed here. If we trained these pigeons to race from A to B with food as a reward, we could receive news from our spies scattered around the country of Saxon troop movements far quicker than we do now.'

Ivar said, 'But some will perish to raptors on their journey. They will easily be picked off by hawks and falcons – especially when flying in a flock.'

'That's why you need to have at least two birds carrying each message. We can set up a breeding programme using Sam's fastest birds and keep breeding them for speed. We can also train them to fly non-stop over short distances and teach them how to avoid being attacked by raptors. Bad weather can also cause problems and they could be blown off course by strong winds. We can teach them to fly alone so they will be at less risk from prey.'

Ubba remarked, 'But this is dependent on Jorvik pigeons being kept in strategic places. If we had some at Repton we would know far more about ships moving up and down the North Sea.'

'Yes, of course! It would take six months to train and test them, but they could be easily transported on longboats and a couple strapped in a basket to a saddle for when you go on scouting missions.'

Ivar clapped his hands. 'Viggo, you bright spark! This could improve communication, lessening the risk to our troops by providing an early warning system. We can start by sending Sigtryggr back to Ireland with some of Sam's pigeons, see if one can make it back here and how long it takes.'

Ubba asked Sulamain, 'Tell me about the Earth's magnetic field so I can understand what is happening here? I have seen salmon swimming upstream and heading north against significant barriers to return to their spawning grounds, which I assume are in Scotland.'

Sulamain used his hands to demonstrate the tilt of the Earth's axis, explaining the angle of 35% as the Earth rotates around the sun.

'It takes one year to complete its orbit. Here in winter we are furthest away from the sun, hence the cold.'

Ivar responded, 'Well done, Viggo. You go and plan how we can implement your ideas and I will support you.'

'You will allow me to direct this project on my own, Ivar?'

'Of course! I trust you to do an excellent job, but you have to continue with your studies as well.'

Ubba commented, 'Your mother and I are very proud of you, Viggo, and amazed at the knowledge you have learned from Sulamain.'

'I apologise for disturbing you all.'

As he left the room his mother grabbed him and whispered, 'Well done, son.' He squirmed in embarrassment and ran.

TEN

Ubba had just returned from a scouting trip. He was at the stables when a young man came running into the courtyard, apprehended by one of his scouts who did not recognise him.

The scout had hold of him from behind, with a seax at his throat. 'Who are you and what business do you have here?'

The young man screeched, 'Hold fast! I have a message for Ubba Ragnarsson.'

He strolled over to the men. 'I am Ubba. What is your message?' Turning to his scout he said, 'Ulf, let the boy breathe so he can deliver his message.'

'Sorry lord, but he should never have got past the palace gate, never mind down here.'

'My master the merchant Torsten sent me to tell you that we were at Loidis yesterday and this morning we passed a single longboat flying a banner with a bear and raven on it. It was heading upriver.'

'Thank the gods, my brother Bjorn is alive!' He turned to his son Arne, 'Quick, find Erik, Refil and your mother and head to the docks.' He pulled a coin from his pocket and gave it to the messenger. 'Have a drink and return to your master and thank him. I cannot express how relieved I am.'

Ubba set off to the docks to await the arrival of his brother. Refil and Erik arrived but although Erik was clearly delighted, he could sense reticence from Refil. He called him over to sit beside him on the loading bay.

'What is wrong, Refil? You don't look overly enthusiastic?'

'Don't misinterpret my demeanour, Ubba. I was beginning to think, like you, that he had died on this last mission. He always said he would come back for us and his intention was to become King of Norway. I don't know whether my battle skills are up to my father's high standards.'

Ubba put his arm around him. 'Refil, you are being too hard on yourself. I know that you are not a natural killer but I have drilled into you the discipline and skills you need to act instinctively when the time comes. There is a huge difference between practising and fighting to stay alive. I promise you your courage and training will be there when the time comes. You have worked hard with men who are battle-hardened and you will give your best. You are an excellent sailor and budding boat designer and that is where your heart lies. Your father knew that when he brought you here.'

'Has Viggo told you that I have promised to build a boat suitable to sail as far as the Arctic Ocean, to Iceland and beyond? There has to be more land further west; we just need to build a boat capable of surviving the rough sea. Viggo has been surveying the geese that migrate here from the west. He is convinced there is rich fertile land on the other side of the Atlantic Ocean.'

'You see, you are a born explorer and Viggo has many talents and a fine brain. If that is your ultimate quest then go for it because you will succeed. Ragnar, Floki and Rollo would be so proud of you, and your mother and father too. Just don't ask me to go with you. I am a definite landlubber – my feet need to be on land, not water.'

'I could never have even dreamt of doing this if it hadn't been for you and Ivar giving me the chance to learn the skills. I love you Ubba for making me believe that I could attempt it. You have been my inspiration.'

The longboat was pulling into the dock and she had visibly taken some hammering. Bjorn was at the helm. This was a chiselled, lithe, deeply tanned version of him and his transformation in frame alone could not have been an easy one. His sons, and Torri, stared at him, hardly able to recognise him. He seemed to have aged a great deal and was clearly in some pain.

As the boat was being tied up, Bjorn made his way to the quayside. Erik and Refil reached him first and hugged him. Ubba turned to Torri, 'There is something ailing Bjorn. Let's get him up to the palace and let Sulamain examine him; he is very ill.'

They went to greet him and Torri hugged him. 'Bjorn, you are ill. What is wrong with you?'

He whispered, 'Just get me to a bed. I need rest and I don't want to frighten my sons.'

Ubba hugged him close. With tears in his eyes he

said, 'My brother, I feared you were already dead but you have returned to us a mere shadow of yourself. We will help you now Bjorn; you are in safe hands... but judging by the state of your longboat and your health, you will be going nowhere for a while.'

Bjorn sobbed, 'I did not think I would make it here. I have a recurring malady that strikes frequently. It started three days ago, and it makes me as weak as a kitten.'

Ubba turned and saw a pack pony that had been used for loading a merchant boat. He ran to untie it and led it over to Bjorn. 'Can you stand on that wall and get on? You are too weak to walk.'

He pulled Refil to one side, 'Go and find Sulamain. Tell him your father is ill and has been in Africa, and to bring all his medicines and his assistant to the palace. Your father needs urgent medical attention.'

He turned to Erik, 'Go and find whoever is second in command on the longboat and bring him up to the palace straight away. Ask him if he knows why Bjorn is so ravaged and weak.'

He led the pony to the palace, with Torri supporting Bjorn's knee on the offside as his balance was compromised. The crowd pulled back in shock, unable to believe that this was the great Bjorn Ironside. At the bottom of the palace steps Ubba gathered Bjorn in his arms and carried him up to the main entrance.

Egil and Ivar were waiting and their mouths dropped open in shock when they saw Ubba carrying someone towards them.

Ivar said, 'Has someone fallen ill on the journey

here?'

'Not just someone, Ivar. Bjorn and is very ill.'

Ivar gasped, 'He cannot be Bjorn! He must be an imposter.'

Ubba replied, 'I can assure you it is Bjorn. I will carry him up to my old room. I have sent Refil for Sulamain. Bring him straight up and when Erik brings one of his men here, question him about Bjorn's state of health. Sulamain will need as much information as possible to diagnose what is wrong.'

He carried Bjorn upstairs and he could feel him writhing. 'I could never have lifted you before. What the hell has ravaged your body so, out in Africa? Ivar has a Moor here teaching our sons, who has served several emirs in Arabia and is a skilled healer. He will know what is wrong with you.'

Torri rushed ahead to open the door and prepare the bed for Bjorn. She ushered servants to fetch hot water, towels, rugs and a nightgown, and Ubba lowered Bjorn into a comfy armchair.

'Your body is sweating but you are icy cold, not blazing hot.'

Bjorn replied, 'I know. My body is shivering like it is surrounded by ice.'

Ubba turned to Torri, 'Should we give him a hot bath?'

Torri replied, 'Not until Sulamain has examined him. Let's get him out of his wet clothes and wrap him up with rugs and furs.'

Ubba undressed him carefully. He could see no new injuries on his upper body, but he was very thin and had no muscle across his chest. His ribs were visible. He had no fat at all on his stomach.

Torri brought him a glass of water. He drank it and asked for more. She only gave him a little more as he was so desperate to have it, but she feared giving him too much until Sulamain had seen him.

They had just got him into bed when Sulamain and his servant arrived, accompanied by a very worried Ivar. Bjorn was propped up on several pillows, shivering and barely conscious.

Sulamain pulled the wolfskin off his chest and shoulders, talking in a very soothing voice to Bjorn, telling him who he was and what he was doing. He took his wrist, felt his pulse and counted the beats. He looked into his eyes and mouth. He checked his heartbeat, shaking his head, then examined his chest in detail. He asked Torri if Bjorn had any new wounds on him that she did not recognise. Over the years Bjorn had taken and survived sword swipes, spear probes and seax wounds.

Torri said, 'I can't see any new wounds except for all these insect bites.'

Sulamain sighed, 'And I am afraid that these bites are the most likely reason for his present condition. Now Bjorn, I need to examine your stomach. I will be very gentle.'

Torri had put a pillow under his bottom to support him. She noticed streaks of blood and urine on it and drew Sulamain's attention to it. He nodded but put his finger to his mouth and shook his head.

Torri turned away with tears streaming down her

face. She was next to Ivar; she sought comfort in his arms and as she looked up at him she saw tears rolling down his face too. Sulamain motioned to Ubba to help him turn Bjorn onto his front. As they did so, Sulamain spotted a small round stitched wound on his side, close to his ribs. It was clean and looked to be healing but Sulamain probed the area around it carefully. He examined his back and then told Ubba to turn him back over, prop him up with the pillows and cover him up. He gave instructions in Arabic to his assistant who set to positioning two stands either side of the bed. He told Bjorn to rest while he prepared his treatment and motioned to the rest of them to follow him out of earshot.

'I cannot stress how ill he is; death is more likely than recovery. He is so weak and dehydrated that the treatment alone may kill him, but it's also his only chance of survival. I am fairly sure after talking to his man who confirmed that he has experienced these attacks previously, that he has malaria. This is caused by mosquito bites, which dwell near poisonous waterholes. They bite humans and animals and infect their lungs, liver and kidneys. He says Sienna nursed him through his infection six months ago using the correct treatment, and he took some more when he was stricken on the voyage home. However, he did not have enough to control it. I have an extract from a type of tree bark and I am going to set up a drip of it into his arm as well as giving him poppy seed to make him sleep. In his other arm I will infuse a salt solution drip to rehydrate his body. He has conquered it before but his body is now in a much weaker state so there are no guarantees – his fate is in the hands of your gods.'

Torri said with great anguish, 'Should we have his sons say their goodbyes now in case he doesn't make it?'

'Yes, I think it would be wise. Once I put him out he will sleep soundly and may never come round.'

'Oh, Ubba! What about Louis, his grandson?'

'Torri, he has to see him and know he has a grandson before he dies.'

Ivar replied, 'I will fetch Marianne and the baby.'

Sulamain said to Ubba and Torri, 'Do you want to explain to him what is happening, or would you like me to?'

Ubba said, 'I will tell him Torri, if you could support the boys.'

Torri sobbed, 'We will do it together.' She ran into his arms and he held her close and stroked her hair.

'Now, my brave queen, you must summon all your strength – and so must I. He made it here and has fought it off before; we must believe he can do it again.'

Holding hands, they went to Bjorn's bedside. He looked at their faces. 'Not good news, then. Tell me the truth, Ubba.'

Ubba explained what Sulamain was going to do – and how ill he was.

'I wanted to die on the battlefield and go to Valhalla. I have had visions of being back in Jormund and of fighting in Norway. I am not ready to go yet.'

Ubba hugged him. 'Then fight brother with all your

strength if you don't want to die. We shall plead for Odin to spare your life. I will guide your sons if you don't succeed, and they will both make their own way in life. They have your courage and curiosity and will honour your name. Now you must say goodbye to Torri alone. I love you Bjorn, and I am honoured to have had you as my role model for all these years.'

'Ubba, you are the most wonderful loyal man with a true heart and soul and love for everyone. You understand what is in our hearts and minds and encourage us to banish our demons. I have huge respect for you having become the warrior you are, because at heart you are a man of peace, not war.'

Ubba left him with Torri. He stood with his face to the wall, trying desperately to stem his emotions as he knew he must control himself to support Erik and Refil. Torri joined him moments later, took his hand and kissed it.

Erik went in first with Torri, Marianne and Louis. Ubba bade Refil wait with him. The boy was stricken with grief.

When Erik came back Ubba put his arm around Refil and ushered him to his father's bedside. As Refil knelt and took Bjorn's hand Ubba said, 'This is your son, the born explorer. He will make you proud and reach new undiscovered land. I have turned him into a decent warrior and when his courage and fighting skills are needed he will deliver.'

Bjorn took his hand, pulled him close and kissed him, knowing the boy could not speak. Ubba helped him to his knees and supported him away from the bedside as Ivar approached.

Ivar sat in the chair and took Bjorn's hand. 'Listen to me, Bjorn Ironside. This is not your time to die. I have seen you in visions both at home and fighting in Norway. The gods will not let a man of your calibre die like this. Valhalla is the only place fit for you. Now go to sleep and fight this affliction like you have before.'

Bjorn chuckled, 'I was hoping you might kill me now rather than letting me suffer; you have always wanted revenge for me killing your mother.'

'No way, Bjorn! Ubba would kill me too and I am not ready to die just yet. I have new lands to conquer!'

'I have brought you another gift Ivar; it is an African eagle and it reminds me of you. Don't let it anywhere near your gyrfalcons. It is a killer with a cruel streak like you. It swoops to catch its prey but doesn't kill it instantly; it soars back up into the sky and then drops it from a great height and enjoys hearing it squeal as it plunges to its death and its bones smash. Then it flies back down to feast.'

Before they left his room and his treatment commenced, Ivar made an announcement. 'In order to ensure the gods are aware of Bjorn's plight we will hold a private ritual at midnight and sacrifice a goat. Only blood relatives can attend, and you must wear white robes and cloaks. I will officiate and make the sacrifice and will implore the gods to save him.'

Erik said, 'I am the closest blood relation to him so I will slaughter the goat.'

Ivar said, 'Very well, Erik – as his eldest son the gods will hopefully listen to your pleas. I will ask Thorin to be there as my assistant. If he does have a link to the gods then we must exploit every avenue available to reach them.'

Ubba said, 'Thank you, Ivar. I appreciate you doing this.'

Ivar replied, 'He is my half-brother Ubba, and I will do anything in my power to keep a Ragnarsson alive.'

Ubba turned to Torri, 'Take the boys away and see that they eat. Oversee their face paint, hair and robes for later. If Arne and Viggo ask to be present then you must permit it. I will stay with Bjorn while Sulamain starts treatment, and will join you later.'

He went over to Bjorn's bed where wooden boards had been strapped to his arms to prevent him from bending at the elbow. Drips had been set up using sheep bladders with an attached needle to inject the liquid into his arms.

Ubba said, 'Ivar is going to oversee an animal sacrifice to the gods to implore them to spare your life at midnight.'

Bjorn smiled weakly, 'I was hoping he might kill me now, but he refused because he said you would kill him and he has new land to conquer like me.'

'Erik insists on doing the goat sacrifice; he knows his duty.'

Sulamain came over with a drink. 'Are you ready now, Bjorn? I want you to drink this to help you sleep. It's just poppy seed and wine. You may have vivid dreams and might awaken at times, but you must not be afraid. Someone will be at your bedside throughout to support you and summon me if necessary.'

Ubba interrupted, 'We will all share the vigil, Bjorn. You will not be alone. Just hurry up and come back to us; we all need you to live.'

Bjorn finished the wine and Ubba plumped up his pillows. As Sulamain set up the first drip Ubba took Bjorn's hand, hoping to give him some of his strength. Bjorn soon settled into a peaceful sleep and Ubba let the tears he had kept at bay fall freely.

Sulamain patted him on his shoulder. 'You go and eat now and prepare for the ceremony. I will stay with him.'

'I intend to take the night watch, Sulamain. I need to be at his side to protect him. I will come straight from the service. Tomorrow we will sort out a rota.'

'Very well Ubba, but this could take days, not hours. If he has not died or responded within seven days then I will withdraw treatment. I won't let him suffer needlessly.'

'Do you think he can make it?'

'Yes, I do. His body may have lost some strength but his will is unaffected and if your gods intervene then he will live. It will take time to restore his strength and fitness and he may still suffer attacks of malaria in the future, but it can be controlled.'

'Thank the gods you were here Sulamain, or he would have died – of that there is no doubt.'

ELEVEN

Ubba went home and Torri put his meal in front of him. He looked at it but for once, his appetite had evaporated.

'Eat, my love. I will not have two husbands at death's door. You have the ceremony and no doubt you will be returning to Bjorn to watch over him during the night.'

'I will try, my dear, as I have to keep myself together. I can't let my emotions overcome me just yet.'

Freya came in and saw his ravaged face. 'Father, I know I should not grieve you any further but I insist on going to the ceremony. I am Ragnar's granddaughter and my uncle needs all his blood relatives to plead his case to the gods. I may only be a little girl but I will not disgrace you, I assure you.'

Ubba looked at Torri, who nodded her assent. 'Sweetheart, you will never disgrace me. You have a rod of iron for a backbone and knowledge far beyond your years. You may even be able to communicate directly with the gods. I will not deny you, Freya. Bjorn needs all the power we can muster to keep him alive.'

Ivar had issued the instructions for where the ceremony was to take place and the family gathered in the entrance hall ready for the procession. Ivar, Ubba and Torri wore the formal white wool tunics and fur-trimmed cloaks of the *gothi* as they had performed Norse ceremonies. Ivar wore a plain gold crown as the leader. The rest wore simple white woollen robes and had cloaks or furs to keep them warm. All faces were painted white and would be marked by the blood of the sacrificial animal during the service. A guard of warriors carrying torches waited outside to escort the party to the ceremony and light the way. They had a short walk to the field where a bonfire was burning, and two pews had been borrowed from the church for the ritual.

Ivar opened the ceremony by summoning the gods to hear their plea to save the life of Bjorn Ironside. Then came the sacrifice. Thorin held the goat as Erik stepped forward to kill it with an axe and then slit its throat, and Thorin held the bowl to collect the blood. Ivar then took the bowl to the pew and each family member knelt and was marked with blood on their face from forehead to chin and across both cheeks. After they were anointed they held hands as Ivar closed the ceremony, invoking the gods to grant their wish.

They returned to the palace and went straight to Bjorn's bedside. Candles had been placed around the room. Ivar asked them to touch Bjorn with one hand and all link hands to pass their strength to Bjorn. He made Torri put her hand on his heart as she had been his wife once. Ivar put one hand on his forehead and Ubba held his right hand. The younger members then filled in to make a complete circle around his body. He remained unconscious throughout and there was no reaction apart from his steady breathing. Ivar recited a Norse poem and issued a final plea for his life.

Ubba changed out of his ceremonial robes and gave them to Torri to take home with the children. He hugged them all and gave Erik and Thorin a pat on the back for their participation in the ceremony. He knelt down to hug Freya and she whispered in his ear, 'The gods were listening, Daddy. They won't let him die.'

Sulamain had been in the background and now blew some of the candles out but kept those closest to Bjorn burning. He turned to Ubba, 'An impressive ceremony, my lord. Combined with this treatment it may help his cause.'

Ubba sank into the chair at the side of the bed. 'Well, considering this is the first time we have ever invoked the gods to spare death and Ivar made the whole ceremony up off the top of his head, I thought he did a wonderful job. My daughter said the gods were listening and as I suspect she has her own link with them, let's hope she is correct.

'Ivar never ceases to amaze me with his knowledge. He exudes the authority of a skilled leader and he has told me that he sees visions that he cannot understand until after the event takes place.'

Sulamain checked Bjorn and said, 'I don't think he will come round during the night; he has had enough sedative to knock a horse out. His body needs to rest to give him the strength to fight. You don't need to stay awake Ubba; just be there in case something untoward happens, and summon me if it does.'

Ubba settled into the chair with a pillow and a footstool and wrapped himself in Bjorn's bearskin cloak to feel as close to his beloved brother as possible. His body was exhausted and emotionally, he felt ripped apart. He timed his own breathing with Bjorn's and drifted off to sleep.

The next time he opened his eyes, sunlight was already streaming into the room and he knew it was well past dawn. He stood up, stretched his long limbs and looked at Bjorn. He remembered one of his Saxon troopers referring to him as "slindgy", which in Yorkshire means tall, gaunt and sinewy. Bjorn was still in a deep sleep but Ubba thought his face looked less pale.

The door opened and his angel of a daughter ran over to him shouting, 'Is he better yet, Daddy? I came as soon as I woke up to see if the gods had answered our call.' She went over to the bed and touched Bjorn's hand. 'His hand feels warmer than it did last night, and he is sleeping peacefully.'

'Well, sweetheart, Sulamain gave him a lot of drugs to keep him asleep so his body can fight the infection. We don't expect him to be healed immediately; it will take some time.'

'I overheard Erik and Refil talking last night and if their father dies they intend to return to Norway and attempt to claim the crown of Norway. Viggo also said he would join them.'

'What are they thinking of? Have they gone mad? Erik is sixteen and has never fought in a battle. Why does he think he can sail to Norway and claim their land? They aren't going to hand their country over to a Dane to rule. They know and fear Bjorn, but it would take an army of seasoned men to even attempt to do it. Viggo is going nowhere, and neither are Erik and Refil. They will remain here under my guidance as their mother and father would wish.'

Ivar entered and asked whether there had been any change overnight. Ubba told him what Freya had said about Erik, Refil and Viggo. A flash of anger showed on Ivar's face and he said, 'Leave this to me, brother. I will nip this in the bud before it goes any further. How they even consider they have the power to do such a thing surprises me and shows the impetuousness of youth. I will avail them of their impossible task and lead them to see sense and withdraw. Frank, Ranulf and Arne will oversee the training of the troops; you must rest, Ubba. I will despatch Erik and Refil to do a full inspection of the longboat and organise a complete refit to make it seaworthy. That will keep them occupied – and they will of course take their turn at their father's bedside. I already have Viggo working on a project for me.'

After Ivar left, Freya settled down with Ubba in the chair and cuddled up to him. She examined his face, running her fingers from brow to chin. 'Are you too tired to talk, Daddy?'

'No sweetheart, I slept reasonably well. Bjorn is heavily sedated.'

'If Bjorn dies will he have a full Viking longboat funeral?'

'Of course he will. He is a king and a great warrior. Unfortunately, he would not have died in battle, which may prevent him from entering Valhalla. However, neither did our father... but we all know he was taken to Valhalla after his death by the Valkyries anyway.'

'If you die Daddy, will you have a Viking longboat funeral?'

'No, pet, I am not a king so would not be eligible. Besides, I would rather be buried in the ground. I am not a seafarer; I am a lover of the land.'

'Why did they used to slaughter wives, slaves and animals at Viking funerals?'

'They did this in the belief that a dead person needed them to serve them in the afterlife. However, it is now considered untenable to end human or animal life, even as a sacrifice to the gods. Promise me that if I die you will ensure that Sleipnir stays alive and well and is given to Arne to continue to fulfil his duty as a stallion.'

'Of course I will Daddy, but I have already told the gods that they must protect you from harm and prevent you from dying in battle. Thorin has already asked his grandfather Odin to spare you too.'

He hugged her and kissed her forehead. 'Well, my little Freya, it seems you have the ear of the gods and I will sleep better for knowing they are watching my back. Now let's concentrate on keeping Bjorn alive, shall we?'

Sulamain arrived to check Bjorn. Freya showed a genuine interest in medicine. She wanted to know how he knew what Bjorn was suffering from. When she asked why there was a third drip draining his urine into a bucket under the bed, Sulamain was lost for words.

Ubba laughed, 'Sulamain, I have learnt from experience that Freya is best supplied with the truth when she asks questions way beyond her years.'

'Well, my little bright spark, I shall speak only the truth as I do with Viggo when he bombards me with questions.' He pointed to Bjorn's left drip. 'This supplies a strong sedative to keep Bjorn asleep to help his body recover, and the one on the right drips saline and nutrients that will give him sustenance because he cannot eat whilst asleep. This third one runs from his bladder to the bucket so that his kidneys can drain and urine is excreted so he does not become infected.'

Freya turned to Ubba, 'Sulamain is a very wise man Daddy. I would like to know how to heal sick people. I have watched Mama apply dressings and nurse injured warriors, but his methods are so much more advanced than ours. Why?'

Sulamain took her hand and kissed it. 'Because as a Moor I have experienced more illnesses and treated very dangerous wounds, and our treatments are passed from one generation to the next. You live where the temperatures are lower than in Africa and Arabia. The hotter the climate, the quicker disease spreads. Pure clean water is essential but often in short supply. In areas with little rainfall it is harder to fight infection. If infection occurs in a wound and it takes hold, a person is more likely to die.'

Ubba turned to Freya, 'Now come on, little one. I have work to do and Sulamain has Bjorn to attend to. I will do the night watch again tonight.'

He met Serena in the entrance hall and she hugged

him. 'You look tired and ravaged, Ubba. Please take care.' She turned to Freya, 'Would you like to play with Astrid and Theo before your lessons start?'

Freya jumped about. 'Oh, yes please, Serena!' She skipped off down the corridor, waving goodbye to Ubba.

Egil was in the entrance hall and Ubba summoned him. 'Could you find me a dark hooded cloak to save me going home for one?'

'Certainly, my lord!' He returned quickly. Ubba thanked him, donned the cloak, pulled up the hood and headed outside. He left the palace grounds, which were still quiet as most people were having breakfast and his personal guards were training in the pool. He headed into the streets where the stalls and shops were preparing for trading. He entered the church from a side door and made his way to the front of the nave on the left-hand side, so he would be hidden from view by the marble pillars.

He was confounded by the desire he felt to plead to the Christian God for Bjorn's life after attending a Norse pagan ceremony as a priest himself. *Why did he think his request would even be considered when he was, in their eyes, a heathen?* He prayed silently on his knees; he so desperately wanted his brother to live. Intent on pleading his case, he did not hear the quiet approach of a member of the clergy until a hand was placed on his shoulder and a familiar voice said, 'Can I help you?' He turned quickly and saw it was Father Abraham, Dean of Jorvik.

'My lord Ubba, you appear to be on a mission and

I suspect I know what it is. Do not fear rejection from me for your cause. Jesus would not have turned you away either. You are a baptised Christian even though you have Norse faith too. If you have finished praying let us sit and talk a while. I do not have any duties until later.'

Ubba sighed, 'Thank you, Father. I would like that.' They moved to an office on the left-hand side of the church.

Father Abraham poured him a glass of wine from a bottle in the desk drawer. 'Drink this. It is not communion wine but good French wine.'

Ubba smiled for the first time since Bjorn had returned. 'I am pleased you appreciate the difference, as I certainly do.'

'I know about the ceremony your family took part in last night and I do not condemn you for it in the least. I do not know Bjorn personally, but I understand why you did this and if it works then your actions will be justified.'

'Father, I would not jump to that conclusion even though my daughter has told me the gods have heard and will not let him die. He is being treated by a Moor physician who is well versed in treating malaria, which it seems is contracted from mosquitos and has struck him down before. Bjorn has the strongest will of all my brothers although his time in Africa has ravaged his body to a shadow of its former self. He is not called "Ironside" for nothing. If he survives it could be down to Sulamain's treatment, or Bjorn's incredible strength, or may be due to the gods intervening. I will keep an open mind if he survives, whereas Ivar will claim it is the Norse gods who have intervened.'

Father Abraham smiled. 'And I suppose you won't be telling Ivar you prayed to Christ.'

'No, I won't. It hurts Ivar that I have Christian leanings, as did my father towards the end of his life. I seem to be trapped in the middle as I am surrounded by people whose lives appear influenced by outside deities. Ivar has always had a strong Norse faith and frequently has visions. Young Thorin is another anomaly and as he grows, the more he resembles Thor. I even suspect my beautiful daughter, who is only eight but has the wisdom of someone far older, is being influenced by the gods. She looks to have mine and her mother's ancestry but was born back in Denmark. My wife cannot explain why she named her Freya, except that when she first laid eyes on her she knew that it was her name.'

'I can understand your concern Ubba, and it must be very difficult to live with, but you are wise to keep your thoughts to yourself. I will not breathe a word to another living soul but will ask God to support you in your travail.'

TWELVE

That evening, Ubba returned to Bjorn's bedside for the night vigil. During the day Erik, Refil and Torri had taken their turn. Sulamain confirmed his lungs were clearing of fluid and his vital signs were stronger already. Though he remained in the same deep sleep, his colour was returning, and he had lost the haggard look he'd had before.

Ubba kissed his cheek. 'Come on Bjorn, keep fighting off this infection. I want you to tell me what happened out in Africa. I also want to show you how well your sons are doing with their fighting skills and their lessons. Even Erik has mastered Latin – *and* he has learnt French from Marianne. I had nothing to do with him siring his son. You can blame Ivar for that when you come around. However, it has been the making of him; he now has a much more mature outlook on life and is accepting his new responsibilities as a father well.' He paused to see if there was any reaction from Bjorn, but there was no outward sign that he had heard.

He settled down in his chair and fell asleep relatively quickly. After a while, a noise woke him; he thought he heard a voice. He thought it could be Ivar, who often had difficulty sleeping and woke frequently after vivid dreams.

The candles had been left burning around Bjorn's bed and as he glanced up he saw a hooded figure with hands either side of Bjorn's face, bending down to kiss his forehead. He pulled his hood back and Ubba gasped in shock. 'Father?'

Ragnar raised his hand as Ubba jumped to his feet. 'Ubba, stay where you are, my son; I cannot touch you for fear of pulling you into the afterlife. I want you to know how proud I am of you and Torri. You are an inspirational and compassionate man who is most like me in character. Torri has produced five exceptional grandchildren and I want you to tell her how grateful I am for her devotion and skill in rearing them.

I am here at the behest of the gods to speed Bjorn's recovery. He is right; it is not his time to die. Nor will you, Halfdan or Ivar die soon. You all still have work to do and lands to conquer. You must follow your heart Ubba, and continue your job of training your children to reach for whichever stars they crave. Freya is protected by the gods. Do not feel guilty about turning to Christianity or moving away from your Norse religion. You can embrace both religions my son. Tell Ivar he has fulfilled his wish to become the most notorious Norse king, despite his disabilities.'

He drew the sign of the cross on Bjorn's forehead then turned and disappeared, causing a draught that doused some of the candles. Ubba took Bjorn's hand. 'Come back to us, Bjorn. The gods have granted our request.' He felt the slightest movement from Bjorn's index finger.

He sat back in the chair and went over exactly what had happened, memorising the words from his father. He had appeared to him as he was when he was in his early forties, at the height of his power and strength. He looked across to the mirror and could see his father's face reflecting back at him. They were identical twins.

He managed to nod off again until dawn and then woke from his dream with a start and looked towards Bjorn, who was peacefully asleep. Sulamain usually came to check on Bjorn early and when the door was flung open he assumed it was him, but it was Ivar. He muttered, 'He looks to have a little more colour in his face.'

Ubba replied, 'I had a visitor overnight, intent on healing him.'

'Who?'

'Our father came and put his hands either side of his face. He kissed his forehead.'

'Are you sure this was not just a dream or a vision, Ubba?'

'No, it was Ragnar as he looked in his forties, fit and well. When I woke he bade me not to come near or touch him in case he pulled me into the afterlife. He said the gods had sent him to heal Bjorn as it was not his time to die yet. He also said that you, me and Halfdan would not die soon; we have more battles to fight and land to conquer.'

'Well, that is good news.'

'He gave me a special message for you. "Tell Ivar he has fulfilled his wish to become the most notorious

Norse king, despite his disabilities."'

Ivar's face lit up with joy as he recalled his father asking him what he wanted to be remembered for. This had been his first thought at the time and he knew then that Ubba had definitely seen Ragnar; it was no dream or vision.

Sulamain arrived and noticed the ebullient mood of both men. 'Have there been some changes overnight, Ubba?'

'Yes, Sulamain. Our father came to revive Bjorn. He said it was not his time yet.'

'Allah be praised! Your gods have answered your prayers. I shall start to withdraw the strength of the sedative, but he needs as much sleep as possible to help him heal. Do not expect him to leap out of bed – he has a long way to go before he will have enough strength to take up his sword again. You will both have to make him realise that if he pushes himself too soon and too fast he will be struck down by malaria again.'

Ubba asked, 'How long do you think he will need to recuperate for?'

'Provided there are no added complications and he behaves and eats to build up his strength again then three to four months at least. To sail the North Sea and fight a battle could take longer – possibly six months.'

'God forbid! Bjorn is never still, except when he sleeps. The only way to keep him quiet would be to confine him to a cell.'

Ivar laughed, 'Well, good luck with that one, Ubba. I suggest you find a female companion for him if you want to confine him to bed. Perhaps you could loan

Serena to him to speed his recovery?'

Ubba glared at Ivar and Sulamain turned away so they could not see his smile.

It was two days later when Bjorn returned to consciousness. Ubba was still on night duty. He woke quickly as Bjorn came round and panicked at his arms being restricted.

He leapt to the bed and held his shoulders down on the pillow. Bjorn looked terrified and finally said, 'Father, is that you?'

'No, Bjorn, it's Ubba. You are not dead, but our father has visited to bring you back to health. Relax, you are in good hands. Sulamain has treated your malaria and saved your life.' He rearranged the pillows so Bjorn could sit up.

Bjorn muttered, 'A drink, please – my throat is so dry!'

Ubba fetched him a glass of water and held it for him. 'Sip this slowly, Bjorn. You have been unconscious for five days and your body is not functioning properly yet.'

After taking a few sips Bjorn asked, 'Will I live, Ubba?'

'Of course you will, provided you don't try to push your body too quickly. It will take time and effort to build your strength up again, so you have to be patient.'

'Ubba, I have had some frightening dreams. Some battles I recognised, but not others. I have also seen the faces of men who died in battle years ago.'

'Sulamain used poppy seed as one of your drugs. That can cause hallucinations. It must have been very frightening for you.' He noticed tears running down Bjorn's cheeks. 'Bjorn, the worst is over now; you will recover to fight again.'

Over the next week Bjorn's health improved. All drugs were withdrawn and he was finally allowed to get out of bed. He struggled to walk at first as his muscles had become weak. Thankfully, his appetite returned with a vengeance and he started to put on weight. Torri purchased fresh fruit recently brought to Jorvik from the Mediterranean; Bjorn was able to benefit from oranges, lemons, grapefruit, peaches and other soft fruits he had experienced on his travels. He had always been an avid meat eater and loved Yorkshire puddings soaked in gravy, which were light and easy to consume.

Sulamain and Torri managed to keep him confined to bed for ten days by having family members visit on a rota basis, which gave him an opportunity to catch up with their lives and relate what had happened in Africa. He admitted to Ubba that he had grossly underestimated the ravages that the burning sun of Africa would wreak on his body, along with the water shortage; he had become seriously dehydrated.

Ubba promised that he could ride out with him after two weeks, provided he swam and took gentle exercise to prepare his body first. Gradually, Bjorn's positive character started to return as his body recovered. Sulamain advised him that the malaria might return – but that he could treat it.

On the day of their first ride out together Ralf insisted that Bjorn ride his grey Barbary stallion Poseidon, as he was well trained and the right height for him. He would also be perfect for practising sword fighting and tilting at the quintain. He was used frequently for hunting and hawking and was ridden out next to Sleipnir often. Ralf had ridden him in the schooling paddock to take any freshness out of him before their ride.

Bjorn was delighted to have such a talented horse to ride on and aid his recovery. He thanked Ralf profusely as he mounted Poseidon, then patted and spoke quietly to the horse to introduce himself. Ubba had decided they would take bows and arrows out with them and see if they could catch some rabbits. It would allow Bjorn to practice, as it was not his usual weapon of choice. Ubba, however, had always used one as his perfect eyesight and tracking skills had been honed as a young boy. Living outdoors undercover was another area where the bow and arrow was essential.

Bjorn relaxed as they headed uphill into the countryside. 'I never thought I would see home or Jorvik again. It really is stunning around here. You have everything you need to farm in this wonderful countryside. Are you going to retire as a warrior and turn to farming if Halfdan and Ivar lose their crowns?'

Ubba laughed, 'Nothing would make me happier Bjorn, but I doubt the Saxons would allow me such freedom. You know I have promised to support Halfdan, but I could not take trained warriors from here as it would leave Jorvik too exposed. I am contemplating going alone to Lincoln. He has built up his troops and trained them well. Halfdan is intending to use his longboat as a means of escape to the North if the Saxons look like they will take Lincoln.'

'I can see the logic in that, but I doubt Torri or Ivar would be happy about your exposure to the enemy. You are a prime target Ubba, and there will be no ransom for you.'

'Neither would I want to be captured or ransomed. I would rather fight to my death than be imprisoned. Remember, I don't endure pain as well as you do; the prospect of torture and confinement is my worst nightmare. All three of us have agreed we will not pay ransoms, and the Saxons would be mad to keep us alive. The same goes for Torri and my children – they would still be considered a threat, even at their tender age.'

'What do you know of young King Edward?'

'Well I taught him to sword fight for two years from the age of eleven. He was better than his father, but Alfred was no warrior. He did not have the strength or constitution. Edward is still relatively young at twenty-six and has his mother Aelswith to contend with. Cutting her apron strings will be no easy task; she demanded he abandon his first wife with whom he sired a son in his teens. He is remarried to a more suitable queen and has a son and daughter with her already.'

'He is ambitious if he thinks he can take over Danelaw and form a united England.'

'Perhaps he is trying to procure the legacy of his

father, which is just what your sons intended to do had you died, even though they were far from capable of taking on your quest to become King of Norway.'

Bjorn laughed, 'Ambitious, arrogant and very unwise, but it cheers me to know they had the balls to contemplate it. That has to be due to the training and education you and Ivar have given my sons whilst they have been here. I will never underestimate your involvement. You have nurtured Refil and encouraged his battle skills to a high level. Even Erik was surprised at the transformation in him.'

'Ivar soon made them see what an impossible mission they faced. I see a lot of myself in Refil and I taught him to hone his fighting skills until they became instinctive, like I did in my early days of training. I never had your courage Bjorn, or your absolute belief. My conscience questioned what we were doing and why, but I did it anyway because it was my duty and was expected as a son of Ragnar.'

'Ubba, that showed far more courage than I ever had. To suppress your doubts and kill for a cause that was not your own showed exceptional commitment and loyalty to our father and to your comrades. You had no desire for wealth, power or fame, whereas these are the primary motives for Halfdan, Ivar and me. You recognised that our father eventually resented the onerous task of being a king, and there's nothing cowardly about that. Erik told me of the lessons you taught him about respect having to be earned. You command the greatest respect from your men than any of us. They truly would give their lives to protect you because you have two exceptional qualities – compassion and trust – that we don't possess.'

Ubba laughed, 'But you have forgotten my essential asset – Torri. She has all the skills and courage required of any king, and has proved it on many occasions. To have Ivar, Halfdan and you recognise that made me so proud, and her so happy. I just want to live my life in peace with her and my children without war looming, but it is not going to be possible. Changes to all our lives are imminent, so like the resilient Yorkshire people I have learnt to love and respect, we just have to get on with life the best we can.'

THIRTEEN

Over the next three months, Ubba supervised Bjorn's fitness regime and guided him in regaining his sword, axe and arrow skills. They spent many hours practising fighting on horseback. Bjorn refused to use a lighter sword whilst his muscles recovered their strength, and he went from being able to fight for five minutes to taking Ubba on for much longer bouts. He also achieved a great deal more balance in the saddle and learnt to control his horse with the lightest of movements. Ubba showed him how to train a horse to stand still even while unattended, and to make it lie down on command to avoid being spotted. Poseidon had already mastered these skills and knew how to fight with his rider. Sleipnir could use his shoulder and rump to push away the opponent's horse and then charge to allow his rider to get closer to make the killer blow. Both horses knew that the shield was there to protect them just as much as the rider. In battle, horses were targeted to bring down the rider. Ubba had designed chainmail for his horse, to cover him from chest to tail, which would protect him from arrows, seax and sword.

Bjorn was also invited to their meetings to discuss tactics for the inevitable Saxon attacks, and his expertise was appreciated by them all. He helped reassure Torri and Ivar about Ubba's plan to go to Lincoln alone, although he implored him to take one or two more men as together they would stand a better chance of survival. Ubba agreed to take Frank with him for reconnaissance and scouting. He would take Raven as his mount, as Sleipnir would be too easy to see and too precious to lose.

Ivar announced, 'I have a suggestion to make to Ubba and Torri, which I have been considering for some time. However, I know you have a temper Ubba, and I would prefer you relinquish your seax to me before I continue.'

There was a moment's silence and then Ubba stood up and leaned menacingly over the table towards Ivar. 'What have you done, Ivar? When it is something you suspect I won't approve of, you usually do it *before* telling me.'

'Calm, brother. I have done nothing yet, I merely wish to make a valid suggestion. Your seax, please?'

Torri was sitting next to Ubba. As he was leaning over the table she slipped her hand under his tunic and down his breeches, and grabbed the seax. 'Let's hear what he has to say, Ubba.'

Ubba glared at her and said, 'You, my lady, are the only person permitted to put your hand in my breeches and disarm me, so I won't kill you... but don't make a habit of it.' He winked at her and took his seat. She moved the seax to a table further down the room. Bjorn and Ivar laughed and the tension was broken.

Ivar continued, 'I know we have discussed that

Torri, Serena and your children should retire to Ralf's farm in Terrington before the battle commences, which is sensible until the outcome is decided. As you know, I intend to go to Ireland if Jorvik is lost.' He paused. 'We know that there is a high probability that if your wife and children are captured, the Saxons will imprison them and possibly kill them. We cannot risk the loss of your line. Let me take Viggo to Ireland with me. He is a very intelligent boy and has the knowledge and attributes of a king. I will keep him safe until you are settled, and will return him to you when it has calmed down.'

There was silence as they considered his offer.

'You would take my son from me, Ivar?'

'Only to preserve his life Ubba; we cannot lose Ragnarssons. Halfdan and I have no heirs. I am assuming Bjorn will take his sons back home with him soon. Viggo has not inherited your looks and would be easier to hide in Ireland. Don't forget I will have Sigtryggr and his men behind me.'

Ubba raised his voice, 'But Ireland is even more dangerous than here. They ambush their enemies on the move.'

Ivar retorted, 'And are you assuming that Edward, being young, would not order the killing of your sons? He is Alfred's son Ubba; he learnt at the knee of his father who may not have been a great warrior, but he was an admirable politician and strategist. And don't forget his wife Aelswith who publicly claimed that "The only good Norseman is a dead one!"'

Ubba took Torri's hand. 'What do you say, my

love?'

'I can see the sense in it, even though I don't wish to be parted from him. I hope Edward and his sister Aethelflaed would have mercy on Freya and allow her to live.'

Ivar snorted, 'Well if they do they are very foolish as she has the gods behind her and will prove more of a threat to their future than any of us. I would willingly take her too if you would let me. Ubba, you may not survive Lincoln or the battle for Jorvik; you have to protect your line.'

Bjorn interrupted, 'I agree that you should protect your children. I know you want nothing more than to have land and find peace with them, but you have to be realistic. I would willingly take all three of them back to Denmark, but I can fully understand your reluctance to part with them due to the distance involved. I think you should let Viggo go with Ivar as I think Ivar will succeed in Ireland. Perhaps you should consider letting me take Freya back home. She will always have status as a granddaughter of Ragnar and will become a queen in her own right.'

Ubba shook his head. 'I need to think long and hard about this and discuss it with Torri. I know my chances of survival are very limited. We will discuss it and hopefully come up with a solution. Let us discuss this together, Torri. We have to decide soon as Bjorn will be leaving.'

They returned home and retired to their bedroom. All the children were at lessons, either in the palace or on horseback in the schooling arena. Torri fetched them a bottle of wine and glasses and they snuggled up together with Torri resting her head on his shoulder.

Ubba said, 'First of all, has Ivar discussed this with you before?'

'No, Ubba. He would not do that.'

'Then give me your initial reaction to sending Viggo with Ivar to Ireland.'

She sighed, 'Like you, I have heard many rumours of Danes fighting in Ireland. The population is made up of many different tribes from all over Northern Europe. Even the Scots hold land in Ireland – as well as Frisians, Frankians, Germans and Anglo Saxons. It has many different religious backgrounds and it is famed for its red-haired short-tempered people. I agree that with Sigtryggr behind him Ivar will be able to conquer Dublin, which has strong trading links. His reputation as a leader and a warrior may be slightly exaggerated but Sigtryggr has made his mark and has ambition to conquer over here. Ivar would be the perfect choice to hold Ireland whilst he comes over here. Viggo has a clever political mind and has been schooled by Ivar personally. Sigtryggr may not have the education and language skills but in a joint alliance, they could prove formidable. Ivar adores Viggo and he would ensure his safety.

'However, Viggo wants to explore and has formed a strong bond with Refil. They are determined to explore beyond Iceland. If Bjorn becomes King of Norway then he will need both his sons beside him. If he doesn't then Refil may take to the seas. This is how I think it could play out politically, but wherever

Viggo settles he will collect followers. He has your communication skills and a thirst for knowledge. Perhaps he does not crave money, power and influence – but he will succeed in acquiring it.'

Ubba stroked her hair. 'So that is your political assessment. But what does your motherly instinct say?'

'My whole life has been based around keeping my children alive and preparing them to make their own fortunes. Of course I will worry about his welfare, but Ivar knows he has a great future and will help him to achieve it. Remember, we could be dead and would have no power or influence to help him. Don't misconstrue Ivar's motives, Ubba. He is not trying to steal him away from us. Now, what are *your* views on Viggo going to Ireland?'

'Much as I want to keep him close, I can see the advantages in it as it may keep him alive. Arne wants to fight with me, but that would be too risky for him and he is resolved to going with you as his family's protector. Arne shares my looks and would be recognised anywhere as a Ragnarsson. He also has my skills for tracking, hunting and survival in the open. He is a good swordsman and a skilled horseman, and has the courage and ability to be a great warrior. However, if the Saxons capture him I think they will kill him as he would be a threat in the future; Danes would flock to serve him just as they do with me. I don't expect they would do it straight away, but they would contrive an unfortunate "accident", I am sure. However, Viggo has to be consulted on this we cannot demand that he goes. Shall we approach him together or separately? He may be more truthful with you about his real feelings, whereas with me he will be anxious to do his duty as a Ragnarsson. Perhaps I should speak to him first and give him some time to consider, and then you could ask him and advise him.'

Torri kissed his cheek. 'And now my dear, what about Freya? I know this will be a very hard choice for you to make but we must discuss it.'

Ubba sighed and took her hand. 'I am torn between acting in her best interests and an overwhelming desire to keep her close to me. If she went home with Bjorn she would have her birthright and status and many offers of marriage... but who can say whether she would be safer married to a Saxon or a Dane? Bjorn has confirmed that he would not take her with him in his fight to become King of Norway – he would leave her at Jormund in Lagertha's care – but she could still be attacked there.'

Torri interrupted, 'But if the gods are protecting her then surely they will watch over her? If they have plans for her then they will ensure her survival.'

'She is still a child, Torri; she needs one of us to guide her future. I think she should remain with you.'

'But if we are captured I may be killed immediately, and so may she. If they were to keep her alive she would pose a threat, purely because of her background. They may think they can force her to become a Christian and follow their ways, but we both know that Freya would not tolerate that.'

A voice announced from the doorway, 'My future is here in this country. I will not flee to Denmark or

Ireland.'

Ubba shouted, 'What have I told you about eavesdropping, Freya? I will remind you that you will obey your father and mother.'

She ran into the room and stood before them like a queen. 'I do not know what the gods have planned for me, but I do know that it is here that my destiny lies. I will remain with Mother and if we are captured then I will take whatever fate befalls us. I have the advantage of being a child and I shall exploit that as best I can to stay alive. They won't kill me or lock me up for ever and I will escape if necessary.'

Ubba pulled her close and hugged her. 'Sweetheart, this is so difficult for us as parents as we know we may be dead and unable to guide you. Do not think that if you left here now you would not return – and if you went with Ivar and Viggo, you would be safe initially. I am convinced Sigtryggr intends to return here, and when you are older you could return here too, as the wife of a Danish king.'

'No, Father. I insist on staying here and taking my chance to survive, even if I am the only member of our family to do so. I will do it and take revenge later. Mother has faced similar problems and reared six children, and I intend to do the same.'

Torri smiled at her. 'Spoken like a true queen, but it will not be an easy option. You will need all your wits about you to survive. We will consider your wishes, but you must remember you are duty bound to obey your parents. We need to consider all the options. Now off you go... and stop eavesdropping on us or

I will have you confined to your room for a week, young lady!'

oOo

After four months of recuperation, Bjorn made the decision to return to Denmark in October before winter set in, to prepare for his assault on Norway in the spring. He was looking more like Bjorn Ironside again. He had spent many hours training with Ubba's men and swimming in the pool. Ubba had coached him on how to train a warhorse and fight in close combat. This he had really enjoyed, and his horsemanship and balance had improved in leaps and bounds. He had also been on patrol upriver with the longboat crew and his sons. Rowing had improved his upper body strength. Ivar had sharpened up his axe throwing and archery skills, and his confidence had soon flooded back.

He had thoroughly enjoyed being amongst his family and having time to spend with them. His relationship with Ivar had blossomed; he was grateful for the education that he had given his sons. They had spent many evenings discussing tactics for his quest to become King of Norway and Ivar's impending fight to keep Jorvik. He respected Ivar's skill as a negotiator and tactician. He praised Torri for her role as a mother and he complimented Ubba on turning his sons into warriors.

They had a party on their last night together. Ubba managed to speak privately to both Refil and Erik and wish them good fortune before the party started. Refil was very fond of Ubba, and Ubba was sad to see him go. But Refil assured him that he would see him again in the future and commanded him to ensure he kept himself alive and well.

Bjorn cornered him just before midnight, slightly drunk. 'Ubba, how can I thank you enough for bringing me back to life? Without your care I would never have made it. I also owe Ivar, Sulamain, Torri and the rest of my family a huge debt. I know how determined you were to keep me alive, and your dedication to overseeing my fitness and coaching my battle skills has proved what an exceptional brother you are.'

Ubba smiled. 'I am just repaying your kindness and patience in helping me when I joined our father as an immature boy. Without your skill and guidance, I would never have survived to this ripe old age. You were there for me when I was throwing up in the bottom of a longboat, crippled with sea sickness. You stood by me in my first shield wall, knowing how terrified I was. You gave me the courage to do my duty, knowing that I had grave doubts about killing someone who had done me no harm.'

Bjorn intervened, 'Ubba, don't ever consider you lacked courage, because to do what you did showed far greater courage than any man I know. You are a man of peace and a great teacher, communicator and loyal family man. Men love you because you inspire them to perform to their absolute limit. Ivar may have secured his reputation as the most feared Dane warrior, and I may have achieved a credible reputation as a warrior, but you will be remembered for your deep love of nature, animals and family, and your compassion for people. You never wanted power, money, authority, status or control. You want to live in peace and harmony. Isn't that what everybody should aspire to, rather than power and greed?'

The next morning, once the boat was loaded with supplies, food and equipment, they assembled at the docks to bid farewell to Bjorn and his sons. Viggo gave them the pannier containing 12 pigeons. He had instructed Refil on their care and given him instructions to release two of them within four weeks of their arrival in Jormund, to give them chance to recuperate from their journey and fly home before the winter storms arrived.

Torri was visibly upset by her sons' departure and Ubba felt desperately sad for her. They both knew that whether they would see them again was in the lap of the gods as their families were facing war. Erik and Refil handled it bravely, both realising that they owed as much to Ubba as they did to their mother. Their survival would rely on the fighting skills Ubba had taught them and the education Ivar had imparted. The responsibility of being a Ragnarsson was a heavy cross for them all to bear.

FOURTEEN

Ubba was enjoying an early morning swimming training session with his men, when Viggo came running in clutching a small piece of paper. He ran to the poolside and leant down as his father finished his final length.

'Father, get out – news from Halfdan – the Mercians are marching north. He has received news from Njal at Repton that King Edward of Wessex has marched troops from Winchester to Wantage to join up with Aethelflaed's Mercian troops. They could reach Lincoln within a week.'

Ubba pulled himself out of the pool and called Frank, 'Time to go, Frank! Wessex and Mercian troops are heading north – we leave today! I knew the unseasonably warm spring weather we have experienced would tempt them to march. It may have been dry down south, but we have had a lot of rain and will cope better than them in the mud. Get a hearty breakfast and we will try to get away before noon. I will go and see Ivar now.'

Ivar was at breakfast and looked surprised when Ubba came striding into the dining room. 'What's up, Ubba? You are moving at speed today.'

'News from Halfdan – Edward has marched from

Winchester with an army to join up at Wantage with the Mercian forces of his sister. Halfdan says they could be at Lincoln within a week. You must prepare to go to Ireland before the army reaches Jorvik.'

Ivar scowled. 'I am not leaving here until I know there is no hope of retaining Jorvik.'

Ubba threw his hands into the air. 'Fine then brother, risk death. But you promised to keep Viggo alive and I will not let you risk *his* life unnecessarily. I may not survive Lincoln and I want my family out of harm's way. Promise me you will ensure they are at Terrington before the Saxons arrive in Jorvik.'

'Of course I will, Ubba. Your wife and children are very dear to me. I don't want you and Frank going alone to Lincoln, but I can see the sense in it. What time do you intend to leave?'

'Soon. I must say goodbye to my family now. Do I have your assurance you will guard Viggo with your life?'

Ivar approached him with arms outstretched and hugged him. 'Ubba, you know I will. I had hoped you would let me take Freya too, but I can understand your reluctance. Be careful, brother. May the gods keep you safe – whichever ones you believe in!'

Ubba pushed himself away from Ivar, fearing he would see his tears... but then he saw Ivar's tears running down his cheeks.

'The gods said we all have work still to do, so we must obey them. Stay alive little brother, and don't piss off the Irish too much!' He fled before anything else could be said between them.

As he walked into his house he could tell that Torri knew. Viggo must have been to warn her. Freya appeared, and had definitely been crying.

'Sweetheart, can you leave us for an hour and then I will speak to you.' He ushered her out and put the inside bolt across.

Torri had not moved. She stood with her back to him looking out of the window, trying desperately to control her breathing.

'Don't crumble on me now, my brave queen. I need all your strength and courage to await my fate, and I do not underestimate the job you are going to have to do to keep the family safe and well. We have discussed our plans; there is no going back.'

Torri turned round. In a tremulous voice she said, 'When Ragnar came to save Bjorn he said all three of you would survive... but he also said you must follow your heart. I just think it is wrong that you may die for your brothers' cause when *you* had no desire to be a king.'

'Torri, the Saxons will not care about that. I am a huge threat to them alive and to be honest, so are you and the children. You know I could not desert my brothers; I feel as deeply as they do about this land. I know it is not ours by right and I have huge respect for those men who will have marched out of their own fields in Wessex and may not even own any land of their own but have walked 400 miles to fight to keep land in Yorkshire under Saxon control.'

'Remember Ubba, Edward is only twenty-six and he does not have the guile or experience of his father.

He cannot afford to defend Jorvik when he is in Winchester. Even if he has done a deal with Guthrun over Daneland, not all the Danes will comply. Who can he trust to hold Lincoln and Jorvik for him? He is surrounded by Alfred's advisors but most of them are priests, not warriors.'

'Are you suggesting that I become his vassal and sell my soul and sword to our enemy? You know I could never do that; Edward would be a fool to trust me. He knows I would betray him in favour of my own interests. Ivar would come back from Ireland to kill me for betraying him, with Sigtryggr by his side. I will die a man of honour and a Dane warrior to the end.'

Torri sobbed, 'Even if Edward offered to spare you and our children? Why can't you do what Guthrun did – become a Christian and rule Northumbria for Edward?'

'Torri, I cannot do it. It is against all my principles and everything my father fought for. If I swore an oath to Edward I would have lost my self-respect and honour, and nor could I take an oath and then betray him. I am sorry but if my children have to die for being Ragnarssons then so be it. Enough talk. I need to make love to you now to remind me why I need to stay alive.' He took her hand and led her to their bedroom.

They made love with passion and fervour as both recognised this could be their last time together. No words were needed; they both wanted possession of each other's body. After their passion subsided Ubba knelt at the side of the bed and touched Torri's face.

'I want you to know that you are the love of my life. You have been my warrior queen, fighting by my side. You have been my devoted wife and lover and are the mother of five incredible children. Your courage and devotion have never been underestimated by me. You are an incredible woman Torri... and if the worst happens, I just want you to know how much I appreciate you.'

She struggled to sit up, but he held her down and kissed the tip of her nose. 'Shush, my love. You don't need to confirm your love for me; you have demonstrated it by your actions throughout your life. I must see our children and Serena before I depart.' He dressed in silence and left the room.

Torri was grateful for Ubba's quick exit. She was able to release her pent-up emotions and sob into her pillow. She knew that she must not break down in front of her children when he departed. She had to maintain the belief that he would be coming back. He was right about their predicament; she would need every ounce of her strength and courage to keep herself and their children alive.

Ubba unlocked the front door. Freya was sitting on the wall outside, swinging her legs and looking very sombre. There was nobody around, so he perched next to her.

She turned to him, 'Daddy, I know how difficult this parting is going to be for both of us, but I want you to know that whatever the outcome I will do my best to honour my family, just as you have done over the years. I will implore the gods to keep you safe. Do not worry about my safety; I may not be considered a threat due to my age and sex, and they may allow me to live. However, rest assured that if they kill you, Mother, Arne and I will avenge your death, just as you did my grandfather's.'

He hugged her to him. 'My precious child, your wisdom is way beyond your years and I can't bear the thought of losing you whilst you are so young. I pray the gods are protecting you, especially if I die in battle. You must guide Arne if your mother and I are dead, as he will be a target too. Viggo will be with Ivar in Ireland and if we are killed and you are captured they will find a way to release you. So never give up hope, my brave daughter; you have family and the gods on your side.'

She looked up at him. 'Will Theo and Astrid be a target too?'

'I don't know, sweetheart. They are both very young and they do not have your mother's genes. I don't think the Saxons kill innocent children as readily as Danes would. Remember, Gytha and Ralf are Saxons too, and they will hopefully be alive and able to protect you. I promise I will try and stay alive to protect you all, but I cannot guarantee it. Now I must go and find Arne.'

'He is helping Viggo prepare a gift for you. He says they will both see you at noon.'

'Then I must go to Serena and the children now. I will see the boys later.'

He went back to the palace and was accosted by several of his troops wishing him well. When he arrived in Serena's apartment Frank was bidding her farewell and she was unable to contain her tears when he came in.

She shouted angrily, 'I have to face the potential loss of my brother, my lover and possibly my children. Don't you dare tell me not to weep, Ubba Ragnarsson. These are not your kingdoms – why can you not just walk away? Why should you die for their cause?'

Frank left the room and Ubba held his arms out to her. 'Come, Serena, you know me better than that. Do you honestly think I could walk away now? I may not be the bravest Dane warrior but Halfdan and Ivar are my brothers – and the land they are occupying may not have been theirs historically, but they both rule it now.'

Serena interrupted, 'But you would risk laying down your life for your brothers' desire for power and land, with no benefit to you or your family?'

'Of course I would. I may not wish to be a king, but this land is worth fighting for and I am an honourable man. I will not desert them now. I am not a coward and they would do exactly the same for me.'

Serena shouted, 'But you are putting yourself on the frontline – asking to be killed!'

Ubba interrupted, 'That is where my skills are best employed. I lead from the front. If I die I will at least die with a sword in my hand and go to Valhalla. Believe me, that is far preferable than being captured and imprisoned. Now let us not part in anger. I understand your reticence, but you must understand my motives too. We have discussed you and the children staying with Torri and there is nobody better on this Earth at negotiating their way out of a crisis than her.'

Serena ran to him and threw herself into his arms. 'Please stay alive, Ubba. All your children need your wise counsel.'

He kissed her and said, 'I leave at 12 p.m. Are you brave enough to see us off? You must not panic the children – you have to believe that I will survive – so no tears.'

'Yes, I will be there.'

Ubba went to the stables to see his other greatest love – Sleipnir. Both Viggo and Arne were there. Arne had Raven tied up in the yard. He was bathing him and washing his mane and tail alongside Josh, who was bathing Frank's horse.

'I am pleased to see you are turning our horses out to perfection.'

Arne replied, 'Of course, Father. You represent Jorvik and even though you may be scouting rather than galloping into battle, the horses require the same level of respect as the brave riders mounted on them.'

'I appreciate that Arne. Now, you know I want you to care for Sleipnir whilst I am in Lincoln. I will need him sharp and fit upon my return. If I don't return then he is yours, son.'

Arne sighed and stopped scraping the water from Raven's shining coat. 'Father, I don't have the experience to ride Sleipnir.'

'Rubbish, Arne. Besides, he will teach you and Ranulf, or Ralf will coach you. You are my son and have the same feel for horses as I do. Use him for breeding, but don't neglect his training.'

Shadow came bouncing into the courtyard, ran up to Ubba and sat directly in front of him, demanding attention. Ubba bent down so he was at eye level with the wolf, fondling his head and ears. 'Now you, Shadow, will carry on protecting my son like you have always done. Keep him safe and away from danger.' Shadow licked Ubba's nose and whined his consent.

He turned to Arne, 'Listen to Shadow. His hearing and smell are finer tuned than any human's – as are Sleipnir's senses. If he is reluctant to go anywhere, listen to him! I know you want to come with me to Lincoln son, but I cannot risk your life. I promise you will have a role in defence at Jorvik, but you must also protect your mother, sister and half-siblings.' He hugged him to him. 'Good luck, my son, and may the gods protect you from harm.'

Arne smiled up at him with tears in his eyes. 'Keeping Freya under control –and her mouth shut – will be harder than fighting in a shield wall. You leave me with an onerous task, Father.'

'I know, son. Now, where is Viggo?'

'Preparing your kit for travelling, in the stables with Sam.'

He went into the large tack room where Viggo was putting two pigeons into a wicker basket attached to the back of his saddle.

Viggo said, 'I know Halfdan has some of our messenger birds but if you are scouting and the castle is under attack and you cannot go back then at least you will have these two with you to send a message back to Jorvik. Promise me you will carry them at all times. The basket has a compartment with food and some water for them, as well as parchment and ink. I know you learnt to read and write later in life, but you did it, so you can use either Latin or Danish to write the note.'

'Thank you son. Now remember, Ireland is a dangerous place. You must not take risks, and always listen to Ivar. The purpose of you going there is to keep at least one Ragnarsson alive. If we are all wiped out by the Saxons do not risk avenging our deaths and coming back here. If I survive and can find a safe house I will send for you. You have the brains and knowledge to go anywhere you want. If you want to keep studying then go east. If you want to explore then join Refil and sail wherever your curiosity takes you. Go to Bjorn in Jormund; if he becomes King of Norway he will need men with your knowledge. Do whatever you want to in your life – not simply what is expected of a Ragnarsson.'

Viggo ran to his father and Ubba hugged him very tightly. 'Father, please stay alive. I am not ready to lose you. You and Ivar have given me the skills to survive but I am unproven in battle.'

Ubba ruffled his auburn curls. 'Rubbish. You will see plenty of action in Ireland and you have Ivar and Sigtryggr to protect you. Ivar is under instructions to send you back to Northumbria if I survive, or to Bjorn in Jormund if he considers Ireland too dangerous.'

'I will make you proud of me one day, Father. I just could have done with your wise counsel and support for a few years longer.'

Ubba turned away to prevent Viggo seeing his tears. He went back out into the yard where the horses were now fully tacked up and ready, and the packhorse loaded with their equipment. Frank had arrived and was checking over the equipment. They were both wearing leather jerkins and breeches so as not to attract attention on their journey to Lincoln. Bows and a quiver of arrows were attached to the front of their saddles, and they carried swords. Armour and shields were concealed on the packhorse.

Ubba unhooked Raven's reins from the post and vaulted into the saddle. 'We must go up to the palace to say our last farewell.'

Viggo and Arne followed them in silence, both struggling to control their emotions. As they approached the palace Ubba was astonished to see Ivar's troops lined up individually on both sides of the steps, forming a guard of honour. His men were lined up on either side of the driveway. A group of family and friends waited on the balcony.

Ubba turned to Frank, 'Christ, I just wanted to disappear unseen with no fuss.' He dismounted and gave Raven to Arne to hold.

Frank smiled. 'Did you honestly think these men would let their greatest commander go into battle without acknowledging him? Ubba, these men would follow you into the gates of hell. Some are angry not to be going with you. They want to be by your side.'

'Shit, I am going to have to make a speech and explain why I chose to go alone.' He ran up the steps and saw the grief he was concealing in the eyes of all of them. Torri had Freya's hand although she looked calmer than anyone else.

'I have already said personal goodbyes to my immediate family, so forgive me if I do not repeat them. I know I carry your good wishes in my heart and I will do my best to see you again soon.'

He walked over to Ralf, Gytha and Thorin. He hugged Ralf to him and Ralf whispered, 'You saved my family and I will fight to the death to keep your family alive.' Ubba muttered an emotional response.

He took Gytha in his arms and kissed her. She whispered, 'Stay alive, my hero. You saved me from certain death twice and my God rewards those who put others before themselves. Rest assured I shall fight to protect your wife and children.'

Ubba moved on to Thorin and he said, 'You know that Odin sent me here, and my first mission is to protect Freya. Have no fear; her future is ordained by the gods and she will live a long and happy life.'

He moved over to where Ivar was and said, 'Ivar, come here. I need to address your men. Some of them are angry that I am not taking them with me.'

They both walked to the top step of the balcony and the crowd fell silent, anticipating a speech. Ubba took a deep breath. 'Warriors of Jorvik, I apologise if I have offended any of you by not taking you with me to Lincoln. It was entirely a military decision made by me alone, without any influence from Ivar or Halfdan. It would have been unthinkable to take you to Lincoln and leave Jorvik unprotected. Halfdan has, over the last two years, raised and trained an army of men including Saxons, Danes, Norsemen and Frisians. I trained you to protect your king and Jorvik. I could not afford to lose any of you protecting Lincoln. I ask you to carry out that work with or without my presence. If I die in Lincoln then so be it, but I will at least know you will keep my family safe and we will meet again in the halls of Valhalla someday. May the gods keep you strong and safe.' A great cheer arose from the men and the gathered crowd.

Ivar patted him on the back. 'Go, brother. And thank you for all your efforts in protecting Jorvik. You may have been a reluctant king Ubba, but no king could ever be as loved as you are as a leader. Remember, everyone here wants you back and will be demanding their gods protect you.'

He turned to look back at his family, waved and blew them a kiss, then bounded down the steps to the cheers of his men and mounted Raven.

Arne said, 'Well done Father; that will have roused them to your cause.'

He ruffled Arne's hair then turned and trotted down the drive and out of the palace gates where he was surprised to find the citizens of Jorvik lining the route and cheering him.

As they left the city gates, Ubba heaved a sigh of relief. 'Frank, did you know some of the men felt aggrieved about not accompanying me?'

'There have been some complaints, but only by those who failed to understand your logic for keeping Jorvik safe. If Lincoln fell and we were all there then

Jorvik would have been open for the taking – and not necessarily by Saxons but by Danes, Irishmen and Scots, too.'

FIFTEEN

They rode until dark then found a spot in a wooded area next to a stream and unwrapped their bed rolls. Ubba had decided to make haste to Roche Abbey and then have the comfort of an indoor bed for one night. They reached Roche Abbey just before dark the next day and Ubba was delighted Father Raymond was in residence.

Father Raymond rushed to greet him. 'Ubba Ragnarsson, welcome. I suspect I know where you are going, but let us not talk of war. I think of you as my "prodigal son" but if you have not read the scriptures then you will not understand that reference.'

Ubba laughed, 'You may be surprised to hear that I have learnt to read and write in Latin and Danish, and have read some of your Christian texts. Unfortunately, I failed miserably mastering Arabic and Greek… but French and Italian I can speak and understand.'

'The greatest warrior Dane in the land has evolved into a scholar too?'

'Not exactly, but Ivar has employed the best tutors to teach my sons about the world beyond these shores and I have seen with my own eyes how much further ahead of us the lands in the East are because of their learning. I saw huge marble buildings in Greece, Rome,

Jerusalem and Paris devoted to housing books, art and sculpture, and did not understand the importance of recording history and culture from previous dynasties. I regret my own actions when raiding monasteries and destroying their beautiful books. I now understand why Alfred kept meticulous journals of what had taken place in Wessex and beyond.'

'Alfred made a pilgrimage to Rome to meet the Pope with his father. He was only a child at the time, but it had a profound effect on him. He may not have been a great warrior himself, but he understood the importance of politics and keeping his throne. This land has always been settled on by tribes from the East who built settlements here and managed to live in harmony with each other, up to a point. However, when the Romans invaded intent on seizing their land for Rome, they realised just how important this green and bountiful land was to them. In the South West pagan tribes held some of the land, resented the Romans and started to fight back, just as we finally woke up to what you were doing here. You are a man steeped in nature – you know how precious this land is.'

'But Father, how come the Roman invasions failed? They had the engineering, science and education to trample the ancient Britons into the ground. Why didn't they succeed?'

'As a priest I have been asked that many times – even by Alfred – and my personal opinion is that the Romans wanted to expand their empire, but the location of this island made it very difficult to control from Rome. It was so far behind Rome in its development, it had a cold climate and was ruled by the weather and most of all, it was an island. That little strip of sea proved a step too far, even though the Romans had their own ships. They took London easily but when they ventured further north, they were horrified at what they found. Thankfully, they still built their palaces with baths and made the roads in stone and left a legacy. They were also having trouble on their own doorstep with Germanic tribes attacking from across Europe. They needed their troops to protect their own land and were losing here as the Ancient Britons banded together and fought back.'

'But why did the Romans want to invade in the first place?'

'The Roman General Julius Caesar was furious that we helped the Gauls to invade their borders. They came to this island looking for riches – land and slaves, but most of all iron, lead, zinc, copper, silver and gold. When they got here they realised that in such an uncivilised environment their chances of mining precious metals was hardly worth the effort.'

'But why did the Romans fail with all their advanced technology, and we Danes actually succeed?'

'You were Norsemen used to coping with extreme weather conditions, and excellent sailors. You came into Northumbria as traders initially, with boats that could navigate the sea and rivers. We were not a violent nation and did not oppose you. You soon realised the value of the land and greed turned you from traders to raiders. You brought your women with you and they fought by your side. The Romans did not bring their women.'

Ubba laughed. 'Did you tell that last point to Alfred, Father?'

'Yes I did, and he agreed with me. Alfred had a keen eye for women and he was extremely jealous of your Danish good looks and prowess with women. Now, if Alfred had possessed a wife like Torri then you would not have needed to raise an axe at all.'

'Father, I think Torri would have resorted to killing Alfred on their wedding night. She only takes real men to her bed.'

Father Raymond laughed. 'Seemingly, only the sons of Ragnar satisfy her very high standards.'

'Exactly, Father. When you have had the best, why compromise? She has received no education at all, but she can beat Alfred and Julius Caesar when it comes to achieving her goals. She is a very wise woman and the love of my life. I made sure she knew how much I appreciated her before I left her.'

'I know that Ubba and I am so glad she forgave you for the one mistake you made. Tell me – which aspects of Christianity appeal to you? Please be open with me; I am not here to judge you or to convert you. You are not the only man to doubt our faith. Even we who have devoted our lives to it are sometimes sceptical.'

'I find the atmosphere in a church comforting. It's a bit like being outside on a beautiful summer's day. You feel warm on the inside as well as on the outside. The calmness and peacefulness envelop you like a bearskin. I like the ritual and music of your services, especially now I understand what your prayers are about. However, I find your attitude to forgiveness difficult to understand. You say your God will forgive every sin, however big or small. Your commandments state, "Thou shalt not kill", and yet you would claim to forgive someone who has. How could your God forgive me when I have killed many Christians? Surely God cannot forgive me? And realistically, neither *should* he. Why do you tolerate this attitude of forgiveness? If you have done something bad you are saying, "Confess your sin… but go ahead and do it again!" because you are not making the person responsible for his own actions.

'For instance, when Arne was a young boy I told him not to ride Sleipnir, and yet he did. He disobeyed me and could have been injured. He said he was sorry but it did not mean I did not punish him. He got a few cracks on his backside with a leather belt for disobeying his father. He had to know that there were consequences for disobeying me. It stopped him repeating this for a while, but soon the temptation became too great. He made the mistake of trying to get on Sleipnir, bareback, when he was running with some mares. One of them was in season and Sleipnir only had sex on his mind. Arne interrupted him as he was lining up to mount the mare. He was lucky the stallion did not trample him to death. Instead, he picked him up by his jacket and flung him over the hedge. Apart from a few nettle stings he was unharmed. He never admitted what he had done, but of course he was seen. If he had admitted to it I would have punished him again, but this time he learnt a valuable lesson – to assess the situation carefully... and never get between a stallion and a mare in season!'

'I hear Arne is the image of you in both looks and personality, and is bound as closely to nature and animals as you are. However, Viggo seems to have a thirst for knowledge, and wisdom far beyond his tender years. He has surprised me with his in-depth knowledge of religion. He understands the difference between the Christian, Moslem, Jewish and Sikh faiths. Ivar has done well to find eminent tutors for his nephews.'

'It was Viggo who taught me Latin and how to write in my own language. He told me about the planets and the Earth's magnetic field. I assumed the Earth was flat before and he laughed and asked me how it could be, as the oceans would run over the edge. Now he has explained about the sun and moon and that the Earth's axis is tilted 45 degrees, which is why in Denmark we have days of no light at all in winter and then in summer, days of no darkness. Viggo needs to visit these countries to truly understand their civilisations, and he has a desire to do so.'

'Come. You must eat with us before compline.'

'Father, could I attend compline?'

'Of course you may – you are a baptised Christian.'

'But I am also a *gothi* and I still hold my Norse faith in my head and my heart. Do you not consider me a heathen?'

'Never. You are a wise and enlightened man capable of great courage and compassion. Any god would want you as a member of his flock. You may be a warrior, but at heart you are a peacemaker.'

After a hearty meal he joined the monks for compline. He encountered a few angry looks at the start of the service. However, when he uttered the responses in Latin, these turned to astonishment. At the end of the service as the other monks filed out, Father Raymond signalled for Ubba to stay. 'Come Ubba and kneel at the altar rail. I wish to give you communion and bless you.'

'Are you sure, Father? You know Edward is campaigning north even as we speak, and I will be defending Lincoln and Jorvik for my brothers?'

'Yes, I am aware of that… but if you survive, I assure you I will do all in my power to protect you and your wife and children from harm.'

'That is very good of you, but I don't rate my chances of survival too highly. But if you can protect my family then I would be grateful.' He knelt before the altar rail and was given the sacrament and blessed.

Ubba returned to his guest room and climbed into his comfy bed. He felt strangely at peace even though he knew he was on the edge of fighting a battle. Perhaps the prayers had calmed his troubled mind.

They left early the next morning, intending to cover the 44 miles to Lincoln in one day. He planned to enter the city in the dark in case advanced Saxon scouts were in the vicinity. The horses were fresh from their break and their fitness was peak. They kept up a steady canter, only stopping for short breaks for food and water. They made good progress and as twilight was falling they entered the city gates. Guards were patrolling the gates but not preventing people entering or exiting. Ubba stopped to inform the guards he had arrived, and was escorted to the stables.

A small unit of scouts was returning to the stables as they were dismounting. He was delighted to see Halfdan with them. He ran up as Halfdan jumped down, and wrapped him in a bear hug.

'Ubba, how glad I am to see you – and so quickly, too. You didn't bring Sleipnir?'

'No, I think I will be of more use to you scouting and Sleipnir is too colourful for that job. Raven is highly trained as a scout and will even lie still when other horses gallop past.'

'Come on, Stefan is due back shortly. We can have some refreshment and then fill you in on the enemy's position. My grooms will see to your horses and cool them off slowly from their exertions.'

He turned to Frank, 'So you managed to persuade him to let you come with him then.'

Frank replied, 'It took some doing, but he saw sense in the end... although some of his personal guards were mightily offended he would not take them.'

Ubba interjected, 'I think I calmed them down before I left. I think they thought it was on Ivar's orders that I go alone, but once I assured them that neither you nor Ivar had influenced me and that it was purely to protect Jorvik, I think they realised it wasn't a rejection.'

Halfdan tapped him on the shoulder. 'Come, I have

someone I wish you to meet. Frank, put your feet up and down some ale. We won't be long.'

Halfdan led him upstairs into a room serving as a nursery, where a servant was spoon feeding a toddler who had dark curly hair. Halfdan picked him up and brought him over to Ubba. 'Brother, meet my son Siegfrid. He is eighteen months old.'

Ubba's mouth gaped open and he stepped back in shock. 'Your son? But you said you would never have children.'

Halfdan laughed, 'I know! And in some part it is your fault.'

Ubba interrupted, 'Surely to God he's not one of my offspring?'

'No, I can assure you he's definitely mine! Stefan and I discussed what Ivar had said about seeing sense and doing the duty of all kings by breeding heirs. Having your sons and stepsons here to train for war and sailing made me realise that I was missing out. Stefan was keener than I was to have a son to rear... then one day I captured a beautiful woman who had been consigned to a nunnery. Because I saved her from her fate, she agreed to bear me a child in return.'

Suddenly, the door opened and a woman in her twenties appeared and came over to them. She smiled at Siegfrid, who was wriggling and shouting, 'Mama!' and trying to reach her. She took him from Halfdan's arms and cuddled him.

She turned to Ubba, smiled and spoke in a lilting tone, 'So you must be the great commander Ubba Ragnarsson, the big brother of Halfdan. May I say his description of you did you no justice at all.'

Ubba was transfixed and totally speechless. This woman was like the many paintings of angels he had seen in the churches. She was tall and slim with red hair falling to her waist and the most translucent alabaster skin and emerald eyes. "Beautiful" did not do justice to her; "stunning and exquisite" was the closest he could come to portraying the extent of her beauty.

Halfdan said, 'My brother seems to be transfixed by you Aoife, and incapable of speech – as many men are when they meet you for the first time. Perhaps you should sit down Ubba, before you faint with shock. I know exactly what you are thinking; let me explain. Aoife was born in Ireland to an Irish mother and Frankian father. She speaks with a French-Irish accent. She was educated in Paris and speaks five languages. She has a very hot temper and she does as she pleases. She had no desire to become a nun but had refused five proposals of marriage, declaring her wish to remain single. Her father lost patience with her and consigned her to a nunnery over here lest her independent spirit filtered down to her younger sisters.'

Ubba managed to find his tongue at last and muttered, 'But she is too good to be wasted on the Church. Most men would pay a king's ransom to have her as a wife. In fact, if all women in Ireland look like her then forget fighting a war – I am off to Ireland now. Maybe that's why Ivar is so keen to go?'

Halfdan roared with laughter. 'Shame on you, Ubba! Have you forgotten your precious wife Torri and your mistress Serena? I doubt Torri would grant you permission to have Aoife as well.'

Aoife giggled, 'You see, this is my problem. I don't want to be a man's property; I want to be free to have sex with whomever I fancy, to swap and change as often as I want, just like a man. Certainly, Ubba has the looks, but I wouldn't fancy sharing him with two other women. I understand Torri is a very beautiful and clever woman and has bred five Ragnarsson grandchildren. She must be very special if she lets you keep your mistress and breed from her too.'

Halfdan laughed, 'We all tease Ubba about his fertility, but he stamps his stock well and has produced a veritable army of little warriors in his time... but is that not what good breeding is all about? Come, brother; we shall have a short war council to update you, and then dine.' He picked his son up and kissed his cheek, saying goodnight and placing him in Aoife's arms.

Ubba left the room in an absolute daze, still trying to reconcile Halfdan's good fortune. He was struggling to understand, but he knew Ivar would be incandescent with rage that his homosexual brother had produced a son to this angel of delight.

At dinner, he enjoyed watching Frank's face when he realised who Aoife was from the conversation at the table. He leaned over and whispered to him, 'Stop staring at her. I know she is irresistible, but I do not know yet how the relationship lies between her and Halfdan.'

Frank laughed, 'Life is so unfair! How can the gods bestow a woman like her on a man who has no desire for women?'

'Halfdan was a full-blooded male as a teenager; he even shared a girlfriend with our brother Sigurd. He is quite capable of pleasuring a woman, especially if she is willing to produce an heir for him. However, jealousy stirs deep in Halfdan's soul, so don't risk provoking him. He is very particular about his possessions, friends and horses. He once killed a man who rode his horse and lamed it. (Mind you, I think I would do the same if someone injured Sleipnir, so I can't condemn him for that.) As a child he protected his toys with vigour. Even Ivar wouldn't' risk stealing Halfdan's toys. He once pinched Halfdan's fishing rod. Halfdan very nearly drowned him in the river. Without my speedy intervention he would have drowned him for sure.'

SIXTEEN

After the meal Halfdan asked Ubba if he wanted to retire, or have a drink with him. Tired as he was, he wanted to know more about Aoife, so he opted to remain with Halfdan.

Halfdan opened with, 'I can see you have a million questions you want answered, so let's get it over with.'

'Do you love Aoife?'

'Define the meaning of "love". I love you as my brother Ubba, but I don't want to hump you. Aoife is every man's dream of the perfect woman and despite preferring men to women, even I cannot resist her charms... but I pursued her only to provide my heir. Our relationship is purely business and if I lose Lincoln I will take her and my son to Jorvik, but she wants to go to Ireland. She has silver from me to finance her next move.

'Leaving her son with you to raise, I hope?'

'Of course! She may be his mother, but through circumstance rather than love. She will have no qualms about walking away from him; she only thinks of herself.'

'Was she a virgin when you took her?'

'Yes she was... in body, but not in soul.'

'Hell's bells, Halfdan. What do you mean?'

'She is a temptress, *volva,* seer or maybe even a witch – she is not an innocent girl. She has been on this Earth before and knows exactly how to lure a man into giving her exactly what she wants.'

'But what about Stefan?'

'Thankfully, Stefan was with me every time I humped her. He is my life partner Ubba, the man I love. I could not in all sincerity take a woman to my bed and exclude him. Imagine how jealous and insecure he would have felt. He never had intercourse with her as he wanted the child to be mine. Before you ask, yes we did indulge in sex as a threesome because Aoife knows how to pleasure a man. She does it instinctively and unashamedly, which is how I know she is a dangerous woman.'

'Do you think she was sent by the gods?'

'Devil, more like. I don't know, but I want rid of her. I know she is the mother of my child and I am aware she could well have used me to spawn the Devil's offspring, but he is an innocent child and I intend to raise him my way. It will become obvious if he has the Devil in him – and if so, I will deal with it as I see fit.'

Ubba hugged him. 'Listen to me, Halfdan. I suspect Freya may have been sent from the gods, for good not evil. I am also certain that Thorin has been sent to replicate Thor. Both of them will know whether she is a force of evil, and how to deal with her. Ivar will have no hesitation in disposing of her if she is.'

'Ubba, I have no qualms about killing her but if she is the Devil's spawn then she may be difficult to kill. You need to be very careful; she has already beguiled you with her looks. Do not fall under the spell of those beautiful green eyes. They will not lead you to heaven, only hell. I have not touched her body since she birthed Siegfrid, but she is looking for her next conquest. Do not let it be you!'

He had broken sleep that night, violently waking several times. To his chagrin it was Aoife's face he saw each time he woke. This had to stop! He knew he must concentrate on the job at hand and banish all thoughts of Aoife. He rose just before dawn as sleep deserted him, and made his way to the stables to prepare their horses for a scouting sortie. Halfdan had built a block of 20 new stables with a wide central aisle for cleaning and feeding, but each horse had an external stable door so they could look out and observe their surroundings.

The grooms were just arriving for work and the stable manager asked him, 'Lord Ubba, may I be of assistance?'

'I woke early and thought I would come here and groom Raven and Noir. I am quite happy to muck them out and feed them too. I would also like to see Pegasus, who was sired by my own stallion Sleipnir.'

'Certainly lord, I will show you to Pegasus and then you can groom your horses… but please leave the feeding and mucking out to my grooms.' He showed him to Pegasus's stable. 'My lord Halfdan is well pleased with his progress under saddle, and he is maturing into a fine beast.'

Ubba cast his eye over Pegasus and was delighted with his conformation, colour and temperament. His mother had been a chestnut mare and he had been born chestnut. He was now four years old and had turned dark dappled grey, but still had some chestnut hair in his mane and tail. He went to Raven's box, put a halter on him and tied him up whilst he was eating his breakfast, and started to groom him.

After a while, he sensed someone observing him from the doorway and as he turned around he saw Aoife. Raven turned towards her and instantly became uneasy.

'What brings you here, my lady? You must have plenty to do in the nursery.'

'I am free to come and go anywhere I please, and I know you are attracted to me.'

'You are very much mistaken Aoife. I have a wife and a mistress at home. Why would I be foolish enough to dabble with you? I do not wish to be a notch on your bedpost.'

She laughed and moved closer to him. 'But you would be missing out on a unique and pleasurable experience.'

Ubba turned around and flung his hand up. 'Do not approach me lady; even my horse senses your malevolence.' Raven was very upset and anxious and pulling back on his rope as she drew closer, desperate to run away.

Aoife stopped and gave him a dark look at odds with her beautiful eyes and face. 'You will not be able to resist me Ubba, however hard you try.' She turned on her heel and stormed out.

Ubba stroked Raven's long neck. 'It's all right, lad.

She has gone now – you are not in any danger. God, I would rather stand in a shield wall facing the Saxons than be alone with her.'

The stable manager came rushing in. 'My lord, what has upset the horses? They are all terrified.'

'They have sensed an evil spirit in their midst, as most animals can.'

He interrupted, 'But the only strangers in the stables are you and the lady Aoife.'

'Well I am still here and they have all calmed down, so I will leave you to draw your own conclusion.'

Raven rubbed his nose on Ubba's shoulder, looking for reassurance. He murmured platitudes and rubbed his nose.

At the previous night's war council, it had been agreed that Ubba and Frank would head up a scouting party going north down the riverbank to ensure there were no troop movements. His grooming of both horses complete, he went to breakfast hoping he would not encounter Aoife. He ate a hearty breakfast and as Frank went to prepare to leave, he told him the horses were ready but he had an errand to run before he departed on patrol.

Within the palace grounds was a small Christian chapel where Ubba headed to ask his adopted God for help in keeping Aoife at bay. He was delighted to find it empty and went to the altar rail to offer his prayer. The only sign he received was a shaft of sunlight coming through the altar window that bathed him in light and lifted his mood. He reflected on how absurd it was that he, a proven Norse warrior, should be concerned about the attentions of a woman when he had slain countless men in his time. However, he knew he was dealing with no ordinary woman; she was capable of using the black arts against him and his family.

Their troop of six set out on their mission carrying no banners, with a packhorse carrying extra weapons should they need them. He kept his promise to Viggo to take the pigeons. They kept close to the river, only leaving it when they reached a forest about five miles south. They turned into the forest and looked for signs of habitation. They each took their shields and bows and arrows from the packhorse. They split up on the perimeter, each scout quartering a section and heading for the middle. Ubba banished all thoughts of Aoife and summoned his vast knowledge of nature and his exceptional hearing and eyesight. The forest was not too dense and there were several tracks leading in all directions. He checked for new tracks – an indication that someone had passed by recently. One track had signs that some horses had been through in recent days. The track was narrow due to the prolific oak and sycamore trees that were nearing full bloom.

He halted as a flock of birds flew up into the sky about 100 yards further down the track. He knew they could have been disturbed by someone from their troop, but it could also be the enemy. Ubba bade Raven keep quiet and he carried on parallel to the path at a very cautious walk. Ubba picked up the sound of a voice on the wind, and he placed the bow over his shoulder and the quiver on his back. He looped his shield onto the hook of his saddle. After 25 yards the track widened and he spotted a large oak tree. He led Raven a few yards in the opposite direction and left a rein dangling over the branch of a Rowan tree, not tied. He covered the pigeon crate and used a hand command to tell Raven to stay still and quiet... then he walked back to the oak tree and shimmied up its branches.

After a 20-foot climb he could see a clearing ahead, which was perfect for a campsite. There were no horses or men there now, but he was certain there had been. He surveyed the area and spotted two of his troop heading towards the campsite. He gave a low whistle, called Raven to the oak tree, shimmied down and jumped onto his saddle to trot off and meet the others. The campsite looked to have been occupied within the last two days. It was difficult to be sure by whom, but he was fairly certain it was Saxon scouts.

When all six were reunited he asked one of them about the two longboats Halfdan had equipped for patrolling the river. This was to ensure the Saxons were not using it to ferry troops or equipment to Lincoln on the river as well as by road. They were also going to use the two longboats as a means of escape should they need it. They inspected the campsite for any clues as to who the last occupants had been, but they were obviously proven scouts and had left none. There had definitely been five horses line-tied there overnight. They returned to Lincoln to report back.

Later that day, Ubba persuaded Halfdan and Stefan to show him round the perimeter of the city to assess the weak points and work out how to defend it. They knew that the Saxons were unlikely to only attack the main city walls; they would attempt to breach the defences at more than one gate. The most likely attacks would be staged on the South Main Gate and the East Gate. The East Gate was closest to the river and was where Halfdan had built his troop training ground. The land sloped down to the river from the East Gate. Ubba remembered that Halfdan had used underground channels to irrigate the water fences on his schooling track. He suggested they made this route a target by funneling the enemy troops into attacking uphill but flooding the field closest to the river, which would seriously impede their progress. They could also block access to other tracks and fields so the intruders would be forced to use this route.

Halfdan had sent scouting parties south to track the Saxons' progress and send messengers back with reports. Latest reports indicated the main body of troops was at least two days' ride away.

That evening after dinner, Ubba joined Stefan and Halfdan for a drink. Aoife had given him filthy looks at dinner but had not tried to engage him in conversation. He watched her charm those around her who seemed completely unaware of her true character.

'Halfdan, why were Aoife's parents sending her to become a nun when they must have known she was no Christian? She would have caused havoc confined to a nunnery.'

'Oh, I am sure they knew, but her father was so incensed at her refusal to marry that he wanted her out of the country and away from her sisters. I am certain she will have cursed him. That's why I avoid direct confrontation and want rid of her quickly.'

'Wise move. Ireland is the best place for her. Do you think Siegfrid will have her powers?'

'I hope not, but it is too soon to tell. His nursemaid Eliza is Stefan's sister. She is watching over Siegfrid and reporting Aoife's every move. Aoife doesn't know of her connection to Stefan.'

'If Ivar agrees to take Aoife over to Ireland then Siegfrid must remain with my household under Torri and Serena's care, along with her nursemaid. I worry about what Aoife may get up to, but I will warn Torri to watch her carefully.'

'You may not have to worry – if Ivar leaves before the battle for Jorvik then she won't need to go with your family.'

They both headed to bed in good time as the prospect of the Saxon Army arriving the next day focused their minds on getting a good night's sleep. However, after several hours of restless sleep, Ubba woke from a terrifying nightmare where he was being seduced by Aoife. Sweat was pouring from his naked body and he was breathing heavily. As he turned onto his back, he sat in a wet patch of ejaculate.

He jumped out of bed and stood still, frantically looking around him, his eyes and ears tuned to any sound. Fortunately, one of the candles he had lit on the dresser was still burning. He froze in horror; he could smell Aoife even though there was nobody in the room. This was something he had noticed when he first met her. It wasn't just lavender or rose used as a scent. The closest description he could find was that it was similar to woodland flowers that were dying. It was an earthy pungent smell, never usually associated with women. He pulled on his breeches, grabbed his sword and checked the corridor then headed towards the nursery.

He carefully opened the nursery door and saw by the moonlight streaming through the window that nobody was there. He moved to the first door leading off it and gently opened it. This was Siegfrid's room, with a single bed occupied by his nursemaid. He quickly departed and opened the second door, which proved to be Aoife's bedroom. She was lying peacefully, facing the door. He held his breath and watched to check whether her breathing pattern was normal and that she was not pretending to be asleep. He left silently and returned to his room.

He poured himself some ale and flung himself into a chair, trying to recall his dream. *How had Aoife implanted herself into his mind when he had no feelings for her other than fear?* The only logical explanation was that she must be a witch and had taken over his consciousness. He hadn't had wet dreams since he was a teenager lusting after Torri when she and Bjorn first became lovers. He had dreamt of Torri when she had been in Jormund, but it had never resulted in him going that far. He realised that if Aoife was a seer then she would have the capability to control his mind, but he had to prove to her that she had no control of him. He gave himself a severe rousting, telling himself to concentrate on the ensuing battle and staying alive. The fact she may have already cursed him for not submitting to her charms also negated his father's words indicating he would survive... but only if he let it concern him or make him doubt his superiority as a warrior.

In the morning, he went down to breakfast and noticed that Aoife kept smiling in his direction. She even asked him if he'd had a good night's sleep, which disturbed him somewhat. He asked to see Halfdan alone after breakfast. They walked down to the stables together.

Halfdan took a measured look at Ubba. 'Are you worrying about the battle? You don't look your usual serene self.'

'No, I had a very explicit sexual dream last night about Aoife. I was certain she was in the room with me; I could even smell her.'

'Come on Ubba; she is playing with your mind. You are trying so hard to evade her sexual demands that you are imagining sexual fantasies with her. What man wouldn't, with the body and looks she possesses? I have her under constant surveillance.'

'Does she know this?'

'She would be a fool if she hadn't worked it out.'

'What if she can become invisible then go wherever she wants?'

'Don't you think that's a bit unrealistic?'

'No, I don't! If she is a witch then she will have all the dark arts to call upon. She has a smell similar to dead woodland – and not only could I smell her, I felt her body and I could taste her.'

'Well, she certainly performs oral sex like a woman possessed, but is it lust or the Devil? She is not interested in sex from a reproduction point of view; she is far too wrapped up in sating her own desire.'

'I don't want anything to do with her and I certainly don't want her reproducing with me.' Suddenly, he realised what he had said. 'I'm sorry, I shouldn't have said that. You must be concerned about Siegfrid; forgive me.'

Halfdan patted him on the shoulder. 'It is my greatest fear.'

SEVENTEEN

Over the next two days, frantic preparation was made for the forthcoming battle. Frank and Ubba had found suitable large trees either side of the entrance to the training field that led up to the East Gate. They had concealed quivers of arrows up in the branches. They had also tested the distance using straw dummies on horseback to assess the best height to release their bows. Their purpose was to pick off key figures as they went through the gate and create a diversion so that Halfdan's escape party could make a dash to the longboats moored out of sight on the river. However, this would make it impossible for them to go through the gate as they would be joining the enemy in the flooded field and would be key targets. Ubba contemplated going into the river and swimming up to the longboats but knew they would be easy targets if spotted. He declared that they would be better heading west and using the fields and woods as an escape route away from the Saxons, then heading north back the way they had come.

The Saxon Army had arrived the previous day and was camped about two miles from the city. The Mercian Army was a day's march behind and had the largest contingent of walking troops, as well as the baggage train. Ubba reckoned they would set up camp and take at least a day's rest before going into battle. That evening, they got as close as they dared to the Saxon camp and overheard some of the troops talking around their campfires. When they had gleaned enough information they returned to their horses and rode back to the castle silently.

That night immediately after dinner, when the others prepared to have a drink before the action the next day, Ubba sought the quiet refuge of the church. His preparation for battle had never been boozy by choice. His survival depended on his innate senses being highly tuned to provoke instant reaction to danger. His sword skills were woven into his psyche without any planning. His eyes locked on to his opponent and he assessed any surrounding danger then went straight for the kill. His reaction speed was his greatest asset. While most men prevaricated, he made the first and final blow. One swipe of his sword followed if necessary, by a seax to the body. His ability to silently track his enemy and kill from behind by garroting was his specialty. Although he preferred fighting on horseback on the frontline, his job tomorrow as a scout and bowman killing from behind, was a major role.

He drew his Ulfberht sword and tested its sharpness. This sword had been gifted to him by his Uncle Rollo, and it had seen a lot of action. When combined with his speed of attack its light thin blade suited his style of fighting – as it had his father. Ragnar had been built like him – fast and athletic as opposed to the larger muscular frames of Rollo, Halfdan and Bjorn.

He moved to the altar rail, laid his sword on it, knelt and made his peace with God. He asked for courage and fortitude to face the ensuing battle. He knew that whether he lived or died depended on his own skill; he could hardly expect help from God in slaughtering his followers.

He returned to the castle and avoided the celebrations. He was content to retire to his bed. Normally, he would have had his wife or mistress at his side but Torri had shown her devotion to him on their last night together in Jorvik and instilled in him that for all their sakes, he had to survive.

Ubba was delighted to find he slept right through to the morning, which would give his body the best chance of fighting well. He dressed and washed quickly, then headed to the stables. Scouting pairs had been out overnight watching the Saxons, and they were preparing to march in sections. He headed to breakfast. Halfdan was just leaving.

'Ubba, keep safe and don't take any chances. I don't want you dying for my cause.'

'Never mind me; you ensure you get away safely. I will make it back to Jorvik with Frank at my own pace. I will cause enough confusion for you to make it to the longboats.'

The brothers embraced but did not speak. He forced himself to eat something as who knew when he would get a chance to eat again. Frank appeared and had some food before they set off to the stables with some spare bread and meat for their consumption later. They had their packhorse loaded with their gear, so they would be able to survive living rough.

They had scouted out a house and barn about ten minutes' walk from the gate into the flooded field. The horses could remain stabled, hayed and safe while they were up the trees, and they could then make their way back and head north. They returned to their selected trees and climbed up to await the enemy. Reportedly, they were making steady progress and would be arriving to assault the East Gate within minutes. They could see a troop heading for the North Gate.

As the first mounted troops approached the field gate, Ubba prepared his bow and arrows for action. He would communicate with Frank via bird calls, a language they had developed to avoid detection. His plan was to wait until the first troop had ridden into the field and realised they were in a bog. They would only attack troopers that managed to ride up the hill towards the East Gate. Then they would pick off riders with their arrows, one at a time. They were both skilled distance bowmen. They did not want to give their position away, just create a diversion so that Halfdan and his party could break out when necessary.

He held his breath as the first riders approached the field. One had gone ahead to open the gate and as it wasn't too deep, he did not notice the state of the field. The first group of ten cantered through. Most of them went down like dominoes as their horses hit the water that came to above their knees, and lost balance as they had no grip. Their momentum flung them to the ground. As a horse lover, Ubba wished them no harm; he hoped they would have a chance to get away if they could find their feet in the quagmire that ensued. There were shouts from the riders and screams from the horses as they thrashed, trying to get up. Several riders were injured in the first attack and some were trapped under their horses, underwater as well. More kept piling in through the gate and made the situation worse. Finally, one rider stopped in time and shouted to the men behind him to stop, and he closed the gate. Loose horses were heading up the field to escape the mud bath below. Six men on horseback who had got through relatively unscathed attempted to follow them. One man diverted his horse up the steep terrain of the field before the gate to find a safer path through, but the field had a solid hawthorn hedge and the rise of the ground was at a steep angle. Some joined him with axes to try and chop a way through or at least make it jumpable for the horses. However, Ubba knew that only the bravest riders would be able to meet the challenges of jumping on a hillside onto sloping ground.

The only sensible route was to risk walking up the hill, but this would expose them to Halfdan's bowmen on the ramparts with no natural cover. Ubba waited patiently until a small band of men, some on horseback, made it up the hill, careful to stay an arrow's length away. Unfortunately, they did not know that Halfdan had a team of ten Welsh bowmen who could assess their target and send arrows raining down on the enemy from a greater distance.

Ubba spotted someone waving a raven banner on

the ramparts and knew this was the signal for Halfdan to break out. He alerted Frank. By now, more men had walked up the hill and as the first tranche of arrows was released from the ramparts, they started to shoot the troops from behind. The first wave was so successful, the enemy went down like flies. He watched as the East Gate was opened and a small mounted troop headed out to take on the enemy. Behind them, Halfdan and his retinue rode out at speed to ride east for the river.

He scanned the area around him to assess his best route out and back to the stable for the horses, and called to Frank to descend. Thankfully, they were far enough away from the action to be unseen climbing down; they walked slowly through the copse and did not encounter anybody. They made it unseen to the stables, tacked up and Frank climbed up onto the roof of the stables to check the area was clear before they came out. They selected a quiet track through a nearby copse and kept walking, listening carefully for any sound of an approaching rider. They headed north, parallel to the road, heading for Roche Abbey.

Ubba had decided to call on Father Raymond for some advice on how to deal with Aoife from a Christian viewpoint. It would be risky if the Saxons had sent out patrols looking for Halfdan, but he was sure that the enemy would know they had left by longboat, and he hoped nobody had seen their departure due to the chaos at the gate into the field. They stopped to water the horses and give them a break for a while. Ubba found a grassy sloping bank to lay on and stretch his back, which had been affected by their long wait in the tree. The weather was turning and the sun disappeared, followed by thick dark clouds. They decided to carry on through the woodland but close enough to the main track to spot oncoming riders – and if they were lucky, find a building to shelter in if the storm developed.

About ten miles further on they found an empty wooden shack in the forest that was used to store chopped wood. They sheltered inside to avoid the heavy shower and Ubba wrote a note to release with Viggo's pigeon. He informed them they were alive and well and making their way home. Halfdan and the longboats would take two days to reach Jorvik, so the pigeon should arrive before them. He also put a warning on the note saying, "Beware of Aoife; keep Freya away from her." He wrote in Latin, knowing that Ivar would translate for Torri. He placed it in the metal tube attached to the ring on the pigeon's foot and then, as the rain was slowing down, he threw the bird up into the air and watched it head north.

As the rain eased off they continued their journey and found shelter in the forest to sleep out in the open overnight. They were about 15 miles from the abbey and as soon as it was light the next day they continued their journey, reaching the abbey gates by mid-morning. They found a good vantage point overlooking the abbey land and could see no riders in the area, so they rode up to the abbey gates. Ubba rang the bell, which was answered quickly by a monk.

Father Raymond came to greet them in the stables. 'Ubba, how pleased I am to see you alive and well...

but do you think it wise to call here? Scouting troops have been sent out by Edward from Lincoln, looking for Danes. We had six men here yesterday asking if we had seen anyone.'

'Father, I need your wise counsel about a religious matter and we will be on our way home soon after some food.'

'Come, then; I will provide a hearty breakfast for you in my office.' He turned to one of the monks and instructed him to send two men out on horseback to watch the road in case any troops were in the area. Frank was shown to the dining room and Ubba followed Father Raymond to his office. A breakfast was delivered and Ubba tucked in with relish.

'So, how can I help you, Ubba?'

'I need your help and advice as to how to deal with removing a malevolent evil force that is intent on harm. I am referring to what your religion would describe as a witch or a devil. Killing them in their original form does not guarantee success as they can recreate themselves into another entity as well as cursing you for life.'

'Good grief, Ubba! I hardly expected a question like this from you. Our religion does have ways of dealing with these evil spirits, but it requires huge courage to do it as the work of the Devil has powers that we do not. We use our devotion to God to exorcise them from humans they have invaded or kill them. However, they manifest themselves in forms that they know will frighten. Sometimes, they may be devils or dragons – and even chopping their heads off does not work because they can recreate themselves in another form. They often appear as beautiful women in order to tempt men, but can turn into old hags in the blink of an eye. Your gods will know how to deal with them, so perhaps you should consult them?'

'Father, I may be a *gothi,* but I know nothing about dealing with these entities. I do recall Norse myths indicating that to prevent cursing you must kill them without spilling blood – such as by drowning or strangling – but I have no idea whether this is true.'

'From a Christian viewpoint they hate our churches, particularly the cross, and if they touch one their skin burns. We also have many myths associated with them, such as that they must be killed by driving a wooden stake into their heart so they cannot manifest into another form after death. They also have superhuman strength and use your fear to weaken you.'

'Have you ever been involved in an exorcism?'

'Yes, but it was very early in my career, so I was on the sidelines. It was very frightening; I had to stop myself from running. The evil spirit had entered a young teenage girl. She was spouting profanities and her whole face had metamorphosed into an old hag. The priest was thrown across the room when he first put a cross close to her face, but he persisted, ordering the Devil to leave the girl's body. We held her down and he put the cross on her heart. I actually saw the evil spirit leave her body.'

'Father, that sounds horrendous and very dangerous.'

'Well, it's not for the fainthearted, I can assure you.

You have to believe you can beat the evil spirit. Some priests have lost their lives trying to do it.'

There was a knock at the door and Father Raymond responded. One of the monks advised him that a troop of six Saxons was heading towards the abbey.

'Martin, go and find Frank and tell him to hide in the loft above the stable.' He turned to Ubba. 'Your horses will not give you away. Had you been on your grey stallion I would be more concerned.'

He pulled a monk's habit off a hook on the wall and threw it to Ubba. 'Wear this. You can join in with the monks at *terce*. The bell has just sounded. Take your breeches off and I will pin the cowl to your hair to stop it falling back and revealing your braids. I suggest you leave your sword belt on in case it is needed. If you are discovered you could take me as a hostage so they won't kill you.'

'Father, I don't want to put you at risk.'

'Don't you worry about me Ubba; you just concentrate on following the service and repeating the responses when required. Now you can read Latin, you should have no difficulty joining in.'

Ubba was positioned in the chapel next to Father Flynn, who was an Irish priest and had led an exciting life prior to being ordained in Ireland. They were in the middle of the fifth row back and conveniently, there was no sunlight shining through the stained-glass windows on that side of the abbey. Within a few minutes of the service starting, Father Raymond appeared in the church door with two Saxon troopers. They walked down the aisle and the troopers looked down the rows of kneeling monks. They did not observe any unusual behaviour and soon left the chapel. Ubba's heart returned to its regular beat. After the service he made sure he gave thanks for the sanctuary offered by the monks. He also thanked God for sparing him.

After Father Raymond had allowed the troops to search the premises and they had gone, he returned to the chapel and signalled for Ubba to join him. As they walked back to his office through the cloisters he smiled and commented, 'You looked every inch the devout priest, Ubba. I know, deep in your heart, you are really a man of peace, not war.'

'Father, I think every man needs to have someone to love and inspire them. Many use religion as their guide, some worship kings, others look to role models within their own families. We all express our beliefs and emotions in different ways but certainly, following a religious faith can have its advantages and disadvantages.'

'I managed to obtain some information from the Saxons, which I think you need to know. They were bragging that Edward has done a deal with the Welsh and there are 200 Welsh bowmen marching north to join them in the battle for Jorvik.'

'Well it doesn't surprise me; they have been sadly lacking in these skills and it can make such a difference to the outcome. I had better get back there to protect Jorvik – having secured Lincoln, they will be marching there soon.'

EIGHTEEN

Ivar was enjoying his breakfast when his peace was shattered by one of his personal guards. Nobody else was at breakfast, as it was Sunday and still early.

'What is it, Erik? Shut the door and tell me.'

'Lord, news has just reached me from a merchant ship that two longboats have been spotted heading north below Loidis.'

'Well, surely that's good news and means Halfdan has abandoned Lincoln and is on his way here.'

'Yes it is, my lord… but the merchant who saw them confirms there was no sign of Ubba on either boat.'

'Erik, there may be many reasons for that. I am not going to leap to the conclusion that Ubba is dead. He may have been sleeping and not visible. He may not have even been on the boat. They should be here soon, so I will not mention this conversation to anyone, and I expect you to do the same.'

'Yes, lord. I just felt I had to pass on the information.'

As he left the room Ivar could not help shivering. He had always underestimated his deep love for his eldest brother. Despite their many scraps and very different characters, Ivar adored Ubba. He treated him as a human being – never as a cripple – and had always been his hero. Despite finding Ubba's popularity galling at times, he knew that Ubba deserved his band of dedicated followers far more than he ever would.

It was mid-afternoon when the two longboats docked, and Ivar was one of the first at the quayside anticipating their arrival. He frantically scanned the boats for Ubba and as Torri and Freya arrived he noticed them doing the same. There was no sign of Ubba or Frank and the shock was clear on Torri's face.

He moved over to her and took her hand. 'Do not panic, Torri; he may not have been able to travel on the boats. Calm down and take a deep breath until we hear news.'

Halfdan was the first off the boat and came rushing over to them. 'Ubba is fine. He is making his own way back on horseback. He created a distraction so that we could get out and onto the longboats. He wasn't fighting on the frontline; he and Frank were shooting arrows from trees at the bottom of the hill. I am certain they both made it safely back to where their horses were stabled.'

Torri scowled at him. 'How can you be so sure? They could have encountered enemy troops anywhere.'

Ivar squeezed Torri's hand. 'Ubba will be fine; there is nobody better equipped or more experienced than him at living rough and making his way home safely.'

Suddenly, Ivar spotted Aoife coming off the boat followed by a young girl carrying a wriggling toddler. Even from a distance, Aoife's beauty was apparent and her red hair caught in the sun and looked like burnished gold. Halfdan saw that Ivar was mesmerised by her beauty.

'Ivar, may I introduce you to Aoife, the mother of my son Siegfrid?'

There were gasps from Torri and several others in the immediate vicinity.

Ivar stuttered, 'Delighted to meet you, madam. Forgive my surprise; I did not know Halfdan had a son. Obviously he was keeping it from his brothers in order to ensure we had no idea of the beautiful mother who bore him. I can understand that he would consider Ubba a possible threat, with his reputation with women.' Torri pinched him hard on his arm.

Aoife bowed and spoke in her beautiful lilting voice, 'King Ivar, how delighted I am to meet you. Halfdan's description of you certainly did not do you justice.'

'Thank you, my dear. With your name, accent and stunning red hair you can only be Irish.'

'Why yes, how clever of you. My mother married a Frankian when he came over to Dublin, but I was born in France.'

They had reached the entrance to the palace and Ivar watched Aoife observe her surroundings. She was clearly impressed by what she saw, and he noticed her looking at him. He realised that he had better wait for Halfdan to reveal whether he had been tempted back by this beautiful woman, whom any man would find irresistible. However, when he saw Stefan giving Siegfrid a piggyback ride on his shoulders as they went up the steps to the palace and heard the little lad's peals of joy, he doubted it. Halfdan had been careful to refer to her only as the mother of his son.

Egil, the master of his household collared him in the salon as refreshments were served. 'My lord, I was not expecting your brother to arrive with family. Will he require rooms adjacent to the young lady and her son?'

Ivar scowled. 'Funnily enough, neither was I aware of this change in Halfdan's circumstances, but as soon as I have extracted the details Egil, I shall convey his wishes to you.'

Freya approached him. 'You can't tear your eyes away from her, can you? Take if from one who knows dearest Uncle, Aoife is not real – just a figment of your imagination. Get caught in the depths of those beautiful green eyes and you will be consumed by fire.' She immediately left his side and he was left speechless, pondering the meaning of her words.

As the guests were ushered out by Egil to their rooms, Ivar approached Halfdan and asked him to remain behind. He agreed and poured himself a jug of ale. 'Well, Ivar, I can see you are transfixed by Aoife and want to know how your homosexual brother managed to sire a son with such a beautiful woman. It's your fault, really; you remarked to Ubba that I should stop all this nonsense and get on with siring a dynasty, which should be the first priority of a king. I saved her from being a bride of Christ, shut away in a convent forever, and in return she agreed to produce me a child. I thought I was being very clever – but believe me, Aoife is no ordinary woman.'

'What the hell do you mean? She is stunningly beautiful and if you took her virginity and bred a son then you have gone up in my estimation, brother. What joy you must have had in releasing her sexuality.'

'Ivar, she may have been a virgin in body, but not in mind. She knew every trick in a harlot's book to please a man. She is a witch, volva, enchantress, sorceress... a she-devil that can turn into an old crone when she does not get her way. She has the spirit of a devil, not an angel, and will tear a man apart to achieve her own ambition.'

'But what about Siegfrid? Is he not human? He has the physical qualities of both of you.'

'I wish I knew the answer to that Ivar. I need your help to get rid of her. I gave her a substantial amount of silver because she wants to return to Ireland. She has no qualms about leaving Siegfrid. She has no maternal feelings for him whatsoever, thankfully. You are closer to the gods than any of us and there must be a way of dealing with her – preferably killing her. However, she will curse anyone who gets in her way, and if she is the spawn of the Devil then she must be disposed of very carefully.'

'You want me to take her to Ireland and kill her?'

'Basically, yes. Alive she will always be a threat to both me and Siegfrid. She was a model of decorum when I wooed her and indulged her sexually. I realised too late that she was a witch. I even contemplated killing her while she was pregnant, but I couldn't do it.'

'Does Ubba know about this?'

'Of course he does; she tried to tempt him and he was bowled over. When I told him the truth he kept away from her, but she didn't like it and it didn't stop her trying to trap him.'

'Freya warned me to keep away from her. She said she was a figment of my imagination and if I was to fall for her I would be consumed by fire.'

'Will you try and find out how to deal with her? I am sure you will have more contacts than me.'

'I will try, but we need to keep this very quiet. I must go and seek out Torri; she looked devastated when Ubba wasn't with you. She has to put on a brave face for her children's sake, but I know she has been very tense since he left.'

He discovered Torri was with Serena in her apartments, so he sent a messenger to ask her to come to his study before she went home, for a private chat. Whilst he waited, he racked his brains to think of someone who would know how to deal with Aoife.

Torri arrived within the hour and she looked like she had been crying. He guided her to the sofa and put his arm around her. 'Come on now, Torri. Stop worrying about Ubba; he will be back soon. It is Ubba that you are concerned about – nothing else, I hope?'

'I suppose I am feeling vulnerable because I desperately want him back safe and sound. Perhaps age is catching up with me. I cannot imagine a future without him in my life. These last two years have been wonderful, being able to have him by my side and see him develop as a father. His children need more time with him and I just don't want to lose him.'

'Facing the fact that he may not survive has shown

me just how important Ubba is in my life. He has always been my hero, no matter how many times we have disagreed. He sees the long-term repercussions of acting in haste. He is a deep thinker and sees the pitfalls of acting violently in anger. I wish he would consider coming to Ireland with me, but I respect his wish to settle permanently here, although I worry for your safety.'

Torri smiled, 'So Ivar the Boneless does have a heart buried deep inside and can love someone other than himself. Be careful – your crown will slip, and you don't want your enemies to realise your vulnerability.'

Ivar laughed, 'I won't have a crown to worry about soon as I won't be King of Jorvik for much longer. I shall have lost my kingdom, and I don't reconcile to failure easily.'

'I am sure Ireland will have some compensation for you Ivar. Now, tell me what you think of Aoife?'

'According to Halfdan, she is an evil witch and needs disposing of quickly and carefully.'

'What? Instinctively, I knew she was not an angel, but where does that leave Halfdan's son?'

'I don't know, but do you have any idea who we can turn to for help?'

'Possibly Thorin or Freya – they have a link to the gods.'

Early the next morning Ivar was fast asleep when someone came rushing into his room and he grabbed the seax under his pillow, fearing an attack. To his surprise it was Viggo. Thankfully, the seax had remained in his hand. 'Bloody hell, Viggo. You nearly got killed! Have you heard of knocking on a door before entry?'

Viggo grinned. 'I did, but you didn't hear me.' He was waving a small piece of parchment. 'My father has sent a message via pigeon and I came straight here to tell you first. He and Frank are returning soon... but my main concern was his final point, which is, "Beware of Aoife – and keep Freya away from her!" Why, Ivar? She is beautiful! How did Halfdan manage to find a girl like her?'

Ivar arranged his pillows so he could sit up comfortably in bed. He motioned to Viggo to come and sit on the bedside chair beside him. 'I can see you are smitten, but have you thought she may be too beautiful to be real?'

Viggo's eyes widened in surprise. 'Whatever do you mean?'

'Sometimes, if a woman is so perfect on the outside and has men falling at her feet to please her, she may not be who she says she is.'

'Then who the devil is she?'

'She's exactly what you said.'

'What?'

'A devil!'

'She can't be!'

'She is what is known as a *volva,* basically a witch, and is here to cause trouble. Unfortunately, Halfdan was reeled in by her and got her pregnant before he realised exactly how evil she was.'

'But if she is not human, how did she have a baby?'

'She can metamorphose into whatever form she wants. She is female but could be very old or revert to being a young fertile woman at any time.'

'But what about Siegfrid? Is he human?'

'I am not sure yet, but I intend to find out. Think carefully, do you know anyone who you suspect may not be all they seem? They don't have to be an evil person; they may well be here to guide and protect someone.'

Viggo scratched his head. 'Thorin. He has always been wiser and stronger than any human and Freya swears he was sent by Odin to protect her.'

'Perhaps your beloved sister is not quite what she seems either.'

'But she is real. I was there when my mother went into labour, and she has the combined features of both of my parents. Nobody could have swapped her at birth. Although, there are times when I wish somebody *would* remove her.'

'Maybe they don't need to make a swap. Perhaps the god who sent her communicates with her spiritually. You have to admit she is far wiser than the average child.'

'But what about Aoife? Is she a threat to us?'

'Her deal with Halfdan was that for a price, she would bear him a child, and then she wants to go back to her birthplace in Ireland. Halfdan wants rid of her and decided to bring her here so she can join us when we go over to Ireland.'

'You mean she will be sailing with us?'

'Possibly, but she may not make it across the Irish

Sea.'

'Ivar, you are not seriously thinking of killing her. If she is protected by the Devil then she won't be an easy target. She could end up killing or cursing you, and you don't want that.'

'I am well aware of that, but intend to have as much information as possible before I risk doing anything.'

NINETEEN

A small scouting party looking for Saxon troop movements was riding in woodland parallel to the main route into Jorvik from the South. Ubba heard hoofbeats well in advance and he and Frank concealed themselves in dense tree cover. As the riders approached, Ubba recognised the leader as one of his Jorvik scouts. He rode out onto the track and shouted a greeting; the four scouts hollered in delight and cantered over to meet them. They set off at a speedy canter for the five remaining miles to Jorvik.

As they arrived in the palace courtyard, Arne was the first to greet him. He ran over to take charge of Raven as Ubba vaulted off him. 'Father, thank the gods you have returned safely. How long before the Saxons attack?'

'The main army is about ten miles away yet. We probably have 48 hours before they attack.'

He was interrupted by Freya running down the steps screaming, 'Daddy, you are back!' She launched herself into his arms. He picked her up, hugged her tightly and whispered, 'You are the sunshine in my life sweetheart, and nothing would ever prevent me from being by your side.'

Ivar, Viggo and Torri arrived and came down to the

courtyard to greet him.

Ivar said, 'About time too, brother. I was beginning to think you had fled south to leave us to fight alone.'

Viggo responded angrily, 'My father would never do that.'

Ivar said, 'I was only jesting, Viggo. I would not want him to think that I cared about him. Now come and tell me everything, brother; we shall have a war council.' But Ubba's attention was fixed on Torri. The look of love and devotion between them was there for all to see.

He walked over to her, wrapped his arms around her and gave her a tender kiss. 'Not now, Ivar. All I want is a tub full of hot water, food, and time alone with my wife. The war council can wait till morning; the Saxons will not attack tonight.' He grabbed Torri's hand and pulled her back up the palace steps, to the delight of the assembled crowd who clapped and cheered him.

Fuming that he had been disobeyed, Ivar snapped at the men, 'What are you men gawping at? Get back to your duties. We are at war!' He saw Freya looking bereft and held out his hand to her. 'Come, Freya. Your parents want some privacy.'

'But I want to talk to my father urgently, about Aoife.'

'Later, child. They need some space.'

Freya was furious, 'They are hardly young lovers in the first flush of youth. I hope sex in reality is as good as they seem to experience it.'

Ivar chuckled, 'Oh, believe me – it is when it's with

the person you have loved since you were a boy. The strength of their relationship is a joy to behold. Not many marriages can survive the traumas they have both experienced. I truly hope you can find a man who loves you like your mother loves Ubba.'

Freya laughed, 'What would I want with a husband? Nobody would be worthy of my beauty or intellect, and I won't be subservient to a male under any circumstances.'

'Spoken like a true warrior and future queen. However, when love strikes your heart you may find you change your mind.'

As Ubba and Torri ran into the palace, Egil was in the entrance hall trying to hide the smile on his face. 'My lord, may I say how delighted I am to have you back safe and well. Is there anything I can do for you?'

Ubba smiled. 'Yes. Have a tub of hot water filled in my palace bedroom, send some hot food and at least two bottles of Ivar's best French wine. Order a guard on the corridor until midnight to prevent anybody entering the room, and that includes ALL my family.'

Erik raised an eyebrow. 'Immediately, my lord. A wise choice indeed.'

Ubba grabbed Torri's hand and set off running up the stairs. They giggled like children as they ran. Torri said, 'Looks like you have not received any injuries.'

'No. In fact, apart from using a bow and arrows I did not engage the enemy at close quarters at all. I expect I won't be so lucky next time.'

There was a knock at the door and two female

servants brought in the barrel and jugs of hot water. They were followed by one of the kitchen staff carrying a tray of food and wine. Torri dismissed them and started filling the tub with hot water, then went to the bathroom down the corridor for some cold water. As she came back Ubba had stripped off his dirty wet garments and as she poured half of the last jug he crept behind her, kissed the nape of her neck and whispered, 'I want your body now, darling.'

She jumped away. 'You are not touching me until you are fully bathed and your hair is washed.' She began unplaiting his braids as he got into the barrel. A wooden seat was fixed halfway down so he could sit on it in the water, fully immersed.

He said, 'Look, you only have to touch my hair and my body craves you.' As she had finished soaping his locks she picked up the jug containing the cold water and threw it over his head, laughing, 'Maybe that will cool your ardour, my lord.'

Ubba spluttered as the cold water hit him. 'Wicked woman, that was unfair, and you will suffer for it now.' He leapt out of the barrel, grabbed her tightly and undid the buttons on her dress. She tried to wriggle away but he held her fast. 'You, my lady, will obey your husband. I am going to have you right here and now, on the bedroom floor.'

'Ubba, stop acting like a teenager. Gone are my days of rolling about on hard floors. I have had six children and am ten years older than you. My back is in no condition to stand such an onslaught. It's the feather bed or nothing, my love.'

Having removed most of her clothes he laughed and scooped her into his arms as if she was a child. 'Very well, my love; your wish is granted provided you do exactly as I say. I beg your pardon now for seeking my pleasure before yours, but I will make it up to you afterwards.'

She kissed his cheek and whispered, 'I love the bones of you, Ubba Ragnarsson. You are my rock, my friend, my husband, the father of my children and definitely my hero. Life without you would be unbearable. My body is yours for the taking.'

An hour of frenzied passion followed, boosted by the knowledge that this could be their last time together. Neither of them referred to it but both knew their time was running out. Even if he survived the first attack and managed to escape with Halfdan, Ubba could not risk compromising his family's safety by joining them in hiding.

They ate some of the food and drank Ivar's wine, and he raised his glass to her and said, 'You, my darling, will leave tomorrow for Terrington, and Ivar will depart for Ireland.'

'Why so soon? You know Ivar won't leave until he knows Jorvik is lost.'

'It will be. There is no way we can defend against the Saxons and the Mercians. They have done a deal with the Welsh and there are 200 trained bowmen on horseback approaching Jorvik.'

'Then you must flee now, Ubba.'

He shook his head. 'Not an option for a warrior, my dear.'

'But Ubba, saving yourself is more important!'

'To you and my precious family it is, but I am the leader of my troops and I owe it to them to stand and fight by their side. I don't wish to be captured either, so I will fight on the frontline as I have always done, and die an honourable man.'

'But Ubba, this is not your kingdom.'

'Perhaps not, but it is still worth fighting for, and I think Halfdan will feel the same. What is more important to me is that you, Arne, Freya, Serena, Astrid and Theo survive. Sending Viggo with Ivar is a calculated risk but may pay off. Your task will be far harder than mine, but our children are the future and must survive. You promised me you would do this Torri... and there is nobody more capable of protecting them than you.'

'Very well, my love. I will do my utmost to keep them safe, but this is war and the Saxons know that unless they eradicate all Ragnarssons, they will keep coming back.'

'The Saxons do not wage war on children. Perhaps the one ace in our pack is Freya. They won't kill a girl provided she appears to be humble and no threat. We know that she has the gods on her side and provided she keeps her own counsel, she could survive and become the matriarch of the next generation.'

'Now tell me about Aoife, whom the gods did not send. She is the Devil incarnate – Thorin and Freya new instantly, as did I. Did she have you in her sights as her next victim?'

Ubba blushed. 'She did, and I admit I fell for her

startling looks, just as any man would… but thankfully, Halfdan warned me in time. She tried her best to get into my bed, but I would not take the bait and she did not take the rejection well. She wants to travel with Ivar and Viggo to Ireland, but Ivar is already aware of her power and is investigating how to deal with her.'

'He must realise that she is dangerous and that killing her will be no easy task.'

'Oh yes, he knows, and he wants to do it properly to ensure she never returns.'

Ubba woke early, refreshed and ready to go. He kissed Torri, told her he was going to find Ivar, and suggested she return to their house and prepare for departure.

The palace was just waking up and he made his way to Ivar's room and knocked on the door. True to form there was no reply, so he opened the door quietly and went over to his bed. Ivar sensed movement and sat bolt upright with his seax in his hand. 'Hell fire, Ubba. What is it about your family? I nearly killed Viggo yesterday for doing exactly the same thing.'

Ubba laughed, 'If you weren't such a cruel bastard with so many enemies you would sleep like a baby – it serves you right. I did knock and am surprised to find you alone in your bed.'

'Unlike you, who will have been humping your wife all night.'

'Of course I have. If I am to die then I am to die happy. Now get up, brother; you leave for Ireland today.'

'I am not leaving Jorvik until I am certain I can't

hold it. I am the King, after all.'

'Well, as commander of your army I am telling you to leave now. There is no way we can hold it. The Saxon and Mercian army outnumbers us five to one and young Edward has done a deal with the Welsh and hired 200 trained bowmen who are here on horseback, right now.'

'The clever bastard! But Wessex has never done a deal with Wales before. Why now?'

'Remember, he learnt at the knee of his clever father. Alfred was no great warrior but he was a brilliant strategist. He wants to make sure he wins. We have possibly 12 men including you and me that can shoot an arrow without seeing the target, and reload instantly. If lured out of the castle to defend the walls by Saxon cavalry, we will die in a hail of arrows without even seeing the damned Welsh bowmen.'

'But the Saxons will die too, Ubba!'

'Not if they are all wearing chainmail, and I can assure you that they were when I saw them in Lincoln five days ago.'

'But we will be defending from the ramparts on the walls.'

'It won't stop the Welsh archers firing flaming arrows over into the city and causing countless fires on the straw roofs of the wooden huts below. I am ordering you to leave now with my precious son Viggo. Take that witch Aoife with you and drown her in the Irish Sea on the voyage. I am despatching the rest of my family, Serena and her children, and Halfdan's son, to Terrington with Ralf and Gytha. There is no guarantee of safety but the sooner they get there, the better.'

'But what are you and Halfdan going to do?'

'I don't know what Halfdan will do but I am staying right here and commanding my men. Death in battle will suit me; I have no intention of being captured. There may be an opportunity to surrender the city when we are sorely beaten, but I will fight to the death.'

'Ubba, you can't do that!'

You won't know anything about it; you will be on the boat from Chester to Ireland before they even attack here.'

'You must flee north with Halfdan by longboat, as we agreed.'

'If the opportunity arises Ivar, I will attempt it, but I will not become a prisoner. I want to go to Valhalla to drink ale with my father, play war games all day long and hump valkyries all night long.'

'Rubbish, Ubba. You need to be guiding your children and raising the next generation of warriors to reach your very high standards.'

'Ivar, I will brook no argument over this. You will leave Jorvik this morning with your personal guard, even if I have to knock you unconscious, bind and gag you to get you onto the cart.'

'You wouldn't dare!'

'I am away to see Halfdan now. I am sure he will back me up on this and if necessary, knock you senseless; he has a better right punch than me. Now get ready! Egil informs me your personal trunks are already packed. By now they will be on the cart. You leave within the hour.'

Ivar scowled at him. 'Are you sure you two are not intent on taking my crown and kingdom?'

He shouted in rage, 'For the love of God, Ivar! Do you seriously think I would do that to you, my own brother? I am giving you a chance to live and am prepared to sacrifice my own life to do it. You are too used to looking at other people's motives, terrified of somebody pulling a fast one on you.' He walked out and slammed the door before Ivar had chance to reply.

Ivar sighed in shame. He knew Ubba would never do that to him, but he wasn't sure that Halfdan's motives were as pure.

Ubba strode into the dining room where Halfdan and Stefan were at the breakfast table along with Aoife. 'Make haste, Aoife; you will be departing with Ivar to Ireland in an hour.'

'Now?'

'Yes, madam. I want Ivar to leave now and my own family is going into hiding. Your son will be under the care of my wife, and his nursemaid will accompany him.'

The lure of freedom stopped her objecting. She finished her breakfast and rushed back to her room.

Halfdan said, 'Has Ivar agreed to go willingly?'

'Not exactly. I may need you to render him unconscious and chain him to the wagon. You have a stronger right punch than I do. I will not let him linger a moment longer as he will be putting Viggo's life at risk if he dallies. I learnt from Father Raymond that as well as Wessex and Mercian troops Edward has hired 200 Welsh bowmen on horseback that are heading this way to join up with them.'

'Shit! That makes the task even more untenable.'

'Precisely, but I have had time to think on it and I intend to stay and lead my men from the front. I would rather die in battle than be captured. I don't think we have a hope in hell of holding them. You must make up your own mind as to what you want to do. You have your longboats; I will not think ill of you if you choose to sail further north now.'

'And leave you to face the Saxons on your own when you risked your life to help me try and keep Lincoln? Not an option, brother. I will fight at your side and if an opportunity arises to escape, we will do it together. Like you, I have no desire to be captured. My 12-strong bodyguard will fight alongside you too.'

Ubba patted Halfdan on the shoulder. 'Thanks for the support Halfdan, but seriously, think about it. We don't want the Saxons to kill two Ragnarssons in the same battle.'

'Possibly not, but you should be the one who survives. You and Torri have bred a dynasty and need to guide your sons to continue to conquer this land.'

Ubba jumped up. 'I am away to see my family depart, and you must take your leave of Siegfrid. Whatever happens, Torri will do her best to keep him alive. I shall suggest that if they are captured, she tries to pass him off as Serena's baby.'

Ubba ran through the palace and all the way back to his house. He heard shouting and opened the door to find Freya and Torri at loggerheads, with Freya screaming that she wasn't going to leave.

'Enough, Freya. I want a word with you outside. Now!'

Torri gave him a knowing look and threw her hands in the air. They went outside and sat together on the garden wall. Freya averted her eyes and awaited his anger.

'There is no way you can stay here, child, and you will not cause your mother any more stress at this difficult time. We are all trying to keep you alive, and throwing tantrums is not acceptable. You will obey our orders Freya, and you will leave and do your best to support your family.'

'I want to stay and fight with you, Father.'

'What good would that do except hasten your death and force me to watch my precious daughter die in front of me? I am ashamed of you; I thought you had more intelligence than that. Can you not understand that you are the ace in the pack? The Saxons will not kill a young girl unless you give them reason to. If you are captured then you must act like a sweet innocent girl as you may be the only Ragnarsson survivor. You may be the only one left to continue the Ragnarsson dynasty, although on marriage you will lose your name.'

'But Father, I can summon the gods to protect you.'

'Sweetheart, how many times have I heard that said by hardened warriors before the battle commences? It is a complete and utter myth – the gods do not intervene in battles. They watch the battle for their own amusement and probably bet on the outcome. We all want to believe there is somebody watching over us but in reality we are the pawns of our own destiny. You need to convince them that you are no threat to them. Keep quiet and observe what goes on around you. The longer you survive, the greater chance you have of freedom. They will marry you off to one of their sons as your bloodline will be highly prized. Bide your time; with marriage will come more freedom, possibly a palace of your own, and maybe somewhere like Jorvik to rule with your husband. There's no reason why Saxons and Danes should not live happily together. Look at Ralf and Gytha; they have a wonderful happy marriage.'

'Father, I don't want to be subservient to any man. I want to do the choosing of my husband myself.'

'Freya, be realistic. If you were a prisoner then marriage would give you some freedom. Your mother and I would have wanted to approve your husband and certainly, we would have been looking for a husband who has wealth and land. We would not let you marry someone below your station.'

'Gytha let Skye go to Ireland with Sigtryggr unmarried.'

'Skye is not the daughter of a Ragnarsson. I do not wish to spend what little time we have together arguing. You will go with your mother and do as you are told.'

Freya sighed, knowing her cause was lost. 'Very well, Father – but please come back safely to us. We need you.'

He threw his arms around her and kissed her. 'I will do my level best to survive but I can't promise I will succeed.'

TWENTY

The majority of their personal possessions had already been transported to Terrington, so they were departing on horseback. Grooms were already leading their horses to the palace courtyard. There was a carriage for the younger children, which Serena and Eliza would be occupying.

Ubba walked back to the palace and had a quiet word with Arne as he mounted his horse, to reassure him. He then said his goodbyes to Serena, Astrid and Theo. Serena kept her emotions under control. Halfdan and Stefan cuddled Siegfrid before handing him over to Eliza. Aoife kissed Siegfrid but showed little emotion at leaving him. Halfdan kissed Torri and thanked her for taking Siegfrid.

Ubba spoke briefly to Ralf, who intended to return to Jorvik to fight. Ubba kissed Gytha and patted Ranulf and Thorin on the back and wished them well. Ivar and Viggo appeared to say their goodbyes. He was devastated at the pain on Torri's face when she turned away after hugging Viggo.

Finally, they were all mounted. Ralf and Ranulf led from the front and Arne and Thorin were the rear guard. The rest followed in the middle, surrounding the carriage. Ivar had given Magpie his favourite horse to Thorin for safekeeping.

Ubba leant against a marble pillar and closed his eyes. He could not bear to see his beloved family departing for the last time. His final view of Torri and Freya had been as they had turned around and blown kisses to him. He felt like his heart had been run through by a sword.

Grooms were bringing up horses and a wagon for the second departure of Ivar's troop. Viggo approached and saw the emotion on his father's face. He flung his arms around him and they clung to one another in total silence. Eventually, Ubba pulled away and said shakily, 'Stay alive, son. Use your intelligence and instinct and the sword skill I have drilled into you, to its best advantage. Keep close to Ivar; he has a natural instinct for sensing danger.'

'I will do my best Father, and will pray to Odin to protect you.'

Ivar appeared in the courtyard. Ubba was shocked as he had been adamant he wasn't leaving. He had expected he would have to carry out his threats to force him to go. Ivar approached hesitantly.

'Have you changed your mind and decided to leave peacefully then brother? May I ask who or what changed your mind?'

'Your viper of a wife tore strips off me with her wicked tongue as if I was still a ten-year-old boy when I admitted I thought you and Halfdan were trying to usurp me. She proclaimed I was not fit to lick your boots, and she was right. I apologise profusely for saying that; it was unforgivable of me to ever doubt your honesty and integrity.'

'Hell fire, Ivar! I shall die happy knowing that you did love, respect and appreciate me. Now go, and I charge you with the care of my precious son – so don't let me down.' They embraced in silence.

Halfdan helped Aoife into the cart. Viggo had mounted up after checking that Ivar's gyrfalcons and favourite raptors were safely aboard, along with the messenger pigeons. Sulamain had chosen to accompany Ivar to Ireland before returning to his homeland. Ivar had four of his personal guards as an escort. They needed to be as small a group as possible to find passage on a ship over to Ireland.

As the small group passed out of the palace gates Halfdan and Stefan approached. 'That must have been gut wrenching for you Ubba, but now we need to get round a table and plan our defence of Jorvik – and an exit strategy for us if possible.'

After Ivar's troop had left, Ubba collared Halfdan. 'We need to talk brother before we have the war council. Bring Stefan with you if you wish, but our original plans will have to be amended.'

Halfdan replied, 'Fine, happy to talk to you now. Stefan will be included in the war council later.'

For certain privacy, Ubba headed to his house. As he opened the door the utter silence hit him hard and a shiver ran down his spine. He had just parted from his family, probably for the last time – if he didn't survive, he knew he would never see them again. He poured himself and Halfdan some strong ale and checked the house was totally empty.

Halfdan looked at Ubba and smiled. 'Well, brother, you had better have something remarkable planned or we will be dead in the next 24 hours.'

'We are not going to win with only 150 men against the combined Saxon and Mercian forces (possibly even 400) plus 200 Welsh bowmen. We cannot rely on those Saxons who are already here in Jorvik fighting for us, so we could be trying to fight to protect the walls and gates and being turned on by Saxons who are already here, too. Ivar and I discussed this a while ago. The only sensible answer is doing something no Ragnarsson has ever done before, and surrendering.'

Halfdan looked at him as if he had gone mad. 'Condemning us to certain death, or even worse – becoming prisoners.'

'Look, Halfdan, I have thought of a possible way of escape. We still have our two longboats as well as your two, which we intended to use for our escape north. Edward will not want to burn the city as he knows he hasn't the time, money or men to rebuild it. He only wants it as a northern stronghold.'

Halfdan interrupted, 'You aren't, by any chance, thinking he will let you keep Jorvik and become his vassal? Jesus, brother. He wants us dead! He knows he can never trust a Norseman to keep his word, no matter how much money he offers.'

'I wasn't suggesting me or you, but he may be prepared to let us leave if we hand over the city without a fight.'

'Ubba, he hasn't marched 450 miles to claim Jorvik

and not kill us and all our men. He will not agree to let us leave peacefully. He may say he will but once he has thrown us in a dungeon, death will be the only release after hellish torture. I would rather die in battle, and so would you.'

He enlightened Halfdan and recounted the plan he and Ivar had discussed the night before. Halfdan listened intently and did not interrupt. Finally, he beamed and said, 'Do you know, Ubba? It is so outrageous that it may just work. If it doesn't, we will die fighting anyway.'

'Ivar spent a lot of time talking about battle strategy with Sigtryggr when he came over. He will be approaching twenty years old now, but he berated our family for losing so many good leaders fighting for land. His opinion was that our wars could have been won more quickly and easily with less bloodshed had we used our brains and brave warriors, and occasionally negotiated better. He related one particular trick he used in Ireland that may help negate the impact of 200 Welsh bowmen and hurry them back over the border to Wales.'

There was a knock at the door. Ralf had returned. 'Everybody is settling in at Terrington and we saw no scouting parties up on the moors.'

Ubba replied, 'How was their mood?'

'Surprisingly buoyant – Torri has changed into her battle gear and reclaimed her position as leader. They don't call her the ice queen for nothing; she is calmer than any man about to face war.'

Halfdan laughed, 'Women have to battle at

every stage of their lives, so they are better equipped than men at viewing the problem and seeing the consequences of their actions. We just fling ourselves into battle despite the odds being stacked against us, with no idea what to do next if we actually succeed. Women are born protectors and will fight like lionesses to protect their cubs. Arne, Freya and Siegfrid are in the best possible hands.'

Ralf said, 'I am away to get some food and will see you in the morning.'

Ubba smiled and turned to his brother. 'Now you understand what our father saw in Torri at a very early age. She was only seventeen when he first met her, and totally uneducated. She watched her husband being blood eagled by him, never flinching but awaiting her death with courage and resilience.'

Halfdan laughed, 'Well, he always had an eye for beautiful blonde women. Why kill her when he could hump her instead?'

Ubba replied, 'She was eight months pregnant with Guthrun at the time.'

'But well worth waiting until after the birth to take her. You had to wait a lot longer – until she finally realised that taming Bjorn would never happen. She married the wrong Ragnarsson first, but what a dynasty she has produced. I missed out; I never had the pleasure of her body in my bed.'

'Obviously, Halfdan, because no man would prefer another man after lying just one night with her. Don't assume that Ivar ever laid a finger on her. He worships her but never attempted to seduce her. He nearly killed me when I asserted dominance over her, and would have destroyed any man who tried to take her from me.'

They returned to the palace, summoned their section leaders and informed them of their new plans. Scouts had been reporting back from the Saxon and Mercian camps. The consensus was that the battle would commence in two days' time. A watch had been kept on all roads north, as well as the river, and there was no sign of enemy troops coming from further north. After a three-hour session they opened up the hall to everybody to enjoy their main meal together. Ubba made sure he avoided over-drinking, as he had a job to do under cover of darkness at midnight.

Egil approached him. 'Lord, are you using your palace bedroom tonight?'

'Yes, I think so. It is a little too quiet at home now the family has gone.'

'Is there anything I can get you?'

'Yes, a black hooded cloak.'

'You will find one in your room.'

Despite his midnight jaunt Ubba woke early, ready and eager to get up and check progress on the defences he had initiated. He went down to breakfast to find Halfdan and Stefan. They were all conscious that they needed to eat well now because they might have little chance to eat after the battle, depending on the circumstances. Halfdan was in a good mood too. Strangely, they both oozed positivity when imminent danger approached.

Frank came to see what Ubba was planning for that day. He reeled off his intentions, which were met with silence from Frank. Then he took a deep breath and said, 'Ubba, I don't think it is a good idea for you or Halfdan to leave the city walls. The enemy will be scouting specifically to target you and I don't want either of you captured or killed. I will check and update you on progress... and as far as going to the longboat hideout, I will have your captain brought here if necessary.'

Ubba looked slightly taken aback.

Stefan commented, 'Frank has a point. Taking any unnecessary risks at this point would be foolish. You have good men capable of doing the jobs you want done. Let them get on with it; you two go and practice your combat skills on horseback in the arena. You could play *hnefatafl* afterwards to amuse yourselves. There are still plenty of women about Ubba if you are feeling frisky.'

He roared with laughter. 'Stefan, I am grateful for your concern, but I don't wish to bed another woman. I want my last night with Torri to remain uppermost in my thoughts and unsullied. But you are right; I would not let Ivar leave Jorvik if he was still here, for exactly those reasons. Provided I can have some feedback on progress, I will obey and enjoy thrashing my little brother off his horse instead.'

Halfdan exclaimed, 'In your dreams, Ubba! I have been working hard on my fighting skills; you will not find me the easy target you once encountered.'

Frank jumped up, 'Well that's settled. I will get on

my way and send someone to instruct your captain if you tell me your wishes… or I will send him here.'

'Go and check on last night's task first, then I will tell you about my instructions for the longboats. You are right – we don't want to give away our hiding place.'

After an interesting and successful schooling session with Ubba on Sleipnir and Halfdan on his half-Percheron warhorse fighting in hand-to-hand combat, Ubba showed him one of his prize possessions, which was kept firmly under lock and key in the tack room.

When he and Bjorn had raided in Italy, they had captured some Italian armour including two chainmail suits of the finest quality and lightest metal ever seen. Halfdan had not been on that expedition and Bjorn had insisted Ubba take them both, as he raided by sea rather than land.

'I have never worn it in battle before because it can restrict movement, but I think with 200 bowmen outside the walls perhaps now is the time to wear it. If the larger one fits you then you should wear it too.' Ubba helped him put it on over his leather tunic. It fitted him well.

'Come on then, brother – let's go back to the arena and try it out with real swords. I told Josh to keep our horses saddled as we were going back out.'

Halfdan helped Ubba put on his chainmail and they went back out to remount. They started with a tentative hand-to-hand fight and found that the mail was cut cleverly around the armpit, shoulders and neck; due to its lightness it allowed a full swing of the arm from shoulder to wrist unimpeded.

After a few minutes they both grew confident that the mail deflected swipes across the chest and arms.

Ubba said, 'Right, now let's pull back and charge against each other.'

'Hell fire, Ubba. I don't want to damage you or Sleipnir. Blizzard weighs a lot more and is taller than him.'

'Oh, don't you worry about that! He will have the advantages of speed and technique.'

They took up their positions and Ubba shouted, 'Go!' They thundered towards each other at a strong canter, both wielding swords and shields. They reached each other in seconds but Sleipnir immediately reared up and struck out with his front legs. This forced Blizzard to turn away from him and gave Ubba a chance to strike at Halfdan. Had he done so with his usual speed he would have sliced into Halfdan's shoulder. Halfdan turned Blizzard to line up against Sleipnir, but he half-passed away from him.

Halfdan roared, 'Christ, Ubba. Just stand still!'

Ubba laughed, 'What, so you can kill me? No way, brother! You will have to find another way to get close to me.'

After three attempts and a rise in temper, Halfdan succeeded in making a strike at Ubba, but Sleipnir pirouetted away and the blow was taken by Ubba's shield. Halfdan screamed, 'Are you commanding that horse or is he in charge?'

'A bit of both. He has become so proficient at close

combat fighting that he now anticipates the next move and instinctively avoids danger.'

Halfdan pulled away and attempted to approach from behind, but Sleipnir let fly with both back legs, narrowly missing Blizzard's chest.

Ubba said, 'Be careful; he is always watching my back and will kick any approaching horse away if I am engaged in fighting another opponent.'

After a few more skirmishes, of which most were thwarted by Sleipnir, they returned to the stables. Halfdan said, 'Thank the gods I am not fighting you again; it is so frustrating! You are there one minute and then gone in seconds. You must have spent some time teaching him all that.'

'Not as much as you may think. He learns so quickly and is so responsive to my reactions... and he carries his hocks underneath him, so he can move fast in any direction.'

TWENTY-ONE

It was 6 a.m. the next morning when a scout came to inform Ubba that Saxon troops were heading into position around the city. Ubba was confident that his men knew their positions, and during the night men and horses had moved out and headed north, upriver to the longboat hideout.

He dressed and headed up to the ramparts. It appeared that the Mercian troops in their blue uniforms were heading up to the north side of the city and the Saxons were assembling at the bottom of the hill at the south side. There was no sign of any archers yet. He went to find Halfdan and Stefan.

'It's decision time! Do we put our plan into action and escape, or do we fight to the end?'

Halfdan replied, 'We can cause much more havoc by escaping, so let's get on with it.'

Ralf and Ranulf appeared in full battledress. Ralf's hair had been shaved at the sides and plaited. They greeted one another and Ralf said, 'Let's get on with it then, and see if I can create enough of a diversion to cover your escape.'

Ubba went to the fire pit, collected some soot from around the edges and rubbed it over his scalp and blond plaits. He hugged Ralf. 'Best of luck, my good friend. May the gods watch over you and keep you safe.'

Ralf muttered, 'And you too, my dearest friend. I will do everything in my power to protect your family. Now go, Ubba! I will despatch a messenger with a white flag. He will ask for surrender terms and time to allow the Saxon citizens who want to depart Jorvik time to leave, if Edward won't accept surrender.'

Ubba took a deep breath and one last look round the hall, then steeled himself to go. He, Stefan and Halfdan ran down to the Roman sewers and made their way underground to the East Gate side of Jorvik. Thankfully, the sewers extended well beyond the perimeter of the city walls and they were met by six of their own guards, who had been waiting to escort them to the copse their horses were hidden in. They made it there without challenge. Ubba vaulted onto Sleipnir with relief.

Ralf ordered the South Gate to be opened and one of Ivar's men rode out waving the white flag. He trotted down the hill to the first line of troopers, bearing the parchment message in Latin that had been written by Ivar before he had departed. This caused some consternation as nobody had expected him. Edward and his commanders were stationed on a hill about a mile further back, watching proceedings. He was escorted by two outriders and taken to Edward. They reached the top of the hill where the horse lines started. One of the Wessex men tried to grab the letter from the Dane, but he shouted angrily, 'My instructions are to give this into the hand of Edward of Wessex, and nobody else.'

'You have no authority to make any demands at all.'

'But Ivar said that under the white flag I would be treated as a messenger and allowed to carry out his instructions.'

Edward had seen the confrontation and he and a woman on a white stallion were already cantering towards them. They halted a few feet away and the Dane approached them on horseback and bowed his head. 'King Edward of Wessex, I have the terms of surrender from Ivar the Boneless.'

Edward repeated loudly, 'Surrender? Never have I contemplated such a move from Ivar. It must be a trick.'

The Dane said, 'With respect my lord, Ivar is no fool – and although he has managed to win many battles against insurmountable odds, there are limits. He is fond of Jorvik and he thinks it would serve you best as a northern stronghold with its walls intact and its citizens alive and well.'

Aethelflaed of Mercia interrupted, 'And he would sacrifice his own head as well as his brothers' heads, to hand over Jorvik to us in good order?'

In spite of the pressure, the Dane smiled. 'Not exactly, my lady – in return for their freedom, along with all his men.'

Edward snatched the parchment and scanned the page. 'Since when has Ivar become fluent in Latin, produced silver coinage for Jorvik stamped with his head anointed by a crown, and adopted a personal seal? My father will be turning in his grave at his audacity to even dare to ask for his life to be spared.'

Aethelflaed laughed, 'But he may also be amused; surely imitation is the sincerest form of flattery. We know Ivar has acquired teachers for his nephews from far and wide and his brothers Ubba and Bjorn have raided as far as Jerusalem and into Africa. Ivar will know that knowledge also wields power and authority.'

Edward turned to Aethelflaed, 'Come. We will go and discuss this quickly with our counsellors.'

The Wessex soldier said, 'May I behead this arrogant Dane now, my lord?'

Edward shouted at him, 'No, certainly not. You will fetch him food and drink and keep him under guard until I have decided on my next move. Unless of course, *you* want to take the reply back to Ivar yourself. Inform the troops to stay where they are, but they may stand down and rest a while.'

oOo

They were making good progress to the longboat hideaway using the thick tree cover that ran parallel to the River Ouse. Ubba was scanning the horizon for signs of Mercian troops and spotted some on a hill about a mile north. They had broken cover and were streaming down the hill to attack them. There was no time to hide and with only ten men against at least 20 Mercians, they knew they would just have to fight them on the run. He informed Halfdan they were about to be attacked and they formed two rows, with the brothers behind. They unhooked their shields and faced the Mercians in a flat field next to the river, at full gallop. Ubba shouted, 'Jorvik!' as they charged, and the men took up his cry.

The Mercians formed one continuous row in an inverted arrowhead shape and the fight commenced. Ubba focused and locked on to his target, a big strong Mercian on a bay horse. The man was wearing heavy chainmail and a helmet. As their frontline hit the enemy, he saw Frank being challenged by a Mercian with an axe. He prepared for the initial clash into his own target. He was already upright in his stirrups with his sword raised. He swung diagonally at the man's shoulder, going for the gap between his helmet and mail. The impact penetrated his neck and cleaved through his shoulder. Blood spurted and Ubba sliced upwards with the sword. His attacker fell from his horse.

Another Mercian attacked him from the right and slightly behind him. Sleipnir caprioled and kicked the horse full on the chest with both back legs. Ubba turned round and Sleipnir reared, then sank his teeth into the other horse's neck. He saw the rider's fear as his sword sliced through his leather tunic and ripped him open across his chest. He raised his sword again and struck him across the neck. He slipped from his horse as it bolted in fear.

He was aware that Halfdan and Stefan were close by and the Mercians were trying to surround their group to hem them in. He turned away from the group, determined to prevent the circle closing, and charged into two Mercians, one of whom he knocked off his horse with his shield and a second whose raised sword arm he swiped through clean at the elbow. As the first rider tried to remount his horse, Ubba stabbed him in the back.

He headed for the gap he had created and shouted, 'Follow me!' As he looked back he saw Halfdan, Stefan and three others following. There was a short pause and then eight Mercians followed in hot pursuit. The quickest route would involve jumping a five-foot hedge and he was fairly confident their horses would manage it, but the Mercians' may not. He shouted, 'Aim to jump the hedge in pairs!'

Halfdan and Stefan set off as front runners. Ubba signalled to one of his men to join him and the other two to follow. He prayed Halfdan's jumping training would yield its rewards. Halfdan had no intention of slowing down to check the landing side, which may have had a ditch. Blizzard leapt into the air without touching the hedge and landed safely, with Stefan a fraction behind. Ubba and the remaining three troopers jumped it in good style and the branches of the yew hedge were kind.

Ubba shouted, 'Keep going! We have the fresher and faster horses and we have only a mile to go on good ground.'

The Mercians did not have an easy jump. On their first attempt four horses refused and brought down other horses attempting to take off in the melee. Ubba allowed himself one look back and then pushed Sleipnir into the lead at full gallop. There were now only six Mercians following them.

As he approached a wooded area he saw two men

waving from the trees. To his delight he realised they were his men guiding them into the copse and creating a path to fire arrows at the Mercians from above. He breathed a sigh of relief, pointed towards the trees and told his men to follow him. As they cantered down the path, more of his men appeared including Josh, his groom.

Ubba shouted, 'Dismount and get these horses onto the boat.'

Halfdan and Stefan were already hiding behind trees, awaiting any enemy troops who had escaped the bow and arrow attack. Two horses appeared and Stefan and Halfdan attacked immediately, cutting them down in seconds.

Ubba shouted at them to head for the boats and ran after them, knowing that more Mercians could soon be on the scene. His bowmen were already running back through the woods to the riverbank. From a distance he saw Josh leading Sleipnir down the ramp to the boat to join the other precious horses. His breathing steadied. He looked at his chainmail, which was covered in blood. His pain returned but apart from a deep cut to his left wrist, he appeared to be largely unharmed, just bruised and battered.

He jumped onto the lead boat with Halfdan and Stefan and threw himself down on the deck, leaving his sailors to navigate the four longboats back out to the Ouse. Egil approached him carrying two bottles of French wine and three pewter tankards. 'Here you are, my lord. I think you have earned this. May I help you out of your chainmail?'

'Yes, Egil, you may.' Stefan was already helping Halfdan out of his. He had a bleeding leg wound.

Egil lifted the chainmail over Ubba's head and said quietly, 'Frank didn't make it then?'

Ubba shook his head as tears spilled down his cheek. 'No. I saw him go down but could do nothing; I was fighting off two men as it was. What am I going to say to Serena? She lost her husband under my command, and now her brother.'

Egil patted him on his shoulder. 'My lord, you have to remember that you and your two brothers, wife, children and mistress are still alive. In the circumstances, that is an incredible feat. Do you know what happened in Jorvik?'

'No, but I heard the Greek fire exploding, so I guess Edward did not accept Ivar's surrender terms. I just pray to the gods that he did not kill Ralf and Ranulf as revenge for not capturing me.'

o0o

After discussion with his advisors Edward, though tempted to take Jorvik without a fight, would not agree to let the Ragnarssons leave Jorvik unchallenged. Rumours had spread through the camp that Ivar may have left already, but he was not going to let Ubba and Halfdan slip through his fingers. The written message was conveyed to the Dane and he returned through the Jorvik gates. Commands were sent out to the troops to prepare for battle.

However, ten minutes later the gates opened and a troop of 20 Danes rode out and lined up in front of the gates. Two riders moved forward slightly, and one was carrying a white flag.

Edward said, 'What the hell are they up to now?'

Aethelflaed said, 'Well, that looks like Ubba, and the younger one carrying the flag could be his son. Shall we ride to meet them?'

'No, we will not move. I will not parley with Ubba; he is not the King of Jorvik. I will not give him the satisfaction of recognition. Send a rider to bring his message to me.'

Aethelflaed interrupted, 'But if Ivar's gone, and possibly Halfdan too, then surely one Ragnarsson is better than none? If he's agreeing to become a hostage provided his men go free, then we should agree. The city remains intact and we walk in without losing the life of a Wessex or Mercian man.'

Edward shouted, 'I promised our mother that I would display all three of their heads on spikes above the gates of Jorvik.'

A rider was already bringing Ubba's demands to the King. He grabbed the parchment from the messenger and scanned it. 'He is offering to surrender himself provided his army is allowed to leave unhindered. Who the hell does he think he is? I will not allow him to dictate to me.' He turned to one of his commanders, 'Order the Welsh archers into position at the bottom of the hill hidden behind my troops on horseback. As soon as Ubba Ragnarsson is taken captive I want them to fire on his army and kill the lot of them. Tell the Mercians to wait for the horn and then start attacking the other gates.'

Aethelflaed exclaimed, 'So you are going to appear to grant his surrender and then renege on it immediately. That hardly makes you an honourable king.'

Edward turned bright red. 'Remind me, sister... since when have the Danes ever been honourable in their battles? Remember what they did to King Aelle. Was blood eagling an honourable death for a king?'

'But he tortured their father and denied him a warrior's death. Ubba is not a king by choice. You would do well to consider the danger you pose to yourself if you murder Ubba. He is not only loved by all the Danes and Norsemen but by many Saxons, too. Imagine what they would do to you to avenge Ubba's death.'

'I won't be killing him immediately. I have many questions I want answers to first. The fact remains that any Ragnarsson is a threat to the safety of a future united England and must be annihilated.' He turned to his commander, 'Have Ubba Ragnarsson and his son brought here. Put them in chains and guarded by five men until we have taken the castle, then transfer them to the dungeons.' He stormed off, shouting for his horse.

Aethelflaed was distraught; this was not the way she would have dealt with it. What Edward failed to understand was that the power and reputation of the Ragnarssons was actually keeping their borders safe from the Scots and Irish and Norsemen tempted to take land in the North. She went to reclaim her horse and find a position from which to watch the ensuing battle.

She saw from a good vantage point that guards were already taking Ubba and his son prisoners, binding their hands, attaching lead reins to their mounts, and escorting them back to the camp. "Ubba" spotted the Welshmen moving into position and as his son still had the white flag, he hoisted it aloft and waved it.

Dane bowmen were concealed both on the ramparts and at various other locations. A church bell sounded and they fired flaming arrows into the narrow ditch containing a thin line of Greek fire powder, which was only 20 feet from the position of the bowmen and six feet from the mounted Saxon Army.

As the first arrows hit the target the Dane army scattered right and left, and some retreated into the South Gate. As the Greek fire shot into the air and then exploded, the Saxon Army turned back. There was not enough room to press forward and the horses, who had never experienced this new phenomenon, panicked and bolted. The bowmen turned and ran back towards the camp; total chaos reigned.

TWENTY-TWO

Eventually, the Mercians forced their way into the city, to find the gates open and few Danes opposing them. A few remaining groups waited for them to thunder in and then fought their way out to freedom.

After fifteen minutes the small amount of Greek fire powder had expired, and Edward and his bodyguards entered Jorvik to find the Danes had escaped and the shopkeepers and Saxon residents were safe and well. They approached the palace to find a small welcoming committee of clergy and Saxon ealdormen outside in the palace courtyard. A small unit rushed up the steps and into the palace to find it practically empty except for servants and kitchen staff, who remained at their posts preparing food.

Edward dismounted and the Chief Ealdorman said, 'Greetings, lord king. Welcome to Jorvik.'

Edward stared around him in total disbelief. 'Where in God's name are the bloody Danes?'

'Gone, my lord! Ubba told us this morning that he had no intention of harming us and would surrender to Wessex without a fight to spare our lives, homes, businesses and the city.'

Suddenly Edward spied Father Raymond and

pointed to him. 'Father Raymond – thank God – someone with a bit of sense. Tell me what the hell has been going on here.'

Aethelflaed arrived with her own personal bodyguard. The ealdorman bowed and said, 'My lady of Mercia, welcome to Jorvik.'

Edward turned to Father Raymond, 'Now, where are Ivar the Boneless and Halfdan? I am pleased to say I have captured Ubba Ragnarsson and his son.'

'Lord king, Ivar left the city seven days ago after Halfdan and Ubba returned from Lincoln.'

Edward's face turned purple with rage. 'Are you telling me that Ivar fled and not one member of the clergy or an ealdorman attempted to get a message to me when I was camped outside your bloody walls?'

Father Raymond continued hesitantly, 'My lord king, we were kept under guard in the church. The ealdormen and members of the Witan were locked in the palace dungeons.'

The look on Edward's face could have turned people to stone, but they were interrupted by the arrival of a small guard escorting the two captives. Ralf was sporting a series of bruises to his face and arms. The crowd that gathered whispered to each other and Father Raymond gasped for breath.

Edward waved them forward. 'Come, men – get this bastard and his son under lock and key as quickly as possible.'

Father Raymond was silently praying for help as he turned to Edward. 'My lord king, that is not Ubba Ragnarsson or his son. It is Ralf Lindholm and his son Ranulf. He is a Dane by birth but is a respected blacksmith, farmer and horse breeder of this parish and is married to a Saxon woman called Gytha who was appointed as one of Ivar's advisers on womens' issues.'

The crowd gasped. Aethelflaed turned to her commander Lord Aldhelm and smiled.

Edward screamed, 'This cannot be true! I can't have lost three Ragnarssons in a matter of hours.'

Aethelflaed rode over to Edward and said quietly, 'You were the one who would not meet him on the battlefield brother, because he was not a king.'

Edward interrupted, 'I last saw Ubba Ragnarsson when I was twelve years old, so I would not have recognised him.'

Aethelflaed raised her voice, 'But I would, as Ubba Ragnarsson saved me when I was a hostage of the Danes ten years ago. He rescued me along with his father Ragnar before the ransom that would have crippled Wessex for years was paid. Of course, our father kept this good deed from public knowledge.'

Edward turned to his men, 'Get both of them locked in the dungeon. They are going nowhere until I have investigated this matter further.'

The Chief Ealdorman said, 'King Edward, Jorvik has been restored to you without significant loss of life or damage to the city as both Ivar and Ubba wanted, which considering their past battle history is astounding. We have great respect for Lord Ubba and would wish no harm to befall him or his immediate family. Ralf Lindholm has never been one of Ubba's troopers, but a respected friend. Ubba helped Ralf release his wife and daughter from Dane slave traders and Ralf swore fealty to Ubba as a result.'

The following morning, Edward called a meeting of his chief advisers to discuss their easy occupation of Jorvik. This was followed immediately by a meeting with representatives of the clergy and ealdormen of Jorvik. The discussion soon centred around Ralf, and various people spoke on his behalf.

Father Raymond said, 'My lord king, I cannot speak highly enough of Ralf Lindholm and beg you do no harm to him or his son. He was a staunch ally of Jorvik for many years before Ivar took control here. He was brave enough to stand up to Ivar when he arrived and ultimately, Ivar and Ubba respected him for it.'

Edward barked, 'He tried to deceive us by acting like Ubba, knowing that he was aiding and abetting his escape from the city. That makes him a traitor in my books and he should be punished as one.'

Aethelflaed interrupted, 'You cannot blame him, Edward. Had you and I gone to meet him, I would have known he was not Ubba. You cannot punish him for that. He cannot die just for being a friend to Ubba. There are many Saxons here who would be proud to be a friend of Ubba Ragnarsson. Some, like me, owe their lives to him – and he did save Ralf's wife and daughter from slavery, so of course he would feel beholden to him.'

Edward looked around the assembled Saxons and said angrily, 'I have sent for his wife to be brought here. I will listen to her side of the story as well as taking advice from some of you before I decide upon his fate. I shall release his son to his mother when she arrives. I do not intend to harm either of *them*.'

Ealdorman Aldrich said, 'I am sure when you have met Gytha and spoken to Ralf, this unfortunate matter will be resolved amicably.'

'Perhaps. Now, Father Raymond, perhaps you could advise me why you let Ubba Ragnarsson a practising *gothi* conduct services in the church when he is an undoubted heathen?'

'My lord king, you will recall the desecration of our beloved church and the savage deaths of nuns and priests that occurred when Ivar attacked Jorvik. This was done entirely by Ivar; Ubba had no idea of what was happening while he was fighting outside the walls during the invasion. I can assure you that he was as horrified as we were to discover what Ivar had done. There are certain saints days and celebrations when the King would be expected to attend. After Ivar's wickedness, Ubba agreed to represent his brother on these occasions as the clergy vowed that Ivar should never be allowed back in the church. He was persuaded by Ubba to restore the church to its former glory in recompense, and Ubba has been a staunch supporter of our religion. I know for a fact he was baptised by King Egbert as a boy, and again as a teenager by your father.'

Edward intervened, 'And this is the same man that holds Norse religious sacrifices and ceremonies within the city walls.'

'My lord king, you know that your father's aim was to lead the Danes towards the Christian path. I have observed Ubba Ragnarsson closely over the last few years. He has more Christian values than many Saxons and his compassion and sympathy extends to anybody, regardless of religion. He is not like Ivar; he has been a steadying influence throughout his reign here.'

Edward shouted angrily, 'Father Raymond, you have been deceived. Ubba Ragnarsson will have slain more Saxons than his wicked brother Ivar. He is the ultimate Viking warrior and has trained many more to his high standards. He is obviously as clever as his brother in conning you. Are you telling me that had I captured him, you would still be begging for his life?'

'Yes, lord king; I would. I would not be the only one either.' He turned to the surrounding company, 'How many of you would support me?'

To Edward's astonishment they all stood up and shouted, 'Aye!'

'Are you mad? Can you not see that leaving even one Ragnarsson alive could jeopardise the formation of a united England? He may not wish to be a king but Ubba Ragnarsson covets this land. He is a force of nature in his own right and will stop at nothing to regain your land.' He walked out of the meeting in disgust.

Edward walked out of the palace and looked around him. He made his way towards the stables, first coming to Ubba's house. His curiosity led him through the door and he walked into the main room that had doors opening out into a small garden. He was startled by the overwhelming feeling of peace. He went upstairs and walked through the bedrooms, pausing in the main bedroom. All the rooms here, as in the palace itself, showed no signs of a rapid eviction. The wardrobes and drawers were empty; there was no doubt that an organised escape had been planned well in advance.

He caught something metal with his foot as it slithered across the wooden floor. He bent down and picked it up. It was a metal comb. He placed it on the dressing table and looked into the mirror. The image he saw was of a beautiful older woman with striking grey hair with blonde streaks. The image was so clear that he turned around, afraid she was in the room. He had only been twelve years old when he had last seen Torri Ragnarsson. Back then she had been married to Bjorn. His father had always maintained that she was behind the power of all the sons of Ragnar. Ragnar chose her as the matriarch of his dynasty for her looks, intelligence and sheer courage as a shield maiden. This idea had been further strengthened when they heard that all four brothers had sworn fealty to her and Ivar had made her Queen Consort. Many had told him of the love and devotion between her and Ubba, despite their ten-year age difference. They had heard about her kidnap and rape, and how she had castrated and killed the man who had raped her.

She had two sons to Bjorn; Erik and Refil, and two sons and a daughter to Ubba. Five children carried her genes and those of their fathers and grandfather, Ragnar Lothbrok. Edward's spies had fed back snippets of information on the progress of those children while they had been in Jorvik. He remembered how relieved he was that Bjorn Ironside had recovered from his ordeal in Africa and taken his two sons back to Denmark. He had been told that Arne was the image of his father in looks and temperament, and shared the same love for animals and nature as his father. However, Viggo had darker hair and was highly intelligent and had surprised all the tutors engaged by Ivar to educate them. Potentially, Viggo could pose the biggest threat to him of all Torri's children. Anger gripped him, and he picked up a candelabra and smashed it into the mirror. He had let not only the three sons of Ragnar slip through his fingers, but the grandsons too. *Thank Christ Ivar was sterile and Halfdan had no children.*

He marched out of the room and down the stairs, flung open the door and slammed it shut, and continued to the stables. He was met by the old Saxon stud groom Sam. 'My lord king, may I welcome you to Jorvik. Allow me to show you around the stables. You have been left with some good quality stock courtesy of Ubba.'

'Only what he could not move in time. I don't see his horse Sleipnir looking over a stable door.'

'Nay! You could hardly expect him to part with his beloved stallion. They are a team and work together as if they were one.'

'Oh, another fan of Ubba the Great! What is it about him that everyone adores? The man is a consummate killer. He is as cunning as a wolf and has their tracking skills as well.'

'My lord, where do I start? He is deeply connected to nature and animals and is the best horseman I have ever seen. He is a great communicator and has genuine empathy towards people. He can assess the strengths and weaknesses of a person very quickly. He strives to get the best out of his men and builds up their confidence and skills. And women just fall at his feet.'

'Sam, you make him out to be a god, and yet he is only human. I do not believe that he doesn't crave power, money, authority and recognition. He has more ambition than all of his brothers. He just doesn't crave the same rewards that his brothers do. He learned from his father that becoming a king was no easy option but a poisoned chalice that devours personal freedom. The expectation of other people to follow in your father's footsteps is a heavy burden with no escape and the fear of failure is omnipresent.'

'I can see you share many of the same predicaments as Ubba, and had to face them at a young age with little life experience. Whatever you do as King, there will always be many who doubt you. But if you take anything from Ubba's example it should be his compassion and devotion to duty. He tackled his fears and doubts head-on and learnt to live with them. Ubba has never been a warmonger, only a peacemaker, but his destiny required him to stand by his family and fight their battles. He has never shirked that duty.'

Edward asked his sister and Father Raymond to be present at his meeting with Gytha. He was surprised at her confidence and composure; she told him plainly what she thought of his mistreatment of Ralf. He had been warned that she was a strong Saxon woman who was used to getting her own way and had held her own with Ivar over many tricky issues.

'Madam, the fact remains that your husband intended to deceive me by impersonating Ubba, thereby giving him time to make his escape from the city.'

Gytha responded angrily, 'How could he intend to deceive? He was outside the castle walls with Ubba's men lined up behind him. None of them would have mistaken him for Ubba; he was well known to them all.'

'Let's move on. What was your relationship with Ivar and Ubba?'

'My lord, I wish you to clarify your use of the word "relationship". If you are insinuating for one moment that I had a physical relationship with either of them, then you are dishonouring my name. King Ivar asked me to be a counsellor on petty disputes brought by local people. It was at the behest of Torri, whom he had appointed to preside over these sessions. She discovered that no women were on the judging panels when she became Queen Consort. You may not know that the Danes treat their women the same as men. If they have brought a dowry or property to a marriage and then their husband mistreats them, they can end their marriage and reclaim their dowry. Ivar upheld this ruling in Jorvik as he agreed that no woman should be treated as the property of her husband.'

Aethelflaed clapped. 'How very enlightened of him.'

Gytha said, 'My lady, Ivar was not the tyrant and monster his distorted reputation would have you believe. He was a good judge of character and wise in determining justice. He did not eat babies for breakfast or rape virgins, as many of his enemies claimed. He made major changes for the better in Jorvik and turned it into a centre for trading from many different countries. The population of Jorvik has doubled under his reign and our businesses have prospered. He has handed you back a thriving city with all its wealth and people intact. That is not the act of a tyrant or a coward in my opinion.'

'Oh God – don't tell me that Ivar was a saint. He was a tyrant who ruled with a rod of iron and crushed anybody who got in his way. Your relationship with Ubba, you have carefully avoided mentioning.'

'Ubba Ragnarsson saved mine and my daughter's lives when he rescued us from slave traders. He also saved me and my son from dying in childbirth. He is my hero and greatest friend. There was never any extended relationship beyond that. Ubba's utter dedication and love for his wife and children is at the centre of his life.'

'I hear his wife accepted his mistress and she has produced two more children for his army of bastards. Why would the great shield maiden and queen tolerate her husband's infidelities? She divorced Bjorn Ironside for his infidelity.'

'Because she loves him! It's perfectly obvious to me.

Her childbearing years were coming to an end and the relationship between Serena and Ubba started when she was back home in Jormund.'

Father Raymond spoke, 'My lord king, Gytha speaks the truth. Ubba has loved Torri since he was a young boy, but he never revealed it until after she divorced Bjorn. When Torri brought all the children over from Jormund he took the responsibility of being a father and stepfather very seriously. He has proved to be the perfect mentor and guide to all those children and would like nothing more than to spend time in peace and harmony with his family.'

'Madam, you may go and see your husband and I will release your son immediately. I have many questions I wish to ask your husband before I decide his fate.'

TWENTY-THREE

Edward had Ralf brought before him in chains, having deliberately kept him waiting for two days. He had hoped to do the interview alone but Aethelflaed had insisted that she and Father Raymond were there. She knew how angry Edward was about losing Ubba, which she couldn't quite understand as he had always loathed Ivar far more.

They were all quite shocked to witness his beaten face and the bruises all over his arms and upper body. Aethelflaed glared furiously at Edward assuming he had sanctioned it when in fact, he had not. He pointed to a guard to bring Ralf a chair and a drink of water. 'Ralf Lindholm, do you plead guilty or not guilty to impersonating Ubba Ragnarsson, thus covering his and Halfdan's escape from Jorvik?'

Ralf looked at his accusers as best he could through the swelling surrounding his eyes. He was surprised to see a woman. No introductions had been made so he had no idea who she was. He took a deep breath, opting to hasten the proceedings along. 'Guilty!'

There was complete silence and then Edward continued, 'Do you admit to being one of Ubba's most trusted soldiers? I warn you that we have testimony from several sources confirming that you were.'

Ralf replied angrily, 'No, I never became one of his bodyguards. I was appointed as a riding instructor to his children and troops. I have my own business as a farmer, blacksmith and horse breeder. Ubba was my friend first and foremost and helped rescue my wife and daughter from slave traders. I owed him for their lives and swore fealty to serve him if he ever required me.'

Edward interrupted, 'So he asked you to impersonate him to allow his escape?'

'I volunteered to do it. I would have followed Ubba Ragnarsson into the gates of hell if he had asked me to. I consider him the most inspiring leader I have ever known, and certainly the best horseman.'

Edward interrupted, 'Rubbish. Once a Dane, always a Dane. You switched your allegiance to him because you knew he would promote your business far more than your existing Saxon customers.'

Father Raymond could not control himself anymore. 'This is totally untrue! Ralf was a loyal supporter of the Saxons here for many years before Ivar invaded.'

Ralf intervened, 'I don't choose my friends by their birthplace, but by how they treat me as a person. Nobody could ever find a more devoted friend than Ubba. He proved it when he helped find my wife and daughter. He was not obliged to do so, but he did.'

'Ah, but I have heard that his motive for rescuing your wife was because he coveted her for himself.'

Aethelflaed intervened, 'Edward, you were told by Gytha yesterday that there was no relationship other than as friends between her and Ubba.'

Ralf said, 'Ivar misread a meeting between them and wrongly assumed they were lovers. You need only take one glance at Thorin to rule Ubba out as his father.'

'So you are prepared to die because of your friendship with Ubba Ragnarsson while he escapes to fight again? Do not be deceived by this rubbish that he and Ivar did not want to harm the people of Jorvik, and spared their lives and city.' He stood up and shouted, 'There is only one reason they did that and that was because they intend to come back. You know precisely where they are and you will tell me, or you will die!'

Aethelflaed shouted, 'Edward, you cannot do that!'

Father Raymond said, 'My lord king, do not do anything hasty. You cannot wreak vengeance on one man for the loss of another.'

Edward slammed his fist on the table. 'He has admitted his guilt Father Raymond, but there is more to this than meets the eye and I intend to investigate every aspect of this case. The sooner he confesses the whereabouts of all three Ragnarssons, the more likely he will be to live.'

He turned to the guard and shouted, 'Take him back to his cell but do not chain him up. Ensure he has adequate food and bedding. If he is touched again by anyone, I will personally behead the culprit.'

Father Raymond left the room, distraught at the possible outcome for Ralf, to officiate in a church service of thanksgiving.

Aethelflaed moved closer to Edward. 'You know he will never reveal their whereabouts. You have information from your own spies Edward, who told you last week that Ivar had left the city and appeared to be heading to Chester. You knew he was heading for Ireland and could have arranged his capture along the route if you had wanted to.'

'There was not enough time to despatch a troop to apprehend him; it would have been like looking for a needle in a haystack trying to cut him off over the Pennines when we have no knowledge of the area. I am quite content to let him escape but my worries are that he may come back, especially as he will join up with Sigtryggr of Dublin.

'Sister, I have no intention of killing Ralf Lindholm or Ubba, but I must make it appear that I am being strong. Nobody else knows that I intend to leave you in charge of Jorvik with Aldhelm, but I must secure your position here. I would be delighted to have both Ragnarssons further north, preferably close to the coastline, keeping the Irish at bay on the West Coast and stopping more Danes invading on the East Coast. They would keep the Scots from risking invasion from the north.'

'I don't know Ubba Ragnarsson well enough to assess whether he would agree to offer you protection to be allowed to remain in Yorkshire without raising an army against us. You heard what Father Raymond said – his loyalty to his brothers ensured he protected their territories, even though he proclaims he has no desire to rule.'

'He is a very different character from Ivar and Halfdan; he is much more like his father. He admits he is lazy and has no interest in politics or governance. I think he just wants a chance to spend more time with his family rather than fighting battles.'

o0o

After an uncomfortable night of tossing and turning, attempting to ease the pressure on his joints, Ubba gave up trying to sleep. He sat up as dawn emerged. He looked over at Halfdan, who was snoring peacefully like a baby. He could not understand why Halfdan's body could take an equal hammering and yet he did not seem to feel the effects. Whereas he could feel every one of his joints and muscles aching and his shoulders and knees felt as though he had been trampled by horses. His low pain threshold could not just be due to his lithe athletic figure compared to Halfdan's size and shape.

Halfdan woke and made his way over to Ubba. He did not even limp despite the deep wound from his thigh to his calf. If that had been Ubba, he knew he would not have been able to walk.

Halfdan gave him a thump on his shoulder. 'Glad to see we are both alive to fight another day.'

Ubba screamed and woke everybody up. 'Halfdan, don't do that! Every bone in my body feels like it's broken, and my joints are seized up.'

Halfdan smiled. 'Sorry brother, but I am not surprised – you took a hammering in that skirmish – but you and Sleipnir were magnificent. You looked like Thor fighting in Norse fables – totally invincible!'

'I never consider myself invincible. I am just striving to stay alive.'

'We will soon reach Richmond and you can rest at the farm you have chosen to use as a base whilst I go and investigate further north. You can then get your family moved up here and assess the situation back in Jorvik. You will be able to rest your aching bones in the meantime.'

Ubba called Kirk over. He was Halfdan's boatman, who had sailed to Repton with him two years ago. He moved around, stretching his body and easing some of the stiffness in his joints.

'Morning, Kirk. How long to Richmond?'

'Probably an hour or so yet, lord.'

'Kirk, I am no longer a lord of anything. Just call me Ubba, please.'

'You look to be in pain, but that's hardly surprising from what the men told me.'

'I will be fine once I get moving and riding again. Are the horses safe and well on the other boat?'

'Yes, Josh seems as devoted to his horses as you are. When will we be returning to bring your family up here?'

'I don't know. I will have to wait for messengers from Jorvik and find out what happened after we left. Hopefully some of my men will have escaped and will make it up here on horseback over the next few days. I just pray to the gods that Ralf has not been harmed by Edward.'

They moored just below Richmond on the Swale

and did some minor swapping of horses and equipment so that Halfdan had all the provisions he needed for his investigations further north. His two longboats left as the horses were being unloaded ready to transport Ubba's supplies and equipment to his farm. A suitably hidden site had been found to moor them until they returned.

Ubba and Egil set off ahead to check the route to the farm was clear and open in readiness for the supply wagons arriving. It was a quiet isolated farm at the foot of the North York Moors and there was only one narrow track leading to it.

Ubba was relieved to be off the boat and back on Sleipnir, able to move his joints again. The farm was only three miles from the river so they proceeded at a steady canter as trotting jarred his joints. When they arrived, they checked the stables and left their horses. The two small wagons would be bringing feed and bedding for the horses. There was a row of ten stone stables, and ten acres of relatively flat grassland. The four Dales ponies they had brought with them would be capable of living outside permanently in one of the sheltered fields. The farmhouse had four large bedrooms upstairs and an adjacent barn with a hayloft above, which could support his small team of guards. Egil turned his attention to the kitchen fire pit and Ubba found some bales of straw to bed down the stables whilst they awaited the arrival of the others.

o0o

After a long night of deliberation, Edward and Aethelflaed came up with a plan. Edward went down to the cell to see Ralf early the next morning.

His prisoner was immediately on guard as he thought Edward's lone presence meant he had decided his fate and death was imminent.

Edward said, 'Ralf, do not be concerned. I do not wish to do you any harm, but I imagine you would not be prepared to reveal the whereabouts of Ubba or his family willingly?'

'No, my lord. I would not.'

'What if I told you that I already know the whereabouts of Torri and her children, as well as Ubba's mistress and her children?'

Ralf smiled. 'Then I would tell you, very respectfully of course, to bugger off and leave me alone!'

'Even though their location incriminates you even more for shielding them?'

'What exactly do you mean, my lord? If you are intent on killing me then perhaps you would proceed. I have made my peace with God and my family and am ready to die. You are the one with the power to decide my fate – not me.'

'My father set up a long-ranging spy network many years ago and I have been monitoring Jorvik very closely. Whilst I am delighted that Ivar has moved to Ireland I am aware that if conditions are not to his liking, he may decide to return. I understand that Ubba would prefer not to spend the rest of his days fighting, and I want to make him an offer. I have no information as yet from my spies as to his whereabouts but I suspect he will not be too far from his family, if not already resting by the fire pit at your farm in Terrington.'

Ralf's head lifted quickly, and he looked straight at Edward. 'My lord if you intend to kidnap or harm his family I would warn against it. Ubba will not accede to your plans whilst you have his family in custody, and he will fight to retrieve them. You may find he will have as great an army as he did when he avenged his father's death.'

Edward raised his hand. 'Peace, Ralf. I reiterate that I do not wish him any harm; I just want to speak to him and I think we may be able to sort out an amicable peace. Aethelflaed and I wish you to escort us to your farm with no escort or spying scouts following. I promise you I will not imprison them; I am doing this without the knowledge of my counsellors, and it is for a very good reason. You and your wife will have an important role to play in the future of Jorvik if I can persuade Ubba to support me.'

'Torri will think I have betrayed her.'

'I will explain that you never revealed her whereabouts and if we go without an escort, this will confirm I mean her no harm. She is a very wise woman and has probably been the guiding influence behind the scenes for many years. I will have you released from your cell after breakfast and we will depart from the stables at 10 a.m. in disguise. I trust you to keep this to yourself and tell nobody.'

'Yes, my lord king, but I do beg you not to harm them.'

The king left quickly and Ralf was brought breakfast along with his riding gear, his own sword and a hooded cloak to change into for the journey. He reflected on what he was doing. He had no choice but to believe Edward sincerely did not intend to imprison them. The presence of Aethelflaed eased his anxiety somewhat.

They set off on their journey. Ralf heard Edward instruct his grooms and guards that they had gone to Ralf's home in Haxby, to explain their absence. Some resistance had been shown by his guards at them leaving the city unescorted, but he made it plain that they would leave without any backup.

As they reached the top of the hill overlooking Jorvik, Ralf paused to show them the view over the city. 'Jorvik is very beautiful. I am thankful the city has not been ravaged and peoples' lives have been spared, just as Ubba wanted.'

Edward remarked, 'No lives would have been lost at all if he had surrendered the city directly to me.'

'When we arrive my lord king, I must impart the news of her brother's death to Serena. I have been told he died in the skirmish to reach the longboats north of the city.'

'I see you have been kept well informed Ralf, in the one hour since your release. I believe they met up with one of the Mercian river patrols and despite being outnumbered, still managed to carve their way out and escape.'

'Ubba will have felt the loss of Frank very deeply as Serena lost her husband under his command.'

They cantered on. Ralf kept scanning the hillside behind for any sign of troops following them. As they approached the last mile to Terrington, Ralf spotted two riders on the hillside across the valley and knew instantly it was Thorin and Arne. They turned back and headed towards the farm to report back. Hopefully, they would not have been too anxious seeing only three riders approaching. He knew they would have been watching for signs of troop movements coming from the south.

As they turned off the open moors onto the track to the farm they discovered Thorin and Arne, plus Shadow, waiting at the gate. Both had swords and shields at the ready, but they must have recognised his horse and known Ralf was with the party.

Ralf said, 'Good morning to you both. I have brought visitors to see Torri. They come in peace, not conflict.'

Thorin responded, 'Are you sure about that, Father? You are not under pressure to reveal her whereabouts?'

'King Edward of Wessex and his sister the Lady of Mercia already had knowledge of her whereabouts.'

Edward responded, 'He is your son, Ralf? But he bears no resemblance whatsoever to you. However, there is no mistaking the other young man. You must be Arne, Ubba's eldest son. Do not be concerned – we come in peace to speak with your mother and should your father be hiding in the vicinity, we would wish to see him too.'

Arne and Thorin both looked startled but Ralf began to open the gate and come in. They all followed to the farmhouse door and Torri appeared at the top of the steps. The boys jumped off their horses, quickly tied them up and came to take Edward and Aethelflaed's horses.

Ralf exclaimed, 'Torri, King Edward of Wessex and his sister Aethelflaed wish to speak to you in peace.'

Both of them removed their hoods and came up the steps to the porch. Torri came towards them with her hand out in welcome. 'Come in. I hope I can trust that this is a private meeting and not a precursor to an army appearing over the horizon.'

Edward took her hand and bowed. 'You have my word, my lady; no harm shall befall you or your family. I merely wish to outline a proposal to you... and if your husband is here too, it would save me repeating myself later.'

Aethelflaed hugged Torri. 'Please do not be concerned, Torri; we have brought no escort to prove we mean no harm. I must also reassure you that Ralf did not give us the details of your whereabouts. We have been informed of your movements by our own spies since you left Jorvik. We knew Ralf would not reveal your hiding place even under torture, so we explained to him why we wished to speak to you without our counsellors present.'

Ralf hugged Torri. 'Is Serena inside? I have bad news for her. Frank was killed in a skirmish when escaping to the longboats. He and five other men were killed by Mercians, but Ubba and Halfdan made it.'

Torri looked shocked. 'Oh, poor Frank. Ubba will take his death badly.'

TWENTY-FOUR

Torri showed them in and asked the cook to make them refreshments. Ralf went in search of Serena. They had just settled around the table when the door flew open and Freya ran in, with Astrid and Theo behind her.

'Mama, why have I to look after these two? I want to meet our guests.'

Torri gave Freya a look that could have turned her into ice. 'Freya, you will do as you are told and look after your siblings.'

Aethelflaed and Edward exchanged a knowing look, having made many unwanted entrances in the past themselves.

'But I want to know if Daddy is safe! And by the look on Ralf's face, it wasn't good news he wished to tell Serena.'

Torri snapped, 'Freya, will you leave the room now, or I will have Thorin confine you in the pigsty for the remainder of the day. Now curtsey to our guests, take the children with you and leave.'

'Curtsey! But Mama, you only ever do that to kings or queens.'

'Precisely! Now leave!'

She hesitated but could not stop blurting out, 'But

Mama, who are they?'

Aethelflaed took pity on Freya and intervened, 'Freya, I am Aethelflaed of Mercia and this is my brother King Edward of Wessex. We just wanted to talk to your parents, but I would love to have a chat with you later after you have finished looking after your siblings.'

Freya's face turned red. She held up her finger and pointed at Edward. 'But you are the enemy my daddy is fighting. You are far too young to be a king. Have you come to kill me and Arne?'

Edward smiled and stepped nearer, at which Freya jumped backwards. 'No, sweetheart. I don't want to be your enemy anymore; I want to be your friend.'

Torri shouted, 'Out now lady or I will put you over my knee right here and now!' Freya grabbed hold of Astrid and Theo and fled the room.

Torri was red-faced with embarrassment. 'I do apologise. She is rather outspoken and has a very enquiring mind. Her father is besotted with her and regrettably, spoils her.'

Edward laughed, 'She is absolutely delightful – very bright, and the image of you. Are the other two Serena's children?'

'Yes, they are, and there's another baby boy in the cradle.'

'And you approve of this extended family?'

Torri hesitated and said, 'Let's put it this way. If you have a good prolific stallion at stud who produces fine youngstock, you will keep breeding them. It just happens to be one of my husband's many talents. I was getting too old to reproduce, but Serena was not. I was content to let her take over, provided Ubba kept his assignations to her and remained my husband as before.'

Edward was shocked at her response but could not argue with the validity of her argument.

'Perhaps it would be easiest if I told you what knowledge I have from my spy network on you, Ubba, Halfdan and Ivar. I do not know your husband or Halfdan's exact location at this time, but I suspect they are looking further north for a new base. I have confirmation that Ivar has arrived safely in Dublin on a merchant ship from Chester, with a small party consisting of a beautiful red-haired young woman, two teenage boys, a Moor, his servant and four personal bodyguards. I suspect one of the teenage boys is your son Viggo, whom my spies tell me is a very intelligent boy whom Ivar is devoted to. Under the circumstances I can understand why you let him go; you feared for his life if he remained here and was captured by me. If, as they say, knowledge really is power, then he is most likely to become a very wise king in whichever country he chooses to settle. Whilst I am delighted that Ivar the Boneless has left these shores, I suspect Ireland may not suit his tastes or ambition and he may choose to return. I know of his affiliation with Sigtryggr and that he visited you last year. I believe it caused a slight rift between you and your husband.'

Torri smiled. 'Do go on, Edward. You don't expect me to deny or confirm any of your points of view.'

'Indeed so, my lady. You are far too clever for that

and in my opinion, you have been the real power behind the Ragnarsson throne for many years.'

Torri laughed. 'I will take that as a compliment, but I cannot claim it to be true. How could I, a mere uneducated woman, influence the lives of Ragnar, Bjorn, Ubba, Halfdan and Ivar? They are all strong enough characters to make their own decisions in life.'

'But the evidence is there, my lady. You are the one lynchpin they all have in common.'

'Rubbish. I slept with Ragnar as I was effectively his slave, then married and divorced Bjorn, and finally married the one who was right for me. Halfdan and I are just good friends.'

'Well, obviously – he is hardly going to bed you if he prefers men. But he did swear fealty to you along with his brothers. Ivar rated you so highly he made you Queen Consort, and Ivar is definitely no fool.'

'You make me out to be power hungry when any of those men had enough power and authority to take any land they desired.'

'It isn't necessarily power or authority you wanted. You bred a dynasty of sons capable of conquering the world. I know about Bjorn's return to Jorvik after his time in Africa, and how ill he was. Without the Moor and Ubba and Ivar's interventions he would have died. However, I am satisfied that he has returned to Jormund and seeks control of Norway, so is unlikely to threaten my united England.'

'What exactly do you want of Ubba? He will never betray his loyalty to his brothers. He has spent his life doing what is expected of a son of Ragnar and he knows most of all that becoming a king is an onerous task for any man. He saw what happened to his father when he became king, and he has no desire to follow in his footsteps. Ubba is a lover of the land, his family, animals and nature. He has spent his entire life doing what other people expected him to do. He is not a born warrior; he is a peacemaker. He is a skilled communicator and he can train men to fight instinctively to save their lives, but he does not enjoy doing it. He wants peace now and a chance to rear his family. But he will not do it as your puppet.'

'I don't want to control him, Torri. I want him and Halfdan to stay in the North and keep the Scots, Welsh, Irish and other European tribes from invading England. I cannot rule Jorvik from 400 miles away. I intend to do something so outrageous that my father will turn in his grave and my mother will disown me. I want to make Aethelflaed Queen of Jorvik as well as ruler of Mercia. I cannot do that unless I know that there is someone who will help her if she is attacked.'

'What more can I say Edward, than I already have? Ubba has no intention of raising an army to retake Jorvik but I cannot confirm that of Ivar or Halfdan. Believe me, nobody can predict Ivar's next move. In all my years of knowing him I have frequently been surprised by his reactions. Some things you think he would do out of spite or revenge, he doesn't... and yet if someone unintentionally offends him he can kill them on the spot.'

'Do you think you can persuade Ubba and maybe Halfdan to meet me to discuss our own private peace agreement?'

'Why would I lure them into a trap?'

Aethelflaed interrupted, 'I promise you Torri, we would not do that. What would it take to convince you of our peaceful intent? We are doing this without the knowledge of our counsellors as they do not know Edward intends to make me Queen of Jorvik. Can you not trust me – as a woman, mother and queen – that no harm will befall them? Even if we cannot come to terms you will all be allowed to walk away unharmed.'

'I have no idea where Ubba is at the moment, but he will be in touch soon. I will ask him, but he will make his own mind up about whether to grant your request.'

Aethelflaed said, 'That's all we want. You contact us, and I suggest we meet here. I cannot guarantee your safety in Jorvik just yet. I would love to meet Arne and Freya again.'

'I will go and fetch them, but I just need to check whether Serena has calmed down after the news of Frank's death.'

As she left the room, Edward turned to Aethelflaed, 'Jesus, she is one hell of a woman. No wonder the Ragnarssons swear fealty to her. To be honest, I am in awe of her as well. What courage, power and authority she exudes. Where do these Danes get their confidence from?'

Aethelflaed laughed. 'You never met Lagertha, Ragnar's wife; she was just the same. Danish women have far more control over their lives than Saxon women.'

Torri returned with the children and a servant followed with steaming mugs of soup for the guests.

Edward approached Arne, who seemed ill at ease. 'Arne, you can rest assured I mean you no harm. I just want to meet your father as I think we can both be of service to one another. Did your father warn you that you may be taken prisoner if captured?'

'He did, but hoped that you would not take the life of a child as you have Christian faith. However, I am prepared for death as I pose a threat to your reign by simply being a Ragnarsson.'

'How does a teenager prepare for that eventuality?'

'With humility and resignation. If the gods have decided that is your fate then you face it with courage. I do not fear death, only perhaps the manner of my death, because I won't go to Valhalla to be with my grandfather.'

'But he did not die as a warrior, so he won't be in Valhalla. He died at the hands of King Aelle, tortured and alone.'

'Yes, which is why my father and uncles avenged his death. I know for certain he is in Valhalla now.'

'Well, if Ragnar is there then I am sure he will be very proud of you.'

'Why? I have done nothing to make him proud yet.'

'Oh, but you will do in the future Arne, I am sure of that. I would hope that we can become friends rather than enemies. I would rather have a Ragnarsson protecting England's borders from invasion than anyone else. I am sure we can live peacefully and work together in the future.'

Torri took the opportunity to talk to Aethelflaed whilst Edward was chatting to Arne. She drew her away from Freya but realised that Freya had the ears of an eagle and would probably overhear anyway.

'My lady, may I offer you my congratulations on becoming Queen of Jorvik. I would also add a warning. My experience over many years has been that ruling can be a very lonely and dangerous life. I know you loved Erik and Aethelred was a cruel husband, but you and Erik would never have been allowed to be together. I know you have sworn celibacy as the Lady of Mercia, but a word of caution from a wise woman. I had the love and support of Ubba and I know how much that helped me. Denying yourself a husband or lover will make the journey harder. You need to have someone who loves you unconditionally to lighten the load and offer you an escape – chance to be a woman, not just a queen.'

Aethelflaed hugged her. 'Torri, I understand what you mean but I will have the support of Lord Aldhelm, who has been my rock for the last two years.'

Torri smiled. 'I am glad, my lady, you have a confidante to support you.'

oOo

Ubba held the torch aloft as they pulled over to the bank of the Swale now they had arrived at Terrington. He was annoyed that their journey had been delayed for five hours after a boat had been grounded when it struck rocks, swinging right across the narrowest part of the Swale on a bend. There was no way they could get past the stricken vessel and so they had offered to help the crew move it before it sank completely.

Their longboat was soon tied to the jetty and Ubba leapt off, ready to make the journey to the farm on foot while his crew stayed on the boat overnight. He would rather go now and see his wife than wait until morning. Looking at the height of the full moon he knew it must be approaching midnight, but he relished the chance to reconnect with Torri and catch up on the news from Jorvik.

He hoped he could remember the way. At least it was uphill, so he was not in danger of falling over a cliff. However, he faltered several times on the steep climb, walking into thorny bushes. Finally, he saw a faint light showing in the farmhouse kitchen. He knew to be cautious as Shadow would pick up any sound as he entered, and could come hurtling through. He was relieved that the lamp was burning when he opened the door, as he saw Shadow framed in the hall doorway with his teeth bared ready to attack.

'Shadow, it is me. Please don't attack!' Instantly, he relaxed and bounded over to Ubba, jumping up to lick his face. 'Down, boy. I could do without that – I am wet enough. Come on, let's get you back to Arne before he wakes and misses you. I don't want to disturb everybody at this late hour.' Shadow led him up the stairs to Arne's bedroom. The moonlight lit the room and he could not resist giving his son a kiss; he looked so peaceful and he was so relieved to see him.

He moved quietly along the corridor, trying to find his wife's room. As he opened the door it was pulled back violently and he was confronted by his irate totally naked wife holding a seax to his throat.

'Christ almighty Torri, it's me! Who the hell were you expecting?' He closed the door, removed the seax, bent down and hugged her. 'I am delighted you met me with such passion, but I can think of far better things to do than cut my throat.'

'It could have been the Saxons coming back to kidnap me, or worse.'

'You have been discovered?'

'Not exactly. Ralf brought Edward of Wessex and his sister Aethelflaed to visit me yesterday. They came unescorted and without the knowledge of their counsellors and soldiers. They want to discuss a peace treaty with you and Halfdan.'

Ubba was divesting himself of his wet clothes; since he had been in the river rescuing the boat, all his clothing was soaked through.

'Do you want me to fill you a tub?' Torri grabbed a towel.

'No, I just want to get dry, cuddle up to you in bed and let your hot body warm me through. I don't want to wake the entire household up. Sorry, darling – you will have to put up with me just as I am.'

'I'll manage, seeing as you are back alive and well. Ralf brought news of Frank's death to Serena yesterday and she is devastated.'

'I have had difficulty coping with it myself. We were so outnumbered by the Mercians I was already fighting two of them and couldn't get to him. I think he was either pulled or struck from Noir and then he was wiped out. Noir had a deep sword swipe on his flank, but he kept up with us and made it to the boat.'

They jumped into bed and clung to each other for warmth. 'How have the children been? Is Siegfrid well?'

'Yes, I passed him off to Edward as your son with Serena; they already know far too much about our business. Edward has spies all over Jorvik and he has received reports of Ivar landing in Dublin. He knew Viggo was with him. Aoife survived the journey so perhaps Ivar did not get the opportunity to kill her. They were on a merchant ship, so it would not have been easy.'

'Enough talking now, sweetheart. I have a much better job in mind for those luscious lips of yours.' He leant over her and kissed her lips tenderly. Within minutes they were making passionate love, each claiming the other's body as though they had been parted for months, not days. After their passion had sated they lay in each other's arms side by side. Ubba nuzzled her neck and shoulders. 'Oh, I never want to be parted from you again my love. Let's just stay here in bed together for a month.'

She giggled, 'Do you want to embarrass Arne and Freya anymore? Freya thinks we are too old to have sex already. She also thinks you should be banned from Serena's bed. She cannot understand why I tolerate your relationship with her; she thinks you should be faithful to me.'

'I can see I am going to have to educate my daughter on the joys of sex from a man's point of view.'

'Oh, don't worry. I enlightened Edward and Aethelflaed as to your superior breeding qualities and said that your destiny was to breed an army of Ubbas to fight our cause.'

'Oh, I bet that shocked Edward – and reminded him that his own father had an eye for the ladies but was not as productive as me.'

'Oh, he's not doing too badly for twenty-six; he has sired twins to his first love and has a son and daughter with his new wife. I think he was weighing up Freya as a potential future daughter-in-law.'

Ubba sat bolt upright. 'Well that's put paid to peace talks. Nobody is good enough for my precious Freya. The gods would never allow such a match.'

Torri laughed, 'But you were only saying a few weeks back that to promote true unity between ourselves and the Saxons would require the marriage of high-ranking individuals on both sides.'

Ubba interrupted, 'But not by sacrificing one of my precious children to the cause. I promised Freya she could choose her own husband.'

Torri could not resist taunting her distraught husband. 'Oh dear! I gave Edward permission to take her back to Wessex to learn how to become a future queen. She hasn't had the extended education the boys have undertaken, but she's a quick learner.'

Ubba's face was red with anger. He grabbed her round the neck and Torri shouted out, 'Stop it, Ubba. I was only jesting! Do you think Edward would allow his heir to marry a Dane who is a true believer in the Norse gods and would never become a baptised

Christian?'

He relaxed his grip and hugged her. 'Do not tease me about Freya; you know how much she means to me.'

As dawn broke, Ubba heard the bedroom door open. Once Freya spotted him she came running over to the bed and kissed him. He pulled her close and kissed her cheek. 'Oh, sweetheart, I am so glad to be back with you.'

'Daddy I knew you were safe, and I dreamt last night that you were around. Ralf told us about Frank and I knew you would be very sad to lose him. I was frightened you may have been injured getting away to the longboat.'

Ubba rolled the still-sleeping Torri over in the bed and made room for Freya to join them. She snuggled up to him. 'I met young King Edward and he said he would not harm me or Arne; he just wants to talk to you.'

'So I understand, sweetheart. But what did you think of him?'

'I thought he was young to be a king and I was cautious in my responses to his questions, but he did try to reassure both me and Arne that he intended us no harm.'

'Ah, but did you believe him?'

'I would like to, but he may be just trying to lure us in to trap you. I liked Aethelflaed and would be inclined to trust her more than him.'

'Good assessment, Freya. You are aware of the dangers and right to be cautious. You did not take the king at face value as you were aware he may be dangerous. Living in Ivar's court has taught you to evaluate the situation before trusting other people and that is a vital skill.'

'Well, there won't be many people who dare take Uncle Ivar at face value because of his reputation. I wonder if he is making new friends in Ireland?'

Ubba laughed, 'Probably many more enemies than friends. Not many get to know the real Ivar; he has been a master of disguise since he was a boy because he has spent all his life in pain. However, he let you, Arne and Viggo into his heart and I know he will protect Viggo with his life. It was not an easy decision for your mother or I to entrust him with Viggo, but it was politically necessary in case we all perish.'

TWENTY-FIVE

As the household started coming to life, Ubba disentangled himself from the bedclothes, then washed and dressed quickly and quietly. He needed to see Serena and commiserate with her over Frank's death. He made his way to her bedroom and knocked on the door.

She was propped up in bed, having only just woken. He ran across to her and scooped her into his arms. She whispered, 'Oh Ubba, thank God you are alive. I was beginning to fear for your safety too.'

'Serena, I am so sorry about Frank. We ran into a Mercian patrol and were outnumbered two to one. We were all fighting more than one man and Frank tried to prevent them from enclosing us in a full circle. I didn't see exactly what happened as I was being attacked by two opponents. He was to my left and then he disappeared; he must have been knocked from his horse. I saw Noir staggering to get up, then he followed Sleipnir as we jumped out of the field.'

Serena sobbed in his arms and he hugged her tightly. Finally, she calmed down.

Ubba continued, 'I know how much Frank cared for me and kept me safe, but I didn't want to lose him this way. We were so close to getting away without any casualties and then our luck ran out.'

'Ubba, Frank loved and respected you so much. He often said he would be willing to lay down his life for you. I know I charged him to protect you for my sake, but he was proud to serve you, along with all your men. No commander has ever been as loved by his troops as you are.'

The door opened. Astrid and Theo came running in. When they saw him they shouted, 'Daddy, you are home!' They were still in their nighties and he bundled them both into bed with Serena and cuddled them.

'I am home. I have work to do now, but I promise I will play with you later. You look after Mummy. She is sad about losing your Uncle Frank, but I am sure you can cheer her up.'

He went outside. Egil, Arne and Thorin were seeing to the horses and starting to turn them out. He hastened to Thorin's stable and told him to keep his horse in; he wanted him to ride to Jorvik and take a message to King Edward to arrange a meeting on his behalf.

When Arne heard, he said, 'I will go with Thorin, Father.'

'No you will not! Think about it, Arne. Did you not pay attention to Ivar's lessons about strategy and the politics of war? You are my son and you would be offering the Saxons a means of forcing me to do what they want if they were to take you prisoner.'

'But Edward said he would not harm me.'

Ubba interrupted, frustrated, 'But how can you trust him? He brought no troops here, but you would be walking straight into the lion's den. Thorin is Ralf's son and he won't harm him because he needs Ralf and Gytha's co-operation. You have to consider your safety; the repercussions of what you do affects the lives of our family. Do you think your brothers Erik, Refil and Viggo would take such a risk? Of course not! Use your brain and think ahead.'

Arne was furious. His blazing eyes and expression were identical to Ivar's when he lost his temper. 'Am I to suffer like you and my grandfather did, just because we are Ragnarssons? You don't like it any more than Ragnar did. You learnt from him how becoming a king deprives you of your personal liberty; that's why you have never wanted power and authority. I don't want it either!'

Ubba sighed. 'I am sorry Arne, but neither of us can escape our responsibilities and the pressure and expectation of being a son or grandson of Ragnar Lothbrok.'

Frustrated at his own stupidity, Arne lashed out with, 'And don't think I overlooked you choosing to save Viggo by sending him to Ireland, and not me! It's obvious all of you consider he will make a better king than I ever would!' He ran off before Ubba had time to respond.

He looked around and saw that Egil and Thorin had heard every word. He threw his arms in the air and said, 'That was never the case at all but he's not going to believe it now, is he?'

Egil said, 'The boy is angry, Ubba. He made a wrong decision and you called him out on it. He was furious at being found wanting by his father and he hit back to hurt you. He knows you love him and that Viggo went with Ivar so that one of them would survive if all your family died in battle here. Give him time to reflect. He may apologise, but he may be too afraid to try. Tell his mother; she will know the best way to deal with it.'

Ubba sighed. 'I will write a note to Edward for Thorin to deliver.' Just as he set off back to the house the longboat crew arrived for their breakfast, expecting to be leaving with Ubba's family and moving them to Richmond that day.

He ushered them inside and was relieved to find that Torri had anticipated that his crew would be coming; the cook had ensured plenty of bacon and eggs were sizzling in the fire pit. He went off in search of parchment, pen and ink and wrote a note inviting Edward and Aethelflaed to a meeting at Terrington at his convenience... but reiterating that if they came with a large escort he would assume it was a hostile gesture.

He hurried back to breakfast, ushered Thorin away from the table and handed him the note. 'If you want someone to accompany you to Jorvik you can take one of my crew. I shall remain here until we have had the meeting. King Edward should give you a response. Do not mention a word about moving up to Richmond. I don't know what I will be doing now, until I know what he wants. He won't risk attacking here as it's your father's home. Whilst you are waiting, amass as much information as you can without giving anything away.

Edward's counsellors do not know his plans for Jorvik.'

Thorin took the note and put it in the chest pocket of his tunic. 'I will do my best lord to assess the situation, and will keep a low profile.'

It wasn't until he and Torri climbed into bed that night that Ubba had chance to mention his row with Arne. Now they both had responsibilities keeping the house or farm running and few servants to rely on, they saw little of one another during the day. Ubba had decided that as he was going to be grounded here for a while, he would put his longboat crew to repairing some of Ralf's farm buildings and building a cattle byre to provide better shelter over the winter.

As they snuggled up together Ubba broached the subject, suspecting that Arne may have already told Torri. To his surprise he hadn't. Torri listened patiently to his version of events and was mortified that her eldest son thought they favoured Viggo over him.

'Oh, Ubba, he tries so hard to please you and if you had mentioned it to me first I could have predicted what Arne's response would be. I know you had to alert him to consider his own safety first, but he is only a teenage boy and his first thought was probably to keep Thorin company. He has never had to consider his position as a target before because up until now, you and Ivar have always been the key players. He hit back with a comment that he knew would hurt you. I don't think for a moment he believes it to be true. Let's be honest; if he wanted to call you out over favouritism then surely he would have attacked you over Freya rather than Viggo. There is always petty jealousy between siblings, not helped by the many historic rows between you and your brothers. I marvel that you all survived to adulthood considering you were constantly at each other's throats, with Ivar stirring the pot so frequently.'

Ubba turned over to face her and stroked her face. 'Do I really give Freya too much attention?'

'No, not really – you are just a besotted father with a beautiful wise daughter. You wear your heart on your sleeve. Freya is jealous when you spend time with Astrid and Theo because she doesn't want to share her daddy. I have talked to her about it and I will do the same with Arne.'

o0o

Two days later Ubba, Thorin and Arne rode out to meet King Edward, Aethelflaed, Lord Aldhelm, Ralf and Father Raymond about a mile from the farmhouse. As their party spotted them on the opposite hillside Edward felt a shiver running down his spine. *Supposing Ubba had a troop of men concealed in the woods behind, waiting for his order to attack.*

Edward turned to Father Raymond, 'Be it on your head if you have misjudged his character and we are all slain within the hour. I can't help but fear that if it was Ivar we were meeting, he would double-cross us without a doubt.'

Father Raymond replied, 'You have nothing to fear from Ubba; he is an honourable man and has given you his word, one commander to another.'

'Let us hope you are right Father, or England will never be created. I have not forgotten that you offered sanctuary to him at Roche Abbey when my troops came looking for him. How you gave protection to an outlaw, pagan, heathen and sworn enemy of your king in a Christian church requires some explanation, does it not? Let's hope your faith in him is justified and our meeting proves beneficial, or you will have some difficult questions to answer.'

'Lord king, Ubba is a twice baptised Christian and although he still serves his Norse gods, he is not entirely opposed to our beliefs. He has benefitted from learning about other religions when he has been in foreign countries.'

Edward laughed, 'But it didn't stop him killing them or raiding their land, did it?'

Aethelflaed interrupted, 'Oh, Edward, leave poor Father Raymond alone.'

Edward replied, 'Well, of course you already have a fascination for these Norsemen, but your trust may well be misplaced. At heart they are plunderers and murderers, which hardly demonstrates Christian tolerance or compassion. What say you Lord Aldhelm, as a true Saxon?'

Aldhelm replied, 'My lord king, they are indeed as you described, but it is difficult not to admire their courage, determination and skill in battle and not wish you could possess more of the same qualities.'

They were approaching the turn-off to the farm. Ubba's greeting party was assembled by the gate a few yards away. Edward had his first close-up view of Ubba. He could not help exclaiming, 'God, he is an imposing figure of a man – and the image of his father. What a magnificent grey stallion. I certainly envy him having such a fine beast, and he sits so still in the saddle; you cannot see him giving any aids to the horse.'

Ralf commented, 'The best horseman I have ever known, and I am honoured to have bred Sleipnir for him. They have an unbreakable bond and are like poetry in motion to behold.'

They paused at the gate and Ubba smiled at the group. 'King Edward of Wessex, we meet again after 12 years when I last recall teaching you sword fighting as a young boy. I hope you have improved significantly over the years.'

Edward smiled. 'Regrettably, I can't claim to be quite as proficient as you. I admit I am green with envy over your incredible stallion. What a magnificent warhorse he is, and Ralf assures me you have trained him to perfection.'

'Lady Aethelflaed, the last time I saw you was in sad circumstances. I hope your life has not been overwhelmed by your loss. I understand your marriage to Aethelred was not harmonious, but I am pleased to hear you now rule Mercia as its rightful queen.'

Aethelflaed beamed at Ubba. 'I was very impressed with Torri on my first meeting. She is a veritable tour de force and your children are an absolute credit to you both. Freya is very confident and knowledgeable for her young age.'

Ubba said, 'Thank you for your compliments my

lady, but Freya has hidden depths and can be quite a headstrong child.'

They entered the yard and Edward was concerned to see more men around than before. Ubba saw his discomfort and said, 'My lord king, these men are my boat crew, not warriors. You need not concern yourself about your safety. You came here on a peace mission and I guarantee your safety will be my top priority.'

Edward felt slightly embarrassed and said, 'Forgive me Ubba, but Ivar's reputation is difficult to dispel.'

'My brothers are all very individual men. You asked to meet Halfdan, but he is out of reach currently and even if he *were* available he would make his own mind up about your proposal and may not come to the same conclusion as me.'

Their horses taken care of, they moved into the house and through to the main hall. A small table was set up with honey cakes and refreshments and Torri approached the group indicating they should help themselves then sit at the large table.

Ubba watched Edward's reaction to Torri and noted the softness of his expression and eyes as he greeted her and kissed her hand. There was no doubt that Edward had fallen under her spell, which he hoped may be useful in their subsequent negotiations.

Edward presented Lord Aldhelm to Ubba. They had never met except across a battlefield. Aldhelm commented, 'A pleasure to finally meet the man who is such a legend – the "ultimate" warrior and commander. I have much admiration for your fastidious training of your troops and their devotion to serve you. Not many soldiers would be so willing to die for their leader; that alone gives you a huge advantage in the field.'

Ubba looked stunned. 'That is a fine compliment, Lord Aldhelm. Thank you.'

Father Raymond hugged him. 'Ubba, I prayed for your survival. Listen to King Edward. He is not asking for the Earth, just a reciprocal agreement.'

Edward spoke, 'Ubba, Father Raymond is your staunch supporter and speaks highly of you. Perhaps he too has fallen under your spell and you have deceived him just like your god Loki.'

Ubba laughed, 'I think you have a different agenda than your father, who would never have studied Norse mythology for fear it would taint his Christian beliefs. I make no secret of my religious beliefs, but I don't think our religions are as far apart as they used to be. Also, I am astounded that you have let your sister rule Mercia and Jorvik in her own right, though she is more than capable. Alfred would not have done that at any price.'

Edward smiled. 'Well I have to admit that your ability to read and write in both Latin and Saxon shows a desire to communicate, which we have never seen before. I commend you and your brother for embracing education and seeking knowledge; it can only lead to a greater understanding on both sides.'

TWENTY-SIX

Edward seated himself at the top of the table, with Ubba and Torri adjacent to him.

'I know you are anxious to know what sort of peace deal I wish to do with you Ubba. I hope you will consider it, as it is not as onerous as you may anticipate. I intend to make Aethelflaed Queen of Jorvik as well as Lady of Mercia. Lord Aldhelm will be remaining here to enforce her authority. I am mindful that Winchester is over 400 miles away from Jorvik and it will be difficult for me to administer from so far away. When setting out on this battle to drive Ivar and Halfdan out of Jorvik and Lincoln, I made sure that I had the number of soldiers available to do the job. It meant offering the Welsh an incentive to join us, but your reaction has rather thrown my plans into disarray.'

Ubba laughed. 'We wouldn't like you to think us predictable.'

Edward grinned. 'I have been keeping a close eye on your activities and have to admit that both Ivar and Halfdan have done well expanding their cities, protecting their boundaries, promoting trade and increasing the population. I must compliment you and Torri on steering Ivar in the right direction. Now that he has voluntarily moved to Ireland I feel disinclined to wage war on you or Halfdan. Who better to keep my enemies at bay than two Ragnarssons?

'Rumour has it that you Ubba wanted a more peaceful life without waging war. It would be extremely convenient for me if you both stayed in the North, preferably one on each coastline. You could keep the Scots at bay as well as deterring other marauding tribes such as Danes, the Irish and Welsh from invading my northern territories. Your mere presence would be enough to deter them; you may not even have to raise your sword.'

Ubba interrupted, 'But I do not wish to wage war on anybody. I want to enjoy raising my children, getting close to nature again, breeding horses and farming. I know how lucky I am to be alive and I want somewhere warmer than Jormund in which to do it. I will not be your hired sword or vassal Edward, I have had enough of that. I don't need money, power or authority; I just want peace.'

'But Ubba, I would not expect you to fight any battles. All I want is for you to keep a watchful eye on Jorvik and report any impending threats. I am prepared to give you land here in Yorkshire to do what you desire. Although, I am reliably informed that there are areas of Cumbria very reminiscent of your homeland with deep lakes, smaller mountains, fewer people and quick access to the West Coast. I believe that Durham may prove a happy hunting ground for Halfdan.'

Ubba laughed. 'Halfdan is very like Ivar in character.

He does not take well to boundaries, even if he is being given money to stay away. I cannot speak for him. He is his own man just like Ivar, and equally ambitious. He may just laugh in your face as he is quite capable of taking any land he covets if he wants to. Should Ivar or Halfdan decide to attempt to retake Jorvik and Lincoln, where does that leave me? I fought for them this time but if I am beholden to you then I would have to choose between Ragnarsson loyalty or my allegiance to you.'

There was unease in the room. All eyes were on Ubba and Edward. Torri flashed a worried glance at Ubba, fearing he would become angry.

Edward watched Ubba closely. 'Then Ubba, you will have to make up your mind. Does your desire to live a peaceful life outweigh your family loyalty? Are you really a peacemaker or will your years of honing your fighting skills and the prospect of fighting beside your brothers again be irresistible?'

'Clever question, but as I have not experienced being a farmer yet, it may be difficult to make that decision.'

Edward sighed. 'You may not want money, power or authority but you will want your children to achieve their ambitions – and without doubt, so will their mother.'

Torri responded angrily, her blue eyes flashing a warning to Edward, 'Ubba is quite capable of making his own decisions without reference to me.'

'Forgive me madam, but you have bred a dynasty of Ragnarssons and I think you will do anything in your power to promote their ambitions.'

Edward felt a touch of remorse. He had come here with the impression that Torri was the power behind all the Ragnarssons, but maybe he was wrong. There was no doubt that she had ambitions for her sons but perhaps she was driven by a desire to keep them alive rather than wanting them to be kings. She had seen enough good men die in battle to know how easily life could be lost. She saw her first husband murdered and blood eagled knowing her life and her unborn son's were likely to be next. She fought in some of the bloodiest battles at the side of Bjorn and then came back with the great heathen army, and Ubba, to avenge Ragnar's death, whereby she had lost her firstborn son. No wonder she had returned to Jormund with her four Ragnarrson boys, carrying a fifth child who would be her only daughter and last child. *Had she come back here because she loved and needed Ubba?* Their love radiated between them like an unseen force.

He remembered his father saying that Ragnar was never the same man after he took Aslaug as his wife when Lagertha lost three more of his children prior to birth. He was doing what all kings were supposed to – reproducing – but at a hell of a price by casting aside the woman he really loved. No wonder Ubba was a champion of women. He had witnessed firsthand the devastation his father had felt at the loss of Lagertha. Ubba had only been ten when he first travelled overseas with his father, and he'd had Lagertha to rear him at the same time as Bjorn. Rumours had circulated that when the news came that Lagertha had murdered

Aslaug, whilst Ivar threatened to kill her, Ubba would not back him. Now he realised why. Ivar realised that if he went after Lagertha then he would have Bjorn and Ubba to contend with, and he needed Ubba's battle skills here in Jorvik.

Ubba turned to Aethelflaed, 'My lady, I can assure you that I have no intention of attempting to become King of Jorvik, but I cannot speak for Ivar or Halfdan; they are their own men. I *can* say that I consider it highly unlikely that Ivar will return to these shores.'

Edward interrupted, 'Maybe not, but Sigtryggr might – and where would you stand then, Ubba?'

Ubba smiled. 'Sigtryggr is not my brother and it is well known that my relationship with him did not start off on the best footing.'

Edward noticed a flicker of remorse in Torri's deep blue eyes.

Ubba said, 'I will be seeing Halfdan soon and I will put your proposal to him and see if he wants to talk with you. I will not try to influence him in any direction; he has his own life to lead. I will not have an army at my disposal, but I would be prepared to warn Aethelflaed of any hostile enemies who may be planning to seize power in Jorvik. If necessary, I will help her by escorting her to safety to avoid her becoming a hostage. I don't want anything in return from you; I wish to live a quiet sheltered life.'

Lord Aldhelm said, 'I can't quite believe that a man of your reputation would be content to be a farmer for long. The thrill of battle is etched into your bones and you are at peak fitness – not a man approaching retirement.'

Ubba laughed. 'You compliment me on the one hand but call me a liar too. You have no idea what a lazy bastard I can be. Winters spent in the dark and cold of my birthplace fostered a love of being at home, tucked up in a warm bed and as far away from a battlefield as possible. I have three great passions in my life: my family, horses and women. I am not a natural warrior; I had to force myself to become one. I found some areas of it impossible to master but others came easily so I pursued those areas and become an expert in order to stay alive. That is what made me able to train other men to reach their potential. I accept my strengths and work hard to overcome my weaknesses.'

Edward said, 'You are a skilled communicator and I find it difficult to judge whether you are being genuinely open and honest or a skilled trickster like your god Loki.'

Ubba chuckled, 'If I had the power of Loki to conjure, hypnotise, levitate, shape shift and change sex, I would not have had to risk my life in countless muddy battles with humans. Unfortunately, I do not possess any of those powers. I am a mere mortal with a low pain threshold, who tries to stay alive.'

Aethelflaed said, 'So who are your heroes then, Ubba? Who has influenced your life most and whose path in life have you followed?'

'My lady, that is a very difficult question to answer as I have never really thought about it in that context. My father has been a great influence on my life, but I have tried not to make the same mistakes he did.

The shining light in my life is Torri. She has been the love of my life, the mother of my children, a wise queen and has the courage of a lion. She is the ultimate warrior, not me. I grew up with Bjorn and he was my hero. Whenever I was struggling he got me through whatever crisis it was, mostly throwing up in a longboat on the North Sea in a storm. On land I have perfect balance, but when I am at sea and it is rough I suffer the most debilitating sea sickness; I cannot even stand up. Without Lagertha and Bjorn I would have died on my first voyage over here. I am most definitely a land lubber and while I think of it, I wouldn't welcome a longboat funeral. Just bury me on top of a hill under the ground with a good view. My uncle Rollo was another hero and taught me a lot about fighting, as did Floki. I sympathised with Rollo's unenviable position as my father's brother. He wanted to create his own fame and fortune and I can appreciate what drove him to forge his own path in Frankia. The expectation of being the son or brother of a famous king is hard to come to terms with. You will always be judged against them and often found wanting.'

'How very true that is. My father was not the first-born son; his brother died in battle and he had to take the lead role. His strengths were not as a warrior but as a scholar and follower of Christ. He did not have a good constitution and he was often ill, but he had to keep going. I note Ubba you didn't mention Ivar as one of your heroes.'

'Very astute, Edward... but do not read anything

into that. Ivar and I have a complicated relationship. I spent a lot more time over here with my father and benefitted from Lagertha as a mother, along with Bjorn. Ivar has always been a little jealous of my closeness to Bjorn and after threatening to kill Lagertha because she killed our mother, he knows he has to tread a very careful line. Thankfully, she is back in Jormund and out of his reach. He knows never to provoke Bjorn – and to be fair, he has never taken it out on Bjorn's sons. He is mindful that the future line of our family relies on Bjorn and me.

'Our mother spent more time with Ivar than any of us because he was a cripple and needed her. He sees her as his champion and does not see the damage she caused in taking him away from Lagertha. Ivar suffers incredible pain every day of his life, but there is nothing wrong with his brain. He has his mad moments but there is a softer side to him. I have never referred to him as a cripple and when I would come home to Jormund he wanted to know every detail of what had happened over here. I have the greatest admiration for him coping with his constant pain and having the courage to overcome his disability. In many ways he is my hero; he has achieved his goal of becoming the most feared Dane of all.'

They broke for lunch as Serena brought in a large trencher of beef and vegetable stew. Edward made sure he maintained a conversation with Torri. His admiration for her was obvious. However, Torri wanted to have a private word with Aethelflaed. As luck would have it she was leaving the room. Torri excused herself, followed her out and showed her to the bathroom, then directed her to her bedroom on the pretext of a private chat.

Torri said, 'I am pleased to have some time alone with you Aethelflaed, and wanted to offer you a piece of advice.'

'I would be delighted to hear it Torri, from a woman who has married two Ragnarssons and borne five children to them as well as being Queen Consort to a third. Your tenacity to survive walking the tightrope between these strong volatile men has to be admired.'

'It hasn't come without many pitfalls, but I just wanted to say that I am delighted your brother is allowing you to rule Jorvik as Queen; it is very rare that a man gives power to a woman on her own. It does happen in our culture, but we maintain the right for women to retain their money and land both in divorce and after the death of a husband. I am not saying it will be easy, which is why you probably agreed to remain celibate as Lady of Mercia after your husband's death, and I know the relationship between the two of you was no love match. However, I must say again that without the love of Ubba it would have been very difficult for me.'

'But you had to put your children's lives before your own Torri, and although I had my daughter Aelfwynn you know she wasn't my husband's child.'

'I do, my lady. And if it is any real consolation to you, I can honestly say it would never have worked had he lived. At that particular time there was no way a Dane could take a Saxon princess and survive. It may well happen in the future as Edward has hinted regarding an alliance between our children – but not back then. Even your father would not have permitted it, and certainly never your mother. But you don't need to take a husband – just a lover to make you happy.'

'Torri, I could not do that as I have sworn an oath to remain single and celibate before God. My people must see me honour that vow.'

'But you are making a huge sacrifice as a woman, denying yourself the love of a good man and bearing children to him.'

'Perhaps, but I will at least be a queen in my own right and not governed by a man. Why did you permit Ubba to keep his mistress and bear more children?'

Torri laughed, 'Because I am a realist. I am ten years older than him and love the bones of him. I know he is my soulmate and the perfect husband, but my breeding days are over. He is a wonderful father and produces strong sound offspring. Ivar and Halfdan have no children, so why deny the best son of Ragnar the chance to reproduce?'

After lunch Edward proposed that he would like to accept Ubba's offer to be back-up protection for Aethelflaed and as he did not want to be beholden to him for land, he would allow him to settle within the Yorkshire area without fear of attack, provided Ubba did not raise or join an army attempting to invade Jorvik or Lincoln.

Aethelflaed confirmed that he would be welcome to visit her or reside temporarily with Ralf at either of his farms, but suggested he did not settle too close to Jorvik for fear of retaliation from other parties.

Ubba agreed and promised to inform Halfdan of Edward's request to discuss a similar arrangement with him. He suggested the meeting take place at Ralf's Haxby farm. He did not confirm where he himself would be living as yet, but assured Edward Ralf would be informed and could convey a message.

Edward confirmed he intended to return to Winchester within the next few weeks, when Aethelflaed's position as Queen of Jorvik had been declared.

TWENTY-SEVEN

Ivar ordered Viggo to stop his chariot on the bridge over the River Liffey flowing into Dublin. He looked across to the south bank, originally named Dubh Linn (black pool) after the lake where the Danes had first moored their boats and settled in the area. Since then small settlements had grown on both banks, reflecting the primitive lifestyles of the settlers. Ireland had never been invaded by the Romans so there were no two-storey stone buildings like in Jorvik and London; everything was constructed from wood. As settlements expanded they joined up on either riverbank. It was a thriving port and had a varied fishing fleet, hunting everything from shellfish to whales.

Ivar turned to Viggo, 'If someone wanted to invade Dublin using Greek fire the whole place would be destroyed in a day as there are no fire breaks or ramparts protecting the coastline. Once fire took hold, the whole city would be destroyed on both banks.'

'Perhaps, but maybe the city is too important as a trading centre for an enemy to risk destroying it. Look at the number of ships and boats moored here from Arabia, Constantinople and many European countries. You would be able to trade everything from silk to whale oil in this busy port.'

'It obviously rates very highly as a port and will have ample wood, wheat, wool, salted meat, fur, leather, fish and ivory to trade for slaves, silver, silk, spices, wine, jewellery, glass and pottery.'

'Are you thinking of becoming a trading merchant, Ivar?'

'No, I'm just impressed that ships from so far east want to trade here. It is so primitive compared to their majestic cities and it hasn't stopped raining since we arrived. Perhaps I am missing something. I need to do more research. Let's move on; we seem to be attracting some attention from passers-by.'

Viggo clicked and his horse moved off at a brisk trot. 'News of your arrival has spread, Ivar. Thankfully your reputation will keep you safe. One of the slave girls asked me if you molest a different virgin every night.'

Ivar laughed, 'Chance would be a fine thing! I have not indulged in sex since we arrived. Everyone assumed Aoife was my partner, but nothing would persuade me to enter her bedroom. I couldn't be sure I would get out alive. It amazes me how easily men fall for women like her. I knew she was a *volva* from the first day I met her. Shame I did not get an opportunity to drown the witch on the way over here. I haven't forgotten my promise to Halfdan, but I need Sigtryggr to find out more about disposing of her in case I make a wrong move. Ireland seems to be riddled with ghosts and spirits, so it does not surprise me that she was born here.'

What I can't understand is if she is a *volva,* how did

she produce a baby? She must be way past breeding age.'

'If they can metamorphose from an old hag into a beautiful woman to deceive someone then surely they can bear a child too. They are not human; they are witches.'

Viggo shivered. 'She certainly looks the part – but was the baby Halfdan's? What if she stole someone else's baby to pass off as his son?'

'That's why I am trying to get more information... but if Siegfrid is not his son then it will become obvious as he grows.'

They pulled into the stable yard and Viggo helped Ivar down from the chariot. He noted the effort it took his uncle, and he felt sorry for him as the constant damp weather was causing him more pain than usual. He helped Ivar into the hall and fetched him cushions and a stool to rest his sore legs on before dinner. Ivar was grateful for Viggo's care.

To his delight, Skye came into the room and his eyes lit up as there was nobody else around, just servants preparing food for the fire pit at the back of the hall. 'Ah, my beautiful girl. Can you spare me some of your precious time for a private chat?'

She laughed, 'For you Ivar, I will relinquish my cooking duties with glee.'

Viggo said, 'Right, I'll see you later at dinner.' He left quickly.

Ivar raised his eyebrows. 'Obviously he has some young lady to court. He is feeling his hormones racing even sooner than his father did.'

Skye giggled, 'Oh, Ivar, leave the lad alone – he is only just in his teens – I don't think sex will be on his mind at all yet.'

Ivar laughed, 'Skye, he has his father and grandfather's natural good looks and easy way with women. He is also very curious to experiment and see whether sex is all that it is made out to be. He might not know what he is doing yet but he is a very quick learner in any subject.'

'You are wicked Ivar, and far too interested in other people's sex lives.'

Ivar leant forward and pulled her closer to him. 'Perhaps, but I have been here nearly a month Skye, and neither you nor anyone else has mentioned your pregnancy. Why is that?'

Her mouth fell open and she was momentarily speechless. 'Damn it, Ivar. How did you know?'

'I only had to hug you when we first arrived to know that you are with child. Don't tell me it's not Sigtryggr's, as he won't be too pleased. I seem to have second sight when it comes to detecting pregnancies.'

'Ivar, of course it is his. I just haven't told him yet until I have proof. He won't be expecting it as we agreed not to try for a baby yet. It's me that messed it up and I just wanted to work out my own feelings before I tell him.'

Ivar hugged her. 'Sweetheart, why don't you want to tell him? You must have doubts if you are not happy to be carrying the child of the man you love.'

'Ivar, I know when I tell him he may well insist on marrying me, but I want to be sure he is fully committed to me before we take this next step. He has given me no cause to doubt his love, but I don't wish to rush into marriage and find it isn't working – or worse still, he ends up dead.'

'Skye, you have to live in the moment. You cannot fear living your life because one of you could end up dead. Death stalks all of us and very few will be able to predict the time of their own demise. If it happens Skye, nobody would be better equipped to cope with rearing a child alone than you. In fact, I can only think of one other woman and that is Torri, who has done it all her life. Now if you have other reasons to doubt Sigtryggr's love then you must raise them with him. He has confessed to me that he loves and adores you but admits he is slightly in awe of you. I told you that you would know immediately when you met the right man for you. Are you sure it is not other influences that are making you have doubts?'

'Oh Ivar, I don't know. I really do miss my home and family desperately. Ireland is more hostile than my beloved birthplace. I thought I could exist on love alone, but I hardly get to see him sometimes because he is so busy being a king and protecting his boundaries.'

Ivar chuckled, 'Oh, my dear, you are learning fast about the responsibilities and duties of kings. Believe me, it is not a great life. Why do you think my heroic big brother rejected it completely? He saw what happened to our father and knew instinctively that it wasn't the path in life he wanted to follow.'

'I guess I should have heeded Ubba's advice – instead of being carried away by my first love affair

I should have thought more about the people I left behind. I miss my mother so much. You don't realise until it is too late that you no longer have your mother in your life, who loves you unconditionally.'

'Take it from me, your mother found adjusting to your departure a very difficult transition, but she did it because she loves and trusts you. I think you need to find yourself a woman whom you can trust implicitly, who will help you through your transition to becoming a mother. Women bond in different ways to men. They need each other for support and succour. Ireland can be a hostile place, especially for women. It's a very male dominated environment and trouble can escalate quickly. Look how many fights and fallouts there are between the men here, escalated by the devil drink. Best friends have killed each other in drunken brawls. Every time a new ship or boat pulls into the docks there is excitement in the air about what they are carrying. That's before the arguments start about what the goods are worth, be it slaves or silver.'

'I am so glad you are here, Ivar. Nobody would ever believe that you could be so perceptive and kind. I will not ruin your wicked reputation as it will protect you from attack here – but do watch your back – there are always people wanting to annihilate rivals.'

'Oh, don't worry. I have lived with that all my life. Do not wait too long to tell Sigtryggr your news. If he thinks you are hiding it he may jump to the wrong conclusion.'

That evening Sigtryggr did not overindulge in drink

after the meal and Skye saw him casting several appraising glances at her, which usually indicated his desire. As she topped up the tankards with ale on the top table, when she poured more into his glass she felt his hand under her skirt, stroking her thigh. He whispered, 'Go to bed, darling. I will be with you shortly.'

She returned the jug to the kitchen and as she came out, she looked over at the table. Ivar was watching her with a raised eyebrow and a smile. *He didn't miss a thing!* She hastened to the bedroom and removed her clothes, but risked putting her nightgown on. She knew he hated her wearing anything in bed, but she could not refrain from covering her body as modesty required, even though he banished her from wearing it in bed. She washed her hands and face and went to the dressing table to release her hair. Sigtryggr adored her hair loose so he could run his fingers through its blonde tresses. He loved to see the combination of his red long curls combined with her silver blonde hair spread out on the pillow.

It had been a week since their last sex session; since Ivar had arrived Sigtryggr had been very busy and at night he indulged in long drinking sessions with Ivar when everyone else had gone to bed. By the time he made it to the bedroom she was fast asleep.

For all his height and size, Sigtryggr had always been a gentle lover. He had never hurt her and was always as concerned about giving her pleasure as taking his own. Most of the time he wooed her before taking her but occasionally, when his desire was uppermost, he took his first. Judging by the looks she had received tonight, she anticipated this would be one of those occasions.

Hopefully, this would be a good time to reveal her pregnancy. Her courses were only two weeks late, but she felt different already in her body and mind. She heard him coming down the corridor and prayed he would be pleased with her news and not angry.

He flung open the door, strode into the bedroom and leant over her, kneeling down and snatching her brush. 'I want to brush that beautiful golden hair.' He brushed her hair gently and with intimate tenderness, and she watched his whole body relax in the mirror as the image of the warrior transformed into a man besotted by the woman he touched. She had never found his scar and missing eye horrendous. Although he had evaded her touching it at first, when she had told him that it was an essential part of him that made him the man he was, he allowed her to touch the scar and kiss it. He had always been ashamed of it because it reminded him of his stupidity and close shave with death. Most women averted their eyes when they looked at him, but she showed neither pity nor revulsion.

He caressed the nape of her neck and gave her butterfly kisses. Suddenly, he groaned and said, 'How many times have I told you not to wear anything over your body? I need to touch your skin to connect with your delicious body. Why do you insist on hiding it away from me?' He pulled her nightgown over her head and tossed it into the corner of the room then continued, 'Look at you, Skye. You are more beautiful than the goddess Freya. Men would die just to see you naked, never mind possess you.' His hands cupped her breasts and her nipples responded and hardened. He turned her round on the stool to face him as his eyes drank in every inch of her upper body. He kissed her left breast and ran his tongue over her nipple.

She was now very aroused and undid his leather tunic. He sensed her desire and took over, removing all his clothing. She watched him and the passion in her eyes drove him into a frenzy. He knelt down, pulled her knees apart and buried his head between her thighs, searching with his tongue. She was soon screaming for release and he drove her to climax whilst desperately trying to preventing himself from coming. The moment she came he entered her and within a minute, he reached his climax. His knees were in danger of buckling on the rough wooden floor, so he stood up, gathered her in his arms, threw her onto the bed and sat astride her waist, intent on seeking his pleasure once more when his body had recovered.

He bent down and kissed her lips. 'Skye, you are the love of my life. Marry me now; I can't risk losing you. I need to know you are mine forever.'

She giggled, 'Is that a proposal, my love? Firstly, I need you to tell me exactly how much you love me, but straight from your heart. I will know if you are just trying to appease me with poetic words.'

'Skye, you know I am a man of few words, but I can show you so much better than telling you.' He leant forward to kiss her, but she pushed him away.

'You will have to do better than that. I know exactly what you are after and I can assure you that you will not possess my body until you have proclaimed your love for me in words. Now, why do you love me? Will you remain faithful to me or will you take your pleasure with other women as and when it suits you?'

'Skye, I am a Dane. I know the difference between sex and love and I cannot promise that if we were parted I could resist the urge for too long. Sex is as much a part of life as breathing is for a Dane. However, I love you passionately and want you to be my wife and bear my children. I want to make you my queen. Why would I stray from your beautiful body once you are mine for life?'

'Once you have married me and I am carrying your child, what if you do not crave my body anymore?'

He howled in frustration. 'I would never do that, Skye. I love you to the moon and back. I will worship you even more when you are carrying my children. I want you in my bed forever. No woman compares to you. I give you my life and my heart and will love you forever. What more do you want?'

'I want you to remain faithful to me. I could not bear to see another woman touch your body; it would drive me insane. I saw your reaction when one of your drunken men pinched my backside. You pinned his hand to the table with your trencher knife.'

'He was lucky; if he had really meant to hump you I would have blinded and castrated him right there on the table. No man touches my woman and lives.'

'But I don't want to be your possession. I am not

your dog, horse or sword – I need to be respected for the woman I am.'

Sigtryggr was now fuming, 'You would refuse to marry me unless I remain faithful to you? Have you gone mad, woman? I know that you love me; your body shivers when I touch you. We crave each other with equal passion. One of us cannot exist without possession of the other. There is already a bond woven between us and I will not let you go. If you refuse me I will confine you to a cell until you promise to marry me. You would turn me into a mad wicked evil man. Skye, you are frightening me now – don't turn me into a monster. Marry me! Please!'

He was still pinning her to the bed and she saw the tears in his eyes. She held up her hand and touched his cheek. 'Sigtryggr, you are right that there is already a bond between us. I am carrying your child and I will marry you because I love you unconditionally, but I have to know you love me too.'

A look of utter shock crossed his face. 'You are already pregnant with my son?' Suddenly, he realised he was sitting across her belly and rolled away from her. 'And all 15 stone of me has been sitting on him for the last half hour.'

They both roared with laughter and he hugged her tightly. She ventured a reproachful comment, 'It may be a girl, not a boy.'

He shook his head. 'I am the King and I command you to produce at least three boys before you have a girl. I also don't know whether there is a crown for the Queen of Dublin. The last king did not have a queen. Don't worry, I will have one made especially for you, my dear.'

TWENTY-EIGHT

Ivar, Viggo and Sigtryggr planned to visit some of the wealthy merchants who traded in Dublin. Sulamain was joining them to help with translation if necessary. He had moved in as a guest with an Arab, Ali Rahman, now settled in Dublin, who had worked for the same Arab sheik as he had many years ago. He had gained quite a reputation as a healer and had stayed in Dublin serving high status clients who could afford his treatment. Sulamain had been slightly appalled at the reduced facilities and lack of grandeur in the accommodation in Dublin. Compared to the grandeur of Alexandria, Constantinople, Rome and other more civilised cities in Europe, Dublin was way down the list of salubrious destinations. However, it had a vibrant multi-national population and an enviable reputation as a port where most items could be obtained at a fair price. It was also the starting point for journeys to Norway, Sweden, Denmark and expeditions to and from the Rus countries.

When Ivar joined them for breakfast he sensed a closeness between Skye and Sigtryggr and assumed she had broken the news, but nothing was mentioned. It was quite common for details of pregnancy to be kept quiet until they became obvious. Miscarriages were frequent in the early stages of pregnancy and parents tended to keep quiet for fear of losing a child prematurely.

The only hint of a change came when Sigtryggr announced that Skye would be joining them that day. Ivar reflected on this decision and concluded that Sigtryggr was intending to marry her and perhaps make her Queen. This would escalate her position in society from mistress to wife, and give her more status. However, as Ivar had learnt very quickly, King of Dublin tended to be a very short tenure indeed. In recent years there had been three different holders of the title. As Ubba would say, it was a very precarious throne to occupy. Although it would give Skye higher status, it would make her a target too. He would speak to Sigtryggr about this later, as he was very fond of Skye and felt duty bound to protect her.

When they met at the stables, Ivar was surprised to find he had been allocated a driver for his chariot and Viggo was given a bay horse to escort him and a raven banner to carry. Skye appeared in a beautiful blue hooded cloak and mounted a spirited dappled grey Irish mare, which matched Sigtryggr's grey heavyweight stallion. Six personal guards escorted them carrying Sigtryggr's banner displaying two ravens and a snake entwined around an axe in the centre. Ivar smiled when he saw the snake as he thought it was very apt and showed Sigtryggr's true character. He was not a man to cross and he was warning his enemies of that. This was definitely a show of power and strength and would be quite intimidating to the people of Dublin. Sigtryggr was announcing that Ivar's arrival in Dublin strengthened his hold over the city and that, perhaps, his ambitions extended further than that. Even Sulamain and his page were given Arab horses to impress their status and show their attachment to Ivar.

Ivar was impressed that Sigtryggr was quick to launch a campaign to show Dublin was now secure in the hands of Danes, and that he would give the ancient clans who ruled some areas of Ireland a warning that he intended to go further than Dublin. Ivar hoped he had the troops required to back him up. People knew Ivar had landed without an army, but they might just be fooled into thinking there was one due to arrive soon.

Their procession soon stimulated interest as they paraded through the city. Crowds gathered to watch and Ivar heard his full name shouted frequently as they trotted along the roads towards the docks.

Their first stop was at a wine merchant. The owners were overcome by the sudden unannounced arrival of their king and the treacherous Ivar the Boneless. Ivar laughed at the cleverness of Sigtryggr, forcing them into treating them as honoured guests, and was determined to ensure he came away with a free crate of French wine with the promise of more to follow.

They were ushered into a large office. Staff hurried to prepare refreshments for their honoured guests. They had no option but to offer their best wines to the King and his party.

Ivar whispered, 'You crafty, clever bastard. I know

exactly what you are doing – and why.'

Sigtryggr whispered, 'I need your help here. You do speak fluent French, don't you? Because the owners are French.'

Ivar nodded as Sigtryggr was shown to the top seat of the boardroom table and he was ushered to sit beside Skye, with Viggo next to him. The owner of the business and his son were sitting directly opposite and Ivar had to stop himself laughing at the fear and desperation on their faces.

Sigtryggr started to make introductions and as Ivar was introduced, he addressed them in French.

The owner Monsieur Beaumond was speechless for a second but said, 'You speak French, Ivar?'

Ivar replied, 'I find it necessary to study the language of the people I deal with, so nobody can misunderstand what is being said in negotiations.'

Sigtryggr continued, introducing Skye and then Viggo. Monsieur Beaumond interrupted and said, 'You are Ivar's son then, Viggo?'

Viggo replied, 'No, his nephew. My father is Ubba Ragnarsson.'

There was total silence as the merchants realised that they were in the presence of not only Sigtryggr of Dublin but Ivar the Boneless, and the son of Ubba Ragnarsson – the most feared warriors in Europe.

In a slightly squeaky voice Monsieur Beaumond asked, 'And will your father be joining you over here too?'

Ivar nudged Viggo's leg but he had already realised what Sigtryggr was doing and couldn't resist joining in.

'Perhaps he and Halfdan my uncle will join us soon.'

Beaumond replied, 'What a shame I may be leaving Dublin sooner than anticipated for France, and may not be here when they arrive.'

Ivar had to pinch himself to keep his composure and he could feel Viggo's body shaking with laughter next to him, although his face betrayed nothing. They sampled the delicious Bordeaux wine on offer and before they left, Sigtryggr had negotiated an excellent contract with them for supplying wine and spirits to the King at a very reasonable rate.

As they went outside to the horses Ivar collared Sigtryggr. 'Where next, you evil son of a bitch?'

He replied, 'We have a busy schedule – next is an Italian merchant. I have a desperate need for marble, armour and clothes. I have a new palace to build, a wife to dress like a queen, and I may need plentiful supplies of armour and weapons to ensure I achieve my next target.'

'I am so impressed with your ability to plan ahead, using your title and my reputation to pay a bargain price to acquire the goods you need. I can hardly believe your audacity and skill. Well done!'

Their last visit was to a Norseman who ran a very successful slave trade business. Ivar could not quite see why Sigtryggr was coming here unless it was to look for potential slaves to build and staff his new palace, but it was surely too soon for that. Their accommodation was full to bursting as it was, but he obviously had his reasons.

The owner was called Axel Haroldsson. He had

started his career as a sailor and after working for several bosses who were trading slaves, he realised it was easier money than risking drowning in turbulent seas. He was in his fifties and mainly bought slaves in the ports he visited when carrying cargo for other people. Slave trading depended purely on the availability of good slaves and he soon realised there was a ready market for strong young men and teenage girls – preferably virgins. He had not met Sigtryggr before, but he had met Bjorn Ironside in Norway and knew all about Ivar.

Axel offered to show them round his pens, but suggested that Skye should remain in the house. She flatly refused as she felt that as future queen of Dublin, she should know exactly what conditions these people endured. After all, she had nearly ended up as one herself. Sigtryggr tried to persuade her to stay and pleaded with Ivar to back him up.

Ivar intervened on the grounds that he would never allow a daughter of his to do this and said she should remain with the ladies in the house. She was not pleased; Ivar knew she would berate him later.

Axel showed them round. The slaves were not chained and they were well clothed and fed. He had two black African men in their twenties whom he had bought in Morocco. They would make him good money as farm labourers and he was waiting for a buyer to come and see them. Sigtryggr said he would need building labourers for a project next spring and asked him to keep an eye out for any men that would be able to do the job.

They went back to the house, where sweetmeats

and wine had been prepared for their indulgence. Even Ivar was beginning to feel slightly tipsy after all the wine and ale they had consumed throughout the day.

Axel made a point of sitting next to him. 'So finally, I meet the renowned Ivar the Boneless. I met a relative of yours this summer in Oslo. He was singing your praises! Admittedly, he was drunk, but they were still compliments.'

Ivar grinned. He rather liked the wit and humour of Axel. 'And who would that be, then?'

'Bjorn Ironside, your half-brother whom you are reputedly not a fan of. He claims you and Ubba saved his life last year and turned his sons from boys to men.'

'He is not lying, but we wouldn't have succeeded without Sulamain over there. He knew how to treat the disease. I only appealed to Odin for his life, and he granted it. He is my brother and a son of Ragnar who follows in his footsteps and I was happy to educate my nephews. How is Bjorn the Bear? Has he conquered Norway yet?'

Axel smiled, 'Not quite. In Norway a king has to be elected by the ruling jarls. He was runner-up in the election to Olaf, who now reigns as King. Bjorn is licking his wounds with Sigurd your brother, who is now King of Zealand in Denmark.'

Ivar was stunned by Axel's news. 'That will have shattered my brother's ego, but he can play a waiting game. Olaf must be 20 years older than Bjorn. I am sure Olaf's life will be shortened knowing that Bjorn Ironside is coveting his throne. I can't believe that Sigurd has become a king.'

'Well, Bjorn's not the only Ragnarsson to have had his wings clipped, is he? You and Halfdan lost your thrones to the boy king Edward of Wessex.'

Ivar gasped and glared at Axel. 'You are either a very brave man or a raving lunatic. I have been in Ireland a month now and nobody has dared even raise the subject with me.'

Axel laughed, 'I only speak the truth, Ivar. Accepting defeat is hard for most men, but in your case as it is only your first ever defeat, I'm sure the wound still festers. What I want to know is how you will take your revenge, and why you have come to Ireland.'

Ivar patted Axel's shoulder. 'I like your courage and curiosity Axel. I think we could become good friends, provided you can cope with my moods and temper.'

Ivar had noticed one of the servants topping up the food platters and he was intrigued. She looked to be around twenty and had a very fair complexion, white blonde hair and deep blue eyes.

Axel noticed Ivar looking. 'No, Ivar, she is not the woman for you. She serves in my household and has caused me no end of trouble since I bought her three years ago.'

'She is your mistress then? Is she a Dane?'

'No way! She is the most vicious untamable bitch I have ever encountered. She claims she is a Rus Princess called Irina, captured by bandits on her way to marry the younger son of the King of Kiev. She is beautiful to look at, but she is dead inside. She will have been raped many times by her captors and has been beaten and close to death. I found her dying in a slave shipment that came to Oslo from Rus. Like a fool I thought I could nurse her back to health. I put her body back together but could not heal her mind.

'She submits her body, but never her mind, and she never breeds. I have sold her twice and had her brought back because she won't breed. She may well be lying about her background but she was obviously born to a wealthy family. Her mind could not cope with reality and so she has shut down. I sold her to a Frankian who actually fell in love with her and treated her like a princess, but she never enjoyed sex – and despite all his efforts, he brought her back. I persuaded her to become a servant to my wife and promised not to sell her again provided she did her job. She is the happiest I have seen her but despite men begging to marry her, she will not contemplate a husband.'

Ivar was intrigued. 'What a desperately sad story; she must have been terrified. Did she try to get away or take her own life?'

'When I bought her, she had been owned by whoremasters and because she refused to give pleasure to a man, she was forced. When she was given to a client she lay there and let them do what they wanted to her, but would never respond to their requests. Believe me, I have tried to get her to breed; she would have a better life than becoming a whore. She tried to hang herself when she was a whore, but she doesn't respond to any of my kindness. She has adopted a stray puppy that came here looking for food. She was so animated by him that I let her keep him. She speaks to him in her native tongue and genuinely loves him.

Thankfully, he is only a small dog; she carries him around with her so the big hounds can't get at him.'

'Is there any way of knowing whether her claims to be a princess are true?'

'None at all. Forgive me Ivar, but I understood that your interest lay in young girls rather than barren troublemakers – even if they do resemble Freya. She is a manipulative hellcat. She pretends she cannot speak our language and even feigns deafness, but I have observed she understands Greek, Italian and French, so perhaps she *was* a highly educated princess... but believe me, she's not for you.'

Sigtryggr and Skye came over to them. Sigtryggr said, 'Well, Ivar, what do you think of this ugly rogue then?'

'I think he is very lucky to have his head attached to his shoulders still. He certainly does not hold back on the insults, even knowing my wicked reputation. It didn't stop him pointing out that I lost Jorvik to the boy king of Wessex without a fight.'

Sigtryggr gasped. 'Hell fire, Axel! You were pushing your luck there, especially as it is not strictly true; it could be interpreted that you were accusing Ivar of cowardice. He took a sensible tactical decision that due to the mass of the armies opposing him he would not win, and withdrew.'

Axel grinned. 'I know, and he took it like a man, although defeat does not sit well on the shoulders of a Ragnarsson for long. I was just interested in knowing why he chose Ireland for refuge rather than going home to Denmark. I will be able to spend many nights around the fire pit this winter telling the tale of insulting Ivar the Boneless and surviving.'

Ivar chuckled, 'Don't speak too soon, Axel. I spent many years dreaming up horrendous slow torture methods for my enemies. I can be very patient at exacting revenge, but I rarely forgive or forget someone who crosses me.'

'I would much rather have you as a friend than an enemy and I am at your service should you need passage back to Denmark at any time.'

TWENTY-NINE

They returned to the less-than-imposing residence of the King of Dublin. Sigtryggr came over to Ivar as he was dismounting from his chariot.

'Ivar, I need your help designing my new palace. Did you take notice of how the Romans constructed your palace in Jorvik?'

'Funnily enough I had other more pressing jobs to do when I arrived in Jorvik. I am no architect, but Viggo showed talent when drawing some of the Roman buildings in Jorvik. I am sure he could work with you and an experienced stonemason to design something fit for purpose.'

At dinner that night they celebrated Sigtryggr's inspired method of securing the goods and materials he required. As they had been drinking for most of the day, they were all in good spirits. Ivar retold Viggo's inspired comments at the wine merchants suggesting that Ubba and Halfdan may be joining them in Ireland. Sigtryggr, keen to plan his new residence, spirited Viggo off to his office to discuss plans.

Ivar and Skye were left alone at the top table. Shielded by the general noise Ivar risked asking Skye how Sigtryggr had taken her news.

'He took it very well actually. He begged me to

marry him and promised to make me his queen. The only bone of contention was that he would not promise to be faithful to me forever.'

Ivar laughed, 'Oh, Skye, you cannot impose your Saxon vow of fidelity on a Dane. Sex and love are two very different activities to us. Sigtryggr does not have a reputation as a womaniser. He thinks with his head, not his cock... and since he met you, why would he wander from the bed of such an angel in search of other sexual conquests? Learn from the greatest queen and most beautiful woman I know –Torri – that imposing fidelity on a husband when apart is just not achievable.

'Look at Torri and Ubba. They have a perfect relationship and Torri turned Serena to her own advantage. Ubba worships her but could never declare total fidelity. For a start, the night before a battle Ubba will seek sex to remind him physically what life means to him. He will use any available woman if Torri is not there. It doesn't mean he doesn't love Torri; he just needs the comfort sex brings him. Now, Bjorn regards sex as food – essential to function, but he craves variety and could never be faithful to one woman exclusively. Don't ruin your life with Sigtryggr by worrying about other women. It is within your power to keep him in your bed. You just have to be inventive, unpredictable and very clever. You have all those qualities; just use them.'

'Oh, Ivar, what would I do without your comforting words and advice? But surely not all Danes are incapable of being faithful to their wife? I don't think my father ever cheated on my mother... at least I hope not.'

Ivar laughed, 'Even I would think twice before cheating on your mother. She would rip the balls off a man with her hand. She doesn't need a sword like Torri. Ralf knows his limits and would never break his marriage vows. He does love her very much and she has made him very happy. He coped admirably accepting Thorin into his family, too... but as the years go by it becomes clearer that Thorin was not sired by Thorsten. Odin sent Thorin here on a mission, and I suspect it was to protect Freya.'

'Do you think Freya is Ubba's child?'

'She definitely has Ubba's genes. I did ask Torri if there was a chance that Odin may have intervened when she was carrying Freya. She admitted she'd had some very strange dreams during her early pregnancy and was so sick on the voyage home she feared she may lose the child, so prayed to the gods for help. Perhaps Njord intervened on Odin's instructions.'

'I know Freya is very forward for her years. She didn't have the benefit of the education of her brothers, but she is very bright and perceptive. Does Ubba think she may have been sent by Odin?'

'Yes, I think he does, and he fears that she will leave at a young age to follow her destiny.'

'Oh, I do miss Ubba. He was another friend and confidante who supported me even though he was not convinced about Sigtryggr being the right man for me.'

'I miss him too, and worry for his future. Edward

is Alfred's son and will be well versed in manipulating people. I sincerely hope Ubba can see through any plots and machinations as he tends to take people at face value... unlike me, always looking for sinister motives.'

'Well, you let Axel live when he insulted you today, which surprised me.'

'I could hardly have murdered him in his own home, and he is entitled to his opinion. It does grieve me to lose Jorvik – it had many advantages as a base – but I don't intend to give up on it. Let's just say it features in my future plans. Axel may well be useful to me and he will keep me informed about what is happening in Norway and Denmark. He told me that Bjorn failed to become King of Norway because Olaf won the votes of the other kings. My brother Sigurd has also become King of Zealand, although I believe it only consists of three small islands!'

'Might you go back to Denmark then?'

'I will if it doesn't stop raining soon. It's only September and I am sure it has rained some part of every day since I arrived. No wonder the land is so green and fertile; these mythical Irish fairies water it every bloody day. It is no surprise the Romans never bothered conquering it.'

'Oh, Ivar, you do cheer me up; it's so nice to have you here. Please don't go back to Denmark. Stay with me and promise to make me laugh every day. Seriously though, I have a favour to ask of you. Our wedding will have to take place soon as Sigtryggr wants no doubts raised over the legitimacy of his son. There's no way my family will be able to come over for the wedding. Both of us would be honoured if you would represent my father and give me away.'

'Of course I will, sweetheart. You are as close as I am going to get to having a daughter, and I couldn't be happier. Perhaps being half-Saxon rather than full Dane is a shame, but you have more than enough Dane in you to make your mark as a queen. I trust you have discussed this with Sigtryggr?'

'He suggested it! You know how he looks up to you Ivar; you are his hero. He commands me to bear him three sons before a daughter – but how can I do that? Is not the sex of a child determined by the male? How can I influence the outcome? It is up to Sigtryggr, not me. If he intends to keep me breeding permanently I will get fat and he won't love me anymore and will seek out other prettier women.' Her emotions took over and she burst into tears.

Ivar hugged her, 'Now stop being a drama queen, Skye. He is only being mindful of his duties as a king. You have to produce male heirs to tighten your grip on the throne. Unfortunately, that's one area I failed in, which is why I have educated my nephews to prepare them for their roles as future kings. I am sure the pair of you will have no problems producing three red-haired healthy little Irish savages over the next few years.'

'Oh no, I forgot about that! Is red hair more dominant than blond? Redheads are renowned for their short temper and stubbornness. My father always moaned if the mares produced chestnut foals

– especially fillies. He said they were flighty and useless for driving and dangerous for riding, especially when in season.'

Ivar laughed, 'What a prospect! You make me want to stay around to see your brood of little Sigtryggrs, to see how he is at stamping his stock. If you get a blond blue-eyed child I suggest you keep it separate from the others for fear they will kill it. Just remember, though... I probably have the shortest temper of most men, and I don't have red hair. In fact, my mother had luscious long red hair but did not produce one red-haired child with Ragnar. Halfdan had flashes of red hair but it petered out when he aged. Ubba and Sigurd were blond like my father and Halfdan and I ended up with brown hair. We are both showing signs of grey now we are deposed kings.'

'Oh, Ivar, you made the right decision and lived to fight another day. What's more, you saved hundreds of lives and left Jorvik standing. Ubba and Halfdan are more than capable of outwitting the young King Edward. Don't forget the female players in this game – my mother and Torri. Between them all they will outwit Edward; he doesn't stand a chance!'

The next day Sigtryggr and Ivar had some rare time alone together and Ivar decided to tell him of his anxiety about Skye. Judging Sigtryggr's mood was hard as he could be loud and happy one day, then hardly speak the next. Ivar knew that the pressure of being King affected people in many different ways. The one thing he had learned was that bottling it all up only increased the pressure. He had found that talking matters over with Ubba and Torri calmed him down, resulting in him making better decisions. However, Sigtryggr did not take criticism any better than he did, so he was mindful not to anger him.

Sigtryggr thanked him for agreeing to represent Ralf at the wedding, which gave him an opening.

'I don't want you to take offence, but I have to say I find Skye seems to have lost her self-confidence. She appears lonely and anxious at times. I knew she would underestimate the loss of her family and environment in coming over here, but I did not expect to find her mentally so low. Ireland can feel quite a threatening place at times and women need other women around them for support. She does not even have her own servant, or any female friends. I don't find the Irish people intimidating, even though they may be frightened of me; they are family orientated.'

Ivar saw anger flick across Sigtryggr's face but then he gave a deep sigh and put his hands up. 'For someone who has no wife you possess considerable knowledge of women's relationships within the home. I admit I am guilty of not ensuring she has enough support. Initially she was content to devote her time to me and because of my duties as a leader, I have had little time with her and failed to see that she was not thriving alone. How do you suggest I remedy the situation?'

'She needs a mother figure she can rely on to get her through her pregnancy, for a start. They should be a female who is not a relative of yours and will not report her every move to you – someone she can trust who has children of her own and can teach her how to be a mother. She needs privacy and time to adjust to being a queen. She may be twenty years old, but she was never bred to become a queen. She will have to learn from experience alone.'

'Many women of her age would have bred three or four children by now over here; surely motherhood comes naturally?'

Ivar's temper was beginning to rise. 'Do you want a wife or a bloody broodmare? You have already frightened her half to death by demanding three sons and no daughters. Look at her! If you wanted a broodmare she hardly fits the bill. She cannot weigh more than eight stone and hardly has the hips required to breed easily. You are at least 6ft 4 inches, probably 16 stone and have the longest legs I have ever seen. Were you descended from giants, by any chance? You must have bred some offspring by now. How many of their mothers survived the birth?'

Sigtryggr was fuming. He was contemplating raising his seax but Ivar spotted him. 'I have only ever let one person live after attempting to kill me and I can assure you I can beat you at throwing an axe. I am trying to help you see the potential problems Skye may face in bearing your children.'

'My first ever conquest at sixteen was a young Frankian thrall. Both her and the baby died during the birth. I avoided virgins after that. I don't sleep around; I need time to establish a relationship with a woman. Do not assume all the red-haired tall boys in Dublin have anything to do with me. I think I may possibly have sired two boys in my early twenties but since I met Skye, I have not touched another woman. I am afraid I don't have Ubba's fertility success rate, so I was greatly overestimating my chances of siring three boys in three years. But surely if Skye's mother produced Ranulf and Thorin then Skye will have no problem?'

Ivar shook his head. 'Actually, she struggled birthing Ranulf and was then assumed sterile. It was only after slave traders took her that she conceived Thorin –and she very nearly died having him. Ubba was there and said it was far worse a bloodbath than in a shield wall.'

'I am sorry. I should have realised how much she missed her family. Like all arrogant men I assumed that I alone was capable of making her happy. I do love her, you know – she's very special and makes me feel safe and content when she is in my arms. I am very gentle with her and not a selfish lover. I promise I will find her a companion of her choice and when the baby is due I will hire a wet nurse to take the strain of feeding. I will ensure she has private rooms and a nursery in my new palace. Who would believe it – Ivar the Boneless, a champion of women?'

Ivar laughed, 'I don't think I quite deserve that accolade, but I do agree with Ubba that they are the brave and courageous ones – not men. They keep going when we leave on raiding missions, and have to fend for themselves in freezing weather as well as keeping their children fed and safe. Skye is not going to take well to you going into battle; she is already terrified of losing you.'

'I have no intention of her being anywhere near a battle, but she will become a target as my queen. I was hoping to leave her under your care and protection. By the way, Viggo has asked if he can fight in the next battle.'

Ivar was appalled. 'What? He's here under my protection and he is still only twelve. Ubba will go berserk if he gets injured or killed.'

'Calm down, Ivar. I was not intending to put him in a shield wall or as a frontline warrior. He would just be holding horses, keeping out of trouble. He is good, you know; Ubba trained him well. He is very quick at picking up what is going on around him. He can fight better than some of my men with a sword and he is a crack shot with a bow and arrow, and a seax.'

'Thank God for that. I taught him to shoot and throw a seax. He is not the scout or tracker Ubba and Arne are, but he is a brilliant strategist. He can quickly assess the best position to fight from. Always, he has a twist up his sleeve to evade trouble; he uses his head and stays calm. But I can't have him killed in a bog in Ireland. The boy needs to expand his knowledge of the world and will be successful wherever he settles. The gods will guide him to his destiny when he is ready.'

'And will Arne be as good as Ubba in time?'

Unfortunately, he has my quick temper and he and Ubba have drawn swords several times. He resents his birthright in some ways. He thinks Ubba lacks ambition for rejecting being a king. He is too young to appreciate the many disadvantages of being a king. He does have ambition and survived growing up behind

Erik and Refil, who are Bjorn's sons. Erik will be an explorer and Refil is a very skilled sailor. They both have Bjorn's curiosity to see what is around the next bay, and they have his courage and determination.'

THIRTY

After they arrived in Dublin, Aoife had only stayed with them for three days, insisting she go to find her family who lived near Wexford in the Kingdom of Leinster, which was south of Dublin on the East Coast of Ireland. She had sensed that Ivar was a threat and wanted to put as much distance as she could between them.

Ivar told Sigtryggr all about Aoife. Between them they had hatched a plan to keep a careful watch on her and if necessary, arrange for her to meet her death under the right circumstances. Sigtryggr volunteered two of his men to accompany her to Wexford and keep a careful watch on her.

Sigtryggr also knew of female seers and witches who would know how to deal with her. It was agreed that when they had the acquired knowledge, they would make a move against her if necessary.

Aoife was happy to have an escort in this strange mythical land; as a woman on her own, she was a target for trouble. The two men chosen to escort her were more than delighted to accompany this beautiful woman anywhere she wanted to go.

Ivar and Sigtryggr were going to visit a seeress who they hoped would advise them on how to proceed with Aoife. She lived about five miles out of Dublin, up in the hills. Viggo accompanied them, along with an escort. Ivar was driven in his chariot as the terrain was quite uneven across very narrow tracks.

They crossed a valley bottom and the ground was getting wetter and softer. Sigtryggr called them to a halt and sent two scouts ahead to guide them onto a safe pathway. He turned to Ivar and Viggo. 'This is dangerous terrain; it is turning into a bog. You must understand how dangerous an Irish peat bog can be. If you fall into a bog your chances of survival are practically nil. It may look like grassy turf, but it is moss and can actually be floating on the bog. If a horse steps on it and it sinks, you will soon be in trouble. Irish horses bred in these lowland areas can become instinctively aware of the presence of a bog. They don't smell strong, but a horse can sense them. If your horse ever stops and refuses to go forward, do not assume he is misbehaving.'

Viggo said, 'What happens?'

'The same as if you get stuck in quicksand, but with even less chance of staying alive. I have seen a man and his horse disappear in less than five minutes. We all carry a rope attached to our saddles whenever riding in this environment and only ride in single file. If the bog is deep then you will have no solid ground to give you purchase. Watch for rushes; there is always water beneath them and they should act as a warning. Again, if there is mist low in the valley it is a sign that water is below. If you have to ride at night you can only do it with flaming torches and scouts marking the route.'

Ivar replied, 'What a damnable place Ireland can be. No wonder it is underpopulated.'

Sigtryggr laughed, 'Peat bogs have one distinct advantage for us natives.'

Viggo replied, 'I can't imagine what it would be?'

Sigtryggr laughed, 'We can lure the enemy into them and wipe them out very quickly without losing a man. We also have coastal areas where rocks stick out into the sea, forming an underwater shelf. A village built along the coastline will attract invaders and then their longboats get smashed on the shelf long before they reach the shore.'

Ivar commented, 'All that to contend with – and permanent rain. Funny how you never mentioned this before.'

Sigtryggr chuckled, 'The West Coast of Ireland is warmer than this coastline, but we don't get frozen solid in winter for long periods like you do in Jormund. However, we do get more than our share of rainfall.'

They arrived at the hidden village halfway up a steep hill where craggy cliffs opened into caves and the occupants lived deep inside. Viggo was not amused when he had to remain outside with the escort. Ivar did not want him to hear what the seeress had to say about disposing of Aoife.

They were led into the cave and the seeress greeted them around a fire pit. They were offered a warm drink, and toasted bread and cheese to eat. The seeress was in her fifties with long silver hair. Her right eye was missing. Sigtryggr greeted her with a kiss to her hand. There was obviously a rapport between them.

Sigtryggr said, 'Morgana, may I introduce you to the renowned Ivar the Boneless.'

'At last I see you in the flesh, Ivar. I have only seen you in my mind before. Welcome to Ireland.' She held out her hand. Ivar kissed it and felt something like a bolt of electricity pass between them.

Sigtryggr said, 'Ivar is not too keen on the Irish weather or our bogs.'

Ivar was still in shock. As he had kissed her hand, her face had transformed into the image of who she had been 30 years ago.

Morgana laughed, 'I see you too have the sight Ivar. Did you like what you saw? You have a direct link to Odin – but where did that come from?'

'I don't know for sure. Probably my mother; she was known for her link with the gods and her knowledge of the dark arts.'

Morgana replied, 'I sense you are aware of your sight but hesitant to pursue going further down the path of enlightenment. Now, how can I help you with this witch who is posing a threat? I need to put my hand on your head and then you can tell me your problems.'

Ivar consented and proceeded to tell her about Aoife, Halfdan and baby Siegfrid. After his long explanation she removed her hand and said, 'What do you want to do about her, and why do you seek to destroy her?'

Ivar replied, 'I fear she will be a permanent threat to my brother and may use her child to destroy him. If the only way to prevent that is destroying her then

I will do it.'

'Ivar, I don't see her future bound to you, Halfdan or her son. She knows you have the sight and recognised her immediately as a witch. The deal with Halfdan to bear him a child for money was completed. He got a baby in exchange for money, so both of them got what they wanted from the deal. She also returned to Ireland, which was a bonus to her. If you attempt to kill her then you will be interfering in something that has nothing to do with you. The baby is Halfdan's and she was just the bearer. I do not see him as a seer with second sight. He is an innocent child whose life will be influenced by those closest to him. She does not want to have him back or destroy him. If you step forward and harm her then you will be in the firing line. Her death is coming soon, but not by your hand. Be patient and let her destiny play out. The Norns do not have your life entwined with hers.'

'So you are telling me to back off because I will have other enemies who will do me more harm?'

She smiled, 'You have spent your life fighting the demons in your head and your body Ivar, to prove you can overcome severe disability and achieve your ambitions. You have become the most feared Norseman, but underneath there is still a very vulnerable man who is not as wicked as he likes to make out.'

Perhaps, but I can't have everything. I have to make do with the life I have got.'

'I watched you approaching. There was a young man with you on a grey horse; I would like to meet him.'

'But why?'

Morgana touched his arm. 'Humour me Ivar, but don't tell me anything about him.'

Sigtryggr went to fetch him. Viggo came bounding in, full of energy and glad to be out of the rain.

Morgana said, 'Young man, come and sit next to me and let me touch your head. I do not intend to harm you; I am just interested in meeting you. Let's call it a little game.' Viggo looked to Ivar for confirmation and he nodded his head. Morgana put her hand on his head and looked him straight in the eyes. She appeared to drift into a trance with her eyes closed for a few minutes. Then she spoke, 'You certainly have a lot of travelling to do in many interesting places. I thought you may be Ivar's son but then I saw an image of your father and it was not Ivar – possibly his brother. You and Ivar have a strong connection and deep respect for each other. You have a thirst for knowledge but no desire to conquer. You are more of a people person than a warrior. You will be leaving Ireland within a year and sailing east to hotter climates, where you will study fervently and become a skilled healer. Later on, I see you on a longboat in very heavy freezing stormy seas with two older men to whom you are connected, sailing west. You will have many dangerous adventures, but you will manage to find your way out of trouble.'

Viggo laughed, 'I have spent my life staying out of trouble. Ivar is my uncle and has been a huge influence in my life, but Ubba is my father for whom I have great affection. Can you tell me what will happen to him and my mother and sister? I fear for their safety back in Yorkshire.'

Morgana touched his hand. 'I am sorry, but I need to touch someone or have them very close by to read into their future. Sigtryggr, you have some good news, which you haven't told me about yet. I forecast you would marry a beautiful girl with long blonde hair, wearing a crown. You have a baby boy already in her womb.'

Sigtryggr interrupted, 'Will the baby be born safely and will there be more sons to follow afterwards?'

Morgana laughed, 'You have always desired to breed a dynasty and I told you that you would. Life has many twists and turns but Skye will keep you safe. She asks for fidelity and you must give it to her in mind, body and soul. Do not be tempted to stray from her bed or you could lose all that you have gained.'

Ivar laughed and turned to Sigtryggr, 'Are you sure Skye hasn't already been to see Morgana to campaign for your fidelity?'

Morgana laughed, 'I haven't met her in the flesh yet, but she is a strong woman and will keep you on your toes.'

Sigtryggr said, 'I will be marrying her soon and will make her my queen.'

Three days later Sulamain paid Ivar a visit and he suggested to Sigtryggr that Sulamain check Skye. He agreed but insisted on being with her.

Ivar said, 'What do you think he is going to do to her? He is a healer, not a pervert.'

Sigtryggr's face went red and he barked at Ivar, 'I am sure he is, but I would prefer to be there if my future wife is being examined in intimate areas. I will fetch her and bring him up to my bedroom when he is ready.'

Ivar went to Sulamain and explained the situation. 'She just needs some reassurance that she is more than capable of bearing this child. I have been concerned about her since I arrived. She is no longer the bright happy girl she was in Jorvik. A year over here with no close family support has made her anxious and withdrawn. She has lost her self-confidence and joy. Mind you, in this country it rains daily, and I think I would be ready to throw myself off a cliff after a year.'

'Sulamain smiled. 'How do you think I feel? It is hardly the sandy warm deserts of Arabia, and it is only autumn now. Do you have concerns about her relationship with Sigtryggr? You don't think he is being too dominant with her?'

'No, I just think he has failed to notice that she needs women around her to thrive. She has thrown all her affection on him and become too dependent.'

'Ivar, he is a young man with a crown to defend and he does not have much experience of women. For all his warrior credentials and bravado, he is not as self-confident as you are, and never will be. He doubts himself and he is being overprotective towards her, especially now she's bearing his child. As you well know, a lot depends on him stamping his authority as King – there are several Irish chieftains who would like his crown.'

They went upstairs. Sulamain saw the anxiety on Sigtryggr's face and resolved to put him at ease.

He addressed Skye, 'Now, young lady, Ivar says you are pregnant, but he has the sight, which I am afraid I don't have the benefit of to assist me. Why don't you tell me when you last bled, and what symptoms you have?'

'I only know that I am about two weeks late. I don't feel any other changes in my body yet apart from being more tired.'

He handed her a large earthenware pot. 'Now, I want you to take this over there and give me a sample of your urine.'

Skye obliged but was slightly flustered. Sigtryggr went to her aid. He brought the pot to Sulamain, who was mixing a potion in a glass jar. He added a small amount of urine and the solution turned green and bubbled. They were all glued to this amazing spectacle.

Sigtryggr anxiously exclaimed, 'What does that mean?'

'It means Skye is pregnant. It has detected a hormone in her urine that confirms it. If she was not pregnant it would not bubble or change colour.'

Skye said, 'You don't have to physically examine me then?'

'No, my dear. It would be almost impossible to detect such an early pregnancy by manual palpation of your womb, and that could cause the egg to detach from the womb as it will barely have started to grow. Now your job is to eat healthily, exercise and sleep well.'

Sigtryggr said, 'Does that mean I must refrain from sex? I don't want to harm the baby.'

No, you cannot harm the fertilised egg – it is safely in the womb – but you will have to be inventive in the positions you adopt so as not to put too much weight or pressure on it. Shall we say... the lady should be on top rather than you.'

Skye blurted out, 'Oh, good! I like that position.'

Sigtryggr blushed from his forehead right down to his feet. 'Skye, stop discussing our sex life!'

Ivar roared with laughter. 'Oh, for God's sake, don't be such a prude. It is a totally naturally act between lovers. It is not against the law, neither is it a sin.'

Sigtryggr rushed to change the subject. 'Should Skye continue riding? She often takes risks jumping obstacles out hunting that very few women would attempt.'

'She has been riding since she was a child. It is a very good form of exercise and a chance to be out in the fresh air. Whilst she should take more care during the first three months of pregnancy, I don't think she should stop riding. She will know when to stop when her bump grows bigger or if she acquires other symptoms that prevent her from riding.'

Skye interrupted, 'Such as, Sulamain?'

'Well, some women experience high levels of sickness in the early stages while the body adjusts to the pregnancy. I have known some women who are so bad with sickness that they risk losing the baby from malnutrition. On the other hand, some women absolutely blossom when pregnant and their sexual appetite increases. My only concern is that if you develop chronic sickness you will also lose weight and condition and you are a little underweight now, so you really must continue to eat well. Make sure you eat lots of meat, fish, eggs, vegetables and milk. You will be able to purchase citrus fruit from the Mediterranean countries from the merchant ships coming into Dublin.'

He turned to Sigtryggr, 'Do you have a family history of twins? This is something that could seriously affect the chances of delivering a live birth in a mother with hips that small.'

Sigtryggr replied, 'No, I don't know of any in my immediate family. I can appreciate that would be a high risk for a first-time mother, but her own mother produced three healthy children – and the last when she was over forty years old.'

Skye said, 'Thorin's birth was very dangerous. He was a breech birth and was double the size of an average baby. It was a miracle and purely down to the dedication of Ubba and the midwife that my mother did not die giving birth.' Skye looked down at her breasts and quietly said, 'Sulamain, how am I going to feed a strong child? Even Serena cannot feed Ubba's offspring on her own. She has a wet nurse helping her until they are nearly two years old. They are always so strong and have such a lust for life. Serena maintains they are born with a seax in their hand.'

Sulamain smiled, 'Skye, give your body a chance to develop. I admit you will probably need a wet nurse as your milk won't come through until two days after the birth, but the more the baby feeds the more milk is produced, so you may find a significant increase in size after the birth, which I am sure your new husband will appreciate. If you start to become too big close to birth then I can try and deliver the baby early, but it is fraught with difficulty. Ideally, babies need to reach full term to develop their lungs; early intervention is not to be undertaken lightly.'

Skye had to attend a fitting for her wedding dress; she was thankful to escape but content that Sulamain would oversee her pregnancy and birth. She was sure Sigtryggr would not forget her faux pas and would remonstrate with her later. She had underestimated his shyness concerning sex; her upbringing had obviously been very different from his. With three men in the house she had learnt about sex naturally and showed no embarrassment about being naked in front of men.

Once she had gone, Sulamain said, 'Skye will be fine, but she needs to have a happy mind as well. Being over-anxious can be as harmful as suffering from physical illness. She looks to you alone to keep her happy, but she needs women around her to support her through the pregnancy. These Irish women are strong and resilient both in mind and body; she needs encouragement from them to deliver a healthy baby.'

Sigtryggr replied, 'I know. Ivar has pointed that out and I will put it right as soon as I can.'

THIRTY-ONE

Preparations were in full swing for the wedding. The kitchen staff were cooking meat and making delicious puddings for the guests. They had freezing cold underground caves where they could store their produce partially cooked or smoked to give it a long life.

Skye was getting more excited by the day. She had been given the order of service and told to learn her lines very carefully in both Latin and Irish. She had been sent on a whirlwind tour of the silk and cloth merchants with a very accomplished seamstress. They purchased rolls of every material to make her any outfit from linen or silk undergarments to thick woollen fur lined cloaks and skirts for the approaching winter. Her pregnancy had been kept under wraps so as not to prejudice the officiating priests who did not approve of sex before marriage, but she had not put any weight on round her middle yet. Sigtryggr had noticed a slight increase in the size of her breasts, which pleased him.

That morning it was sunny and warm and as she looked down to the courtyard she saw a small troop preparing to ride out. Viggo was among them. She leant over the first-floor balcony and beckoned him over. 'Viggo, where are you going?'

Viggo came towards her and looked up. 'Delivering invitations to the merchants and leading figures in Dublin. Ivar insists I go because I can speak several languages and translate for those who cannot understand Latin.'

'It's a lovely day. Can I come with you? I need some exercise and fresh air.'

Viggo replied, 'Only if you come dressed like a man, not a queen, so you won't be recognised.'

Skye replied, 'Give me five minutes to change – and don't tell Sigtryggr; he would not approve.' She ran to her room and pulled out her leather breeches, a white shirt, leather tunic and riding boots. She carefully twisted her long blonde hair into a bun and pinned it firmly out of sight under her thick sheepskin cloak. This adventure would ease her boredom and acting as a man appealed to her. She went down the backstairs and came out into the courtyard striding like a man.

Viggo came over with a troop horse and whispered, 'I daren't bring your mare out or the men would know something was up. This horse is safe enough and is very skilled at covering uneven ground. We have one delivery to make outside the city, so keep a very low profile until we are well away from here.'

She mounted, stroked the neck of the horse and murmured platitudes to him, and he stood quiet and still. The horse knew instantly she was an experienced rider and settled into his job sweetly and quickly.

They set off through the wooden gates, both looking around for Sigtryggr or Ivar. There was no sign of either, but they didn't spot a man mounted across from the gates, wrapped up in a black hooded cloak with a goatskin draped around his back. He watched the troop of six horses go down the road then he pirouetted his horse and set off at a strong gallop in the opposite direction.

It wasn't until they stopped at their first delivery that the troopers realised the man riding in double file with Viggo was not a man at all. One of Sigtryggr's older warriors realised first when they dismounted at the wine merchant's warehouse. He had gone to hold their horses while they went in to deliver the invitations. He saw her bright blue eyes and braided hair as her hood fell back when she jumped down off her horse.

Skye whispered, 'Shush, Merewolf. I am here in disguise on a mission for Sigtryggr.'

As he took her horses' reins he leant closer to her. 'I hope you are not lying to me young lady, as I know he would not take any risks with your life. Be very careful; with only four of us we cannot offer you enough protection if we are attacked.'

Viggo had heard some of the conversation but ushered Skye into the merchant's office as Merewolf shook his head in disdain. Monsieur Beaumond was sitting behind his large oak desk when Viggo and Skye came in. She stayed by the door and let Viggo take the lead.

Beaumond said, 'Ah, young man, we meet again. What can I do for you?'

'I have a personal invitation from Sigtryggr for you to attend his wedding and the crowning of his future queen.'

Beaumond looked delighted and then he remembered the threat of two more Ragnarssons potentially making their home in Dublin. 'I assume your father and uncle will be arriving for this special occasion?'

Viggo managed to keep his face straight. 'That depends, of course, on what is happening in Jorvik now King Edward has retaken possession. I hope my father will be able to attend but there are only two weeks left and we have no confirmation yet of them having received their invitations.'

Beaumond said, 'I am currently planning a trip home for more wine, but I will ensure that the couple receive an appropriate wedding present.'

As they were shown back out to the courtyard they refrained from speaking in company, but Viggo gave Skye a beaming smile.

They continued their deliveries and nobody else detected her disguise. Their last delivery was to the outlying farm around five miles outside of the city. It was amazing how quickly they were in open countryside with Merewolf leading. The other men were amused at their young queen's audacity, but it only endeared her to them even more.

They cantered in full sunshine. Skye was anticipating Sigtryggr's reaction to her willful act when they passed a copse of trees and six horses and riders came flying out, followed by a further six blocking their path further up the road. Her heart missed a beat as she pulled up and Merewolf immediately rode next to her on the left, as Viggo was on the right. The group surrounded them and closed in.

Viggo whispered to her, 'Stay quiet and keep your head down.'

Their leader moved in closer and Viggo demanded, 'Who the hell are you and what do you want?'

'Never mind who I am, young pup. I have the advantage of knowing who you are, but you don't know me. These are Sigtryggr's men, except for the one next to you. She is the prize we are here for.'

Viggo surveyed the ugly brute before him and his heart sank. He knew they were here to kidnap Skye; he would have to try to talk his way out while keeping his identity hidden.

Skye felt her body stiffen with unease, but she had to be brave and appear as calm as possible.

Merewolf said, 'Kalen Murphy of Tara, I believe. You grew up with Sigtryggr. What possible reason could you have for challenging us?'

Kalen laughed, 'I wish to deprive Sigtryggr of his wife and queen to settle old scores. How dare he marry a Saxon when there are many Irish princesses who would have earned him more power and influence?'

Viggo responded, 'Her father is a Dane.'

Kalen replied, 'And how would you know, pup?'

Viggo shouted, 'Because I am her brother. I came over here with Ivar to attend the wedding as my family's only representative. They are trapped in Jorvik under King Edward's occupation.'

Kalen came closer. Merewolf and Viggo moved their horses as close to hers as they could. He commanded his men, 'The guards won't be joining us and will have a long walk back to Dublin. I am only interested in the girl. Merewolf, you can tell him I spared you because you are native Irishmen. I will send a messenger with our demands soon and will enjoy entertaining his bride until he comes up with the money.'

Merewolf's horse was pulled away from Skye's. Two men pulled him off it and he had a seax held to his throat and a sword at his back. Skye saw a gap and kicked her horse, intending to swerve past Kalen. However, he was very quick and grabbed her reins, stopping any escape. 'Not so fast, my dear. Now let us look at the woman Sigtryggr thinks is fit to become Queen of Dublin.' He grabbed her hood, pulled it back and the hairpins caught on it. Sections of her blonde hair cascaded onto her shoulders.

His lascivious look of appraisal made her spine shiver. He laughed loudly, 'Merewolf, you take as long as you like getting back to Dublin. I am going to be enjoying myself in bed with this new toy for quite a while.' He was now towering over her and he never saw her hand fly up and strike him across his right cheek. He grabbed her with one hand around her neck and whispered menacingly to her, 'You want a fight lady, then I will give you one. I enjoy breaking young fillies in and I never spare the whip.'

By now Viggo had been grabbed from his horse and checked for weapons, as had the other guards, but he heard Kalen's threat.

Skye shouted, 'I will not go with you without my brother!'

'What bloody use is he? He's not going to protect you from me, unless of course you want him to watch.' She gave him a determined look and tried to pull her hands away from the man who was trying to bind her wrists to the saddle. Kalen acceded in exasperation, 'Hell fire and damnation woman, you can have your little brother to comfort you if it shuts you up. We can put a price on him too – and kill him if Sigtryggr doesn't want him.' He turned to his men. 'Get him back on his horse, but tie his hands to the saddle and lead him. If he gives you any trouble, kill him.'

As they were preparing to set off and Merewolf and the other two men were disarmed and led away, Skye cast a mournful look at Merewolf. She imagined him telling Sigtryggr of her fate. *Enough of this – she must prepare herself for what horrors lay ahead. At least she had Viggo with her, but he was heading into danger just like her. What would Ivar say when he got the news?*

They barely went above a trot and dark was already falling on a day where the weather now threatened heavy rain. Her mind was full of scenarios of what Kalen had in store for her. She wasn't as brave as Torri and knew she would never be able to fend him off – and if she tried, he would soon have the upper hand. She also had to focus on the baby, knowing that any beating administered by her captors could put an end to his life too. She offered silent prayers to the goddess Freya to protect her.

At the same time Viggo's brain was working fast. He knew he must find a way of telling her not to disclose her pregnancy; he had an awful image in his mind of what they might do to her if Sigtryggr failed to pay the ransom. He knew Ivar would not be keen to capitulate but with his life at risk too, he would insist they paid.

It felt like hours before they reached the gates of the fortress and with the light failing, he would never be able to remember the way they came. He knew at one point there had been bogs on both sides of the track and the thought crossed his mind of throwing himself in to avoid a laboured death. His mother's face drifted before him and she said, 'Now, come on, Viggo; you are a Ragnarsson. Use your head to figure a way out.'

As soon as they were in the courtyard he had his hands untied and was roughly pulled off his horse and bundled through the door, followed by Skye and Kalen. The hallway sconces were being lit by servants and he saw a wide oak staircase and balcony above. A fortress like this would have dungeons and he wondered whether he would be kept with Skye in a cell until Kalen came to take her to his bed, or put in one alone.

He spotted an imposing older man coming down the stairs with red hair sporting grey streaks. He was wearing a red and green tartan woollen kilt. He looked shocked at the two prisoners. Skye had put the hood of her cloak up as it had started raining.

'Kalen, how come you failed in your mission to kidnap Sigtryggr's woman, returning with two bedraggled teenage boys?'

'I did not fail, Father.' He strode over and threw back Skye's hood. 'She was in disguise as a male, but I can assure you there is a woman under there. She may be a bit on the bony side, but she will soon fatten up when I have tupped her.'

His father shouted, 'Do not speak like that in front of a lady, you foul-mouthed imbecile.' He turned to a man servant. 'Take them into my study and let them warm up by the fire with a hot drink and cake.' He strode over to Kalen and pulled him away, out of hearing.

The servant ushered them into the study, which had a roaring log fire and a big settee. Skye collapsed on the settee. When the servant left, Viggo hugged her and said, 'Skye, please be careful what you say. His father may look like less of an ogre than Kalen, but it could just be an act. Ivar taught us how to cope with questioning. You give as little information as you can and in your case, you must pretend you are terrified. Do not reveal your condition; it will only escalate the stakes and would tip the balance even more in their favour to extract more of a ransom.'

'But what if he rapes me and beats me and I lose the baby?'

'Skye, you will have to do what your mother did to save you from the slave traders. Do not offer any resistance; just let him do it. Once you are no longer a challenge he will tire quickly of you.'

'But what if he makes me pleasure him? I couldn't do it, Viggo. I would feel disloyal to Sigtryggr.'

Viggo decided that tough love was required. 'Now, you listen to me; you will do whatever it takes to stay alive – and that includes pleasuring him in whatever way he wants. I can give you some tips on how to contain his ardour.'

Skye was shocked. 'Viggo, have you experienced sex already? You are only twelve years old!'

He blushed and replied, 'Well, what better way to learn than from experienced women who enjoy teaching young boys the ropes? I have always had a thirst for learning and it is no different than learning to play an instrument.'

'Hell fire, Viggo. You have your father's lust for sex, but hopefully not his fertility rate.'

'I make sure they are not likely to get pregnant. I am enjoying learning the art but don't want saddling with the responsibility just yet.'

'I don't think Arne has been as forward as you and he is two years older.'

'I think he is getting there, but a bit more steadily than me. I followed Erik's sex life very closely and he certainly had an appetite. He caught me hiding in his room one night when he was with Marianne. Although he beat me up, it was worth it for what I learnt from them both.'

THIRTY-TWO

The door opened and two servants appeared, carrying hot drinks and warm buttered scones. Following closely behind was Kalen's father. They both jumped to their feet.

'There now, you look a lot warmer and less scared than half an hour ago. I am Donal Murphy, the chieftain of Tara and regrettably, Kalen's father. Who are you two?'

Viggo, having been taught how to conduct himself at court by Ivar, stepped forward and bowed, 'Sir, may I introduce you to my sister Skye Lindholm. I am Viggo Lindholm, both formerly from Jorvik.'

Donal stretched out his hand to Skye, bowed and kissed her hand. 'My lady, welcome to Tara. May I assure you that I mean you no harm. This unfortunate incident was planned by Kalen, largely without my knowledge, and was done to exact revenge for a previous falling out he had with Sigtryggr when they were teenagers. However, I am not one to miss an opportunity for profit and agree that a little more money in the pot would be useful with a harsh winter approaching.'

Skye interrupted, 'So you will not let Kalen rape me? I am due to marry Sigtryggr in two weeks' time and he is expecting to marry a virgin. I would like to arrive at the altar unsullied.'

'Young lady, I may be a rogue Irish chieftain, but I am not in the habit of raping women. I can assure you that you are a guest in my house rather than a prisoner and I will endeavour to protect you at all times. Therefore, for your own safety I will have you locked in your bedroom at night and suggest you keep close to your brother during the day. Provided he does not cause trouble he may move freely in the house.'

'Oh, thank you, my lord; that does make me feel safer. Please tell us why Kalen and Sigtryggr fell out.'

He went to pour himself some whisky and returned to his comfortable chair. 'Sigtryggr's father and I formed an alliance to attempt to take Dublin on behalf of his grandfather Ímar ua Ímair. His cousin Ragnall was also a grandson of Ímar and we all lived in Meath together. Unfortunately, his father died when he was twelve years old. I treated him as one of my sons after that. Sigtryggr and Kalen are opposites in both character and temperament. Sigtryggr is an intelligent deep thinker and though he lacks education, he is a clever assessor of situations and thinks hard before he acts. Kalen overreacts to every situation without any thought of the consequences. He has a cruel streak and will torment man or beast for pleasure. This trait is not something I have myself, but his mother could be that way inclined. I have tried to discourage his excesses, but without success.

'Sigtryggr is a loner who takes ages to form friendships because everyone he ever loved either died or left him. His reputation is that of a wise strategist and he relishes finding ways to solve problems. He can be brutal, but only if someone lets him down. He does not tolerate liars and cheats and so he will destroy them.'

Skye interrupted, 'When he first came over to Jorvik, he was an imposing and interesting young man and found a kindred spirit in Ivar. Unfortunately, he flirted with Torri and my mother and found himself at loggerheads with Ubba. I have never known Ubba to be jealous before – he thought Sigtryggr had gone further than flirting – which was never the case. Ubba is normally the most well-adjusted and kind person, but his love for Torri is deep and very precious. He felt usurped and threatened by Sigtryggr and inadvertently took Torri to task about it.'

Donal commented, 'I have never met Ubba but men who have served under him say he is a natural born leader and his men would follow him to hell and back. There are not many leaders you can say that about. Plenty of women admire his looks and power, but he prefers to form relationships that will last. Kalen says that Sigtryggr has no hope of founding a dynasty with you as your hips are too narrow to bear his children. From what I know of him I am sure you must have qualities that he admires that will make you a perfect partner and queen, even though you have some Saxon blood.'

There was a knock at the door and two servants appeared.

'Ah, Morag and Isaac are here to show you to your

rooms. I have put you in the nursery wing where you can have adjoining rooms. If you wish Skye, Morag can sleep in your room. You will both be locked in but only I or these two will have access to the keys. You must both be exhausted; have a good night's sleep and I hope you will join me for breakfast tomorrow.'

Viggo said, 'Thank you very much my lord for your kindness.'

Skye said, 'Has a messenger already gone to the court to inform Sigtryggr?'

Donal laughed, 'No, not yet. I think your men should have made it back on foot by now. I will send a ransom note first thing tomorrow morning. This is not ideal terrain at night.'

'You do realise that taking me away from Sigtryggr by force will provoke an instant vengeful reaction from him? Ivar has a very short temper too.'

'I know just how much this will have affected him and I regret I was unable to stop it happening.'

'Then just let us go home in the morning and I will persuade him that it was a misunderstanding that you played no part in.'

Donal took her hand and kissed it. 'Skye, you know that he will not take this lightly and will seek revenge regardless. Kalen has no idea of the retribution his childish act will reap.'

Skye declined to have Morag sleeping in her room. They had an interconnecting door and after the servants left, Skye went into Viggo's room. 'Would you mind sleeping in the other bed in my room? I know we are not siblings, but I would feel safer if you were close by in case Kalen breaks in.'

Viggo hugged her. 'Of course I will, Skye… but not until I have found something I can use as a weapon against him. I think there is a metal poker in the fireplace, but it is hardly a sword or spear. Promise me you won't tell Sigtryggr I slept in your room; he might kill me.'

'No he would not, Viggo; he will realise it is for my protection and at my request. What do you think he will do?'

'I haven't known him long, but I am sure he will take this very badly – even worse than Ivar would. He loves you Skye, and the thought of Kalen even touching you will drive him mad. He will certainly kill him, and it will be a painful death. I can't see him letting Donal get away with it either.'

'What can we do to prevent it?'

'Give me chance to sleep on it and I will see if I can come up with anything. Ivar will be just as angry about me. How many men can Sigtryggr raise overnight to assist him?'

'Probably around 200 men. Certainly enough to storm this place and kill everyone.'

'Neither of them will pay a ransom unless there is no other option – and as soon as Sigtryggr appears on the horizon our chances of survival reduce. They will threaten to kill me unless Sigtryggr backs down, and Ivar will not want to risk my life. At least Ivar will be there to calm Sigtryggr down. He will be distraught that Kalen has power over you if he has destroyed other treasures he has loved as a child, and he won't be capable of thinking objectively. I don't think Kalen will listen to his father either; this really is about him and Sigtryggr.'

'Oh, Viggo, why will Kalen threaten you first rather than me?'

'To test Sigtryggr. He will know that you would not want to lose me. However, he doesn't know who I am, and Ivar will capitulate even if Sigtryggr doesn't.'

'Viggo, how will you face death?'

'Ivar taught us all that death in battle tends to come quickly and without too much pain. It gives you a chance to go to Valhalla. Not everyone who dies in battle goes to Valhalla; only the bravest warriors selected by the Valkyries. Death by slow torture is horrendous and requires real courage and fortitude. It is something my father has a real fear of as he has a low pain threshold. Ivar says you have to pray to the gods and not reveal anything as you will likely be killed even if you give your enemy the information they want. Both my grandfather and uncle have been captured and tortured. Rollo survived but my grandfather did not. I have no idea whether I will be silent and brave until it happens.'

Skye hugged him. 'Oh, Viggo, you have already proved yourself brave when you rescued your comrades when the boat sank in the North Sea. You were only eight years old then. You have all your father's attributes and Ivar's intelligence. Ivar always said you have a great future. The gods will not let you die so young.'

oOo

Sigtryggr and Ivar were discussing plans for the wedding and coronation. A question was raised and Sigtryggr wanted Skye's opinion, so sent for her. It was a long time before a servant returned and his face showed his fear.

'Where is Skye?'

The servant stuttered, 'My lord, she has gone out with Viggo delivering invitations.'

'But surely that was this morning? They should be back by now.'

'Yes, lord. Kettil has taken a small troop to go and look for them. They may be being entertained by one of the merchants, which has delayed their progress.'

'Send him straight to me when he returns. The same with Viggo and Skye.'

Ivar picked up on the uncertainty in his voice and knew he was concerned. Kettil returned within an hour and came to report back to Sigtryggr, who was now pacing up and down like a lion.

He announced, with trepidation in his voice, 'My lord, they made their way around Dublin and out to the farm, but have not been seen coming back into the city.'

'How many men were with them?'

'Merewolf, three troopers and the two of them.'

'Not enough to fend off a kidnap attempt.'

'But my lord, Skye was dressed as a man. Everybody reported that Viggo and one male escort entered their premises to deliver the invitations personally. If someone was intending to kidnap Skye they would have had to have been watching her movements very closely.'

Ivar intervened, 'Well, if that was their objective then spying is easy enough to do. They may have gained access inside here. Have any strangers been seen?'

'Lord Ivar, there have been many deliveries for the wedding going in and out of the gates every day.'

Sigtryggr was pacing back and forth at speed.

Ivar said, 'Stop it, Sigtryggr. Until we hear from the kidnappers we can do nothing. They won't kill Skye – but what about Viggo? He is a bright lad and a trained fighter, but also an easy target.'

Sigtryggr growled, 'What worries me is what they will do to Skye whilst waiting for the ransom.'

Ivar replied, 'Just concentrate and think who might want to do this to you, and for what reason. Has anybody showed dissension about you marrying Skye? Have you made promises to wed in exchange for land and then broken them? Did your father promise you would marry another chieftain's daughter when you were still a child?'

Sigtryggr threw himself down on a chair and put his hands over his eyes. 'Not as far as I am aware, but there has been some resistance to her not being Irish. Nobody has brought it directly to my attention.'

Ivar turned to Kettil, 'You may go, but alert us as soon as anyone comes. I need to speak to the messenger; don't let them leave a note.'

'Yes, Lord Ivar.' He departed with a sigh of relief.

Ivar poured two jugs of ale, handed one to a distraught Sigtryggr and patted him on the shoulder.

'I know the waiting is crippling, but do not think the worst yet. They will not harm their prize if they need the money. How much can you raise for a ransom and how many men can you rally to your cause if we have to fight?'

'The cost of the wedding has taken up a large chunk of my silver stocks. It could not have come at a worse time. I have probably 100 men here and I'm sure I can raise some citizens to join us if necessary. Hell fire, Ivar. What am I going to do? She's carrying my child and I need her by my side.'

Ivar interrupted, 'Is the child more important than her? You are only twenty years old. If she died in childbirth you would have to find another wife and breed again anyway. You must realise that the sensible thing to do is to pretend you don't care. The reply should be, 'Keep her. I have many years to found a dynasty; I will find another wife.' If they object to her being a Saxon then ask them for suggestions on who they would like you to marry.'

'Ivar, what are you saying – that I should leave her to die?'

'No, fool. It reduces her value and whatever they ask for, you can halve it. However, that does not help me get my precious nephew back, who I promised to keep safe and sound. We could speculate all night but until we have the name of the kidnapper and know his history, we cannot do anything.'

'But Ivar, they may be raping her one by one as we speak. What chance has the baby at only ten weeks old?'

'No, they won't – I have taken earls' wives and children as hostages before and would never damage valuable goods. Calm down and wait and see.'

It was four hours of pure hell for both of them before Merewolf and the three troopers made it back. Merewolf came up alone to the room. One glance at Sigtryggr and Ivar warned him to be very careful. 'My lords, I regret to inform you that Kalen Murphy of Tara took Skye and Viggo hostage as we were returning from delivering invitations.'

Ivar intervened, 'How come they took Viggo hostage?'

''He told them he was Skye's brother and she pleaded to take him with her. There were 12 men. They ambushed us quickly and easily and held a sword at her throat.'

Ivar said, 'Clever Viggo. So they are not aware of his true identity?'

'No, lord. She refused to go without him and they agreed, to keep her compliant.'

Tears were running down Sigtryggr's face. 'If Kalen Murphy has captured Skye he will definitely rape and kill her. He destroyed everything I loved when I was a boy and lived with his father after mine died. Merewolf, is his father still alive?'

'I believe so, but he was not with them at the ambush. Certainly Kalen was fully in charge of that. At least he did not kill us; he just took the horses and left with the hostages.'

Ivar said, 'Did he tell you how much he wanted as a ransom?'

'No, lord, he just galloped off. I assume he will send someone with his demands soon.'

'Sigtryggr said, 'You go and get something to eat and rest; we may be leaving as soon as it is daylight, to attack.'

Ivar turned to Sigtryggr. 'Tell me everything you know about Kalen, so I can understand how his mind works. We are going to have to handle this very carefully.'

Sigtryggr sank onto the sofa. 'He is a jealous cruel bastard and hates me because I was everything and he was nothing. His own father, whom I loved and respected, was appalled at his behaviour. He tormented me in a cold calculating evil way. If I had equipment or horses that were better than his, he would steal them and destroy them. If he saw me looking at a girl he would molest her and make her his own. That is why I am not a womaniser, Ivar. I have learnt to keep my emotions hidden for so long now, it has become second nature.

'After my father died Kalen had increased opportunities to taunt me but I didn't complain to Donal his father, although other members of the household will have informed him. Kalen was eight years older than me and built like a bear. He made sure his acts of torture were invisible. I was not strong enough to fight him off then, but I am now. All bullies are cowards at heart, but the only way of settling this is to challenge him to single combat and a fight to the death.'

Ivar replied, 'A man like that will not risk his life.

He knows you will be twice the warrior he is now and he won't agree to fight.'

Sigtryggr said, 'It may well be that he has done this without his father's knowledge. Donal will be mortified as he is an honourable man. He will protect Skye. He may even insist Kalen takes the challenge because he will know that I now have the strength and power to kill him. Donal would not have sanctioned this kidnap and it may just be the trigger that pushes him to remove his son permanently.'

Ivar smiled, 'There is some hope then. But are you sure you can beat him? You have a lot to lose if he wounds you and you die later. I have never seen you in battle, but you are going to have to be the equal of my brothers Ubba and Halfdan to do it.'

'Ivar just promise me you will kill him if he gets the better of me. Don't kill his father; it is not his fault his son is despicable. Donal always deserved better and deep down, I love him.'

Ivar patted him on the back. 'I promise you Kalen will wish you had killed him; if I have to finish him off he will regret it. Now go and tell your men to prepare to ride out before dawn. We won't bother waiting for the ransom note; we will go and surprise them. I need to ensure Viggo gets out alive.'

Sigtryggr managed only a short nap as he kept waking with a vision of his upcoming fight with Kalen. He prayed to Odin to protect him and promised he would uphold and promote his religion far and wide. Finally, he gave up trying to sleep and went to prepare his horse. He was like Ubba in that whenever he was at his lowest, he turned to horses as a source of strength. However, he was not as communicative as Ubba; he always measured his answers carefully before speaking. He did not like to give away any indication of the state of his mind under pressure, instead becoming quieter and withdrawn.

THIRTY-THREE

They set off for Tara. Merewolf led the way and all Sigtryggr's men accompanied him, including Ivar in his chariot. Kalen had posted lookouts on the ramparts, but the rescue party was given extra cover by a low-lying mist... as Ivar saw it, a sign that the gods were watching over them.

Kalen was roused from his bed to find his fortress encircled by Sigtryggr's troops, and Ivar and Sigtryggr banging on the gates for admission. His father was alerted and came storming down to the gates, instructing his men to open them but only to admit Sigtryggr and Ivar. Kalen tried to countermand but his angry father replied that he was still Chieftain of Tara and he would invite in whomever he wanted. Ivar and Sigtryggr were admitted on foot into the courtyard. Kalen and Donal stood at the top of the stone steps outside the front door.

Donal shouted, 'Sigtryggr of Dublin and Ivar the Boneless, welcome to Tara. I know your business is with my son Kalen, but I want you to be aware that I knew nothing of his intention to kidnap your future queen. I can assure you that she and her brother have been kept safely under my protection since they arrived.'

Sigtryggr ran up the steps. Donal moved forward and embraced him. 'Sigtryggr, what a fine man you have become. Your father would be so proud of you.'

Ivar said, 'We wish to see Skye and Viggo before any negotiations commence.'

Kalen and Sigtryggr were staring at each other. Sigtryggr smiled as he drew himself up to his full height, which was six inches taller than Kalen. Instantly, he knew he was no longer the boy that had been tortured and intimidated all those years ago. He was going to kill him.

Donal said, 'It is a little early in the morning but to put your minds at rest, I will take you to their rooms for reassurance.'

Kalen shouted, 'No, you cannot see them. I forbid it.'

Donal responded, 'Whilst I still live and breathe Kalen, you have no authority whatsoever over me. Gentlemen, follow me, please.'

As they arrived at their bedrooms the servant was unlocking the door. When the door opened and Skye saw Sigtryggr and everyone else, she leapt out of bed in her nightgown and launched herself at them.

Sigtryggr hugged her tightly and kissed the top of her head. 'Are you all right, my darling? Has that bastard touched you?'

She shook her head. 'No. He threatened to harm me, but his father has kept us safe.'

Viggo emerged from the adjacent bed and Ivar exhaled in relief. He gave him a wry smile and winked.

Kalen was furious and shouted, 'You have seen that

no harm has come to them. Now let's get down to business.'

Skye looked up at Sigtryggr, 'Have you come to pay a ransom?'

Sigtryggr said, 'Yes, sweetheart. I will have you and your brother out of here in no time.' He could not tell her that he would fight for her rather than pay the ransom, but he was now more determined than ever that Kalen would die for what he had done. He could not bear to see him even look at his precious queen.

They were shown into the main hall and faced each other on opposite sides of the table.

Kalen spoke first, 'If you want her back in one piece then you will have to pay a fortune.'

Ivar interrupted, 'How do you know he wants her back? He is a young man and can soon find an alternative wife to found his dynasty.'

Kalen laughed, 'Well, she's no broodmare and will struggle to birth your hell-spawn offspring, for sure.'

Ivar saw Sigtryggr's hand instinctively go for his seax, which had already been removed before they were allowed through the gates. He nudged his foot in a warning to him to hold his temper.

Ivar said, 'And what price are you anticipating for her and her brother?'

Kalen replied, 'At least three times her weight in silver. As an added incentive I will not charge you for her brother.'

Ivar grinned at him valuing his nephew so low.

Sigtryggr leant over the table threateningly towards Kalen. 'I will not pay any money or silver for the release of my queen and her brother. You have insulted me as your rightful king and broken your family's allegiance as a vassal. I wish to settle this by challenging you to *holmgang* – single combat to the death – right here and now.'

Kalen spluttered, 'But my father swore allegiance to you; I never swore fealty.'

Ivar intervened, 'Donal Murphy, Chieftain of Tara did not kidnap his king's future wife – you did – and he has every right to punish you as he sees fit. This was a personal vendetta against a boy you have tormented many times before. He is demanding you fight for your life against him.'

Kalen gabbled, 'I do not accept the challenge and will give her back untouched and unharmed, with my apologies.'

Sigtryggr slammed his hand on the table. 'Not acceptable. You will pay with your life for this insolence. Unless of course you beat me; then you will have the prestige of killing me.'

Donal intervened, 'Kalen, it is a matter of family honour that you accept this challenge. You have brought this upon yourself and I insist you fight. You always bullied and tormented Sigtryggr when he was younger and now he reaps his revenge, and I support him.'

Kalen screamed, 'You would condemn me to death. This only proves that you have always loved and favoured him over me.'

Donal laughed, 'There is nothing I can find in you that is worthy of my love. You are a total embarrassment to me and I would rather die leaving no heir than allow you to inherit Tara.'

Ivar clapped his hands and declared, 'Well, gentlemen, we are all in agreement. Shall we proceed outside to form the square and see justice done?'

Kalen panicked, jumped up and attempted to flee, but his father tripped him up and grabbed him by the collar of his tunic. 'If you refuse to fight then Sigtryggr may dispose of you however he wants. You can't even die in an honourable way; you would rather run away. You cannot be my son, you have no backbone.' He pulled him to his feet and punched his face so hard that his head bounced off the wall. His knees buckled and he slumped unconscious to the floor. Sigtryggr and Ivar exchanged a worried look.

Donal called for his guards and instructed them to remove Kalen to the courtyard, tie him up until he came round and prepare a battle square for a fight. He turned to Sigtryggr and calmly said, 'If he refuses to fight, you may execute him however you wish.'

Sigtryggr grabbed Donal's arm. 'You really want me to kill him?'

Donal shrugged off Sigtryggr's hand. 'You would be doing me, and yourself, a great favour. He is not worthy to be my son and he will be a continuous threat to both of us if left alive.' He walked off, tears streaming down his cheeks.

Sigtryggr turned to Ivar. 'I can't murder him in cold blood, surely?'

Ivar said, 'If you can't, I will. He has kidnapped your queen and is guilty of that. You could waste time putting him on trial, but the outcome would be the same. Behead him with a long-handled Dane axe if he won't fight you.'

Sigtryggr went to release Skye and Viggo with the intention of sending them out to join his troop. After he explained what had happened, both of them refused to leave. Skye was terrified he would be hurt in a fight, but Viggo agreed that he should implement his right to a fight to the death.

Kalen had come round and realised he was in a no-win situation. He knew he would have to accept the challenge, or he would be forever branded a coward. He realised that Sigtryggr would triumph, as his reputation as a warrior had spread far and wide.

Ivar announced the rules of the challenge and both men prepared for their fight. They were allowed a long sword, a seax and a maximum of two shields each, and they would fight to the death. Both of them were checked for any extra hidden weapons and Donal's men formed the square. Ivar reminded them that only he as the adjudicator could issue a second shield – and that no men were allowed to give either contestant additional weapons. Sigtryggr had his fine chainmail under his leather tunic. Kalen wore only a leather tunic and declined any further protection.

They squared up to each other, about six feet apart. Sigtryggr looked imposing and terrifying and raised his sword and shield. Kalen looked a beaten man already and did not even raise his. Ivar called time and only Sigtryggr moved. Kalen raised his shield but the force of Sigtryggr's downward swing split it in half.

Ivar immediately called a halt and threw him a new shield. Sigtryggr stepped back to allow him to reposition himself, then as Ivar shouted to continue, he advanced on him again. This time Kalen protected his left side but Sigtryggr leapt forward and swiped his sword in a fast downward arc that carved a line through Kalen's right shoulder and chest, which immediately spurted blood. The force dropped him to one knee. This was followed by a second swipe, which caught Kalen on the left side of his neck and opened his throat. He fell forward onto the ground and Sigtryggr finished him off with a slash to the right-hand side of his throat.

There was silence from the spectators. Skye had turned her back to the fight and whimpered in fear. Kalen lay unmoving in a pool of blood as his life ebbed away. His sword was still unused in his hand, underneath his body.

Sigtryggr walked over to Donal and embraced him. He whispered, 'I am so sorry it had to end like this. I do not hold you responsible in any way for the kidnap and I will not harm you or take any of your land in revenge.'

After they returned to Dublin they were having lunch and the mood was sombre. Sigtryggr was holding Skye's hand as if she might disappear at any moment. There was no doubt he was bemused at what had transpired at Tara. He had expected a proper fight from Kalen and was appalled that he had effectively not even defended himself... He knew that Kalen was a coward, but he had not enjoyed killing him like that.

Ivar was relieved at the outcome and turned to Viggo, 'I am very proud of how you behaved under pressure. You displayed a brave and quick reaction in attempting to stay with Skye to protect her, yet keeping your own identity safe.'

Viggo replied, 'Well I learnt at your knee, Ivar. The tuition in political strategy will hopefully stay with us for the rest of our lives.'

Skye interrupted, 'Viggo was wonderful; he kept me safe and cheered me up at the same time. He prepared me for what Kalen might do. Thankfully, he did not have the opportunity thanks to your quick intervention. I do feel sorry for Donal; it must have been very hard to admit to everyone what a bastard his son was and to support his death. He will be devastated Sigtryggr and fraught with grief.'

Sigtryggr replied, 'I intend to go and see him in a few days and would like him to come to the wedding so that everybody sees I bear no animosity towards him.'

Skye said, 'Oh, I do hope he will come and that you will continue to support him. He was like a father to you after you lost your own so young.'

After lunch, Sigtryggr insisted that he and Skye retire as he just wanted to sleep entwined around her body, knowing she was safe and sound. They showered together and he soaped her all over to wash the grime away. He knelt in front of her and gently soaped her stomach. 'Thank the gods you were not showing any signs of carrying my child. My second worst fear was that he would rape you, but my first was what he may do to you if he discovered you were pregnant.'

She bent and kissed the top of Sigtryggr's head. 'I told Donal I was a virgin and he instantly put me under lock and key to protect me from Kalen. I feared he would attack me and so did Viggo. He told me not to resist for the baby's sake, but I don't think I could have just laid there and let him rape me unchallenged.'

Sigtryggr stood up and hugged her tightly. 'I knew he would harm you. He always destroyed everything I loved and he would have taken evil pleasure in raping you. That's why I came immediately – the longer you were there, the more likely he would be to attack.'

He wrapped a big towel around her and carried her to the bed. He pulled the covers back, positioned her on the pillows and took the towel off. He knelt down beside her and carefully dried her all over.

She watched him in amazement. 'How can you be so sweet and gentle with me within hours of killing a man? These two opposite sides to you are difficult to reconcile.' She noted that Sigtryggr was aroused by her body but did not make any attempts to touch her sexually. As he climbed into bed beside her she whispered to him, 'I am not made of glass and I can see your desire. Take me to heaven and back and reclaim my body.'

He laughed, 'Whatever you desire, my love. I am your faithful servant.'

THIRTY-FOUR

Ivar was supported down the steps by Skye and cheered by the remaining servants. They made their way to the newly decorated farm cart that would take them to Christ Church Cathedral for the wedding and coronation (in place of a typical Viking inauguration). The six boys and six girls who made up their attendants were already in the back of the hay cart on benches, brimming with excitement. Sigtryggr had made a clever move by inviting the young sons and daughters of other chieftains to form their retinue. The one requirement they all shared was bright red hair. The boys were dressed in leather braided tunics with blue shirts and fur-trimmed cloaks. They had miniature swords and seaxes on a leather belt at their waist and would carry a smaller version of Sigtryggr's adopted shield. The sides of their hair were braided and tied back in blue ribbon.

The two women who were in charge of them had already collected up the shields as they had been fighting with each other while getting dressed. They were told that if they took their swords out of their scabbards they would not be allowed to take part. The girls wore miniature matching blue wool dresses with tartan shawls and their red hair was braided with coronets of flowers.

As the noise reached a crescendo in the back of the cart Ivar turned round and glared at them. 'Children, I am Ivar the Boneless, and you are here as representatives of your families. Do not misbehave as I will not tolerate insubordination in my troops – and neither will King Sigtryggr. You have been given a great honour and you will keep the noise down and behave as your fathers would in battle.' The boys looked uneasy and the girls gasped in shock. Ivar's cruel reputation had circulated very quickly when he had arrived in Dublin.

He turned back and patted Skye's hand. 'That should keep the noise down on the way to the church.'

'Oh, Ivar, you are wicked! However, I made sure the swords were not sharpened.'

'Good idea – we don't want blood all over your beautiful dress. May I say you look absolutely stunning, my dear? You are making me regret my decision not to marry you. However, you wanted to fly free Skye and I think your temperament will balance Sigtryggr's well. He is a deep thinker and can be a little too morose at times.'

Skye laughed, 'And you don't think you can be the same, Ivar?'

'Of course not. I may be a tyrant, but I have a wicked sense of humour and can't resist being unpredictable. Now explain to me why you are marrying in a Christian church when you are both Odin's followers.'

'To appease the chieftains and people of Dublin.

The marriage will be conducted as a Dane ceremony with Christian elements and the coronation has to incorporate their coronation vows as well as ours.'

'Well, I am just warning you that the Christian God does not like me entering one of his houses. I see a lot of apparitions. They resent my presence and I have witnessed arrows flying around quite frequently. In fact, if the roof falls in I wouldn't be surprised.'

Skye said, 'When you hand me over to Sigtryggr perhaps you should sneak out of the vestry door. I don't want to die on the day of my wedding and coronation.'

They were now approaching the main street leading to the church. People thronged, shouting and pressing to see the bridal party.

Sigtryggr was already in the church, sitting in the front pew with Donal McCarthy as the ring bearer at his side. He had been to see Donal again to ensure that their friendship was still intact after what had happened. Donal had been shattered by the whole wretched business, but he did not regret the outcome or blame Sigtryggr for challenging Kalen to a duel. In fact, Donal realised that he had always loved Sigtryggr because he had been the opposite of Kalen. They had a drunken night reminiscing and Sigtryggr had asked him to be the ring bearer at the wedding. Donal was overjoyed.

He glanced at Sigtryggr's anxious face and said, 'Christ, lad, you look like you are at your own funeral! Lighten up; it is supposed to be a joyous occasion.

What are you fretting about?'

'I am worried someone might assassinate her on the way to the church. I have ten armed men either side of the vehicle, but somebody could shoot an arrow from one of the higher buildings.'

'Who would dare do that after you stamped your authority fairly convincingly by killing Kalen? As far as I am aware nobody is against your bride or you. They just want peace. Someone with your reputation – and with Ivar the Boneless behind you as well – may just be enough to create peace for the first time in many years. I know that you have greater ambitions than just being the King of Dublin and if you rule carefully, you may find others will support you to become King of Ireland. Learn from Ivar's historic journey. Who would believe that a crippled son of Ragnar Lothbrok would achieve such greatness? He has no heirs, so use him to forge your ambitions.'

There was a rustle at the door of the church and one of the clergy close by came and directed them to stand to the right of the altar steps. Sigtryggr turned to look back down the aisle to catch the first glimpse of his bride. His heart missed a beat. She looked stunning. She was lit by a shaft of light coming through a window, which gave her an ethereal look. Her blue velvet dress was overlaid around the bodice in silver running down the front of the skirt and reflecting in the sunlight. Her blonde hair was woven at the sides and covered in flowers that met in a circlet around her forehead, but otherwise, her hair had been left loose to fall down her back.

She had not revealed any details of what she or her attendants would be wearing. He was overjoyed at the boys' replica warrior outfits and the girls looked so beautiful with their long red hair cascading over their blue dresses and cloaks. He saw her staring intently at him, clutching Ivar's arm. He blew her a kiss and turned towards the altar to await her arrival. Ivar was wearing a red velvet tunic overlaid in silver, with a red fur-lined cloak. He intended to stand out and impress, but not to overshadow Sigtryggr on his big day.

As Skye arrived at Sigtryggr's side she looked up into his eyes and saw love and tenderness radiating. He leant in to whisper, 'Welcome to your big day, when you finally become my wife and queen forever.'

The children were organised and the girls ushered to a pew, but the boys formed a half-circle guard of honour around the wedding party. Ivar was highly impressed and turned round and gave the mini warriors a look that had them standing to attention and puffing out their chests.

The wedding ceremony commenced, conducted by a *hofgothi*. The exchange of family swords provided Skye with another surprise. Unbeknown to her, Ralf had forged a sword for her wedding day and given it to Sigtryggr before they left Yorkshire. The handgrip was overlaid in silver with scrollwork entwining two "S's" in a heart. A sapphire centrepiece glittered in the sunlight that streamed from the windows behind the altar. Ralf had also made the two silver wedding rings with the same scroll and inscription. Donal presented them proudly to the priest and shed a tear at the joy on Skye's face.

Ivar placed Skye's hand in the Gothi's hand. Then he took Sigtryggr's hand and bound them together with white rope. They both gave their vows with authority and commitment. Finally, Sigtryggr was able to kiss his bride and he took his time, savouring every moment.

They were escorted by the Christian priest into the vestry to sign their wedding certificate. This was required by the clergy as proof of the King's marriage. Ivar had taught Sigtryggr to sign his name and translated the Latin wording. Ivar and Donal were the official witnesses and the priest asked Ivar what he would like to be called. He opted for "Ivar the Boneless". Regrettably, the title of King of Jorvik was now lost to him. However, he signed "Ivar Ragnarsson," as this was his birth name.

They then processed down the aisle with the bride and groom in the lead, followed by Ivar and Donal together and then the six girls and mini warriors reformed their lines. The reception from the guests was incredible; they clapped and cheered. Even the Christians were generous in their applause and the women were enamoured by the young boys and girls.

As they reached the doorway Sigtryggr's men formed a guard of honour tunnel, raising their swords for them to walk underneath. The crowds at the church gates went wild when the mini warriors came out, and started cheering and clapping. The parents of the attendants had left by a side door to come and see their children. Ivar organised everybody into position, with the mini warriors on one side of Sigtryggr and Skye, and the girls on the other. He and Donal stood next to the happy couple. Behind them were his warriors, chosen for their size and presence.

Ivar grinned at Sigtryggr and whispered, 'I have to say it was an inspired idea to have the mini warriors. It will have boosted your reputation and sent a message to the chieftains that you intend to include them in your political decisions. Just make sure you do, as acting as a judge between fighting groups is not an easy task. Take it from someone who has plenty of experience in these matters.'

There was a short break whilst the clergy set up the church for the coronation. Sigtryggr had been officially crowned a year ago, so his silver crown was blessed already and he put it on his head before the service started. It had been made larger as it had been too small when he was crowned, and they'd had to pin it to his hair. He had designed a simple silver crown for Skye using the snake and axe emblem from his banner.

His throne had been placed at the top of the steps leading up to the altar. He insisted the mini warriors were included in his retinue as he walked down the aisle. His own men were positioned one on each step leading down from the throne to the nave. Horns were used to announce the arrival of the King and everyone stood and bowed their heads as he walked up the aisle. His mini warriors were positioned two steps below him and allowed to sit down facing the pews.

Skye and her attendants followed. Sigtryggr moved to meet her and she knelt before him with the clergy on either side of them. Sigtryggr made his proclamation in both Irish and Latin, to make her Queen. There were several vows and prayers made by the Archbishop and then the crown was handed to Sigtryggr and he placed it carefully on Skye's head. As he helped her to her feet the horn was sounded and the Archbishop shouted, 'Hail, King Sigtryggr of Dublin and his anointed queen.' The congregation replied in affirmation.

They returned to the top of the steps where a second smaller throne carved especially for Skye under the King's instructions, had been placed next to his. They sat down and one by one, the chieftains and leaders who had already sworn allegiance to Sigtryggr came forward and bowed before their new queen, swearing allegiance to her. This reinforced their vow and made them unlikely to threaten her. Any one of them who took up arms against them would automatically be a traitor and condemned to death.

Sigtryggr had also had a brainwave during the service. He rose and went down the steps to his mini warriors and told them to stand. He waved for the girls to come up from their pew and stand on the same step, all facing him.

He announced, 'As a token of my appreciation for the services of my mini warriors and my wife's handmaidens I would like to formerly offer the boys an opportunity to learn fighting skills and become warriors in my army, if they wish. The girls will be offered a place in my household to serve if they wish.'

He instructed them to kneel and as he blessed each one of them they had to say their name, which he announced to the audience. He then sat down to be at their level and said, 'You have all been on your best behaviour and have made your families very proud. I also gift you your uniforms, dresses, shields, swords and seaxes, provided you do not harm anybody with them. If you do boys, I will come and personally remove them from you.'

The boys' eyes lit up and they grinned from ear to ear. One boy turned round and shouted to his family, 'Father, King Sigtryggr has let me keep my clothes and all the weapons!'

The church filled with laughter and they clapped and cheered. The horn was sounded and they processed back down the aisle with the boys hardly able to contain their excitement.

They headed back to the palace for a feast with 500 guests. Sigtryggr made sure he spoke to everyone and thanked them for attending. He did not drink heavily as he wanted a clear head to concentrate and remember what he was told, and he was determined not to disappoint Skye on their wedding night.

The wedding feast was in full flow and Ivar was enjoying chatting to some of the merchants he had met previously. To his surprise and delight Axel had brought Irina with him, probably to serve as a reminder that selling slaves was his business. He had kitted her out with a very expensive dress that showed off her exquisite figure. Ivar went over to their table for a chat.

Axel grinned, knowing that Ivar was more interested

in Irina than in him. Ivar complimented her on her appearance but although she responded politely, evidently, she was alert for any signs of him wishing to become her new master. Axel had promised her that he would not sell her again, but she knew that if someone offered the right price, his greed could make him renege on his promise. She knew several men had shown interest in her that day and had even asked Axel if she was for sale. He had turned them all away with a definite refusal, neither confirming nor denying that she was his woman.

Another man came up to Axel and asked if he could have a private word. They left the table, much to Ivar's delight.

'Now we are alone Irina, I would like to ask you about your background. Axel has given me some information, but I would like to know more about Rus and life in your country.'

Irina laughed sarcastically, 'I am surprised, as Axel does not believe my claims. He thinks I fabricated the whole story. Kiev is a beautiful city, but you have to be acclimatised to the cold weather. There is snow on the ground for half the year at least. It is colder than Denmark, but the wooden houses are well insulated against the cold and I had a happy childhood surrounded by my family in my hometown. Axel has told me of your exploits; you have certainly made an impression on the Irish.'

'Madam, my reputation may not all be true as the tales expand into fantasy the more often they are repeated. I can confirm I do not eat babies and

I generally only kill my enemies or those who have betrayed me.'

Irina smiled, 'Perhaps you are not as wicked as you make out... but why have you no wife or children at your side?'

Ivar's eyes showed a flash of anger closely followed by sadness. 'Because there would be no point; my affliction makes me sterile. The first duty of a king is to reproduce and unfortunately I cannot, even though two of my brothers only have to lie with a woman once to breed.'

Irina put her hand on his. 'I can see it is a deep disappointment to you and something we have in common. I cannot breed either and I have wanted to be a mother since I played with my dolls as a child. However, it is probably a blessing that I cannot, or I would have spent my life producing offspring with my abusers, which would have been a fate worse than death.'

Axel returned and commented, 'Why do you both look sad? Surely this is a day of celebration? The King has a queen to breed his sons... although I am sure his father taught him how to select broodmares, yet he seems to have ignored his advice. I doubt she will birth easily at all with those narrow hips.'

Ivar intervened angrily, 'One selects a queen for many reasons more important than the width of her hips. She is half Dane, half Saxon and comes from good Yorkshire farming stock. She may not be as well educated as a Rus princess, but she will be a valuable asset to Sigtryggr in ruling the hotbed of multi-national renegades here in Dublin.'

Axel said, 'You admire her then?'

Ivar said, 'I once considered her as a potential wife, but she declined and my brother threatened to kill me if I married her.'

Axel replied, 'Why? Did he want her for himself?'

'No, he was a firm friend to her mother and father and did not want me to ruin her life. Sigtryggr will benefit from her many qualities and believe me, he loves her deeply. I will always protect her. She is very special to me and I will destroy anybody who attempts to harm her.'

THIRTY-FIVE

It was well past midnight before the newly married couple managed to slip away from the feast. Everybody was enjoying themselves thanks to the copious supply of ale, and dancing was in full swing for the younger guests.

Sigtryggr was anxious to ask Skye if she would join him in one more traditional wedding vow. 'Skye, there is another tradition that I would have liked to have included in our wedding ceremony, but it would have offended the Christians and may have caused uproar with the ladies. I know we had the hand-tying ceremony, but this is usually followed by the bride and groom having one hand slit and the blood mixing and marked on their faces as a symbol of their joining. Would you be willing to do it now?'

'I have seen it done at Dane weddings. I am already bound to you in mind, body and soul but if you need to do this I will gladly do it.'

Oh, thank you, Skye; it would make me happier still. It is a tradition that our family has always carried out. I promise I will use my sharp hunting knife and will not cut deep. I will seal it with a heated knife to prevent infection.'

She was determined to be as brave as possible and

prayed she would not faint. Sigtryggr prepared by putting one knife in the fire to heat it up. He placed a bowl and a hunting knife on the dresser. He took her hand and kissed it and then made a diagonal cut across her palm. She managed not to scream. He sliced his own hand and massaged her hand over the bowl to extract the blood. His cut was deeper and the blood ran freely. He murmured the vow in Norse then stirred the blood in the bowl with his finger and marked her across her brow, nose and cheeks before doing the same to himself. He made her sit in a chair while he fetched the knife to cauterise her wound. It was not as deep as his, so he only left the knife on for a few seconds. She whimpered a little and as he applied the knife across his own wound he gasped in pain.

Skye leant back in the chair and closed her eyes. 'You sure know how to dampen a woman's ardour, husband.'

He smiled. 'Don't you worry, my angel – I will have you screaming for me in a few minutes.'

'But we can't make love without using our hands! And what if we bleed all over the sheets?'

He laughed, 'The servants will be able to report that you must have been a virgin on your wedding night.'

'You must be joking after the times we have been caught indulging in sex since I came over here. Even your men caught us in the hay barn and got a view of our naked backsides.'

'Skye, they would have been more worried if I hadn't been humping you. One or two have even questioned my fertility because I haven't impregnated you in all this time. They are not used to women deliberately avoiding pregnancy with the help of nature. A Dane likes to score a bullseye every time he humps. I was so enamoured with my mini warriors that I think you will have to produce six boys before you can start on the girls.'

'Now listen to me King Sigtryggr of Dublin, I am not spending the next ten years as your broodmare confined to the stable. I am your queen and will rule at your side, not from a birthing chamber. If you go to war then I will go with you.'

'No you bloody won't madam, not while you're carrying my precious child. Even Ivar would back me up on that. It is imperative that you produce an heir as quickly as possible.'

'The sex of a child is determined by the male, not the female. Ask Sulamain if you don't believe me. I have the egg, you supply the sperm with the sex already determined. It will be your fault if I produce girls and not boys, not mine.'

'I will see Sulamain in the morning. If it is true he must know a way of increasing the chances of producing a boy.'

'Apparently, it is all down to timing – something you can struggle with at times.' She giggled.

How dare you insult me, woman! Now, get undressed and into that bed and let me make mad passionate love to you on our wedding night. You swore to obey me today, my queen.'

'Shame you didn't realise how deceitful I can be.'

'Why do you always have to have the last word?

Rest assured I shall impose my conjugal rights on you, in or out of the damned dress.'

He marched up to her and started undoing the buttons down her back, but could not resist kissing her forehead. 'For someone so small you are very determined and far too stubborn.'

'I was just waiting for your assistance; the buttons are at the back and you just mutilated my hand.'

'Oh, just excuses, my dear – you still have one fully functioning hand.'

'I know my love, but I was saving it for a special assignment that I think you will enjoy.'

Her dress fell to the floor and he picked it up and threw it over a chair whilst pulling her shift over her head. He unbuttoned his tunic and discarded it over the same chair with the rest of his clothes, picked her up and carried her to the bed. He looked at her beautiful body, lay down next to her and whispered, 'Skye, you melt my heart with joy. My body aches for you and you have unhinged my mind.'

'For a man of few words my love, I will take that as a declaration of your love for me.'

The next morning those who had not made it home after the celebrations were given a hearty breakfast and sent on their way. The servants were going to have a massive job clearing up and Skye was about to help them. Ivar saw and swooped on her before she could. 'Where do you think you are going, my lady?'

'To help clean up, of course.'

Ivar shook his head. 'No way. Skye, you are the

Queen now; you have to assert your authority and demand respect. Did you ever see Torri cleaning the palace?'

'Ivar, be reasonable – this is a one-off occasion. We don't have the staff to cope with all this mess. We need all hands on deck.'

'Well, command your troops to assist. They are all wandering about still drunk; it will clear their heads. The fact that they think they are warriors does not rule them out of menial duties.'

'But Sigtryggr may not agree and they are his men.'

'Rubbish. Now follow me!' He marched her outside to the courtyard, saw Merewolf and called him over. 'Now tell him what you want done and he will instruct the men.'

She realised that Ivar was right. 'Merewolf, I need the men to restore order. Can you send some to the kitchen, main hall and upper floors to report to the managers of each section?'

Merewolf looked shocked but was not about to argue with Ivar. 'Yes, of course, my lady. We will do our best, provided someone instructs the men.' He bowed and turned away with a smile on his face. He knew whose idea this had been and he approved.

Ivar said, 'Well done, Skye. These men are not just Sigtryggr's; they are sworn to serve you too. Whatever jobs need doing they should do it, whether it be farming, haymaking, shepherding, cooking, cleaning, building or defending you. I know it is hardly the court of the King of Wessex, but Sigtryggr has big ideas for his new palace and will need their labour too.'

He took her hand to lead her indoors and she cried out in pain as he caught the scar on her palm. Ivar turned her hand over and his cheeks started to colour. 'And how did you acquire this since yesterday, my dear?'

She daren't look him in the eye. 'I cut my hand on a knife.'

Ivar interrupted angrily, 'Do not lie to me Skye. I know exactly what this is and I suspect Sigtryggr has a similar cut across his own palm. This is a pagan ritual and not a Norse one, and I do not like him using it on you. It is rarely used in marriages today. You are not his dog, sword or chattel and are in no way subordinate to him. You are his equal in this marriage. Come over here and listen carefully to me.'

Tears were running down her cheeks as they sat on a bench well away from prying eyes and ears. Ivar hugged her and she felt tears on his cheek too. 'I know that Sigtryggr has lost many people he loved and it has had a profound effect on him. However, there is a very fine line between love and possession and I fear that he may turn into a very jealous husband and dominate you completely. I gave him some criticism for the way he ignored your needs when he brought you here. To be totally fair, he agreed with me. It could have been ignorance of women in general.'

She stuttered, 'He didn't force me, Ivar. I agreed to do it. He does have a lot of insecurities and my kidnapping did not help. But you must believe me when I tell you that he has always been as gentle as a lamb in his dealings with me. He has the same anger and rejection issues that you do, but he hasn't learned to deal with them yet.'

'Sweetheart, I am only trying to protect you. I know it should not be my business but just as Ubba protected your mother when she was in danger of dying in childbirth, I want to help you. As long as you promise to tell me immediately if he starts being overly possessive or jealous then I won't challenge him on this issue. However, if I sense a problem, I will not stay silent. I love you both, but I won't see him destroy you. He has huge potential as a king, partly because he has experienced many losses, just as I suffered with pain and was determined to overcome my disability. Rejection hurts hard in whatever form it comes.'

She threw her arms around him and kissed his cheek. 'Oh, Ivar, who would believe it – you championing women's rights just like Ubba? I had a long conversation with Torri about how to deal with jealous husbands and she told me that she did not think Ubba had a jealous bone in his body until Sigtryggr arrived.'

Ivar interrupted, 'Now they have the perfect marriage and relationship, and that is what I want for you. They work as a team and weather whatever storms come their way. Ubba was mortified when Torri was kidnapped and raped. He wanted to kill the bastard and he did make the initial blow, but he knew how much it would mean to her to castrate and kill him herself. Every man wants to protect their wife and Ubba took some time to reconcile with that. You know, there is no reason why your mother should not come over here for the birth next year. If Ubba is still playing at being a farmer rather than a warrior then he and Torri may come too.'

'Oh, Ivar, do you think they would come over here? You sound as though you think Ubba will be bored as a farmer.'

'Yes, he is a people person and he likes excitement in his life. A few months of breeding horses and children will be enough to drive him insane. He will be back in action soon. He is not as lazy as he thinks he is and he enjoys the politics of warfare just like my father did.'

Sigtryggr came rushing out of the door and saw them. He shouted angrily, 'Skye, why are my warriors changing beds and washing up in the kitchens?'

Skye stood up and raised her hand. 'I believe they are "our" warriors, not "yours", and they will be deployed wherever they are needed. Is there an army at the gates? Are we under siege?'

'No, of course not!'

'Then they will carry out my orders until they are finished and the palace is restored to my satisfaction.'

Sigtryggr folded his arms across his chest and glared at Ivar. 'I assume this was nothing at all to do with you?'

Ivar shrugged his shoulders. 'Of course not. When would I take an interest in domestic matters? I always had someone to take care of those areas.'

'Trouble is Ivar, it has your hallmark of meddling written all over it.'

He turned to Skye. 'Very well, my dear wife – as you wish – but just remember that it works both ways.

I trust you will think carefully before you get yourself kidnapped again as next time I will send the cooks, housemaids, washerwomen and servants to rescue you. You may find they will be too late to save your neck.'

He flounced off, trying not to laugh at the astonishment on their faces. To his delight, Ivar applauded him, but he daren't turn around.

Ivar laughed, 'Oh you see how quick he is – what a brain!'

Skye retorted, 'Especially when he accused me last night of always wanting to have the last word. You have got to admit he is a lovable little boy at heart, for all his size and bluster. The prospect of producing six sons just like him is enough to make any woman flee from his bed. Promise me you won't leave me, so you can rescue me if I need you.'

'I will always be your protector, as long as I am alive.'

THIRTY-SIX

Halfdan glared at Ubba. 'You have given your support to Edward and promised to protect his sister, who will take the throne of Jorvik? Have you gone mad, Ubba?'

Ubba raised his hand. 'Halfdan, hear me out! Edward is not averse to us remaining in Northumbria, as he wants protection from the Scots, Welsh and other Norsemen. He cannot rule from 400 miles away and would rather we stay here than leave it open to other raiders. If you want to try and take Durham he will not send an army to prevent it. I told him I had no wish to become a king of anywhere and would find my own farm and retire.'

'Are you saying you would not support me in an attack on Durham?'

'No, of course I will. I did not accept Edward's offer of a Yorkshire property for that very reason. I will be living in Richmond and will join you whenever you need me. I have sworn no bond with Edward or Aethelflaed over Jorvik. I have, however, offered to remove her from harm should I be aware of an impending attack on Jorvik by other Danes or invaders. How I will know about them while living 50 miles north remains to be seen. Edward just wants to talk to you. Any arrangements you make are between the two of you.'

'If I agree to see him will you accompany me?'

'Yes, if you want me to – but I do not have Ivar's political flair. I will send Thorin with a message for us to meet at Ralf's farm in Haxby. It will be more convenient for them as it is closer to Jorvik.'

'Yes, but what if he sets us up and plans to kill or capture us there?'

Ubba said in exasperation, 'Look, he has been here twice and come without an army both times. He does not want these negotiations known about by his counsellors; he does not want them to think he has made any deals with a Ragnarsson. We have to show some trust too. He intends to appoint Ralf and Gytha as advisers in Aethelflaed's court, so he needs to tread carefully – and attacking us at Ralf's farm would hardly be conducive to that. For the record, I think he is brave to make his sister Queen of Jorvik. His own father would never have done that and his mother is expecting three Ragnarsson heads to be spiked on Jorvik's gates.'

Halfdan laughed, 'But can we ever be at peace with the Saxons?'

'Well, look at it from their point of view. Better the enemy you know than one you don't. He wants us to stay to protect Northumbria and he may be willing to pay you for that privilege. I would not accept any payment as I couldn't guarantee that I would know about an attack in advance.'

'Well, I will agree to meet him, but I don't want

him to have any warning. The less time Edward has to plan our capture, the happier I will be.'

'But we could be in danger of running into a Saxon troop on the journey.'

'Why do you think I want you there? You and Sleipnir are the best scouts I know and if you bring your son's wolf, we will have another alert set of eyes and ears. I appreciate you may not want to put Arne at risk by bringing him.'

'Very well. We will leave at first light.'

Halfdan nodded. 'Now, where's my son?'

'Probably still using Stefan as his hobby-horse, where we left him. Forgive me but is he the more maternal member of your family? He certainly has a natural way with children. For someone so tall, strong and powerful he has amazing gentleness and patience. My Astrid and Theo adore him because he tells them fairytales and lets them ride on his back.'

oOo

They set off at dawn. As predicted, Arne was furious about being prevented from going, but begrudgingly sent Shadow with them. Ubba rode Sleipnir for his speed and close-combat fighting skills, although he knew he would stand out more than Raven. Halfdan's Percheron was grey too, so they would both be at risk of being spotted, but he knew the most secluded routes to use when they got closer to Jorvik. Shadow lolloped along at speed and tried to keep in front of them to check out surrounding areas. They were well wrapped up in cloaks trimmed with bearskin as the wind was biting after an overnight frost.

Stefan's horse was a dark bay and they used him to scout the valleys from the hill tops as they descended from the Wolds and North York Moors. They used the old drover's route, with Stefan and Shadow scouting ahead.

They spotted a group of Dales pack ponies heading their way and pulled into a covert of pine trees to let them pass. Ubba touched Sleipnir's nose and gave him the command to be silent. Shadow was called to heel. Halfdan and Stefan had learnt from Ubba's earlier training and issued their own commands to their horses. They could see the line of five ponies with three drovers who were taking sheepskins to sell at local farmers' markets further north. All three horses stood quietly, resisting the urge to whinny to the new arrivals and Shadow sat alert and ready for a possible attack.

As they came closer to Jorvik Ubba led them back up into the hills away from the tracks. They had to continue cross-country, jumping into and out of fields, which was far more interesting for both the horses and the riders. They skirted around Jorvik, heading to the west side to approach Haxby. Ubba hoped Gytha would be there, even if Ralf was not.

He found a good viewpoint up a hill behind Ralf's farm and they observed a rider checking the field of weaned foals and filling up a hayrack. It was one of the farm labourers, not Ralf. They observed that the road from Jorvik was clear and then cantered down the hill and headed down the narrow track to the farm gates.

Ubba leapt off Sleipnir and opened the gates as one of the farm dogs came, barking frantically, towards the gate. When he recognised Ubba his tail started to wag and he bounded forward to greet him... until he spotted Shadow and accepted his dominance, staying back as the horses headed up the drive to the house.

Ralf appeared from the barn and Ranulf from one of the stallion boxes.

'Ubba, my friend! How pleased I am to see you and your brother and Stefan. Are you here for a meeting with Edward and Aethelflaed?'

They hugged and Ranulf came forward to take their horses as Halfdan and Stefan dismounted. The kitchen door flew open and Gytha ran down the steps and threw herself at Ubba. 'Oh, Ubba, I have been worried about you and the children. How are they all coping at Terrington?'

Ubba hugged her. 'I was worried that Ralf and your family may have been harmed because of your connection to me, but thankfully Edward seems to want to make a deal and keep us in Northumbria to protect Aethelflaed.'

They went into the welcoming kitchen where thick bacon slices were already cooking on the fire pit next to a pan of fried eggs. The cook had seen them arrive and knew that the three Danes would have been on the road for three hours and would be hungry.

They caught up with the news from Jorvik while they tucked in. It appeared that Ralf's family had endeared itself to Aethelflaed, who was determined to give Ralf and Gytha special adviser roles in her new government. The news of Aethelflaed becoming Queen of Jorvik had been well received by the Witan and ealdormen. She was regarded as clever and fair from her dealings in Mercia.

Ranulf departed with a handwritten message from Ubba to Edward, asking him to meet them at the farm.

Halfdan wanted to see Ralf's stallions and horses as he wanted to purchase a youngster of the same calibre as Sleipnir. Ralf agreed to show Halfdan and Stefan around but Ubba said he would join them later. He wanted a private word with Gytha first.

To ensure privacy she led him to her bedroom and he couldn't resist commenting, 'Heavens above, Gytha! Is this a sexual invitation?'

She slapped his shoulder. 'No you great oaf. You have seen me at my worst giving birth to Thorin in this bed. Even you, great lover that you are, would find it difficult to hump me and not recall the horrors of that night.'

He laughed and hugged her. 'I miss you Gytha, and my time in Jorvik... and you may be touched to know that I miss sparring with my wicked brother whose obsession with my love life was overwhelming. If he witnessed us together right now, rumours would already be circulating in Jorvik.'

She pushed him down to sit on the bed and joined him. 'Ubba, surely you are not already bored with your new life when you have all the time in the world to enjoy your wife and mistress? What else do you want if not sex?'

'Your opinion on Edward and Aethelflaed's sudden decision to want two Ragnarssons to remain in Northumbria. Is it genuine or is he setting us up?'

'I think he does want you to stay here to keep other invaders away. Even Ralf can see that it would make sense, although he is just as confused as you about the sudden about-turn. He knows it will not be popular news back in Wessex that he has not captured and killed all three sons of Ragnar. Having spoken to him several times, Ralf believes Edward holds you in high esteem and would like you as a valuable friend, certainly not as an enemy. He admires your honesty and integrity, and your skill in rallying your troops.'

'And at the same time he is confused by my lack of ambition. You see, I saw how my father struggled inwardly with the onerous task of ruling and I don't want to make the same mistakes as him, which ended his life far too soon. I want to see my children grow up, but it is becoming more difficult than ever because of our family name.'

'Have you heard any more news from Ireland? I am sure you are missing Viggo too.'

'No more than confirmation from Edward of their safe landing in Dublin. I was hoping to hear more news of them whilst I was here.'

'Sam has been watching daily for any of our pigeons returning from Ireland. They may not have made it back here. What worries me is that Sigtryggr and Ivar may have come under attack from other chieftains and could be busy fighting. The responsibility of being a parent weighs heavily on both of us in these turbulent times.'

She was crying. He hugged her tightly. 'I know how hard it is waiting for news, but Skye has Ivar protecting her now, alongside Sigtryggr.'

Immersed in their grief they had failed to hear the door open. Ralf stood in the doorway, observing them quizzically. 'Most men would be horrified to find Ubba Ragnarsson in their wife's bedroom and her crying in his arms, but I know better than that.'

Gytha replied tearfully, 'We are both missing our children and worrying about their survival.'

Ralf touched her shoulder. 'I know you are Gytha, but we have to trust that Sigtryggr is protecting her. She wanted to go with him and we both chose to let her fly the nest.'

Later that day Ranulf came back from the palace with a note from Edward. They all congregated around the kitchen table and as the note was written in Latin it was handed to Ubba to translate.

'He, Aethelflaed and Aldhelm will come here tomorrow morning at 10 a.m. with no escort and he assures us that we will be unharmed.'

There followed a long discussion about what Edward may hope to achieve. Halfdan was adamant he would not swear to desist from taking any cities other than Jorvik. He intended to take Durham in the future if he could raise enough men capable of attacking such a well-protected city. He reckoned he would need to attack from both land and sea. The ramparts at Durham were 20 feet high and would require the skills of men used to attacking with battering rams and climbing towers. He looked at his brother and Ubba smiled but made no comment.

After the conversation had abated, Ranulf pulled out another piece of parchment from his pocket and placed it on the table. 'Now for the other message given to me by Sam just after it arrived by pigeon from Ireland today.'

Gytha shouted, 'Is there news of Skye?'

'I don't know. I can't read it. It is from Viggo. Here, Ubba – you will have to translate this one too.'

Ubba grabbed the note and the further he read, the more excited he looked.

'Basically, they all arrived safely in Dublin and Ivar's reputation assured nobody objected. Sigtryggr strengthened his hold on Dublin with the support of some Irish chieftains. He and Skye are married; she was crowned Queen two weeks ago.'

Gytha screamed, 'Oh, how wonderful, Ralf! Our daughter is a queen!'

Ubba laughed, 'Viggo has suggested we all visit Ireland in June next year, as Skye would like some support from her mother.'

Halfdan said, 'That sounds like Viggo's way of telling you she may already be carrying a baby.'

Gytha shouted, 'A baby too! Oh, Ralf, we must be there. Our daughter needs us.'

Ralf laughed, 'Calm down, my dear; a lot can happen in nine months. You know well enough the perils of bearing a child.'

Ubba said, 'Well, I would certainly like to go and see them all and now I am just a farmer I am sure I can spare the time to go. Halfdan, you will have to plan your attack on Durham for after I have been to Ireland.'

Ralf produced some wine he had purloined from the palace cellars and they had a rowdy night celebrating the news.

The next day the royal party of four arrived exactly on schedule, with no sign of any followers. The family assembled outside and Ranulf and a groom came to attend to the horses.

Ubba ran down the steps and assisted Aethelflaed in dismounting from her horse. He bowed and said, 'My lady, pleased to meet you again.'

Edward was slower to dismount as he was looking at the stallions who were excited by the new arrivals in the yard and were squealing. The chestnut mare Aethelflaed rode was calling back to the stallions and flirting vocally. Ubba waited for Edward to dismount and ascend the steps and then gave Aethelflaed his hand to steady her. She smiled as it was unnecessary, but she enjoyed the attention.

At the top of the steps Ubba moved towards Edward and said, 'My lord King, may I introduce you to my brother Halfdan and his righthand man Stefan.'

Edward grinned at the reference to Stefan. He greeted them both cordially and marvelled at the difference in features between the two brothers. Both Ubba and Halfdan were at least 6ft 2 inches tall but

Halfdan was built like a true "berserker" in size and stature, whereas Ubba was tall, lean and agile – the image of Ragnar.

They were shown into the house by Gytha and congregated around the kitchen table. Gytha asked Edward if he wished to be alone with Ubba but he said he was happy for Ralf and her to be at the meeting.

Lord Aldhelm had not been keen on what he perceived as Ubba's overfamiliarity with Aethelflaed. He was concerned that with his wife not there he was making a play for the future Queen of Jorvik, and resolved to keep a careful eye on the Dane.

Edward said, 'Halfdan, I am sure you are aware of my discussion with your brother about remaining in Northumbria. Have you decided on your next move? I want you to be aware that I am not averse to you settling further north.'

Halfdan laughed, 'And you truly expect that I would reveal to you what my next move will be? Perhaps you could explain your sudden desire to keep me on your shores and tell me whether you have any preference as to where you would like me to settle? Of course, it could be achieved a lot quicker if you were to supply me with an army too.'

Edward responded with a wry smile. 'Very clever, but I cannot supply you with an army... though there are ways I can assist if necessary. I believe Ricsige of Northumbria is proving to be an inadequate king since the death of Ecgberht.'

Halfdan smiled, 'Well at least we are both receiving similar intelligence. No doubt yours is from the clergy.

Mine is from the citizens and merchants. However, when I left Lincoln my army was dispersed and I have nothing like the number of men I would need to launch such a campaign at present.'

Aethelflaed said, 'Shall I put it more bluntly? I would feel happier with you in that region rather than Ricsige. The Scots will not be repelled by him, but they would fear tackling you. I can't send an army to assist you but as Edward suggested, there may be other ways I can support you. If you are on the East Coast of Northumbria then it will dissuade Norsemen from invading.'

Halfdan replied, 'I may have to recruit Norsemen to strengthen my army, which will require money.'

Edward intervened, 'But Ireland is nearer than Denmark. I would not want Ivar the Boneless back in the county, but Sigtryggr, I believe, is young and ambitious.'

Ubba remarked, 'Be careful, Edward. Your father would not have contemplated becoming King of England with the help of Danes. Why the change of heart?'

Edward replied, 'I don't regard all Danes as my enemies. Both Halfdan and Ivar brought prosperity to Jorvik and Lincoln, although Ivar's cruelty was restrained by you, for which I am grateful. I admire your courage, tenacity and resilience to overcome whatever setbacks threaten to prevent you achieving your objectives. You may not all be trustworthy, and greed can overcome you, but I would far rather have you on my side than as an enemy.'

Ubba laughed, 'I think you may have problems convincing your mother of our virtues; there could be repercussions.'

Edward responded firmly, 'My mother is no longer the Queen. Times move on and many things change – hopefully for the better. I will be going back to Wessex soon, so I suggest you keep in touch with Aethelflaed via Ralf. Ubba, I cannot guarantee your safety in Jorvik, even after the coronation. There are always bounty hunters looking to make a profit.'

Ubba said, 'I don't intend to be within 50 miles of Jorvik, but I will keep in touch with Ralf. And if Aethelflaed needs me, I will come to her rescue.'

Edward turned to Halfdan, 'Well I hope we can work together in the future.'

Halfdan said, 'I was quite happy and settled in Lincoln until you came along and ousted me. It may take me some time to get over that.'

They all laughed and Edward raised his glass. 'A toast to the future of this rich and pleasant land.' They all raised their glasses and Edward reflected on what his father would think about him co-operating with Danes to realise Alfred's ambition for a united England.

During the lunch that followed Aethelflaed managed to engage Ubba in a private conversation in the corner of the large room, much to the annoyance of Lord Aldhelm. 'Ubba, I just want you to know that I will instruct my army that you are not to be considered an enemy of Jorvik and there will be no price on your head. I anticipate though that this will not please some of them, so I think you are wise keeping your distance for the time being.'

Ubba laughed, 'I can see I have already ruffled Lord Aldhelm's feathers – and he won't be the only one. I assure you Aethelflaed, I will not be leading an army against you. I am pleased that your brother has been brave enough to put you in charge of the city. I doubt a Dane would have done that, even though we do treat our women more equally than Saxons do.

I remember when we rescued you from captivity with the intention of you and Erik fleeing the country to start a new life together. The gods took control that day and Erik fought his brother, lost his life and shattered your dreams. It would never have worked but I remember how devastated you were after witnessing his death. I was still a teenager then and deeply in love with Torri, even though she was married to Bjorn; I had plenty of experience of unrequited love. Returning to your bullying husband carrying a Dane's lovechild cannot have been easy – and yet, once again, you denied love when you became Lady of Mercia, vowing never to remarry. You put your duty to the crown first and denied your own happiness. The curse between the crown and personal happiness takes its toll once again.'

She smiled and touched his hand. 'I don't regret it Ubba; it allows me to make the best decisions for the people I rule over. Had I been married it would have been more difficult to have my voice heard. A man's opinion is always taken more seriously than a woman's. Men do not like deferring to a woman in marriage, never mind ruling a kingdom.'

'I suppose I have been spoilt by having the perfect queen at my side. I am more than happy for her to have the upper hand. She does it so well and fights like a lion to protect her children. I am looking forward to my retirement as a farmer and being free to please myself rather than my warring brothers.'

'Ah, so Ubba the reluctant king and Ubba the peacemaker are really true descriptions of you.'

'Along with a few other sexual references describing my love of bedding beautiful women and producing children.'

'I have seen the results of your favourite pastime Ubba and you certainly rate highly in the stallion stakes. If I ever wanted to reproduce and breed a future king then you would be at the top of my list.'

Ubba laughed, 'Best not to mention that to Edward or he may change his mind about leaving Jorvik in your hands. I am flattered that you would even consider me. Obviously Erik did a good job of persuading you that not all Danes are violent heathen rapists.'

'No, I think there are many similarities between us.'

THIRTY-SEVEN

That evening, after the royal party had left and they had finished dinner, Halfdan asked, 'Well, come on, big brother... Tell us what happened when Aethelflaed was kidnapped by Siegfrid and Erik. How did Erik manage to bed himself a Saxon queen?'

Ubba smiled. 'I know you won't believe me, but I was never aware of exactly what happened; it was kept very quiet at the time for obvious reasons. Ragnar was asked by Alfred to be the go-between in negotiations for the ransom to free her. He wasn't well acquainted with either brother as they had never actually met. However, reputation, as you well know, is all. Our old friend Haesten was also involved with Erik and Siegfrid and was in charge of guarding Aethelflaed.'

Halfdan interrupted, 'They put Haesten in charge of a female prisoner? That's like putting a chicken in a wolf's den and expecting it not to eat it. His lust for young women was well renowned.'

Ubba laughed. 'Well, Haesten probably thought that as she was no innocent virgin but the wife of Aethelred, he would enjoy humping a princess — especially Alfred's daughter. It started when she insisted on bathing in the river. Both Haesten and Erik escorted her and got an eyeful of her naked body.

Haesten tried his charm offensive and it did not go down well with Aethelflaed. She fought him off by kicking him in the balls, and Erik walked in on him. Thus ensued a scrap between the two men and of course, Erik was seen by the princess as her protector. Aethelflaed loathed her cruel bullying husband and was impressed by Erik, who probably had exactly the same idea as Haesten. The inevitable happened and Erik was soon besotted.'

Halfdan laughed, 'No different than you then, Ubba. I have seen the connection between you and Aethelflaed, so don't deny it.'

Ubba threw his hands in the air. 'Look, I only came into this debacle totally innocently. I was there when we attempted to rescue Aethelflaed and had no idea she had fallen in love with Erik and that my father had agreed to help them escape. However, by then, Siegfrid had guessed that Erik was in love with her and he imprisoned her in a cage hung in the rafters of the great hall. I was tasked with releasing her whilst a fight broke out between Siegfrid and Erik and our men. I managed to get her out, but she witnessed Siegfrid killing Erik and was distraught. I threw her onto my horse and left at full gallop. The great hall was set on fire. We hid in the forest that night and she wept in my arms.'

Gytha intervened, 'Ubba, if you took advantage of that poor girl I will be so disappointed in you.'

Ubba smiled. 'I am hurt that you would even think that of me Gytha. Am I not your knight in shining armour, who frequently rescues damsels in distress without harming them? You once referred to me as such and I was only twenty years old when faced with this dilemma. Of course I did not do such a thing – especially when she told me she was carrying Erik's baby.'

Halfdan laughed, 'I bet you could not wait to hand her back to Alfred to sort that one out. I trust our famous father managed to restrain himself too, on this occasion.'

'Oh, he knew just how badly Alfred and Aelswith would take this news. Their daughter was carrying a Dane's baby while married to a future King of Mercia who had raped her on her wedding night and hadn't touched her since. Thankfully, he was responsible for putting her in danger by being too close to the Dane camp, so Alfred blamed him for that and secured his silence.'

Gytha said, 'And was it you who persuaded her to go back to her odious husband?'

'She really had no option. Her mother had no sympathy at all – she had "supped with the devil" as far as she was concerned and betrayed her father. I persuaded her not to take her life, which is what she wanted to do at the time. Father promised that if life became untenable with Aethelred he would kill him.'

Halfdan slammed his hand on the table. 'Now I understand why you are keen to protect her as Queen of Jorvik. You feel obliged to carry on our father's promise. But why, Ubba, is she so important to you?'

Ubba was flustered; he really had no answer. He stammered, 'I just think she has had a very raw deal in life. Yes, she fell in love with a Dane – but what woman wouldn't, married to that feckless cruel bastard? Thankfully, she bore a daughter, which made her life easier, but she has always put her duty before herself. She chose celibacy so that no man would rule Mercia and deny her happiness yet again. I think that Edward has been very brave in acknowledging her as Queen of Jorvik and Mercia, as the Saxons are a far more male dominant society than we are.'

Gytha ran over and hugged him. 'Oh, Ubba, the champion of women. This is why we love you so much. You must explain this to Torri as unless you do, she may think you hold a torch for Aethelflaed when in truth you are saddened that she has had to live without the love and support of any man, and has denied herself the joy of more children. A heavy price for any woman to pay.'

'I know from experience how hard women have to work to keep their families together. I appreciate that I have the perfect partner to support me and my children. I regret that not many men understand the sacrifices their wives make; it saddens me.'

Halfdan said, 'Ubba, you know Ivar would not be too pleased to know you are supporting the usurper of his throne. Where does that leave you if he decides to come back and fight for it again?'

'Ivar made a choice to go to Ireland of his own free will, and only time will tell. I will tell him; I am certainly no coward. If he decides to come back to try and retake Jorvik then it will be without my help. I will keep my word to Edward and Aethelflaed.'

Halfdan smiled. 'You would prioritise the Saxons before your own brother?'

'If he was claiming Jorvik. Ivar will not come back over here so it will not be a choice I have to make.'

o0o

Ubba breathed a sigh of relief; they had made it back to Ralf's farm in Terrington with no problems. He just wanted to wrap his family in his arms and thank the gods he was still alive. He had harboured a fear all along that Edward may be deceiving them and would attack. He craved some peace away from the stress he had felt over the last few months. The trouble was, he wasn't sure whether he would ever achieve the peace he desired.

Thorin and Arne came to take their horses. He dismounted and could feel the stiffness in his joints. His feet were numb with cold. He hugged Arne, who came for Sleipnir.

'I'm happy to see you are safe and well.'

Arne replied, 'Did you run into trouble?'

'No, but the fear that one might keep the mind and body on constant alert.'

He opened the door and the warmth and comfort of the scene hit him hard.

Freya ran up to him shouting, 'Daddy, you are home again!'

He hugged her and whispered, 'My sweet angel, you don't know how much I want to remain by your side forever.'

She pulled away from him and remonstrated with

him, 'Daddy, an angel is a Christian entity. Do not call me that!'

Torri intervened, 'Enough, young lady. Your father is tired and hungry and will call you whatever he likes. I certainly don't consider you an angel. Now finish laying the table.' She sloped off, giving her mother a defiant look.

Torri looked closely at Ubba, who looked very tired, dejected and wet. 'Ubba, are you all right? Have you had bad news?'

He hugged her tightly. 'No, sweetheart. I am just tired and so glad to be back here in one piece. Nothing went wrong at all.' Torri unfastened his heavy wet cloak as he seemed to be frozen to the spot.

She served them dishes of piping hot stew straight from the pot and managed to catch a moment alone with Halfdan when Ubba had gone to change. She caught him just outside the hall as he returned. 'Ubba does not look well. Has something upset him?'

He replied, 'No, I just think he has been on high alert for so long that he was expecting an attack and when it did not happen the fear drained away and left him exhausted. He just needs time with you. Once you get to Richmond just let him sleep as much as he wants. When he starts chasing you and Serena round the bed, you will know he is healed.'

Torri laughed, 'Thank God there are two of us to satisfy his needs.'

Halfdan laughed, 'He just needs you all to bring him round.'

As they ate, Ubba thawed out and told them the

news of Skye and Sigtryggr's wedding and coronation.

To everyone's utter shock Freya said, 'Oh, I already know that. I saw it in a dream a while ago. Skye wore a beautiful blue dress and they had six girls as attendants and six boys dressed as mini warriors carrying swords and shields. At the wedding Skye presented him with a sword designed and made by Ralf with a silver handle and scroll showing a snake. Ivar looked splendid in red and gold. He gave her away on behalf of Ralf. Then they had the coronation; they took the oaths in both Latin and Irish. The church was full of people and they had the boy warriors as a guard of honour. Sigtryggr put the crown on Skye's head and they all cheered. Then the chieftains declared their oath to Skye, one by one.'

Ubba interrupted, 'That was very clever of him and was probably suggested by Ivar to bind them even more to his cause. What about Viggo?'

'Oh, he was there Daddy, strutting about like a peacock as usual in a dark navy and silver tunic.'

Torri snapped at Freya, 'Peacock? How dare you insult your brother?'

Arne burst out laughing. 'Oh, come on, Mother – you know how much Viggo loves silk and velvet, and richly coloured clothes. She is only being truthful.'

Freya continued, 'They had a big dance back at the palace. Ivar talked to a beautiful blonde-haired Rus princess called Irina. They are attracted to each other.'

Torri commented, 'Has Ivar found love at last?'

'Perhaps, but it is too early to say. I feel there are some serious hurdles to overcome. Oh, and Skye is already carrying Sigtryggr's son.'

Halfdan said, 'So Viggo *was* hinting about a baby next year when he suggested Gytha goes over to support her.'

Ubba said, 'I see no reason why we can't visit them at the same time. We have our own longboats and could navigate the river network to Ceaster and then sail across to Dublin on the shortest route.'

Torri said, 'Oh, that would be wonderful.'

Freya said, 'Daddy, why did Sigtryggr perform the blood ritual of binding hands with Skye on their wedding night and not during the service?'

Ubba was horrified. 'Why did he even consider it necessary? It's a pagan ritual not a Norse tradition and would not have been well received by the Christian community.'

'Oh, I know that. Ivar was furious when he saw it, but Skye made him promise not to challenge Sigtryggr about it. He thought it showed too much dominance and was totally unnecessary.'

Ubba said, 'Well, he was absolutely right. I appreciate that Sigtryggr descends from Dane and Irish tribes, but it is a ritual frowned upon now by gothis. I hope he is not treating Skye as a possession rather than a wife.'

Torri said, 'Oh, come on, Ubba. She has had her mother and me as role models. She is a very determined girl and won't let Sigtryggr bully her. Ivar won't let him get away with it either. Look what he did to you when you asserted your dominance over me.'

Ubba sighed, 'Don't remind me – my ribs have not

forgotten it.'

As they climbed into bed that night Ubba was asleep within minutes of his head hitting the pillow. Torri was worried about him but she snuggled up close, vowing she would soon have him full of vitality when they reached Richmond and he was away from any more stress.

Halfdan took his leave the next day and promised he would return to collect Siegfrid as soon as he had a suitable home for them sorted.

Ubba expected he would have to organise the packing of goods and equipment to sail to Richmond, but he was told in no uncertain terms by Torri that Egil had sorted out the packing and stowing of their belongings on the longboat. Arne had overseen the provision of supplies of feed and hay. All the horse equipment had already been loaded too.

He sought out Thorin, who would be remaining at Terrington to run the farm with their workers whilst Ralf was in Haxby. He was under orders from his father to keep a very low profile in case Mercian troops mistook him for a young Dane warrior. He was banned from riding out alone.

Ubba asked, 'Thorin, was everything Freya related about the wedding true?'

'Yes, sir. Freya will have dreams showing her what is happening in other places. However, as she reaches puberty this gift may fade. Girls are much more intuitive than boys in these matters.'

'What did you think about Sigtryggr enforcing the

marriage binding on Skye?'

'I think you should look at it from his perspective. The Irish Danes will still be doing that wedding ritual like their ancestors before them. I know you see it as a sign of dominance but beneath all that bravado and his warrior looks he is quite an insecure character. Remember he lost his mother early and his father died in battle. Now he has found Skye he may just be frightened of losing her too. If it makes him feel more secure then so be it – and as Freya said, Skye went ahead with it willingly, not under duress.'

'I suppose you are right. At least Ivar is there to keep an eye on them – and believe me, he does not miss a thing. But what of your future, Thorin? Do you know what the gods have in store for you?'

'I'm afraid not. They will send me where they need me when I have reached puberty. For now, I am content watching Freya's back; that is why I am here.'

'Of course it is, and as soon as we are settled in Richmond you must come up and spend Christmas with us, unless your parents need you back in Jorvik. Be careful, Thorin. Some Saxons will not want Aethelflaed as queen and may take it out on you. Watch your back!'

'Oh, don't you worry about me, Ubba. You go up to Richmond and spend the winter in the valley rather than up here on the moors. You look like you need a rest. Arne is quite capable of looking after the horses. He has your ability to sense when a horse is not right and to act quickly. He will soon have his shepherding skills tested during spring lambing.'

Serena was heading to the dairy for milk. Ubba took the chance to speak to her, following her in. She was filling a pitcher from a barrel and had not heard him. As she turned around and saw him, she nearly dropped the milk.

'Ubba, you great lumbering oaf. You frightened the life out of me.'

'Charmed, I am sure. I just wanted a little chat with you. Come here and sit next to me at this table.'

'Why do I feel like a naughty child? You always say that when one of them has been naughty.'

'I just wanted to know if you have something important to tell me that for some reason you are reluctant to confirm.'

She tossed her head. 'Such as? You have been away a few days and Torri said you were tired and needed to rest.'

'All right then, lady – if you are not for telling me, I will tell you. As wolf leader of this pack I know instinctively when one of my females is carrying my child. You were pregnant before I left for Lincoln. Why did you not tell me?'

'Oh, dammit, Ubba. I didn't want to make the parting harder for you than it already is. You said a couple of months before you left that now would not be a good time to have a baby. When you came back I kept quiet for that reason. When Frank was killed I was so heartbroken, and so were you; I just didn't want you to have any more upset.'

He hugged her to him. 'Serena, I only meant from a practical point of view that an extra baby could have waited... but as long as it is mine and there is no other reason you are trying to hide it, then of course I am delighted.'

She looked daggers at him. 'What do you mean? Do you think I have been with someone else?' She slapped him across his cheek. 'How dare you accuse me of being unfaithful, you arrogant bastard? Who the hell did you think I had been with?'

Ubba was nursing his rapidly reddening cheek. 'Christ, woman, I didn't think you had been unfaithful. I was just concerned when you did not tell me. I don't know how, but I can tell when a woman is pregnant. There are changes in her body, both in touch and smell.'

Torri was standing in the doorway. 'For heaven's sake Ubba, stop digging yourself a bigger hole. Apologise to Serena and beg forgiveness. You know very well there is nobody else involved. We have a household and four children to move tomorrow and I can do without a hormonal mistress and bad-tempered husband to cope with as well.'

Ubba left by the other door quickly, knowing that he could suffer a far worse beating with two of them ranting at him. He escaped to the farm office and asked a servant to fetch Arne.

When Arne received a message that his father wanted to see him in the office he knew he must have done something wrong, but he couldn't think of anything specific. He went back to the house and his trepidation mounted with every step he took.

He knocked quietly, wanting to flee back to the stables. He heard his father summon him to enter and made himself walk in.

Ubba looked at him in surprise. 'Good grief, Arne! You look as though you are about to have your head chopped off. Can a father not have a conversation with his son on equal terms without you assuming you have done something wrong?'

Arne tried to control his rising panic, but he knew that whatever his father was going to discuss, it would not be to his liking. 'I just know that I am not going to like it.'

Ubba smiled, sensing Arne had picked up on his own tension. 'You are approaching fifteen soon and it's time you mastered the essential life skill of sex.'

Arne jumped up and leaned menacingly over the desk. He raised his hand. 'Stop right there, Father! I would have had to be deaf, dumb and blind not to know about sex having lived with you for the last two years and in Jormund before that. Three-year-old Theo already knows exactly what you and Serena are up to in the bedroom without seeing what is going on, and knows to keep out. I don't even want to imagine what you and my mother get up to and I certainly don't want to know the graphic details. Leave me to find out for myself; I am sure I will get there in my own time.'

Ubba was visibly shocked; Arne was blazing with anger and looked the image of Ivar when he lost his temper. 'Calm down, Arnie – you look exactly like Ivar when he is about to kill someone. It's quite unsettling. I merely want to help you to master something as essential to life as living and breathing. Am I to assume that you are still a virgin?'

Arne was still on his feet. 'None of your bloody business, Father. End of conversation.' He started to move towards the door.

Ubba grabbed him and hugged him tightly. 'Now listen to me, son. When you first came over here I told you that communication was a vital tool and that if you have any problems you must tell me straight away because I will likely have encountered a similar problem. You are angry about something far more serious than sex.'

Arne tried to break free but Ubba would not let him go. He pushed him back into his chair and sat on his desk, facing him, holding his right hand. 'You have to get this off your chest. Something is festering in your mind and it needs sorting.'

'I am angry that you kept me away from harm. As you stated, I am turning fifteen soon. You were fighting in battles at twelve years old and I fear if I don't have an opportunity to learn I may be found wanting when I do have to fight in a battle.'

'Oh, son, I can appreciate your frustration but that was 30 years ago and at that age I was mainly catching loose horses behind the lines, not facing seasoned warriors at the front.'

'You chose to keep me here under your protection and sent Viggo with Ivar. You must consider him more capable of fighting than me.'

He hugged Arne to him again. 'Son, that was never the reason for Viggo going with Ivar. It was precisely the opposite; you have a natural talent for fighting, which is a gift from your grandfather and me. You are bonded to nature as we were and your sight, athleticism and hearing are attuned to observe minute details that will keep you alive. You can hear an arrow flying through the air. You can sense the slice of a sword coming from behind. You feel the change in air patterns when a seax is thrown at you from a distance. Very few men can do that and Viggo is not one of them. These attributes cannot be taught; they are instinct.'

'But if I don't practice them in battle, how will I know if I have the courage to kill an enemy?'

'Because your mother has more courage than any man I have ever witnessed, and I see it in you. You also have Ivar's short temper and quick intelligence, which will get you out of a difficult situation at speed. You will not lack courage or ability when you face your first battle. Add to that your empathy with a horse, and a wolf watching your back. I think you will have more than enough skills to survive.'

'But father, I am not going to get the chance. You surrendered Jorvik and have agreed with King Edward not to attack there again, and to protect Aethelflaed should other invaders attack. Retirement as a farmer may be an option for you, but where does that leave me – an untried teenage Ragnarsson – while my brothers forge their paths as warriors, scholars, sailors and explorers?'

Ubba sighed, 'At least you are alive, son. Surely that must count for something. I know you may find it difficult to adjust from palace life in Jorvik to hill farming, but I will not neglect your education.'

'Then let me join Halfdan if he is fighting for territory in the North East, or let me go to Ireland and join Ivar and Sigtryggr. I need to prove myself in battle Father, and survive. I know I will always have a price on my head for being your son, but I need to forge a reputation that will prevent enemies considering me an easy target. If I had been with you when you fled Jorvik and ran into the Mercians, do you think I would have survived?'

Ubba sighed, 'Son, the Mercians would have spotted you were the youngest and likely the weakest target. You may have made it to safety, but I would probably have died trying to save you – just as Frank was killed trying to protect me.'

'Then all the more reason why I should make my own path in life. Did Ragnar protect you when you were a teenager in battle?'

'No, son. He was often leading the charge, but he saw I was positioned with Bjorn further back, with Lagertha keeping a watchful eye on both of us. When I became more proficient I was proud to serve at the front with him, Rollo, Floki, Bjorn and many other good warriors. Speed, agility, sword fighting and tracking were my strengths, and I honed them.'

'Then let me have the chance to do the same and prove my worth. I know you don't want to put me at risk, but I have to fly free some time.'

'I promise I will discuss this with your mother. You think about what you would like to do with your life and we will work something out. I don't want the same distance between you and I, that I had with my father.

'Son, let me assure you that you will never please everybody and someone will always be ready to stick a seax in your back. You have to do what you think is right and keeping my family alive will always be my top priority. I also understand your anxiety at not being proven yet, but there is a very fine line between life and death – and nobody can predict the outcome.'

Arne sighed, 'Very well, may I go and finish mucking out the stables? At least you ensured I mastered that skill at an early age.'

'Arne, I do owe you an apology. I appreciate you may not want to discuss such intimate details as your sex life with your father, but I think I may be more than qualified to give advice.'

Arne grinned, 'As if living up to your warrior reputation is not hard enough, you highlight another of your many talents I need to master. You may not have noticed but the chances of finding a partner have somewhat diminished since we left Jorvik.'

'I will talk to your mother once we have settled in to our new home and will ensure your education is not forgotten. I think I have upset enough people for one day. I will go and lie down before I upset anyone else!'

He went upstairs, took his weapons belt off and threw himself onto the bed. He was supposed to be a good communicator and he had upset his mistress and his eldest son, and been caught in the act by his wife. He could almost see Ivar laughing at him, heaping scorn on him like he used to do. He missed his little brother more than he had ever anticipated.

Torri came to bed and found him fully dressed, fast asleep on top of the bed. She shook her head and went to find Serena, who agreed to give her a hand undressing him and getting him into bed. Even when they had to sit him up and remove his breeches, he did not wake up.

Serena said, 'Are you sure he is not ill, Torri? Could he have been poisoned at the meeting?'

'No, I think Halfdan is correct – his body is just drained from being on high alert for so long. I have noticed it before, after battles. Remember he uses every one of his senses to their absolute limit and that drains him of his energy.'

'Maybe I should not have reacted to his confrontation about the baby. On reflection, him assuming that as I didn't tell him I had something to hide is a very fair perception.'

'Rubbish, Serena – don't make excuses for him. He knows damn well that you would never be unfaithful. If he had accused me of that, he would not have any balls still attached.'

Serena laughed, 'You wouldn't have done that to him, surely?'

'In fighting mode I would have, but he is such a

lovable rogue it is hard to be truly angry with him. He has all the charm of his father; one look into those deep blue eyes and you fall under his spell.'

'Oh, that's a lovely thing to say, Torri. I know men tend to be little boys at heart but there is something very special about Ubba.'

'Perhaps, but it is unusual for him to upset three of his closest family members in a matter of three hours. He should never have tackled Arne. Once you drive an arrow into Arne's heart you have to contend with an Ivar-esque tantrum of epic proportions.'

Serena smiled, 'Perhaps blaming Ivar is unjust, Torri. You also have a wicked temper when roused.'

Torri blushed. 'Maybe. Arne has inherited Ubba's looks and skills, but he finds the weight of his birthright hard to bear. He is a very private individual and will never be the lothario Ubba is with women. Arne needs to love and trust a woman before he develops a sexual relationship. He will get there in his own good time if Ubba will just leave him alone. Whereas Viggo is totally out to experience what all the fuss about sex is, just to make sure he doesn't miss out.'

'Really? I hadn't noticed him being particularly precocious.'

Torri laughed, 'You mean you didn't see my twelve-year-old son lose his virginity with one of Ivar's warrior's young wives?'

Serena shouted, 'What?! Who?'

Ubba stirred but did not wake.

'Tynan's wife Anna. Viggo fancied her and – don't ask me why and how – she agreed to show him the ropes. And boy, did she make an impression on Viggo, on many occasions!'

'But she only married Tynan in the summer and is carrying his child.'

Torri interrupted, 'His, or Viggo's?'

'Surely Viggo would not be fertile at just twelve years old?'

'It's not beyond the bounds of possibility, Serena. I had no idea; Ivar told me but by then it was too late. We both agreed to keep quiet as Viggo was going to Ireland with Ivar. We thought it best not to alert Ubba or tackle Viggo. He knew exactly what he was doing – and the consequences, as well. If Tynan had caught him there would have been bloodshed, but he is wily and clever. He just wanted the experience. Now Ivar has the problem of containing his sexual appetite in Ireland.'

THIRTY-NINE

The household was up bright and early. Ubba found he had slept from early evening right through until morning.

'Did I really sleep a full twelve hours? No wonder my stomach thinks my throat has been cut! I am starving.'

Torri leaned over him. 'Ubba, we are moving out in precisely one hour. There is no cooked breakfast; we need to get down to the longboats and sail. Can't you hear the horses are being taken down to load? Arne will be in charge of them and you will be on the other longboat. I want no repeat of yesterday's trauma. You had better think about how you are going to mend fences with Serena, as she is very hurt. Really, Ubba, it is so out of character – usually, you think before you speak. Upset anybody today and I will personally have you thrown overboard.'

Ubba pulled the covers over his head. *Christ, he was in the shit with Torri.* How he was going to dig himself out of this hole, he had no idea. Torri had already left the room, slamming the door. Knowing it was best do as he was told, he went to wash and fortunately, banged into Egil in the corridor. 'Thank God it is you, Egil. Can you do me a big favour and find me some food?'

Egil shook his head. 'Really, Ubba, you have caused a major storm. Usually it is only Ivar that can upset three people in three hours, but you have certainly upped your game. Your wife gave me strict instructions not to feed you, but I know how hungry you will be and will see what I can find to sustain you on the journey, provided you eat it surreptitiously. If caught, my name is kept out of this.'

A while later, having eaten, Ubba went to the door. The children were climbing aboard the wagon. There was no sign of a horse for him, so he shouted, 'Where is my horse to ride down to the river?'

There was stony silence and then Torri shouted back, 'All the horses are already loaded; you will have to drive or ride in the wagon like the rest of us.'

Ubba's temper flared. 'I don't want to ride in the wagon. I want a bloody horse!'

Torri fired back, 'Ubba, it is either ride in the wagon or bloody walk!' She turned to Egil, 'Now drive on, Egil.'

Egil's face was a picture; he was unsure who to obey. However, after one of Torri's ice maiden looks, he took up the reins and they set off.

Ubba ran down the steps, screaming obscenities. He ran to the stables where Thorin was. Magpie was saddled up ready.

Ubba shouted, 'Is he for me, Thorin?'

'Yes, lord. I took pity on your plight.'

'Well, thank God *someone* cares about me. I intend to be on the longboat well before the wagon arrives.

Torri would not let me have breakfast, threatened to throw me overboard if I upset anybody else, and has now left me to walk. She is no longer a queen, but boy does she act like one.'

Thorin managed not to laugh. They set off at a brisk trot into the field and headed for the wall at the far end. They jumped about ten different obstacles before they started descending towards the river. Ubba was enjoying himself. Nothing pleased him more than being out in open countryside on horseback. He knew Torri would not relent and go back for him, just as she knew he wouldn't walk to the river. They soon made it to the quay and could see the wagon coming slowly down the hill. They would all have seen their mad cross-country gallop.

Once on the longboat he checked on the horses and could feel Arne's eyes boring into the back of him.

'Good morning son, looks like a good calm day for travelling.' He was unsurprised when no reply was forthcoming, but he saw Josh grin and roll his eyes towards Arne. He went to the other longboat before the wagon pulled up.

Egil looked very uncomfortable. Clearly, he could not wait to get off. The children were scrabbling up the gangplank onto the longboat and he reached out and lifted Theo into his arms as Astrid and Freya boarded. Freya pulled his cloak and he bent to put Theo down. Freya whispered conspiratorially, 'Daddy, you really are in trouble with Mama. She says we are not to talk to you because you have been beastly to Serena and Arne. You are going to have to apologise to both of them. Mama said she hopes the stables are big because you will be sleeping with Sleipnir, not her or Serena.'

Ubba laughed, 'Sweetheart, have no fear. I will have them both eating out of my hand before we reach our destination.'

As her mother bore down on them Freya said, 'Good luck, you are going to need it.' She shot off, clutching Theo's hand, and ran to Torri.

Ubba paused while the children caught up with their mother, then he strode forward with a smile on his face. 'Ladies, how beautiful you look on this lovely calm morning.'

Torri gave him a look that could have melted a glacier, shook her head and turned her nose up at him like the true queen she was. Serena just looked shocked and stared at him. The entire crew was silent, hanging on every word.

Ubba, not to be thwarted, homed in on the easiest target to deflect and said to Serena, 'Would you like me to look after Theo for you, darling?' Serena was so confused by this charm offensive, she didn't know what to say.

However, Torri took the bait, 'I wouldn't trust him, Serena; he is likely to fall asleep or end up throwing up all over him before we get to the Swale. He will need more looking after than Theo does.'

Keir his captain approached and said, 'My lord, everything is loaded. Permission to cast off?'

'Of course, Keir. Ladies, please sit down. We wouldn't want anybody falling into the water, would we?' He glared at the back of his wife's head.

Keir shouted, 'Cast off away from the bank!'

Ubba picked up Theo and waved to Thorin. 'Thank you for the horse. I won't forget your kindness.'

Keir ordered, 'Take up oars... and pull!'

The boat powered out from the bank and sailed sweetly upriver. Every member of the crew's eyes were firmly fixed on Torri, waiting for her next move.

Ubba swept towards Serena, took her hand to move her into the stern, and perched her on some crates while still holding Theo firmly. He put Theo on the deck and let him play with some ropes.

Ubba took Serena's hand and kissed it. 'Forgive me, Serena. I did not mean to suggest you may have been unfaithful. I know you would never do that but like a stupid man, I assumed there may be a serious reason why you did not tell me sooner about the baby. I should have realised that I had inadvertently suggested that having a baby would be inconvenient. You were grieving Frank too and I should have been more attentive but I felt guilty that he died protecting me, and I blamed myself. It was all a big misunderstanding; of course I am delighted you are having another child. If it's a boy we will call him Frank and if it's a girl, maybe Frankie.'

He grabbed Theo, who had managed to climb up by pulling on the ropes of the crates. As he turned around he saw Torri glaring at him. He winced and knew she was going to be a much harder nut to crack. However, he had made his peace with Serena, which is what she wanted him to do.

Egil appeared and gave him a bag of food. Ubba

sat down on the crate next to Serena and tucked in to the meat pies and slices of cold bacon, sharing it with Theo. 'Thank you, Egil. I can see my wife is still fuming. Any suggestions on how I can melt her anger?'

'Not really; she was threatening to do some very nasty things to you when she saw you galloping across the fields. Some were even worse than Ivar's torture methods. I do think you should be very careful; for such a tiny woman she has a mean streak.'

Ubba smiled, 'Bjorn did warn me she can be venomous when roused. Luckily, I have usually managed to stay in her good books. This calls for drastic action, Egil. Be prepared to put me back together if she rips me apart.'

Egil looked horrified, 'Please tread carefully, lord. I think I would rather fight in a shield wall than take her on.'

Ubba laughed, 'Me too!'

He picked Theo up and said to Serena, 'Come, sweetheart; let me take you back. I need to try and make peace with Torri before she becomes more vindictive.' He led them back to the others and Freya climbed on the bench and whispered, 'Good luck with Mama!'

He strode purposefully up to the masthead where Torri had perched to gain more height to observe what Ubba was doing and be in a higher position than him.

'May I have a word with you, my dear?'

The crew practically stopped rowing, craning to hear what was going on and holding its collective breath.

Torri looked down her pretty nose and levelled him with a haughty look. 'But it never is just one word with you, is it, Ubba?'

'Perhaps we could retire to the stern to continue this private conversation – unless of course, you want everybody to hear what I want to say.'

There were audible gasps from the crew and Egil moved closer to the masthead.

Torri regarded him defiantly and replied, 'No, you carry on!'

'Very well, I will, because I need you to listen and understand how I am feeling. I have reflected on what has transpired with the loss of Lincoln and Jorvik to the Saxons. When I thought about it from a personal point of view I realised that the three things I most wanted were within my grasp – and we should take the opportunity to explore them.'

'And what exactly are these three things?'

'Life, peace and freedom. A month ago, I thought I would not see you or my precious family again. I thoroughly expected to die defending the walls of Jorvik. However, we were able to withdraw with minimal loss of life, though I bitterly regret that Frank did not make it. I don't regret that the majority of us escaped with our lives.

'I do not seek power, money or authority; what matters most to me is my family and having a chance to see my children mature. Not many Danes have ever had that luxury. As it happens, Edward of Wessex wants us in Northumbria because our reputation will keep other invaders at bay. He has been brave enough to make his sister Queen of Jorvik, but he cannot protect her from 400 miles away in Winchester.

'I love this land and want to farm it and breed horses, and if I can be left in peace to do that then I will. My father realised too late what a poisoned chalice being a king is, and he regretted it to the end. I know it won't be the life that you are used to, and we may fall out many times as we both have volatile temperaments. And who knows? Maybe sitting by the fireside in winter and breeding sheep and horses will not fulfil me, but I have the opportunity to try it and the freedom to do it. What say you, my love?'

Torri jumped down from the masthead and ran to him. He scooped her into his arms and kissed her. The crew cheered.

He put her down and she said, 'That was a very brave and courageous speech to make coming from one of the greatest warriors of our time. You know that I have never coveted power, wealth and authority either, but have done my best to keep my children alive. If the gods have given us life, peace and freedom then we must take it with open arms. We cannot predict the future and peace may not last very long, but I would welcome the chance to grow old at your side rather than losing you in battle.'

Freya came running up to them. 'Well done, Daddy! But does that mean I will never be a princess and live in a big palace again?'

Torri laughed, 'I am afraid so my dear, but you wanted to choose your own destiny, so now you will have a chance to make your own way in life.'

Freya replied, 'But Edward hinted about me marrying one of his sons. He won't want a farmer's daughter as a wife for his son, will he?'

Ubba patted her on the head. 'Perhaps not sweetheart, but freedom means we can go where we please... and we will start with a trip to Ireland next year to see Ivar, Viggo and Skye.'

o0o

Aethelflaed woke early on the day of her coronation, feeling excited and anxious at the same time. There had not been many objections to her becoming Queen from the ealdormen or previous holders of positions in Ivar's government. She wondered whether this was because they had become used to Torri's fair governance as Queen Consort. However, there were still some men who obviously felt that a female ruler was not to their taste. The possibility that someone may assassinate her at the coronation had been raised with Edward and he had made sure that she was only seen in public after the coronation for fear of giving someone the chance to kill her on the way to the church.

There was a knock on the door and Edward entered. 'I am glad you are awake. I could not sleep either. Visions of Mother's anger when she hears what I have done kept haunting me during the night.'

'Oh, do come in. I could do with a distraction to steady my nerves.'

Edward sat in the chair by her bed. 'We haven't really had chance to discuss our opinions of Halfdan. He is a very different character to Ubba. He is not as open and probably not as honest as Ubba. However, he did lighten up when he knew that I would support his bid for Durham. Do you think Ubba will join him?'

'I don't know. I think Ubba does want to live in peace rather than forever be at war. It doesn't concern me if he joins Halfdan in a battle for Durham, just as long as he doesn't invade Jorvik.'

'You seem to empathise with one another because of your shared experience of the kidnap.'

'When I was rescued after witnessing Erik's death, Ubba looked after me. I was an emotional wreck and there were no women around. He never condemned me for falling for Erik, but he did confirm we would never have been accepted as a couple by either side and would have had to leave both families and this country. He knew I was suicidal. When we were riding along the top of a steep hill I kicked my horse into gallop and intended to throw myself over the cliff. He was so quick and one hell of a horseman. He jumped onto the back of my horse, pulled him up and cradled me in his arms. When I stopped crying and thanked him, he commented that he'd had no intention of saving me; he just did not want to lose a perfectly good horse. I still don't know whether he meant it, but it was so absurd it actually made me laugh. His father found it highly amusing too.'

'That Ragnarsson charm and wicked sense of humour certainly turns ladies' heads. Ragnar was not a wordsmith like Ubba. He did not say a great deal but when he did, it certainly had impact.'

'Surprising as it may be, people tell me that Ivar also has a wicked sense of humour and though he is prone to violence, they say that when told bad news he will often laugh about it. He used to really taunt Ubba over Torri. As long as Ivar remains in Ireland I shall be happy, but if you hear he has sailed you must let me know straight away. There will only be one place he is heading.'

Edward nodded. 'Question is, will he be the only Ragnarsson coming back, or will Ubba be at his side? That would be a real test of loyalty my dear, even though he did promise to warn you of any impending attacks. I suppose only time will tell.'

'Father Raymond seems convinced that Ubba wants to pursue his farming interests and raise and educate his young children in peace. Both Ivar and Ubba gave Bjorn's sons and his own a thorough grounding in languages, religion, history and fighting. There is no doubt that Viggo is an exceptional scholar or that Bjorn's sons have inherited his sailing and exploring skills. Let's hope they go west in search of new lands and do not covet ours.'

Her maid appeared with her breakfast and to help her dress for the ceremony. Edward left to prepare for the coronation and change into his ceremonial gown.

o0o

The longboat was nearing its destination. They had sailed through the valley with rich pasture on both sides. When Ubba had selected the farmhouse at Richmond as his new home he had been delighted at the lie of the land. He had discovered that the river ran close to a copse and although narrow, it ran into it and created a perfect hiding place for two longboats. This would ensure they would be unseen by passing river traffic. The jetty would be his own personal landing place; it was visible from the farmhouse, which was on slightly higher ground about 500 metres away. His land extended up to moorland. He had over 100 acres perfect for horses in the valley and for sheep higher up on the moors. He had no immediate neighbours either, which gave him total privacy, for which he was extremely grateful. Another distinctive feature was the farmhouse. It had been constructed with stone and was two storeys high, which gave him beautiful views across the valley and surrounding hills. It was ideal from which to see an enemy approaching both on the land and river.

Keir guided their boat into the jetty to allow the passengers to disembark, then pulled away to let the other longboat unload the horses and the cart that would be needed to take their food and equipment to the farm. Ubba jumped on board to take Sleipnir off and the horse nuzzled him, looking for titbits in his pockets. It was only a short walk, but Theo begged Ubba to let him sit on Sleipnir, so he threw him and Astrid onto him without a saddle and led them towards the house.

The staff and farm labourers came down to the jetty to help unload. There was still sun shining through the valley even though the breeze blowing through had a hint of autumn about it. Torri was waiting by the gate as Ubba and the children approached.

'Oh, Ubba, it is in a beautiful setting and two storeys as well, but built of stone, not just wood. It will be far warmer because of that and it is not on top of the hill and exposed.' She reached up and lifted Astrid off Sleipnir as Ubba grappled with Theo to remove him while he objected loudly. 'Shush now, Theo. This is your new home and you can start learning to ride like Arne and Freya.' Theo listened carefully and decided not to throw a tantrum in case his father would not allow him to ride again.

Ubba took Torri's hand and led her into the garden, which had been planted by the farmer's wife. The dahlias were still in full bloom.

'I bought it from a retiring farmer, including all its contents – what was in the house and the farm buildings – plus some heavy horses to work on the land. It took a fair bit of our silver from the hoard we buried, but I thought it would be perfect for a family-run farm. I am sorry, my queen – it is not the palace you are used to – but I think we will be happy and safe here.'

Torri stood on a bar of the garden fence, threw her arms around him and kissed him. 'I don't need palaces and wealth. I am content to have you alive and well to watch our children grow up. I know it will be a new start for all of us, but we have the freedom to please ourselves for the very first time in our lives.'

He kissed her longingly and hugged her tightly.

Freya came running into the garden but when she saw them kissing she turned and ran back into the house. She ran off happy in the knowledge that her parents were reconciled. Claiming her bedroom would have to wait a little longer, but she was determined to have her own room rather than sharing with Astrid.

www.ingramcontent.com/pod-product-compliance
Lightning Source LLC
Chambersburg PA
CBHW051310190726
48290CB00001B/85